THE TRAVELER'S DOOR

End of Days Publishing
Copyright © 2023 Carl Alves
ISBN: 9798860034280

Cover art and design by Kealan Patrick Burke

Created in the United States of America
Worldwide Rights

THE TRAVELER'S DOOR

CARL ALVES

DEDICATION

This novel is dedicated to my wife, Michelle, and my two boys, Max and Alex, who have made this journey through life and writing an excellent adventure.

ACKNOWLEDGEMENT

A special thanks to Kealan Patrick Burke for his usual standout job on the novel's cover. I hope you enjoy it as much as I do. A special thanks to my readers who continue to support my writing and make this worth doing.

CHAPTER I

Julian closed his eyes and massaged his temples. In the bed next to him, Nancy stirred awake. Had she done something to her hair?

"Did you sleep well, honey?" Nancy asked.

Julian shook his head. "I've got a monster headache."

"Take something for it."

"Good idea." Julian got out of bed, walked to the bathroom, and opened the medicine cabinet. He blinked a few times in confusion. Picking up a few containers, he didn't recognize a single one. What did Nancy do, replace the regular medicine with ones from a Mexican pharmacy? He didn't want to think about it. He just wanted to dull the pain.

"Um, what should I take for my headache?"

"Take Anstin."

Nancy said it like it was the most obvious thing in the world. How was he supposed to know he should use Anstin for headaches? He had never heard of this brand before.

He popped three in his mouth and washed it down with water. Hopefully these Anstins would kick in soon. He got back in bed.

"Are you all right?"

Julian groaned. "Not really."

"Maybe you ought to take it easy today."

Julian stared at Nancy's eyes. "When did you start using colored contacts?"

Nancy frowned. "What are you talking about? I don't wear contacts."

Julian propped himself on his elbows. "Of course you do. You're wearing green tinted lenses."

Nancy put her hand across his forehead. "I don't wear contacts, and my eyes have always been green."

"No, you have brown eyes."

Nancy opened her eyes wide. "Take a look for yourself."

Julian stared closely and couldn't believe what he saw. She wasn't wearing contacts, and her eyes were indeed green.

"What the hell?" Julian muttered.

"Are you sure you're okay?" Nancy asked.

"I'm having my doubts."

Damn, he must have had a bender last night. He thought back and was sure he hadn't drunk any alcohol. He and Nancy had stayed in and watched a movie. It had been too late to get a sitter, and he had been tired from a tough week at work. Still, it felt like he had slammed down half a bottle of mezcal and eaten the worm.

It did not take long for his head to feel better. This Anstin had to be a wonder drug. He had never taken anything that worked so quickly.

His throat felt parched. After checking on Natalie, he would help himself to a glass of orange juice. Fortunately, she had slept through the night. Lately, Natalie had been coughing up a storm.

A sudden urge, almost a panic to check on his daughter, seized Julian. At age three, Natalie was the cutest little girl he had ever known. He knew he was biased since she was his only child, but he was convinced of this. She had her mom's curly blonde hair and facial features. At work, he couldn't stop himself from constantly glancing at the pictures of her he kept on his desk. Whenever he had to work late or travel, horrible guilt overcame him. If he wasn't there to tuck her in bed at night, he felt hollow.

Julian opened the bedroom door. This wasn't possible. He gripped the doorknob to maintain his balance, his head spinning. The kitchen was somehow situated outside of the bedroom. Their kitchen was located down the hallway in their townhouse that they rented. Had been ever since they moved in two years ago. Unless the landlord had done major reconstruction overnight while he slept, he had to be losing his mind.

He crept outside before coming to a dead stop when he encountered a pale skinned, pre-teen girl with long, dark hair sitting on the floor watching TV. Who was this girl, and why did their living room look vastly different than it had yesterday?

The dark-haired girl looked up at him. "Hi, Julian. Can you help me with my math homework?"

He felt like saying, *who the hell are you?* Instead, he mumbled, "Um, maybe later. I'm not feeling so well."

On the verge of hyperventilating, Julian tried to control his breathing. All sense of normalcy in his life had exploded like the detonation of a bomb. He nearly collapsed on the ugly, checkered couch—something he would never own—staring at the stranger in his living room who acted as if she belonged here.

It took him a few minutes to find the strength to get to his feet. His legs felt as if they were weighed down by leaden boots. He trudged back to the bedroom and looked around now that the lights were on. This bedroom had to be three times the size of the one he had gone to sleep in the night before. The furniture was new and not remotely to his liking.

He knocked on the bathroom door. The light was on, so he presumed Nancy was inside. He had to talk to her before he lost his mind. With any luck, she could set him straight.

Still brushing her teeth, Nancy opened the door. He waited for her to finish. He needed to have a real conversation with her, not one clouded behind a toothbrush.

Julian took a deep breath and pressed his palms together. When he had spoken to Nancy earlier, she didn't give any indication that anything was out of the ordinary. She should be as confused as he felt. "Nancy, why does our townhouse look different, and why is there a strange girl sitting in our living room watching television?"

Nancy put away her toothbrush. "What are you talking about?"

"Our townhouse. It's totally different than it has been for the past two years since we started renting here. And there's this strange girl in our living room."

Nancy scrunched her forehead. "I have no idea what you're talking about. This is the same house we've been living in for years. You should know. You designed the house. It was your pet project. As far as a girl, I don't know who you're talking about. Kathie didn't have any friends sleep over last night, and it's a bit early for any of them to come over today."

Julian raised his hands. "Hold up. Who's Kathie?"

Nancy folded her arms. "Kathie. As in my daughter."

Julian's hands shook. He felt like vomiting, bile rising in his throat. This was getting out of control. He tried to keep his voice steady. "We don't have a daughter named Kathie."

In a panic, he bolted out of the room. He had to find Natalie. He walked past the girl he presumed was Kathie. To his left was the kitchen. The bedrooms had to be upstairs. This house was enormous.

He ran up the stairs two at a time and found a girl's bedroom, probably Kathie's. A young girl he had never seen before, maybe eight or nine years old, was sleeping in an adjacent bedroom. A third bedroom contained file cabinets and bookshelves, but no bed. That left the corner bedroom.

He peeked downstairs at Kathie and thought back to his conversation with his wife. Nancy had told him that Kathie was her daughter, not their daughter. Did she have kids he didn't know about? Could the younger girl be her daughter also? That was impossible. He had known Nancy since they were in the second grade.

Julian took a deep breath. The corner bedroom door opened. Out stepped a tall man in his late thirties with fair skin, dark hair, and a goatee. He wore boxer shorts and a gray shirt.

The man tapped his shoulder. "Hey Julian, up and at 'em early I see. I was thinking we could hit the links today. I wanted to check out that course in Oak Valley. We could try out your new clubs."

"Maybe some other time." He hated golf, not to mention he didn't know this fellow. He peeked into the bedroom over the man's shoulder. This was a man's bedroom, no sign of Natalie anywhere. His desperation grew.

"Well, let me know."

"Sure," Julian said.

Julian walked down the stairs. The world felt like it was collapsing on top of him. The spacious house made him feel claustrophobic. He was in a foreign house with two girls and a guy he didn't know, his daughter was nowhere to be found, and his wife acted like nothing was wrong.

He racked his brains, trying to think how this could have happened. Last night, he and his wife had put Natalie to bed, watched a movie, then went to sleep. Nothing out of the ordinary occurred.

Julian sat on the sofa near Kathie. She was watching a reality game show he had never seen before.

Kathie took out a textbook, laid it on the table and sat next to him. "Can you help me with my Algebra?"

Julian nodded. "Sure. Let's take a look at it."

He cringed. The numbers were familiar, but the symbols were gibberish. He bit his lip. It was as if it were written in Cyrillic. He was good at math, damned good at it. In college he had taken extra Calculus classes even though they weren't required, but this made no sense to him.

"Can we start with problem seven?" Kathie asked.

"Um, I have a massive headache. Can we wait 'til later? I can't think straight."

"Why don't you take some Anstin?"

"I just took some."

The girl closed the book and went back to watching the show. He stared at the television. The logo on the bottom left of the screen said VX2. What kind of television station was VX2? Nothing made a damn bit of sense.

Looking around the house, he found a few familiar knickknacks and furniture he and Nancy had collected along the way, but much of it was foreign. He stared at the television set. The manufacturer was Reo. Never heard of them.

Loud music blared from outside. "What's that?"

Kathie looked up at him. "It's just the band."

"The band?" Julian walked to the window. Their house had a large plot of land. The edge of the property bordered a high school. Why would anyone want a house next to a high school? Doesn't this band bother you?"

Kathie shrugged. "Not really. Plus, I know people in band."

"So, you're not in high school yet, right?"

Kathie scrunched her face. "You know I'm in eighth grade."

"Of course," Julian said. "And you would say we get along fairly well, you and I?"

Kathie took a long look at him. "Are you all right, Julian?"

"Um, sure. So, we get along okay?"

"Of course we do."

Julian nodded. He wanted to ask the girl more questions but was flummoxed. He did not know what he could ask that wouldn't have the girl think he had lost his mind.

Think, Julian, think.

Some things were the same as he remembered, but most were not. It had to be one of three things: either his memories were false; he was delusional and none of this was actually happening; or he was in some Bizarro World. He didn't know which of the three scenarios he preferred.

Inside his bedroom, Nancy was painting her nails, something she rarely did. He walked to the bathroom and frowned. Something was wrong. There was no shower or bathtub.

"Nancy, uh, how come there's no shower in our bathroom?"

She stopped painting her nails. "You're acting really strange. Why would you think we have a shower in the bathroom? It's out back."

"Out back?" He didn't like the sound of this.

"Yeah." Nancy said it like it was the most obvious thing in the world.

He had to see for himself. The sneakers next to his bed looked and felt like Nikes but had an inverted swoosh. He put those on and grabbed a jacket from his massive walk-in closet and went outside. Circling the house, he found a wooden hut in the back. He opened the door gingerly. The room had a tiled floor, a wooden bench, and shelves with soap and shampoo.

He took two steps in, and hot water shot from the ceiling. He stepped back before the water soaked him. The shower clinched it. He was in a Bizarro World. There was no way he was creative enough to conjure up the operation of these showers, and the stinging water told him this was really happening.

Julian left the hut and went back to his house, feeling as if the world around him had gone crazy, and he was the only sane one left. Julian left the hut and went back to his house, feeling as if the world around him had gone crazy, and he was the only sane one left.

CHAPTER II

Julian walked back into the house, resolved not to freak out. Something far beyond the ordinary was happening. He didn't know how or why, but if he was going to get through the situation, he had to think rationally despite the insanity of his predicament. What was the alternative? Curl up into a corner and rave like a lunatic?

If this place was real and not a hallucinogenic dream, then that left the question of how and why he got here. The only thing he could do now was to gather intelligence and find out about his surroundings, who these people were, and who he was in relation to them. His biggest obstacle was doing this without asking direct questions. If he did, the people living in this house would want to check him into the loony bin.

He found his brown-haired *niece* working on her math homework. She looked up at him.

"Hello…Kathie?"

The girl smiled. "Hi…Julian." She laughed, apparently thinking they were playing some sort of game. "Are you feeling better?"

Julian frowned.

"You said you had a headache."

"Oh, yes. I guess that Anstin is working. I'm still going to have to take a rain check on that math homework."

Kathie frowned. "Rain check?"

"I can't help you right now. Maybe later. You're not in school today?"

Kathie rolled her eyes. "It's Friday. Isn't it enough that I have to go to school four days a week?"

Julian put his finger in the air. "Right. Friday." If the kids only went to school four days a week, would that mean that he was not scheduled to work today? The guy he met upstairs mentioned going golfing. Just who was that guy, anyway? There was so much he needed to learn, the most pressing was where was Natalie.

He looked at the portraits in the house and spotted pictures of five people. What really disturbed him was there was no picture of Natalie. Whatever was going on here, he could deal with it if only he could see Natalie's smiling face. Sure, his wife was here, but she acted differently than his Nancy.

Julian entered an office in the house. He rummaged through files until he found the deed to the house. It was jointly owned by he, his wife, and a guy named Sean. That had to be the man he met upstairs.

Going back into the family room, he found Kathie working on her math problems. "Hey, Kathie, do you know where Sean's at?"

"Dad went for his morning jog."

That answered one question but brought about a slew of other ones. Nancy had mentioned that Kathie was her daughter. That probably meant his wife and this Sean character must have been married or at least had a child out of wedlock.

"What about your sister?" Julian assumed the young girl he had seen sleeping upstairs was Kathie's sister, but around here, who could tell for sure?

"Maddie's taking a shower."

Julian nodded. Probably that outside shower thing. As he went back into the office, he wasn't sure if he should feel relieved that the two girls living in the house weren't his children. He loved his Natalie and couldn't imagine fathering any other child. There was always the possibility that Maddie could be his daughter, but he doubted that. He saw a distinct resemblance to Sean in her facial features. If they were Nancy's daughters, and this guy was their father, then why were they all living together?

In the office inside the house, Julian found paystubs with his name. The company he worked for was Advanced Design Concepts. The paystub had an eleven digit phone number, but Julian did not have a cell phone in his pocket, nor could he find one in the office. He went for another visit with his stepdaughter. "Kathie, I can't seem to find my phone."

She fished her pockets for a phone and tossed him something that was half the size of his palm. He had never seen a phone this tiny.

"Um, I think this one's a little different than my phone."

Kathie rolled her eyes. "Do you want me to dial it for you?"

"That would be great," Julian replied.

He gave Kathie the number to dial. She pulled up a tiny, digital screen and punched the numbers for him. When she handed him the phone, she gave him a look like he was an alien from Mars.

Julian took the ringing phone, brought it into the office, and closed the French doors behind him. When the receptionist answered, he said, "Hi, I'm looking for one of your employees, a Julian Dawson."

The receptionist told him to hold. When she returned, she said, "I'm afraid Mr. Dawson isn't in today. Would you like to connect to his voice mail?"

"No need. I'm coordinating a conference that Mr. Dawson is attending. Can you please verify his position with your company?"

"Mr. Dawson is the chief architect," the receptionist said.

Julian thanked her and disconnected the phone. Interesting. Here, he was an architect. In college, he had tinkered with the idea of going into architecture. Torn between that and business, he had ultimately decided on a marketing degree. After working for a few companies, he had opened his own consultancy firm, which was struggling to get off the ground, hence the small townhouse and not this palatial abode. Maybe he should have been an architect.

Julian encountered the other young girl who lived in the house. From their conversation, he was able to gather that Sean was her father as well. She was in first grade, and everyone in the house got along fabulously.

After getting nowhere with a computer he could hardly understand, Julian went to find his wife. He had been purposely avoiding her. She was in many ways similar to his Nancy, but in other ways distinctly different. Being around her weirded him out. It was as if aliens had abducted and made a clone of her but forgot important details.

She was in the kitchen making lunch.

"Nancy, we have to talk."

"Sure. What's on your mind?"

Julian put his knuckles to his chin. "Don't you think it's a bit weird that Sean and his daughters are living with us?"

Her brows rose. "His daughters? They're my daughters too."

"Yeah, I know, but don't you think it's odd that your ex lives with us?" He hoped Sean was her ex-husband and that this wasn't a polygamous relationship.

She folded her arms. "Why's that odd? It's perfectly normal."

"It is?"

"Lots of people have similar arrangements. Your sister and her husband live with her ex-husband and your nephew."

Julian didn't know what to say that wouldn't upset Nancy. In this place, this sort of arrangement might be normal, but where he came from, he didn't know anybody who lived like this.

Nancy's lip curled the way it always did when she was mad. "If this bothers you, why haven't you ever said anything before? Why is it a problem now?"

"I feel uncomfortable with your ex-husband living here. Why's that so unusual?"

"Well, I find it disconcerting. You and Sean are good friends; at least I always thought you were."

"Don't get upset." He needed to clear his head. "Look, I'm going for a ride. Which car should I take?"

"I made you lunch."

"I'll be quick." Julian wanted to get away from Nancy and get a better feel for his surroundings.

Nancy waved her hand. "Why are you asking me? Take the RL8. It's your car."

Julian eyed the keys on the hooks. He saw the one that said RL8 and took it.

The unusually bright sun temporarily blinded him. He had to squint several times and hoped that he had shades inside the car. He found a red sports car with high curves in the front and back. Upon further investigation he found a logo with RL8 on the back of the car. A sharp-looking ride. It looked Japanese, which made him wonder if there was a Japan in this place.

Not wanting to take a chance with the key fob, he manually opened the door with the key. He went inside and stared in exasperation. Instead of a steering wheel, the car had what looked like a joystick and two small circular wheels. He normally drove a stick, but this car had a crazy contraption with levers and gears between the driver and passenger side. If he tried driving this, he would crash it in 4.6 seconds.

As Julian leaned his head against the high headrest, the seat rose and shifted. A harness came down from the roof. Near panic, he opened the door and stumbled out of the car.

How could people drive these things? This was a death mobile. Nothing about this place made the least bit of sense.

He got to his feet, not sure what to do since his idea of going for a drive turned out to be an epic failure. Glancing around the serene neighborhood, he wondered just what else was different here from the world he knew.

Seconds later, the answer came loud and clear. Julian gaped at what looked like a combination school bus and monster truck driving down the street. This thing looked more like a futuristic prison vehicle than something that should be transporting children. Inside, were school-aged kids who looked as happy as can be. He nearly lost his balance as he stumbled back to the house.

CHAPTER III

After eating lunch, Julian spent the afternoon wandering on foot. Every so often, he encountered something that threw off his sensibilities, such as the top traffic light that was hot pink instead of red. When he first saw the light, he stood gawking at it like an idiot.

As he attempted to cross the street, a woman driving a tiny car that was slightly larger than a golf cart nearly ran him over. She must have been doing ninety miles per hour. He hadn't seen her until the last minute and she gave him the finger to top it off.

On the verge of hysteria, he tried to control his breathing.

I have to get home. I have to get home.

It was becoming a mantra for him. He calmed down by reminding himself that there had to be an explanation for his being in this twisted world. With time, he would find out. Until then, he had to be patient and learn as much as he could about his new environment.

Not sure where to go, he walked toward the school. He wasn't sure what to expect, perhaps some deranged educational system, but the school and the grounds seemed normal. They even had a football field. At least they had football here. It was a small point, but comforting nonetheless.

Beyond the school was a shopping center, where he bought cigarettes at a convenience store called The Koolah. Even that transaction was difficult since the currency was different here. His attempt at smoking lasted five seconds. The cigarettes he bought were stronger than anything he had ever tried and reeked of cow manure. He tossed the pack in a nearby trashcan.

Walking around the neighborhood wasn't bringing him any closer to the answers he needed, so he returned to his opulent house. His legs felt heavy as he walked.

How was he going to get the information he needed? He felt little connection with Nancy 2.0. He certainly felt no connection with Sean. Kathie had a quick wit about her, and out of everybody he met, she seemed to be his best bet. Apparently, she and the other Julian got along well, and he had taken a liking to her.

Outside of the house, he found Kathie shooting hoops. She hit a short jumpshot.

"Hi, Kathie."

"Hi, Julian."

Without warning she tossed him the ball. He caught it, spotted up for a jumpshot and watched the ball sail over the basket.

Kathie turned and stared at him. "What was that?"

The ball had to contain helium or a similar gas. It was lighter than any basketball he had ever shot. "I guess my shot is a little off today."

"It sure is. Wanna play some seventeen?"

Julian could only assume that was some version of a basketball game. "In a bit. Hey, I wanted you to help me out with something."

Kathie went to get the ball. "Sure thing."

"I know this might sound weird but work with me here."

"Okay."

"Let's say I was a visitor from another planet, what could you tell me about the place you live in?"

Kathie chuckled. "That's silly."

"I know. Just play along."

Kathie hit a short shot, nothing but net. If he played her in a game of hoops using this ball, she would smoke him, even though he had always been a good basketball player. "Okay, let's see. We live in United States."

"Interesting."

"What's so interesting about that?" Kathie asked.

"Nothing. Go ahead."

"Charles Bear is the president."

"Never heard of the guy," Julian muttered.

"What do you mean you never heard of him? You voted for him. Anyway, we live in Fultonville in Philadelphia."

"You mean Philadelphia is the state we live in? Not Pennsylvania?"

Kathie scrunched her face. "What's Pennsylvania?"

"Never mind."

"Julian, you know, you're acting really weird today."

"Well, if it's any consolation, I'm feeling really weird." There were any number of questions he could ask Kathie, but he wasn't sure which ones would get him closer to what he needed. Not to mention, his headache was coming back.

"Tell me one more thing," Julian said. "How are you with this whole dynamic of everybody living in this house?"

Kathie frowned. "What do you mean? Like you being married to my mom and stuff?"

"Well, yeah. That and your dad living in the house."

"It's fine," Kathie said.

"Fine?"

"Why wouldn't it be? This way I get to see Mom and Dad every day, and you're a pretty cool guy when you're not acting so weird."

Julian sighed. Despite his misgivings, this relationship seemed to be working for the rest of the family. If he was going to stay here long term, he didn't know if he could live with those conditions.

"Thanks for your help. You seem to have a good head on your

shoulders for a teen-aged girl."

Kathie rolled her eyes. "And you seem to have it together for an old guy."

"Old guy? I'm barely over thirty."

"Well, you're old to me."

"No matter how this shakes out, it's been good getting to know you."

Kathie shook her head as if he was some clueless adult.

When Julian returned to the house, Sean and Nancy sat at the kitchen table staring at him intently. He closed his eyes and sat.

"Julian, we're concerned about you," Nancy said.

Sean folded his hands. "You've been acting a bit odd today."

Nancy spoke in a high pitch voice. "What's going on?"

"We want to help you in any way we can. We're family."

Julian got up from the table. "I'm going to need another one of those Anstins." Walking to the bathroom, he had the distinct feeling that he wasn't going to enjoy this conversation very much.

Sean had a lot of gray hair mixed in with his brown hair both on his head and his beard. The guy looked closer to forty than to thirty. There was something about him that didn't sit right with Julian. Perhaps it was the fact that he shared the same house as his wife. He could buy into this version of Nancy as his family, but not Sean.

"What's going on?" Nancy asked.

Julian sighed. "You have no idea."

"You're right. We don't. Why don't you let us in on it?"

Maybe the best thing was to tell them the truth.

"Listen, I don't know how this happened. This morning I woke up in this strange place. At first, I thought things were normal because I woke up next to you, Nancy. The only difference I noticed between you and my Nancy is the color of your eyes. Otherwise, you look alike."

Nancy put her hand on his hand. "Julian..."

"Let me finish. The rest of this place is way different. Where I come from, I have a different job. Your cars are different, your shows are different, and that whole outdoor shower freaks me out.

"Although this house is nice—much nicer than my real house—I can't stay. First off, nothing against you, Sean, but this whole thing with you living here is…well, strange to me. This type of situation is atypical in my world. Perhaps over time I would be able to reconcile that type of arrangement, but the most important thing is that I desperately need to get back to my daughter, our daughter."

Nancy's brow furrowed. "Our daughter? But you said you didn't want kids. Kathie and Maria were enough."

"Maybe your version of Julian doesn't want kids, but I love my Natalie more than anything. She means the world to me, and I can't imagine not being with her. I need to get back. I don't belong here."

Sean took a deep breath. "Julian, I think you should see a doctor. I once went through a rough patch, and Dr. Everett really helped me out."

"Thanks for your concern, but I'm not crazy. Believe me, I've considered the possibility, but this is all too real. Some of the things I've seen today have been mind-numbing. Somehow, I woke up in a world that is fundamentally different than the one I come from and I need to go home."

"Julian, you are home." Tears formed in Nancy's eyes. He wanted to comfort her, but this woman was a stranger to him. If it were truly his wife, he would know just what to say to make everything better. Perhaps Sean would be better equipped to comfort her.

Julian slowly shook his head. "Look, I don't know what happened to your Julian. I can only hope that he returns, but quite honestly, that's not my problem. I have to get back to my daughter and my real wife."

Nancy shook her head. "You're not well, Julian. Let me call Dr. Everett and make an appointment."

Julian stood. "I don't need to see a shrink. I'm perfectly sane. All I need is to find a way out of here and back to where I belong.

If you're not going to help me, then I'll figure this out on my own."

Nancy appeared to be on the verge of a breakdown. Sean had this forlorn look in his eyes. Neither of them was going to help him. Kathie was only a young girl, and he did not want to involve her. For better or worse, he was on his own.

CHAPTER IV

Julian walked out of the house, not sure where to go. He was certain of one thing—hanging around this house and neighborhood would not get him home.

He eyed the red sports car in the driveway. Trying to drive that contraption would probably get him killed.

Kathie was no longer outside. Up the street, a kid was zooming by on a skateboard. He could not see the motor, but the kid was moving fast and not using his feet for propulsion.

Julian stared in fascination. The kid was going to get into a horrible accident, but he seemed to have no concern at all. It took a few moments before Julian realized he was coming straight at him. Just as he was about to move to the side and avoid getting splattered, the skateboarder slowed and shot out his hand, which held an envelope.

His heart racing, Julian made eye contact with the skateboarder, who gave a nod.

Extending his hand, he took the letter from the skateboarder as he passed. As soon as they completed the handoff, the kid accelerated down the street. Julian remained baffled, trying to determine the mechanism of acceleration, since he did not appear to do anything to make it go faster.

The outside of the envelope had Julian's name. He opened it and found a letter inside. After hastily unfolding it, he read the letter.

By now I am certain that you are quite confused, Mr. Dawson. I have the answers you seek. Find me at the Swanson Building inside of the city.

Finally. This was his first glimmer of hope. Whoever wrote this letter had to know about his situation and could help him.

Where he came from, he lived a half-hour outside the city. If the geography of this world was similar, he could navigate his way there and try to find the Swanson Building. The only problem was he had no confidence in his ability to drive that red sports car.

One of the neighbors was about to enter a car that looked similar to a Buick. Julian ran over to him.

"Oh, hi Julian." The older man frowned.

Julian probably looked frantic. At least that's how he felt. "Hi. Listen, I need a big favor. I need you to drive me into the city."

The man's brow furrowed. "Well, I wasn't planning on going. Your car is right there. Why don't you drive it?"

Julian took a deep breath. "I don't mean to put you out, but I really need this favor. I would sincerely appreciate it and I don't have an alternative right now."

"Um, okay."

The old man got in the car, and Julian went into the passenger's side. The crazy harness contraption descended from the roof. This time Julian was ready for it.

They drove out of the development and onto a bigger road. Within a few minutes, they were on the highway.

The old man glanced at him. "What's wrong with you, Julian? Is everything all right? You're acting a bit strange, well more than a bit strange if I'm being honest."

"No. Nothing's all right. Everything's backwards. I have to find something called the Swanson Building in the city."

"Well, I've never heard of the Swanson Building, but I can certainly give you a ride. Pardon my asking, but why didn't you ask your wife or Sean for help."

Julian sighed. "It's complicated. Let's just say that under the circumstances, they would not be particularly keen to help me now."

"You all seem to get along so well. I'm sorry to hear that you're going through some difficulties."

Julian waved his hand. "It's nothing to worry about. I just have extremely urgent business, and I couldn't wait for Nancy or Sean to come around to my way of thinking. And I couldn't drive my car…" Julian didn't want to get into the entirety of his situation with his neighbor. He just needed transportation.

Conversation remained sparse for much of the ride. Although the highway and some of the buildings looked familiar, the highway numbers were different.

The old man kept his eyes on the road. "Is there anything I can help you with?"

"No. I just need you to drive me where I need to go."

Julian closed his eyes, praying that when he opened them, everything would return to normal, but alas that was not to be. He glanced at the letter once more. There had to be a reason he was here. The only thing that made sense was that he had been purposely transported here, although he could not fathom a reason why, let alone how. The situation, just like his mind, was a jumbled mess.

When they approached the city, Julian felt more at ease. This looked like the Philadelphia he remembered. When talking to the old man, he purposely had not mentioned the name of the city in case they called it something different.

"Where to now?"

"Get off the highway, drive a mile or so and drop me off."

The old man stopped at Market Street, which was the same as back home. "Is this okay?"

Julian nodded.

"I feel really bad about this situation. I've always gotten along well with you and your family. Is there something you want me tell Nancy? Maybe let her know I dropped you off here."

Julian waved his hand. "It doesn't matter. Do what you want. If things work out the way I'm hoping, I'll never see them again."

The old man gaped at Julian.

"Listen, I'm sorry I dragged you into this. Thanks for the ride. I really appreciate you willing to help me here."

"Um, sure."

Julian exited the car. He had no doubt the old man would go back and tell Nancy and Sean about this. He didn't care. The only thing that mattered was getting home.

Now he had to find the Swanson building. He travelled into his own version of Philadelphia several times a year, so he was familiar with the city, but he had never heard of a building with that name. He began walking with no specific destination in mind.

He approached a young woman with multiple piercings on her nose and ears, as well as a woman who had the appearance and demeanor of a librarian. Neither had ever heard of the Swanson building. As he continued walking, he asked more people, but had the same results.

Wonderful. Whoever the mystery person was that had sent him the letter chose an obscure building for them to meet.

Cursing under his breath, he passed the sports arena. For some reason it was called The Hive. What was the name of the team playing there – the Bees? He did a double take at the flashing billboard. Tonight was the first of three sold out concerts featuring Kevin Federline.

What the hell?

In his world, he was the loser who had married Britney Spears for two minutes. If he didn't already have enough motivation, there was no way he could stay in a world where K-Fed was a big star.

Every time he passed a building, he looked at its name. Perhaps a detailed map of the city would list building names. At this rate, he would still be wandering by nightfall.

Sighing in frustration, he entered The Donut Heaven, which looked suspiciously like Dunkin' Donuts, and got himself a coffee and a donut. The coffee was stronger than Dunkin' Donuts coffee, but at least it managed to clear his sinuses.

Julian felt claustrophobic as he sat at the table. How was he going to find the Swanson building? Nobody in this damn place knew a thing about it.

Staring out the window into oblivion, Julian snapped out of his daze at the sight of a thin man with shaggy blond hair, a long black coat and jeans walking past him on the sidewalk. It took him a moment to realize there was something drastically wrong with the man. It was only until the man was leaving his line of sight that he figured it out. The guy's sneakers. He was wearing Nikes. Not this world's version with the upside down swoosh, but the Nike shoes with the regular swoosh.

Julian leapt out of his chair, knocking it over, leaving the potent coffee on the table. He bolted out the door and ran outside as the man was crossing the street.

"Hey, you," Julian yelled.

As the man crossed the street, Julian chased him. The light turned red. Neither that nor the oncoming traffic would stop him. He had seen at least a dozen people with the funky Nikes, but only one wearing the real deal from his world. He dodged two cars, forcing a driver to slam his brakes. The driver gave him an angry gesture.

"Hey, you in the black coat." Julian ran up to him, panting for breath. He grabbed the man's arm and turned him around. "Hey, I need…"

Before Julian finished his sentence, the guy ran.

Damn.

He was already out of breath. He exercised regularly back home. It was probably just an adrenaline dump from the excitement of finding this man.

Julian would not relent. It would take a lightning strike to stop him. "I just need to talk to you." They crossed two more blocks, the passersby staring at them. "Hey, you're wearing Nikes. They make them where I come from."

When the man finally slowed, Julian mouthed a silent thank you. The man turned, his eyes sharp like that of an eagle. His nose was hooked, and he had a scar on his left cheek. He was no stranger to trouble. No wonder he had run.

He jogged until he caught up with the man. "Your shoes. They make those shoes where I come from. They're Nikes. Joe Biden is the president."

The man's eyes narrowed. "So they are, and so he is."

"Listen, I don't want any trouble. I just desperately need to go back home. I have a wife. Well, my wife's here too, but I need to go back and see my daughter, Natalie." Julian closed his eyes. "Please help me."

"Follow me. The name's Cutter."

CHAPTER V

They walked into a dark bar filled with shady characters. A man with shifty eyes and arms covered with tattoos glanced at Julian.

Cutter motioned to a table away from the bar. "What do you like to drink?"

Julian shrugged. "I usually drink Yuengling."

Speaking with an Australian accent, Cutter said, "Then you'll want a Knox."

Julian sat at the table while Cutter got two beers from the bar. He had a million questions, but where to start? "So, do you come from my world?"

Cutter shook his head. "The right term is plane. That's not my native plane, but I've been there many times. And yes, I am familiar with Joe Biden, and these shoes are the Nikes you can find in your home plane. I have eclectic tastes and like to pick up items from different planes. So, tell me what happened, friend. I can see that you're a bit confused."

Julian was finally feeling normal again. He wasn't crazy and he had found a person that could relate to his situation. "Confused doesn't even begin to describe it. When I woke up this morning, I found myself in this crazy, backwards world."

Cutter swallowed his beer. "Backwards is a relative term."

Julian gave him a brief synopsis of the day's events. Cutter let him tell his tale without interrupting. Julian still could hardly believe he was actually living through these bizarre events. "So, what's the deal? Did I come here by accident?"

Cutter shook his head. "You're here for a reason. People can't accidentally go between planes. You either have to be a traveler like me, or someone sent you."

Julian frowned. "What's a traveler?"

Cutter took a deep breath and folded his hands, as if determining how much he should tell Julian.

"Look, I know you're reluctant to give my any trade secrets or anything that can get you in trouble, but I promise you I'm just trying to get home and won't do anything that will put you in danger."

After a few moments and a couple swigs of beer, Cutter's shoulders slumped into a relaxed posture. "There are certain people who have an innate ability to travel between planes. It's a genetic trait. We have a society of sorts. I am one such individual. There are others like me, not many mind you, but they are out there. Since you're not one of us, that can only mean somebody sent you."

Julian had so many questions about travelling and planes that he wasn't even sure where to start. "Who would send me?"

Cutter sighed. "The only one capable around here is the Game Master."

"The Game Master?"

"I don't know his actual name, but that's what people call him. He likes to create games, the kind where people get hurt or worse."

Julian didn't like where this was going. "Why?"

Cutter took a long draft. He sighed. "I don't like to cross the Game Master and I do all I can to stay out of his business."

"Look at it this way," Julian said. "If he's the one who sent me to this plane, I'm sure he would appreciate you helping me to get to him. And whatever you tell me, I'll keep it in confidence."

"He's not the nicest person. He controls doors. He is one of a handful of, I don't know how you would describe it, but they're almost super beings, at least super intelligent. People like him have figured out how to manipulate travel through planes by the creation of doors."

"Doors?" Julian rubbed his eyes. His headache was coming back with a vengeance. "Like you just open a door and then you're in another place?"

"It sounds somewhat simple when you put it that way, but I assure you the manipulation of these doors is anything but simple. As a traveler, I can go back and forth between planes with little effort, but I can't take anyone with me, in case that thought's going through your head. If you're not a traveler, you need a door."

Julian's face lit up. "So, he can get me back?"

"If he brought you here, he did it for a reason." Cutter leaned in. "He wants you to play one of his games."

Julian's brow furrowed. "Like what? I don't even know what the hell I'm doing here. How can I possibly help some super-being?"

"Who knows? Only one way to find out. Let's go see him."

While they finished their beer, Julian thanked the Lord he found Cutter. At least now he had a chance.

Julian paid for drinks. After exiting the bar, they took a cab to Thirtieth Street Station.

"So, do you live around here? I mean like permanently."

Cutter chuckled. "Not exactly. I suppose I'm a bit of a gypsy."

Julian frowned. "Oh?"

"You see, I don't like to stay in one place too long. Start to get antsy. I keep residences in five planes. That way, I can make a quick getaway if need be."

"So, when we first met, you thought I was somebody who was after you?"

Cutter shrugged. "I have some enemies out there. Fact is, you weren't. Just an honest guy in a bit of a pickle. I can relate."

Cutter told the driver to stop. They had spoken freely since the driver did not appear to understand English.

From the outside, the warehouse looked abandoned. It had drab walls and boarded windows.

Julian surveyed the place, suddenly filled with trepidation. "So, what's this Game Master like?"

Cutter rubbed his stubble. "If I'm being truthful, he's a real son of a bitch." His face tensed. "We've crossed paths. I've done a couple of jobs for him, and things didn't turn out so well, so I generally keep my distance from the man. Haven't seen him in a few years. It's better that way. I don't know what kind of scheme he's conjured, but you need to be real careful when dealing with him. Don't trust the bastard. He'll deceive and manipulate you."

"Well, if he really is behind this like you suggest, then I might not have a choice. Hey, before we go in there, I just wanted to thank you for your help. I really appreciate it."

Cutter gave a slight nod. "Ready to go inside?"

"Sure. Let's do it."

CHAPTER VI

From the outside, there didn't appear to be much activity in the building. Once they entered through the aluminum door, the situation changed dramatically. The place bustled with movement. People walked through corridors, some sat at desks, and others worked in laboratories.

Cutter spoke in a low tone. "This is the Game Master's center of operations, at least in this plane. He keeps a low profile, so nobody of an official capacity bothers him. He's Joe Average Businessman as far as they're concerned. Of course, they have no idea what he actually does, very little of which is legal or moral."

"So what jobs have you performed for him in the past?" Julian asked.

"Nothing you need to concern yourself with."

The seriousness of Cutter's tone told Julian that it would not be a good idea to pursue this matter any further. The last thing he wanted was to alienate his only ally here.

The workers largely ignored them, preoccupied with their own business.

"Do you know where to find the Game Master?"

"Not entirely sure," Cutter replied. "But if I remember my way around from the last time, I think I know where he keeps himself. Follow me and act like you belong here. Project confidence."

They walked up three flights of stairs, down a long hallway, and into a large room. Inside, a man was tied to a chair. A strip of tape covered his mouth. Dry blood was crusted on his forehead. Julian took a closer look and realized that he was missing an ear. Coagulated blood covered much of his left ear, which had been partially severed.

Julian gasped, but Cutter acted as if everything was normal.

A bald man stood nearby holding a syringe. He was not an inch over five feet tall, with narrow eyes and a face covered with acne scars.

Staring at the man on the chair, Julian wanted to help him, but couldn't take the risk. He had no idea what kind of business had transpired here with this unfortunate soul, but if the short man was the Game Master, he was not going to jeopardize his only chance of getting home. Maybe this guy was a criminal who deserved his fate.

Julian turned away from the man tied to the chair. Cutter cleared his throat to get the bald man's attention.

He turned around, syringe still in hand. He wore a wide smile that revealed crooked teeth. "Ah, Julian Dawson. It's good to see you. I am glad you received my letter." He put down the syringe and held out his hand.

With some reluctance, Julian shook it. He doubted the contents of the syringe contained a vaccination or an antidote that was going to help this man.

"You've proven to be resourceful in finding me, but that comes as no surprise. I knew you would prove to be a man of high character, capable of doing important things. That is why I selected you."

Julian gulped. "You selected me?"

"I need your assistance in a matter, and then you can return to your old life."

Julian stole a sideways glance at Cutter, who had a blank expression. "That would be great. What exactly did you have in mind?"

The Game Master turned to Cutter, his wide smile never leaving his face. "Mr. Cutter, if you don't mind, this is a private matter."

Cutter nodded. "I understand. I need to be on my way. Got things to do. Hadn't intended on coming here, anyway."

The Game Master reached into his pocket, pulled out two gold coins, and handed them to Cutter. "This should compensate you for your efforts this afternoon."

Cutter pocketed the coins and nodded. "I'll be on my way."

Julian intercepted him before he left the room and shook his hand. "Thanks for everything. I really appreciate it. If I ever have the chance to help you, don't hesitate to ask."

"I have a feeling we'll cross paths again. Until then, good luck. I hope you find your family."

"Thanks. I appreciate it."

After Cutter made his exit, the Game Master excused himself and left the room, leaving Julian alone with the man tied to the chair. He wondered if this was a test. He stared at the man. The man looked at him with pleading eyes. The tape covering his mouth stifled his screams.

Julian spent the next few minutes rationalizing his indecision. In the end, this guy was not his problem. He had to think of Natalie.

The Game Master returned with a briefcase. "I'm glad you decided to stay. You have questions?"

"Of course I have questions." Julian leaned inward. "How did I get here? How can I get back to my family?"

The Game Master raised a long, thin finger. "First things first. I brought you here. I am assuming your friend, Mr. Cutter, told you about me, so you must know a little about your situation."

Julian frowned. "But how? I woke up in bed this morning and found myself in this…place."

"The how is not very important for your purposes. For your

immediate concern, Mr. Dawson, the why is more important. If you recall at lunch yesterday, you ordered iced tea. Immediately afterward, you felt light-headed. That feeling dissipated throughout the day. The teleportation took place when you went to sleep."

Julian narrowed his eyes. All of those things had happened to him yesterday.

"Okay. Why am I here?"

The Game Master smiled as he lifted the briefcase. "I have a very important delivery, and I need someone I can trust, someone motivated to complete the delivery as if his life depended upon it."

Julian folded his arms. None of this was making a damn bit of sense. "You brought me here to deliver a briefcase. Is this some kind of joke?"

"Not a joke, I assure you."

Julian once more glanced at the man in the chair. There was no way his assignment could be as simple as delivering a briefcase. The Game Master was malicious and cunning. Cutter had told him that the Game Master was into creating games, the kind where people got hurt. Regardless, what alternative did he have? If Cutter could not help him get home, then the Game Master was his only option.

"Okay, I'll do it. Where do I deliver this briefcase?"

"I knew I could rely on you, Mr. Dawson. This briefcase contains information of a most sensitive nature. If it got in the wrong hands, then it could be quite damaging. You are not to open it. You are to give it to nobody until you arrive at your destination. Do you understand?"

"Of course. You can count on me."

"Very well then, Mr. Dawson. I will verify receipt of the briefcase, so please don't think about ditching the package. I will provide you explicit instructions on the delivery. Just to give you a little extra motivation, I have something else for you."

The Game Master handed him a photo of Natalie.

Julian tried to contain his anger. This son of a bitch had ripped him out of his world, all to complete some scheme. He took the photo, resisting the urge to thrash the little man.

"I'll deliver the briefcase," Julian said through gritted teeth. "Just tell me what I need to know."

CHAPTER VII

The Game Master was gracious enough to give him a plastic card that would allow him entry onto the train that would take him to his destination. He didn't know what kind of game the man was playing. Julian had little doubt that he was a pawn in some plot, but he didn't see a way out of it. He had to complete his assignment and put this whole weird experience behind him.

He found his station and swiped the plastic card to gain entry. In his hand, he carried the brown, leather briefcase. Regardless of the Game Master's warnings, he had no intention of examining its contents. He had a feeling he would rather not know.

His stomach was roiling by the time the train reached the station. The train looked exactly like the ones he was used to riding back home. He had been expecting something that looked like a combination monster truck and bullet train.

After the train came to a stop, he boarded the half-full compartment. They left the city and travelled to a more rural area. The tall buildings gave way to trees and bushes. After over an hour of travelling, his stop was next.

Julian exited the train along with a dozen other passengers.

He took out the directions. The building was five blocks from here. Shops, restaurants and office buildings populated the area. He walked alongside a park. Not far from him was a running stream. He found kids at play, people walking and jogging, an all-together normal day for these folks.

He made a left onto Applecorn Street and searched the addresses for his destination. The building with the address he was looking for was a moderate sized, brick building. He entered the building. He was supposed to find a Trevor Kennedy. There was a Senator Trevor Kennedy listed on the directory. The Game Master had not mentioned anything about meeting a senator.

He went to the guard at the front desk. No ordinary receptionist, the man looked like he ate glass for breakfast. He had a big head with a protruding forehead, short brown hair, and no neck.

Julian tentatively approached the big man. "Um, I'm here to see the Senator. I have a package for him."

The big man had no reaction. "And you are?"

"My name is Julian Dawson."

"He's expecting you," the guard said. "Take the elevator to the fourth floor, then go to the end of the corridor. He'll be in the office on the left."

The entire fourth floor belonged to the Senator and his aides. People scurried about talking on the phone, typing on computers and otherwise looking busy. He took Cutter's advice when they had visited the Game Master's complex and pretended to belong. Despite his shabby dress, nobody stopped him.

He went to the office at the end of the hallway and knocked on the door. A woman dressed conservatively with a plaid dress greeted him.

"I'm here to see Senator Kennedy."

The woman eyed his attire. "The senator isn't seeing anybody today."

Julian frowned. That was odd since the guard had sent him up without hesitation. Apparently, this aide had not gotten the same message.

A man wearing a dark suit with salt and pepper hair entered the room. He looked very much like a politician. "That's okay, Adrien. I'm expecting him."

Despite the aide's interference, getting a hold of Senator Kennedy was easier than he had anticipated.

The office looked conservative with muted tones, mahogany furniture, and pictures of the Senator posing with others he suspected were people of great importance. One of them looked like George Clooney.

Senator Kennedy turned to Adrien. "I'll let you know if I need anything further."

Adrien took that as her cue to leave the room. Julian could only surmise that the esteemed senator did not want his aide to know what was in the briefcase.

The Senator smiled. "I take it you arrived here without issue?"

Julian shrugged. "Everything went okay. Look, I just want to get this thing over with. I don't know what business you have with the man who sent me and I don't want to know. I just want to complete this task and be done with it."

Senator Kennedy looked at him appraisingly. "I like a man who is straight to the point. Very well, I won't keep you long. May I have the briefcase?"

"Sure." Julian handed him the briefcase.

The Senator inspected it before laying it down and entering a combination on the lock. He opened it so that the contents were only visible to him, then gave an approving nod. "Everything appears to be in order. I will send a message that the package has been received." He closed the case.

"Great," Julian said. "If you don't have anything else for me, then I would like to be on my way."

"Of course." Senator Kennedy extended his hand. Julian shook it, mostly as a reflex reaction. "Thank you for your service today. It is much appreciated."

He found the Senator to be too cool, too confident, a consummate politician, which made Julian immediately distrust him. In his business dealings, he had encountered a few local politicians and had always found them to be conniving and fake. Kennedy was no different.

Julian exited the office. On his way out, Adrien gave him a suspicious look. He smiled and waved at her. Perhaps she was unaccustomed to getting surprise visitors at the Senator's office, or maybe she was just aggressively uptight.

He found his way to the train station. According to the posted schedule, he had twenty minutes before his train was due to arrive. He couldn't imagine the Game Master was going to let him go home. There had to be something else, something more dangerous and sinister involved. From what Cutter had told him, and judging by the fellow he had tied up to a chair, this task was far too simple to fulfill his bargain.

Julian picked up a newspaper and began to read. The lead article indicated that China was on the verge of declaring war on the Soviet Union. Apparently, over here, the Cold War was still in effect. The United States was staying out of the conflict for now, but was deeply concerned about the nuclear implications.

Julian shook his head. As if the threat of terrorism and global unrest in his own world wasn't bad enough, the problems on this plane seemed worse. He continued to read the newspaper after entering the train, the ache in his heart growing as he thought about his wife and daughter.

When he exited the train, his hunger overtook him. He found a pizza place and decided to get some food. With the currency left in his wallet, he ordered two slices of pizza and a soda, and found a table to sit. While eating, he watched a television monitor. He froze at the sight of his own image on the screen.

Julian put down the pizza and got closer to the screen so he could hear the commentary. Below his image read something about a terrorist attack.

The newscaster said, "We are still awaiting further details from law enforcement, but right now the information we have is that there has been an attack on the water system that feeds the city and the metropolitan area's water supply as well. A biological agent has been unleashed, and local and national experts have been brought in to contain the situation. At this point, they are not sure how widespread the damage is, but for the time being, they are telling people not to drink tap water. Several people have died and many more are reported to be ill from drinking the water."

"Holy shit." Julian tried to remain calm, but his heart was racing into overdrive. Why had his picture been on the television screen?

Up next Senator Kennedy was speaking. "We believe that this was the vile act of a terrorist. Our first objective is to keep our citizens safe, but rest assured we will hunt down whoever is responsible. This act of aggression will not be tolerated, including if any state or nation is associated with it."

Images flashed on the screen of Senator Kennedy on the front lines working with police emergency personnel.

"Channel 10 News has been informed that the lead suspect in this attack has been identified as Julian Dawson, who lives in Ebersville, Philadelphia. It is not known at this point if Dawson has ties to any terrorist organizations, but he is currently the lead suspect in this case, and we have been told that the FBI has hard, physical evidence linking him to the attack."

The news feed showed the briefcase he had given to Senator Kennedy. "Surveillance footage reveals Dawson transporting this briefcase, which was left at the scene of the crime, where he is believed to have dumped the contaminated vials directly into the feed system that supplies most of the area's water."

Julian bubbled with rage. That no good, rotten, son of a bitch.

It was never about the delivery of the briefcase. The Game Master had selected him so that they could have a fall guy for this attack.

He had to get out of here. The police were certainly looking for him. He had to get back to the Swanson Building before they captured him.

Julian left the pizza joint without looking back. He was about five blocks from the building.

Fear replaced his rage. He had to get home. If they caught him, he would rot away in prison. Who even knew what the legal system was like around here? They might just kill him on the spot.

He walked at a brisk pace, not wanting to attract attention. It was with great relief that he made it to the Swanson Building. The seemingly mundane building, which now he knew to be a place of malevolence, loomed before him.

There were fewer people now than when he had originally set foot in the building. Everywhere he went, eyes were on him, following him, tracking his movement.

He proceeded straight to the laboratory in which he had met with the Game Master earlier. This time, he was nowhere to be found, nor was the man tied to the chair. There was, however, dried blood on the floor. He found a short Asian woman wearing a lab coat, pouring liquid into a beaker. He grabbed her by the shoulder and turned her around.

"Where is he?" Julian asked.

The woman looked wide-eyed and startled. "Who?"

"The small, bald guy. The one who goes by the name the Game Master. Where is he? He was here earlier."

She shook her head. "I don't know."

Julian could tell she was lying. He gripped her more firmly. "Take me to him now."

"Let go of my employee, Mr. Dawson."

The Game Master walked into the room. Standing by him was the guard he had met at Senator Kennedy's office.

The Game Master smiled. "Mr. Dawson, I am glad that you have successfully completed your mission. I must commend you on a job well done."

43

CHAPTER VIII

Julian must have had a look that suggested he was going to thrash the little man because the guard from Senator Kennedy's office stepped in between them, almost daring Julian to make a move. He wasn't foolish enough to press his luck against this massive beast that looked like a human wall.

Julian gritted his teeth. "You son of a bitch. You unleashed a biological weapon in the water supply. People are dying from it."

The Game Master waved his hand. "You saw the gallant way Senator Kennedy stepped in to handle the situation. He took charge and saved many lives. That is going to resonate with the voters in his upcoming presidential election bid. I think he has significantly increased his chances of defeating the incumbent."

"You're insane."

"On the contrary. All of this was well calculated and planned out. You will find that I am both sane and meticulous."

Julian clenched his hands into fists. "You set me up to take the fall for your little scheme."

"Mr. Dawson, I made a bargain with you, one that I have every intention of fulfilling. Nothing has changed in that regard."

"Then you set up the other Julian Dawson."

The Game Master shrugged. "What happens to your shade is of little concern to you. The police investigation into this heinous assault will find that the other Mr. Dawson has ties to the Soviet Union, and, in fact, is working for them as a spy. He committed this act of treason on their behalf."

Julian remembered the newspaper article he had been reading on the train. "This is all a ploy for the US to join China in this war against the Soviets."

The Game Master glanced at the guard, a bemused look on his face. "Well, I can see that you've been paying attention to the political tidings in the short time you have been in this plane. Let's just say that there are many forces at work here, and the game has just begun."

Julian folded his arms. "I can't let you get away with this. I'll tell the police."

The Game Master gave a hearty laugh. "Now that's rich. What do you propose on doing, telling them that you are not of this plane? That you were transported here and were unwittingly involved in this attack? You would be serving your time in a padded cell. Not your best idea in the brief time I have known you."

Julian wanted to refute this statement but couldn't. He was stuck here and could not see a way out.

"Mr. Dawson," the Game Master said in a placating voice. "Do the sensible thing. What happens to your shade on this plane does not matter. The man is a stranger to you. Your concern is getting home to your beautiful wife and precious daughter."

"And I'm supposed to forget about all this? Pretend none of this ever happened?"

"Whether you remember or forget what occurred is of little consequence." The Game Master opened a folder on his desk and removed a photo of Julian having a picnic lunch with his family. Someone must have taken the picture a year ago, based on Natalie's appearance.

"How long have you been tracking me?" Julian asked.

"For some time now," the Game Master replied. "I have to be very thorough when I recruit candidates."

"Why me?"

"For one thing, you have an uncompromising and often times stubborn streak. You are determined to accomplish your goals and are not easily deterred. It would have been easy for someone to have devolved into a life of crime after witnessing your drunken father murder your mother."

Julian took a step back. It felt like someone had punched him in the gut. He never spoke about his family to anyone but Nancy, and that had taken years before he opened up to her. Even now, all these years later, it felt like a horrible dream. He had been a boy of six. His father used to get drunk and often slapped his mother around. One time he had taken it too far and killed her. Julian had run into his closet and hid there, crying hysterically until the police came. If the Game Master knew about that, then he probably knew everything there was to know about him.

"Yet you overcame those difficult circumstances and even earned a scholarship to Villanova University, holding down a part time job, yet still achieving top grades."

"How do you know all of this?"

The Game Master waved his hand. "I do my research. It's important in my line of work. When you finished school, you could have gone the conservative route and worked for a large firm, earning a decent living with full benefits and all of the things that go along with it, but you took quite a risk by starting your own firm in your early twenties, one that is starting to show some dividends over a decade later through your hard work and dedication after some lean years."

Julian stared at him. It was unnerving that this man knew so much about him.

The Game Master got up from his chair and moved toward Julian.

"Although important, those weren't the main factors in my selection. Most importantly, you are completely loyal and devoted to your family. When an old college flame sought you out in what seemed to be a random encounter—and mind you, she was quite a beauty—you rejected those advances out of loyalty to your wife. Despite the requirements of your job, you make every effort to be there for your young daughter. That is what made you ideal. Your motivation would be pure and unbridled. You'll do anything for your family."

Julian trembled. His mind felt frayed from what he had been through today. He rubbed his eyes and dug his fingers into his skull. "How do you know these things?"

The Game Master chuckled. "I am a man of great means and resources. It would be unwise to underestimate me, Mr. Dawson."

"I don't." Julian felt defeated and powerless to change the horrible injustices that had been committed. The role he had played in today's tragedy would be something he would have to live with for the rest of his life.

"I fulfilled my end of the bargain. Take me home."

"I shall," the Game Master replied. "What do you take me for, a liar? You did well in your task, and I'm sure you will do well in future tasks."

Julian eyed him warily. "I have no interest in future tasks. I've completed my end of the bargain and I want to go home."

The Game Master said, "To do so you will need to go through a doorway. Ah, and based on your reaction, I see that our mutual friend Mr. Cutter has already told you about these doorways."

"Yeah, he mentioned them, but didn't really explain."

"That is because Mr. Cutter's knowledge of such things is rudimentary at best. Other than their existence, it is not likely that he knows much about them."

"So, how does this work? I walk through a physical door, exit on the other side and I'm back home."

"The door is more metaphorical than physical, although in some cases it can be both, as it will be in this case," the Game Master replied. "There is more to it. I will give you a beverage, a fruity concoction, to drink. Then you step through and are on the other side, back to where you want to be."

Julian felt rotten about this whole situation. The Game Master had used him, and people had been hurt as a result, but his overwhelming urge was to return home. "All right, let's just get this over with."

"If you'll excuse me." The Game Master exited the laboratory, leaving Julian in the company of the goon. The man looked like he could bench press a Cadillac.

As he waited for the Game Master to return, Julian stared at his shoes, the desk, the ceiling, anywhere but the big man in front of him. The lab room itself was devoid of decorations or personal touches. It had files, miscellaneous laboratory equipment, some futuristic looking gadgets, and a computer.

A few minutes later, the Game Master returned with an opaque cup in hand. He handed it to Julian. "Drink fully. After a few minutes, I will take you to the door that will lead you home."

Julian stared at the beverage. It was pink and foamy and had a citrus smell to it.

"How do I know you're not trying to poison me? Tie up loose ends?"

"Mr. Dawson, if I wanted you dead, my associate here could snap your neck with ease. I've seen him do it. Trust me. No, we still have future dealings, me and you."

The logic was unassailable, so Julian put the cup to his lips and drank. It tasted a bit like fruit punch with an acidic aftertaste. He downed the entire cup without stopping. When he was done, he put the cup on the Game Master's desk and looked down at the short, bald man. Whatever was in there didn't have any immediate physiological effect.

"Now, that wasn't so bad," the Game Master said.

Julian shook his head before letting out a long belch. "Excuse me."

All of a sudden, a wave of dizziness hit him. He held onto a file cabinet for support.

"Would you like a seat?" the Game Master asked.

Julian took a moment to clear his head. "No, I'm fine. Can I go now?"

"Wait a minute. Give the formula time to work its way through your system." The Game Master looked at his wristwatch. Although it had a different emblem on it, the watch resembled a Rolex.

As Julian waited, the dizziness he felt continued to ebb and flow.

The Game Master looked up from his watch. "That should be sufficient. Now, if you will come with me."

The goon followed Julian and the Game Master. They went down a hall and made a right. Midway through the corridor, they stopped at an elevator. The Game Master pushed the up button, and the elevator immediately opened. He punched a code on a number pad on the wall, and they ascended. When they reached the top floor, they exited, the goon in the rear. At the end of the corridor was a set of stairs. They climbed the stairs and found themselves on the roof of the building.

The Game Master motioned with his hand. "Do you see the door?"

Julian frowned. In front of him was a single, brass door. He did a double take. Nothing supported the door. It stood on its own with no frame. "Um, yeah. I see it. You mean you don't?"

The Game Master shook his head. "Nor does our friend here. The door is for you alone."

Julian moved closer, not sure what to make of it. "It doesn't exactly look like it goes anywhere."

"I can assure you it does. I suppose you will have to make a leap of faith. What do you have to lose?"

"Nothing."

"Indeed."

Julian stepped in front of the door that apparently only he could see.

"I look forward to working with you again, Mr. Dawson," the Game Master said.

"I don't think so." Julian opened the door and stepped through it.

CHAPTER IX

A dizzying array of images flashed past Julian. It seemed as if there were hundreds of scenes moving at such blinding speed that he could barely make sense of them. It was as if he was racing through a tunnel at the speed of light. Disoriented, he thought he was going to collapse until it all stopped, saving him from insanity.

Having a difficult time breathing, Julian dropped to one knee. The Game Master had not told him to expect anything like that.

Just another one of his little games.

When Julian took a good look at his surroundings, he let out a long, guttural scream. He was not in his home plane, not by a long shot. This looked nothing like home. Whereas the plane he had come from was similar to his own with only minor differences, this time he had landed on the set of a science fiction movie.

That son of a bitch had lied to him. Of course, the Game Master wouldn't let him go home yet. The task had been too easy, even if it had produced devastating results.

He turned to go back through the door, to return and confront the scheming sociopath, but it had disappeared.

Julian clenched his fists, wanting to smash something. He was standing on a long platform near a body of water. The smell of sulfur permeated the air, blasting his nostrils, watering his eyes. The night was dark. Above him vessels, about the size of cars, flew past. The night sky was lit by a multitude of lights.

Out in the water were numerous flashing illuminations. A brilliant blast flashed off in the distance. This was followed by a thunderous sound. A surge of heat blasted him, and waves crashed against the platform on which he stood.

What did he land himself in, some kind of war zone? His frustration and anger bubbled. Here he was, caught in another of the Game Master's ploys, far from home. To make matters worse, he had no idea what he was supposed to do. If only that little man was in front of him now. Julian would choke out the son of a bitch.

He began walking with no destination in mind. Unlike his experience in his last plane where he had been in the house of his Julian counterpart with people to speak with, here he was the proverbial stranger in a strange land.

More explosions far off in the water caught his attention. Streaks of red shot across the sky. Whatever had been fired upon was now firing back. The last thing he wanted was to get caught in the crossfire. He hurried off the platform to the street.

Looking around, he appeared to be on the outskirts of a city. He jumped as a motorcycle zoomed by as if shot from a cannon.

He walked past a drab building with a sign that read J.P.'s Fish Market. He didn't smell fish or see any sign that this place was in business. Above the building were monorail tracks. Up ahead was a man that appeared drunk. The man's clothes were tattered, his eyes bloodshot, and he reeked of booze.

Julian cursed loudly. How was he going to get home? If he had to perform another task for the Game Master, couldn't he at least have the dignity of letting Julian know what he needed to do?

The drunk looked up at him with a scowl. "You gotta problem?"

"Yeah, I have a problem. I don't know where the hell I am?"

The drunk frowned. "You must be in worst shape them me. You're in New London, pal."

Like that was any help. "I have no idea where New London is. Is this at least the United States?"

The drunk grinned. "Whatever you've been drinking, I want some of that. Never heard of no United States. Is that some new third world country? They're always popping up."

Wonderful. This plane didn't even have a United States of America. "What country am I in?"

"You're in New England, of course."

Julian frowned. New London. New England. George Washington and the colonials must have had less success in breaking away from the mother land in this plane.

"Say, you got some credits?" the drunk asked. "We could talk about this over a bottle."

"No, I don't have any credits."

Julian created some distance between him and the drunk. This man would be of no help to him, and he needed answers, not wasting his time with some dreg of society.

Julian spotted three men in uniforms that looked similar to the Power Rangers. They had high top red and white boots, red suits with a black belt, and a helmet with a dark visor.

One of the Power Rangers pointed at him. "There he is. Get him."

Julian looked around. The drunk was no longer in sight, and there was nobody else nearby. They were coming after him. When they drew their pistols, he decided that he did not want to find out why they wanted him. He bolted toward the end of the block, then made a left at the intersection. His pursuers chased after him. He had no idea where to go. These Power Rangers knew the area better than he did and had guns. He was in deep shit.

He glanced back, his heart racing. They were still in pursuit. One of them fired at him. He ducked for cover.

He had just arrived in this plane. What could he possibly have done to upset them so much? They continued to fire. One of the shots took out a light pole. He was pretty sure they weren't firing bullets, seeing as how the shots were blue streaks of light.

He found an open shop selling clothes and handbags. He went into the shop only to encounter a startled shopkeeper. The man had an olive-skinned complexion and slicked back gray hair. Julian ran to the back of the store to the protests of the old man. In front of him stood a door that led to a storage room and another door that exited the store. He took the exit and found himself in an alley. Winded and breathing hard, he was not about to stop.

He ran down the alley. His pursuers were back on his trail.

Damn.

He knew it was wishful thinking, but he was hoping he had lost them. They fired at him again. Initially, he had thought they were law enforcement types, but if so, why would they be openly firing at him?

He spotted a fence to his left. Operating out of instinct, he climbed the fence, trying to create some separation from the Power Rangers. He had never been shot at in his life, had never been in a situation remotely this dangerous.

After scaling the fence, he ran to end of the street, knocking over trash cans in his wake. He found a bigger street at the end of the block. Maybe he could get lost in the middle of the crowd.

The ground vehicles were sharp, angular, and compact, not much bigger than smart cars. Even the larger one was sleek and built low to the ground.

Unfortunately, there weren't crowds to get lost in. His lungs were on fire. His legs felt as if they were made of rubber. He didn't know how much longer he would be able to keep up this pace. He was going to collapse before long with no real plan on how to elude his pursuers.

He looked up and found a flying vessel descending toward him. He wondered if it belonged to the people chasing him. The vessel, about the size of an SUV, was still flying in his direction. He looked across the street and contemplated running to the other side.

A dark-skinned man with a shaved head leaned out of the vessel. He wasn't wearing one of those funky red suits his pursuers wore.

The man shouted, "Julian Dawson." His voice was deep and powerful. "I'm here to extract you. Grab my hand."

Julian glanced back at his pursuers. He was on the fence about taking the man's offer, that was until the guys in the red suits opened fire on him. When he raised his arm, the man grabbed Julian's wrist and forearm. He had a powerful grip as he lifted Julian off the ground. The vessel began to ascend as the Power Rangers continued to fire at him.

The man pulled Julian inside of the vessel. Down below, they had stopped firing and were staring at him with contempt. Julian stuck his middle finger out at them as they faded from view.

CHAPTER X

Once Julian escaped the people trying to kill him, he turned his attention to his rescuer. The man had to be at least seven feet tall with a muscular build. He had a thin beard and a tattoo of a star underneath his left eye.

Julian found himself in the vessel's open cabin. The walls were lined with electronic gizmos and components that Julian couldn't begin to comprehend. Up front, the vehicle's driver or pilot was a man in his sixties, wearing shades and a headset. A single long bench lined one side of the vehicle. Two swivel, bucket-chairs were at the rear of the vessel.

Julian stared up at the man who had lifted him to safety. "Who are you?"

"I'm Manny." He motioned to the pilot. "That's Coyote. We were sent to retrieve you."

Julian frowned. "Who sent you?"

"I think you know the answer to that, Julian."

"The Game Master?"

Manny didn't reply.

"What does that son of a bitch want?"

Manny gave a slight grin. "Tsk, tsk, tsk. That's no way to speak about the man who just saved your ass. Without our intervention, you would have been roadkill."

"You'll have to excuse me if I'm not overly effusive in my thanks. If not for that little bastard, I wouldn't be in this mess."

Manny narrowed his eyes. "It would be wise to unsharpen your tongue. He's our boss and pays very well. Therefore, he has my allegiance, and I'm not the guy you want to mess with. Anyway, he thought you might be in a bit of a pickle, so he sent us to save your ass. You can say 'thank you' now."

Reluctantly, Julian said, "Thank you." If not for them, he would be dead. "Why were they trying to kill me?"

Manny shrugged. "Who's to say? My guess is that it would have something to do with your wife."

Julian frowned. "My wife?"

"Uh-huh."

Julian had a lot to learn about this plane and his role here, but Manny and Coyote weren't going to be the ones to answer his questions. "When can I speak with him, your boss?"

"Don't know. I was just told to get you out of harm's way and take you to a safe house. Don't have any instructions after that."

Julian yawned. He wasn't sure how many hours had passed since he had awoken in that strange bed with his strange wife, but he was damn tired. "This place you're taking me to, does it have a bed?"

Manny nodded. "Food and beverage too. You look like you had a rough day."

"You can say that."

"Where are we going?" Julian asked.

"Somewhere safe," Manny replied.

They flew for a few minutes in silence. Julian looked out the window. They were flying at a high velocity and a low altitude, maybe thirty meters off the ground over sparsely populated land.

"We'll be landing soon."

Julian's brows rose. "Don't we need to get in position and buckle up or something?"

"You're not from around here, are you?"

Julian narrowed his eyes, wondering if Manny was talking geographically or if he realized that Julian was from another plane. "I'm far, far away from home, trying to get back."

"If it makes you feel better, you can buckle yourself up back there in one of those seats, but it's not necessary."

Julian made his way to the back of the cab. He couldn't see any reason why he wouldn't want to buckle up on this flying vessel, something he always did at home. Manny laughed at him, but he would rather be safe and look silly than take an unnecessary risk.

The descent was quick, and the landing gentle. After coming to a stop, the vehicle's hydraulics lowered it further. They exited to a farm house. There was a one lane road a short distance from the house. He didn't see much traffic, either on the road or in the air. Corn fields surrounded them on all sides. He was glad to see that even in this land of technological advancement, they still had farms.

"Not much to do around here, I take it," Julian said.

Manny, carrying a large duffel bag over his shoulder, glanced back at Julian. "We're not here to entertain you. We're here to make sure those guys shootin' at you don't waste your sorry ass."

Coyote made a big pot of chili for dinner. Julian tried to engage the man in conversation, but the pilot had little to say. The only thing he could glean was that he was a combat veteran of several wars, but the only reconnaissance missions he did these days were against aliens.

Julian's jaw hung open. He was tempted to further question the man, but didn't want these people suspecting that he was not from this plane. If only Cutter were here. He still did not know all that much about the man, but from the start, he had gotten the feeling that he could trust him. It would be nice to have an ally who knew his situation and could provide him with the information he needed.

After dinner there was nothing to do, and Julian was beyond exhausted. Manny wrangled up a toothbrush and toothpaste for him but not a change of clothes. He crashed onto his bed and was out within seconds.

* * *

A knock on the door awoke Julian. Judging by the flooding sunlight assaulting his eyes, he surmised it was the next morning or maybe even the next afternoon.

In his deep, gravelly voice Manny said, "Wake up, sunshine. You got a visitor."

Julian tried to keep his eyes open, a struggle in the bright light. He let out a deep yawn and put on the pair of pants he had kept folded on the side of his bed. His visitor could only be one person. He was going to give that son of a bitch a piece of his mind.

Before Julian went to meet his visitor he made a trip to the bathroom to splash water on his face. He still wasn't fully awake and needed to be alert for this meeting.

Sitting on the sofa was the Game Master. He looked ridiculously small next to Manny, almost as if they were of different species.

The Game Master smiled. "Mr. Dawson, I am so glad to see you whole and well. I was informed that there was an incident yesterday."

Julian gritted his teeth. "You lying son of a bitch. You promised to send me home. We had a deal. I completed my end of the bargain, and instead of going home, you send me to this place where I nearly got my head shot off. I want to go back to my family."

The Game Master folded his hands. "Yes, about that. I understand your concern. You see, you are uniquely positioned to help me out with a current endeavor. And you must admit that the previous task was not particularly taxing. A simple delivery is hardly a suitable challenge for a man of your talents."

"Cut the shit," Julian said. "I want to go home."

"And you will," the Game Master said. "You just have to do this one thing for me."

Julian closed his eyes. He wanted to strangle the bastard, but he would have to get past Manny. Even if he were able to kill the little weasel, he wouldn't have the first clue on how to make his way back to his family.

He didn't have much leverage and he knew it, so he went back to what he knew in the business world. "I want a contract."

The Game Master frowned. "A contract?"

"Yes. I complete this task and you send me home."

The Game Master chuckled. "Very well. I will draft a contract and we will both sign it prior to this next little task."

"And why exactly am I so qualified for your little task?" Julian asked, trying to keep the venom out of his tone.

"Because it involves your wife," the Game Master replied.

Julian's brows rose. "My wife? Nancy?"

The Game Master shook his head. "In this plane, Julian Dawson is married to a powerful woman named Freena Monroe. She is the Secretary General to the Supreme Chancellor of the planet Earth. An especially difficult undertaking as the planet is on the brink on intergalactic war."

Julian was having a hard time wrapping his head around this concept. This plane was so radically different than his home plane. "You mean there are aliens here?"

The Game Master raised his hands, palms up. "Mr. Dawson, look around. This is a vast universe. Do you think humans are the only intelligent life forms out there? What a waste of space that would be. There are many truths that are unknown in your plane. You must broaden your way of thinking, my friend."

Julian glanced at Manny. Based on his neutral expression, talk of planes was not new to him. Maybe he was a traveler like Cutter, or maybe the Game Master had brought Manny into his confidence.

"You're not my friend," Julian said. "You're an evil bastard who ripped me out of my life and away from my family. Not to mention, you tricked me into killing those people."

The Game Master shrugged. "Perhaps we are not friends, but you still must complete another task for me. You are still in my debt."

Julian gritted his teeth. "What do you want from me? I'm not going to kill anyone for you."

"Don't be silly. If I wanted someone dead, I certainly would not turn to you for such an assignment, especially since I have Manny to do such jobs. Manny, how many people have you assassinated on my behalf?"

With deadpan eyes, Manny replied, "Seventeen."

Julian gaped at Manny, who was standing across from him just to the Game Master's right. He figured the guy was muscle but didn't realize he was a straight-up killer. He was starting to see a pattern. The Game Master, for all he lacked in physical size and stature, surrounded himself with some very dangerous men. Their massive size made up for his lack of it, something he would catalog for possible future usage.

Julian took a deep breath and looked around, but there was no way out, not unless he could figure out a way of travelling through one of those doorways. "So what do I have to do to get back home?"

The Game Master leaned in toward him. "I won't lie to you. You're task won't be an easy one. But, quite frankly, it will be an altruistic one."

Julian raised his brows. "Altruistic? You'll have to pardon my skepticism."

"Perfectly understandable. From your perspective, you only saw people becoming ill and dying. What you don't understand is that the end result will greatly benefit society."

"You'll have a hard time convincing me of that." Julian leaned away from the Game Master. "What do you want from me?"

"I need you to convince your wife, or rather this Julian's wife, that the United Federation of Earth must preemptively strike the aliens from the planet T478. Our planet's forces are ready to strike and are waiting for an official declaration of war. There is no more influential person than your wife. She is scheduled to testify in front of the World Council this week, and her testimony will likely decide the move to go to war or not."

Julian folded his arms. The setting may have changed, but the story sounded the same. "Go to war. Where have I heard that before? The last time I was involved in a plot for the United States to join China in their impending war against the Soviet Union. You're a warmonger, positioning pieces on a chess board to serve your needs."

The Game Master's eyes narrowed, and his mouth tightened. "Mr. Dawson, you lack the necessary information to formulate that opinion. You were in your last plane for less than a day. Similarly, you have been here for less than twenty-four hours. These are complex issues that even the residents of these planes, who have lived here their entire lives, cannot comprehend. Don't pass judgment upon me."

"Maybe you're right." Julian seriously doubted it. This guy was rotten to the core. "So, I have to talk this woman into making a decision in which many sentient beings will die?"

"It will serve the greater good," the Game Master said.

"And if I refuse?"

A stern look crossed the Game Master's face. Julian got the impression that not many people defied him.

"Then you will not see your family again. Make no mistake; I am the only one who can make that happen. You do not want to cross me."

"And how do I know you'll return me back to my plane?"

The Game Master smiled. "You will have a contract in writing."

Julian ground his teeth and held back the acidic comments he wanted to unleash. He had no assurances that the Game Master would stay true to his word. He also had no other means of getting home. There was not much to think about. He sighed heavily. "Okay. I'll talk to this woman. But you damn well better bring me home after I finish this task."

CHAPTER XI

Manny and the pilot transported him to his counterpart's home. After boarding, he soon discovered the vessel was equally adept at travelling on land as it was in the air. They drove away from this rural area toward the city. The massive high rise buildings loomed in the distance.

This plane felt foreign to him. It smelled different. Hell, it even tasted different. When he opened his mouth, he could almost feel a metallic taste in the air. He couldn't be sure how real that was, or if it was just his mind playing tricks on him.

The roads didn't appear to have speed limits, or if they did, Coyote ignored them. He drove at speeds in excess of one hundred miles per hour. Even when there was traffic, his zipped in and out of the lanes as if he were in a NASCAR race. Julian seemed to be the only person troubled by his hyper-fast driving.

Julian tapped Manny's shoulder. "How's it possible that you can drive and fly these vehicles?"

"I take it they don't have anything like this where you come from?"

"I've never seen anything like this in my life."

Manny chuckled, his now familiar guttural, deep-throated sound. "Then there will be lots of things around here you haven't seen."

Julian felt foolish asking, but he needed more information. "What can you tell me about my wife?"

Manny gave him an appraising look, his one brow raised to a side. "You serious?" When Julian didn't respond, he said, "Don't care much for her politics, but you could do worse." Manny chuckled once more as he looked out the window.

At least this asshole was having fun here at his expense.

A few minutes later, Manny said, "We're coming up on the destination. The boss man don't want to hear from you until you got the job done."

"What if I run into problems?" Julian asked.

"Said you would be able to handle things. Not sure why the boss man has this kind of faith in you, but I'm not the one making the decisions around here."

"Thanks for the vote of confidence."

Manny shrugged. "What can I say? You haven't exactly shown me much."

Julian grumbled. He would like to see if Manny, despite his size and the fact that he was a killer, could do better if he had been thrust out of his home and sent to these foreign planes with people trying to kill him. Given the circumstances, Julian felt he had performed admirably. At least he was still alive.

"What do I do when I've completed the task?" Julian asked.

"Send a vidmail to the boss man at this address." Manny handed him a chip about the size of a penny.

Julian looked at him incredulously. "What am I supposed to do with this thing?"

"The boss man said you were smart. You'll figure it out."

He had the distinct feeling that Manny was trying to make life difficult for him, having fun making him look foolish. Not that it was especially difficult. Julian was getting played by the Game

Master and couldn't figure out a way to get over on him.

They came to a stop, pulling over to the curb on a quiet street in what appeared to be the outskirts of the city.

Manny pointed down the street. "You see that big orange house at the end of the block. That one belongs to you. Have fun. Make sure you give your wife my regards. Let me know if she's good in the sack."

Julian wanted to say that whoever this woman was, it wasn't his wife. Nancy was back home with his daughter. Instead, he said nothing, his mind occupied by his task at hand.

After exiting the vehicle, he walked up the street without looking back. Numerous trees and bushes lined either side of the street. Although he did not recognize the makes and models of the cars, he could tell by looking at the shiny frames and their sleek elegance that they were high end. Each of the houses on the street were large but not quite mansions with neatly tended and manicured plots of land.

He walked over to his house, unsure of how to get inside. It's not like he had a key. If there was an alarm system, he wouldn't have the slightest idea how to disable it.

A thought occurred to him. People who lived here or, judging by its opulence, worked in the house, would recognize him and let him in. If nobody was around, then he wasn't sure what he would do; perhaps wander until he encountered somebody who recognized him.

He slowly ambled to the front of the house, pretending like he was looking for something. He opened the gate attached to the metal fence. There was no lock on the gate, just a simple latch. He pretended to observe the flowers in the garden. Stalling for time, he checked out the landscaping in the back yard. Everything seemed to be in order. Unless his counterpart was a skilled gardener, he guessed they paid somebody to take care of it. He certainly couldn't have managed to make it look this professional.

If someone didn't come soon, he was going to run out of things to do. He got on his knees, examining a bed of flowers. He was no botanist and didn't have the slightest idea what kind of flowers these were. They were light blue with specks of green in the middle and had a pleasant fragrance. The thought occurred to him that perhaps they didn't even exist in his plane.

When he looked up, he found a middle-aged woman wearing a green dress standing with her hands on her hips staring at him. He guessed she was Jamaican or Haitian. For a moment, he thought Manny had set him up and had given him the wrong house on purpose just to mess with him.

"Mr. Dawson, what are you doing in the garden? You never go near the garden. Is there something wrong?"

Julian breathed a sigh of relief, glad the woman wasn't going to summon the police thinking he was an intruder.

"And where have you been?" the woman asked. "You were supposed to arrive yesterday. The missus has been so worried without you calling or nothing. She had half a mind to have the police searching for you."

Julian didn't know what to say. He always tried to be well prepared when dealing with clients and business associates. He prided himself on doing his homework so he could handle all eventualities. He had to fight and claw for every client, and work his ass off to keep them happy. It was his livelihood, a skill that put food on his family's table. In this situation, he had gone in blind, not knowing what Julian's family or home situation was like.

Julian got up and dusted off his pants, wishing he knew this woman's name. "Yeah, things got pretty hectic on my trip…" He wished he knew where the other Julian had gone. "You know how these things can go."

"I know you get tied up in your business, Mr. Dawson, and it's not like Paris is around the block or nothin', but the missus gets worried. I was worried too."

Julian gave her a crooked smile. "You know how those crazy Parisians get. They drive a hard bargain. Um, is my wife home?"

The woman shook her head. "Mrs. Dawson still be at work. You know she's involved with that very important business with the aliens. You should call or send a vidmail."

There was that whole vidmail thing again. He would have to get a handle on this plane's technology. Once he got inside the house he would have a chance to learn more about his new situation, but he could learn more from this woman.

"Just out of curiosity," Julian said. "What's your take on this whole alien business?"

The woman appeared taken aback. Julian was under the distinct impression that his counterpart would never have asked her opinion about anything.

She looked down.

"Please," Julian said. "I would like to hear what you think. Speak freely and honestly."

She folded her hands. "Well, to tell the truth, I don't trust the aliens. I know you be friendly with them, but I never like them. There have been the attacks, and they look so strange."

He found it interesting that this Julian had developed a friendly bond with the alien forces. That would make his position all the more curious. It was a great strategy by the Game Master, the more Julian thought about it. If Mrs. Dawson's husband, who was allied with the aliens, gave an impassioned plea against them, then perhaps that would sway her opinion.

"But have they done anything specifically that makes you distrust them?"

"Well, there was the attack at the mine and the fire and all that, and those other bombings," the woman replied. "They say that the aliens were behind them. Who's to say for sure?"

Julian's impression was that she wasn't terribly knowledgeable about current world events. He was going to have to gain intel in order to present a cogent argument to his wife.

* * *

Unfortunately, finding the information he needed was more complicated than he thought it would be. Apparently, people in this plane they were not big believers in paper records. He found various digital devices in the house, but he had a hard time figuring out how to use them. He presumed at least one of them would allow him to send vidmails, but he would probably need a tutorial on its use.

He found a few correspondences directed to Freena, but nothing that would help him glean information about the current situation.

Freena arrived at six that evening. He still needed to learn more. In his last plane, there had been people to speak with. Here, the only person he encountered was the woman who worked here, and Julian didn't even know her name.

He was taken aback when he first laid eyes on Freena. She was stunningly gorgeous. She had an olive complexion that defied any notion of race, possibly a mixture of different ones. She had long, luxurious brown hair, luminous eyes, and elegant facial features. Her body was taut and well-muscled. She looked as if she could be a runway model instead of a politician. He hated to admit it, but Nancy wasn't on the same playing field in terms of beauty as Freena.

By the expression on Freena's face, he couldn't tell if she was angry or glad to see him. She had a haughty look that was difficult to read.

"Where have you been? I've tried to contact you about a dozen times. You've ignored all my messages and vidmails. I've been worried sick."

"Yeah, about that," Julian said. "I ran into some trouble. I was attacked. It was an assassination attempt."

Freena put her hand to her mouth, her eyes wide. "What are you talking about? Who would try to kill you? I don't understand."

This was the basis of the story that had been forming in his mind for the past couple of hours. The best part was that he wasn't even lying. Of course, he was omitting a whole lot. "They tried to take me out, but I managed to escape them. I've been on the run ever since. That's why I haven't been in contact with you."

"You're not making any sense. Who would want to kill you?"

Julian tried to compose himself. He was getting worked up from his own story. "A group of aliens. I barely made it out alive."

Freena touched his face. He had a nice cut from his encounter with the Power Ranger aliens. "Oh my. But why would they want to kill you?"

Julian sat on a nearby chair. "I have some theories, but I don't want to say anything until I have a better idea of why. I would hate to incriminate anyone unnecessarily."

"But you already said they were aliens," Freena said.

"I realize that, but there are many aliens out there and they have varying motives." That seemed to pacify Freena for the time being. Julian was winging it, hoping his story sounded credible.

Freena folded her arms and began pacing. He hated that he was putting this woman through such worry but couldn't help it. He thought about her real husband, and what he was doing right now. The Game Master had never explained that part of it to him.

"I'm going to get Arnie at the WC to provide increased security both for you and our home. Obviously, I have my own security detail and we have the one that protects us at home, but I didn't think you were at risk."

Julian shook his head. The last thing he wanted was people tracking his movements. "That won't be necessary. I don't think they'll be attacking me again."

"Why not? If they attacked you all the way in Paris, why wouldn't they attack you here?"

That was a good question that Julian did not have an answer for. "Look, I'll be fine. I can take care of myself. I eluded them in Paris; I can do so here as well. For what I need to do, I can't have a shadow following me."

Freena frowned. "I don't like it. If I see even the slightest hint of trouble, I'm going to have guards accompany you at all times. You know this is a delicate time. Tensions are high on all sides."

Julian nodded. "I understand. How are things at work?"

Freena tilted her head upward and sighed. "Time keeps growing shorter. We're going to have to come to a resolution, but Krupp is wavering. There are a million special interest groups who have his ear, and they all have their own agenda. He's waffling and can't make a decision."

"That must be difficult."

"Tell me about it. I don't know what to do. I have prepared arguments on both sides."

"I'm working on something that may help you out," Julian said.

Freena smirked. "Well, time is running out."

CHAPTER XII

Julian felt lost with the gadgets and gizmos of this plane. He had a hard enough time figuring out how to turn on the lights or flush the toilet. Every time he did something correctly, it felt like a small victory. He always considered himself to be tech savvy, having designed his company's website, but around here he felt like the village idiot.

He and Freena apparently had no children. The only other people living in the large house were servants. Freena and his Julian counterpart were well off. The house had many niceties, not to mention hired help. No matter in which plane he found himself, his Julian counterpart was more successful than him.

What the hell? If these people are basically a version of me, why are they all doing significantly better than me?

The other Julian was either self-employed or didn't have a standard nine to five job. There was no mention of him going to work from either Freena or the servants.

He spent most of the morning trying to figure out how to use the computer in his office. The thing was the size of a tablet. It had no keyboard, and after about three hours and many choice curse words later, he figured out how to work it enough to get information.

The main screen of the computer consisted of a holographic image that launched in front of him and operated like a touch screen, allowing him to navigate through images and texts on the virtual screen.

He gleaned from this super-high-tech computer that humans had first made contact with aliens over forty years ago on this plane. Astronauts had been exploring the furthest reaches of the solar systems when aliens had contacted them via a message sent through space. When the astronauts returned to Earth, this plane's version of NASA sent their own messages back through space. They exchanged more messages until nearly a decade ago when the first ships arrived from a neighboring solar system.

Julian was fascinated reading all of this. If there was intelligent life in other solar systems in this plane, then it stood to reason that the same held true for his plane. The wonderment and elation of the people was evident in the articles he read. Contingents from Earth travelled to planet T478 on their space vessels, while a segment of aliens stayed behind on Earth.

In the last few years, tension had started to mount. When trade between the two worlds occurred, various interests surfaced on both sides. They each wanted what the other had without having to pay fair value. There had been allegations of corruption and graft. In the last year, the mounting tension had turned violent. In recent months, there had been talk of war with many humans believing the Byraakys, the aliens from T478, wanted to take over the planet.

In his limited time researching the subject, he could not delve into the intricacies of the arguments, but the possibility of conflict between the two sides seemed senseless. Why couldn't trade happen peacefully? Both sides had much to learn from each other. Yet he had been tasked to advise for war. That was the only way the Game Master would allow him to return home, unless he was deceiving him again.

Julian's eyes felt heavy. Sitting on a comfortable leather chair, he started to nod off when the doorbell rang. Moments later, a sixtyish man with gray wisps of hair on his mostly bald head knocked on the door. He couldn't remember the butler's name but figured him to be of Eastern European descent given his pale skin and slight Russian accent.

"Mr. Dawson, you have a visitor."

Julian frowned. He wasn't expecting anybody, but then again he had little knowledge of his counterpart's affairs.

He followed the butler to the front door. He was stunned but not the least bit displeased to find the familiar disheveled face of Cutter standing at his front door. Julian was so taken aback that he could not even speak. He still didn't know the man well enough to know if he could trust him, but just then it didn't matter. Seeing a friendly, familiar face was a beautiful thing in this twisted plane.

Julian surprised himself by embracing Cutter. "Come on in. I'm really glad to see you."

Cutter smiled and stepped inside of the house. "That was a better greeting than I had hoped for. Nice place you have here."

Julian looked around at the vaulted ceilings, as well as the sculptures and paintings fashionably distributed throughout the house. "Yeah, I guess so."

The butler excused himself.

"I would give you a tour, but the place is still new to me. So how did you find me? What brings you here, anyway? I figured I wouldn't see you again."

"I'm full of surprises. Somewhere we can speak in private?"

Julian looked around. There were many rooms in the house, but he directed Cutter to the room he thought was his shade's office. "We should be away from any prying eyes and ears here. Unless of course, the place is bugged."

"Yeah, about that." Cutter took out a device about the size of a smart phone. He walked around the room, waving the device. After about a minute, he put the device away. "Unless they are using some serious tech, we should be fine. Just wanted to make sure our mutual friend or anybody else isn't listening."

Julian closed the double doors to the office. "Would you like something to drink? There's a liquor cabinet here."

Cutter perused the contents and nodded approvingly. "High quality stuff. Very expensive. I think I will help myself to the Marslen. Would you care for some?"

Julian nodded. "I could use it."

Cutter poured them each a shot of the liquor. It smelled like Scotch, but didn't identify itself as such on the bottle. Julian took a swallow. It was strong and smooth, and burned going down his throat.

"So, how did you find me?" Julian asked.

Cutter drained his glass and put it down. "I suppose the why is more important. I don't trust the Game Master, not a little bit. He's a nasty little bastard. I knew he wouldn't be sending you home. I figured you could use some help."

Julian folded his arms, the alcohol starting to have an effect on him. The reasoning sounded flimsy, and he thought there was more to it, but didn't want to press Cutter just yet, not wanting to alienate his one potential ally. "Why didn't you say something then?"

"Because it wouldn't have made a difference. You wanted to get home and would do whatever the Game Master was asking of you. I didn't have an alternative way of getting you home, so I was of little use to you. Anyway, I knew his game wasn't going to be over and he would be sending you elsewhere. I figured you needed help."

"Well, you got that part right," Julian said. "I do need help. As soon as I arrived in this plane, people, or rather aliens dressed up like Power Rangers, tried to kill me."

"Hmm, strange." Cutter frowned, his brows furrowed.

"What is it?"

Cutter poured himself more Marslen into his glass and took another swig. "Good stuff."

Julian could tell he wasn't going to expand upon his previous thought. "So how did you find me?"

"Well, the first place I went was your home plane, the one where Joe Biden is the president of the United States and Nike makes non-inverted swooshes on their sneakers, and you weren't there."

"How could you know that I wasn't there?"

"When you travel from one plane to another," Cutter said, "you leave behind a trace, almost like a scent. Normal people can't detect it, but travelers can. After the dust up with the poisoning of the water occurred, I traveled to roughly the location that would correspond to the Game Master's headquarters in your home plane. There, it's a regular office building. Since there was no trace of your arrival, I knew you couldn't be there. I then proceeded to travel to different planes until I found you in this one. Fortunately, it only took me five attempts to find you."

Julian grinned. "You're like a bloodhound or something."

Cutter raised his glass. "Never thought about it like that. Once I got here, it wasn't hard to find you. Although there must be other Julian Dawsons here, there is only one married to Freena Dawson. Knowing the Game Master's ill intent, it wasn't hard to determine that your Julian counterpart would be the one married to her. His schemes are grand, so he wouldn't concern himself with Julian Dawson the schoolteacher. But the one married to one of the most powerful women in the world, now that would be who he was interested in."

"Good deduction."

"So, what is that creepy weasel making you do this time?"

Julian sighed. "I have to convince my wife to deliver a speech at the World Council calling for a declaration of war against the aliens."

"Oh, just that. No problem, right?"

"What's your take on this whole war issue?"

Cutter raised his hands. "Don't get involved in politics. In fact, I avoid it like the plague. I've been in many, many planes and have seen lots of people itching to further their own goals. I stay out of it, and when the heat gets too high, I leave that plane."

"I thought you were going to help me out."

"I will, but I'm not going to tell you whether or not to go through with this, or whether a war against the Byraakys is justified."

Julian waved his hand. "Look, I appreciate you just being here. I realize you don't owe me anything. By the way, how do you work this vidmail thing? The Game Master gave me a chip that I'm supposed to use once the job is done to get back into contact with him."

"You'll need a vidmail player. I can get a hold of one for you. Then we can figure out how to get into the other Julian's account. Probably get some helpful info by digging through his vidmails."

"You have a place around here —I mean in this plane?"

Cutter nodded. "I have houses and apartments on many planes. I don't necessarily own these places, mind you. I share them with members of my family —other travelers. Comes in handy."

"All right," Julian said. "Since I have you here, can you help me work this computer? I'm trying to learn as much as I possibly can about the current situation with the Byraakys."

"No problem with that."

Not only was Cutter helpful in terms of working the computer, but he also explained much of the culture of this plane and gave further insight into the issue with the aliens. Despite his claim to have no interest in politics, he was very opinionated about the situation, making Julian question the sincerity of that statement.

After a couple of hours of research, Julian sighed in frustration. "I can't do this. I can't play God. Who am I to decide if people should live or die?"

"You're not going to decide anything. Freena and this plane's power brokers will. You will simply nudge her in a certain direction, if that's what you choose to do."

Julian poured more liquor into his glass. "What would you do if you were in my position?"

Cutter sat back, a sad, mournful look on his face. For a while he said nothing. "I'd want to get back to my family."

Julian glanced at the old-fashioned grandfather clock. Everything else was so futuristic that it looked out of place. "Freena told me she would be coming home soon."

Cutter nodded. "I'll be going. Don't want to arouse suspicion. I'll get a vidmail player for you. You want to reconvene tomorrow?"

"Definitely. Can you make it here by ten AM?"

"I can," Cutter said. "You'll be interested to know that a day has twenty-six hours in this plane."

"Everything else is strange around here. Why shouldn't that include the rotation of the planet?"

Cutter laughed. "See you tomorrow. Good luck with your task, my friend."

CHAPTER XIII

The doorbell rang. It sounded like the chimes of a grandfather clock. Out of instinct he went to answer the door, but the older gentleman he assumed was the butler intercepted him.

Julian figured Cutter had forgotten something and was returning, but the hulking figure at the door was Manny. The butler turned to Julian with a wide-eyed inquiry, as if asking if this man could possibly be his visitor.

"Hi, Manny." Julian went to the front door and led him inside, trying to make this exchange seem as natural as possible. Just as Cutter's appearance had taken him aback, this visit was equally surprising. "Thank you for coming on such short notice."

"Will you be requiring anything, Mr. Dawson?" the butler asked.

Julian shook his head. "We'll be fine." He led Manny into the office.

When they entered the office, Julian closed the door. Being inside of the room with this giant, he felt intimidated, but he had no reason to suspect that Manny would do him harm. After all, he could have just let the Byraakys kill him on the day they first met.

"Didn't think I would see you here. Can I offer you something to drink?"

"You sure could." Manny opened the liquor cabinet and helped himself to a bottle.

Julian figured the big man would find a glass and pour himself a drink, but it became apparent that he planned on keeping the entire bottle. Asshole. "Help yourself. So, what can I do for you?"

"Boss man thinks you're going to need some help pulling this off. I tend to agree."

Julian rolled his eyes. "I know. You've made it clear that you don't think very highly of me."

"Anyway, the boss man gave me this to pass on to you." Manny handed him a silver chip about the size of his thumbnail. "This should add credence to your argument."

"What exactly should I do with this chip?" Julian asked.

"Put it in your vidmail player."

Julian raised his hands. "Slight problem. I don't have a vidmail player."

"Thought that might be an issue, so I brought you one." He handed Julian a slim device about half the size of a smart phone. It was sleek and black. He showed Julian how to insert the chip, turn it on, and play the video.

"You planning on sticking around?" Julian asked.

Manny shook his head. "Got things to do."

"Well, I wouldn't want to cramp your style. Can I offer you something to take home along with that bottle? Maybe like a Thanksgiving turkey or something?"

"Yeah, I'll take a second bottle."

Julian gaped when he actually went for another bottle of liquor. "Well, I've really enjoyed our conversation today, but since you have to be going."

"I'll see myself out." Manny tucked the bottles in his jacket.

"So what can I expect in this video."

"See for yourself," Manny replied. "Even you will find it self-explanatory. Tick tock. Time's running out. You need to get to work on that hot wife of yours. I'm sure the two of you don't have as whole lot going on in the bedroom, so you should have plenty of time to figure this out."

"It's been a pleasure seeing you again, Manny. Can't wait to do it again." He walked Manny to the front entrance and closed the door behind him. "What a dick." He felt like punching a wall after the big man left. He glanced at the clock. There was little time before Freena was due back. In fact, she should already be here. Things were probably getting heated at the World Council.

There was no time to waste. He flipped open the tiny vidmail player screen. There was only one file on the chip. He entered in the encrypted code to play the video, which was no easy feat since the buttons on the player were tiny, making him wonder if the people in this plane had small hands.

The scene nearly exploded in front of him. He was so taken aback that he nearly tripped over the chair in the office. He hadn't been sure what to expect, but he wasn't ready for anything so lifelike. Holographic images of aliens in power ranger suits, over a dozen in total, breaking into a building occupied two thirds of the room. The action was happening right before him.

He sat in the chair, transfixed by the scene. The aliens gunned down two guards with those same laser type guns they had shot at him with. They proceeded to take cases of...he couldn't make out what it was, so he got up from his chair for a closer look and stared at the cases they were hauling away. The label on the box had inscribed XC-390—8FT on it. He wasn't sure what that meant, so he jotted it down. By the appearance of the inside of the building with wooden boxes arranged in shelves, he guessed they were some type of munitions or weapons storage.

He jumped back when an eruption of firefighting exploded in front of him as guards opened fire on the aliens. The battle was fierce between the two sides, but in the end the aliens prevailed, eliminating the humans. They made a hasty exit with the boxes in tow.

The video faded to black. He thought it was over, but a few seconds later, more images appeared in front of him. This time it looked like a conversation between two individuals. He peered closer and found that one of them was a Byraaky, but he wasn't wearing a Power Ranger suit. Julian walked toward the image. His heart beat rapidly as he stared in fascination.

The alien had a humanoid appearance, something he should have surmised based on the fact that with suits on, he hadn't realized they were aliens at all on his first encounter with them. This one was tall in comparison to the human he spoke with and had spotted, pale-green, wrinkled skin. He had a short stubby nose and a long, wide chin. He had a peculiar scar below his left ear. His ears were long and thin, triangular, and very pointy. The scar was in the shape of a crescent moon and was dark purple. He didn't want to be prejudicial since he always thought himself as being open-minded, but it was damn ugly.

He couldn't get a good look at the human in the image. The man's back was turned to him, and he wore a long coat. Trying to get a different view, Julian moved to the other side of the room and was surprised that the image completely disappeared from that vantage point. He quickly moved back to where he had been.

"I have the information you need," the man in the long coat said. "With it you can destroy the planet's main defense system. Earth will be vulnerable to your attack. Destroy these targets and the planet will be yours in a matter of weeks, maybe even days."

"How can there be any such assurances?" the alien asked. "Conflicts by their very nature are unpredictable."

The man in the trench coat seemed unimpressed. He folded his arms. "Let's cut to the chase. We both know that your goal is conquest of the planet, regardless of what you say publicly. I can make that happen. The question is, are you willing to pay my price?"

The alien paused, as if in thought. "These negotiations promise to be fruitful. We indeed can provide what you need and are amenable to a trade. I am sure that we can find terms that are agreeable to both parties."

"It's agreeable if you meet my price," the man said. "So, do we have a deal or not?"

"I believe a deal can be reached."

That was the last of the conversation as the images faded from view. Julian waited for more images to appear in front of him, but there were no more.

He poured himself another drink. "Damn." He hadn't been sure if he could go through with giving this pitch to Freena, but after seeing what he had just seen, how could he not plead the case for war? The Byraakys clearly intended to take over the planet. He had to act for the safety of all the humans on this plane. If he didn't do something, they would be doomed.

He was still sitting on the chair, sipping his drink, which went down smooth and sweet, when Freena entered the house. He once more marveled at her sight. She was a breathtaking beauty. He felt terrible comparing her to Nancy, who came up short. It didn't matter. Freena wasn't his wife. She was somebody else's wife.

It felt awkward being around her since he had no idea how close their relationship was despite being married. Last night, Freena had been so tired that she had crashed in bed and was asleep before he got ready to join her. He slept beside her, but there had been no physical contact.

He grabbed her hands and kissed her on the cheek. "I'm so glad to see you. We need to talk. There's something important I have to tell you."

She took a step back, frowning. "What is it? Is there something wrong?"

"Yes." Julian led her to a chair. "Please sit."

She did as he requested.

"I was purposely vague when we spoke yesterday about what happened in Paris. Before I spoke with you, I wanted to get the full story and make sure I had my facts straight. What I tell you might seem a little shocking, but it's important that you know, especially in light of current events."

Freena folded her arms. "What are you talking about?"

"I've been investigating the Byraakys' true motivations. That was the reason behind my visit to Paris."

"But you were there for your conference."

Julian shook his head. He wished he had been able to find out more information about his Julian counterpart, but he had been focusing on researching the alien problem. "Sorry for being so secretive, but it was a cover. I was there to meet some contacts. This is something I have been working on for some time.

"What I discovered is that the Byraakys intend on taking over the planet. It's something I suspected for some time, but now I know definitively. Before I spoke to you about this, I wanted proof, and now I have it."

"But I don't understand," Freena said. "You have always been sympathetic to the Byraaky cause. You have been doing business with them since they entered the planet."

"When we first made contact with them, I had been so excited about the possibilities. It was thrilling when they first landed on our planet. There was so much to gain by interacting with another intelligent and advanced civilization, but slowly I learned things that disturbed me. As much as I wanted to, I can't deny the truth. If we don't act now, the human race will be destroyed, and we can't let that happen."

"How did you come across this information? And why haven't you said anything before. It's late in the game." Freena wore a neutral expression.

"I didn't want to influence you until I had something concrete. I came upon this accidentally through a business contact. He had heard scary rumors and passed them on to me." Julian had no idea if this made sense, since he didn't know who his counterpart dealt with or what sort of things they discussed. Nothing like going in blind. "I started poking around and then I did some serious digging, and it all pointed to some pretty nefarious deeds by our visitors."

"You said you had proof," Freena said. "Can you show me?"

"Absolutely. Follow me." Julian led Freena to the office, which, based on the male style of furnishings and décor such as the stuffed deer head on the wall, he assumed was used by his Julian counterpart. "I was able to get a hold of this footage. What's on here is pretty self-explanatory and incriminating." The only thing he couldn't know with absolute certainty was its authenticity, given that Manny had provided it to him. But he figured if it was a fake, Freena and those she worked with would be able to determine that. Despite some misgivings, this was the right thing to do.

He accessed the main screen of the vidmail player and started playing the footage he had seen earlier. He paid little attention to it, having already seen it. Instead, he concentrated on Freena's reaction. At first, her face shown bewilderment, then growing concern. By the end, her outrage was visible.

After the vidmail was over, Freena began to pace around the room, her hands on her hips. "I can't believe that. I had been holding out hope that the reports were false. I certainly did not have anything this solid to substantiate them. Do you know what was in those cases?"

Julian shook his head.

"They were filled with Trulifiam 7," Freena replied. "There was a break-in at a secret facility in Antarctica. We thought the Chinese had done it. This is devastating. Trulifiam 7 is the most lethal weapon on the planet. I can't imagine how they could have learned of its location. There were only a handful of people who knew about it."

The more he heard from Freena, the more he was convinced this was the right action to take. If the aliens had taken this incredibly powerful weapon, the humans in this world had to defend themselves.

"I don't think there's any alternative," Julian said. "We need to defend our planet. Their intentions are obvious. It's time for war."

Freena closed her eyes. "I truly wanted to avoid this, but we can't afford to let them use the Trulifiam 7 against us. We have an invasion fleet ready. We're going to have to attack. After I present this new information, I'm going to call for a vote tomorrow in the World Council. God help us all."

Julian inwardly sighed. God help him most of all. It seemed like Freena had bought into his story, and now there would be an interstellar war. The wars of his plane were highly destructive. He could only imagine what this would be like. But he took solace that this was the right thing to do.

CHAPTER XIV

Julian spent most of the night with Freena as she prepared for her speech. She spoke with the Chancellor, who called for an emergency assembly. She would give her speech, and they would call for a vote. Although there were strong factions on both the pro-war and anti-war sides, she expected that even the most anti-war members would vote her way, or at least not voice opposition.

He helped her arrange her thoughts for the speech, making her coffee, being there for her to bounce ideas off of, but mostly just keeping her company.

He had a great deal of empathy for Freena. He hadn't had any intention of feeling anything for her. He just wanted to complete his task and return to his family, but it was hard not to care about this beautiful woman. Rightly or wrongly, she felt as if she had the weight of the world on her shoulders. It had to be an incredible ordeal to bear, and she maintained it with grace. She was thoughtful and conscientious, strongly motivated by doing what was right. He could hardly believe she was a politician.

It was well past midnight when she looked up at him from her computer screen, her lips quivering. "Am I doing the right thing?"

His heart melted. He took her in his arms, hugged her, and kissed her forehead. He was asking himself the same question. With the information he had, he was convinced this was the right course of action, but what if he wasn't seeing the whole picture?

For a while, he said nothing and just held her. It seemed like this was what she needed. She certainly didn't protest.

"I'm sorry that I've been so distant," Freena said. "I know I haven't always been the easiest person to be around. It would have been easy for you to leave me after my affair, but you've always stuck by me. You have always been there for me. You don't know how much that means to me."

Julian shifted uncomfortably. He felt like a voyeur, prying into someone else's relationship. This private moment wasn't meant for him.

He felt compelled to say something. "You have to do what you feel is right. You're intelligent. You've obviously done your homework on this subject. Nobody wants to go to war, but sometimes it's necessary."

Freena furrowed her brow. "That's sounds so strange coming from you. You have always struck me as a pacifist. What happened to the anti-war rally guy I met in college?"

"I guess I grew up." He had no idea if this Julian had changed his stance or if he would be in support of this action.

Julian stood and held Freena's hands. "Look, you need to get some sleep if you're going to be functioning properly tomorrow."

Freena closed her eyes and nodded. "I'm exhausted. I'll have a fresh perspective on things tomorrow morning. It's going to be a long day."

"It sure will." Julian led her upstairs. He felt horribly guilty about sharing a bed with this gorgeous lady, even without any physical contact. He had always been loyal to Nancy, not just when they were married but also when they had been dating. Apparently, the same could not be said about Freena.

He couldn't help but to be mesmerized as Freena undertook her nightly ritual. He momentarily contemplated telling her that he would be sleeping in the spare bedroom down the hall, but that would be too strange to explain. The best thing would be to try to act as natural as possible.

He felt like a nervous schoolboy as he went to bed wearing boxer shorts and a tee shirt. He had no idea what his counterpart's nighttime attire consisted of, but if this was different from what he usually wore, Freena made no mention of it.

She rolled over toward him, her eyes heavy and tired. "Wish me luck tomorrow."

"Good luck," Julian said.

She gave him a kiss on the lips, squeezed his hand, and turned over. He gazed at her on the other side of the bed. After a few minutes of watching the steady rise and fall of her breathing, he came to the conclusion that she had fallen asleep. Before long, he joined her in slumber.

* * *

Julian awoke the following morning to the sounds of Freena showering. He had not heard an alarm. For a moment, he was tempted to waltz in and get a glimpse of her, but he shook that thought away. This woman wasn't his wife. She was some other man's wife.

Grudgingly, he used the bathroom down the hall, consoling himself that at least he wasn't being creepy. Travelling between planes brought a whole new set of complication to his life, complications he did not want.

It would all be over today. Freena would do her thing in front of the World Council, and the Game Master would return him home. The first task was merely a diversion. This had to be the real reason the Game Master had recruited him. It made sense to select the shade of a man whose wife had the power to bring the world to war for such a task.

He went back into the bedroom, where Freena was mostly clothed and preparing herself for her day. She looked professional and intense. Gone was the vulnerability from the previous evening.

"Are you ready?" Julian asked.

Without taking her eye off the long mirror, Freena nodded.

"Good," Julian said. "I'll be keeping you in my thoughts today."

"Send me your positive vibes," Freena said.

"I will."

He wondered if this would be the last time he would see her. With this task complete, he did not see any reason to stay around. He hardly had a chance to get to know her, but he would miss Freena. Before she left, he kissed her cheek and once more wished her luck.

Shortly afterward, Cutter arrived.

"I brought a vidmail player," Cutter said.

Julian waved his hand. "It doesn't matter anymore. Manny, that goon I was telling you about that works for the Game Master, was kind enough to bring me one. Not only that, but he brought me some startling footage. It really indicts the Byraakys. I showed it to Freena. This is all the ammo she needs to make her argument. She plans on showing it today when she makes her speech. It's all over now except for the shooting."

Cutter brushed back his dirty blond hair. He wore it just past the shoulder. The top of his forehead had a quality scar that extended from one brow to the other. Just by Cutter's demeanor, Julian could tell that he ran in some dangerous circles. Julian also had the impression he could handle himself when things got rough. "All the same, it might be beneficial to take a look at the other Julian's account."

"That's all well and good, but it's not like I have his passwords. I assume you would need that sort of thing in order to see his messages."

"You do," Cutter agreed. "Fortunately, I have certain skills that will help us in that area."

"You can hack into his account?"

"Hack is such an ugly word. I can allow us to temporarily view his messages."

Julian grinned. "You're a man of many talents."

While Cutter went to work, Julian asked the butler to brew coffee. He had tried some this morning and could have sworn it was laced with alcohol. Perhaps that was how the coffee tasted in this plane or perhaps that was how the other Julian liked his.

While Cutter was trying to get into the account, Julian rummaged through the office. Despite the lack of paper, there had to be something in here that could give him insight into the life of his shade. He was trying to find pictures, correspondences, anything that could paint a picture of this man.

Cutter perked up. "I'm in."

Julian sat next to him. "Oh yeah. What do you have?"

"A number of messages." Instead of working off the tiny screen that came with the vidmail player, Cutter expanded a virtual screen that hovered in front of him. "Hmm. There are messages from someone that keep popping up over and over again for the past few days. They are texts, not vids."

"What does it say?"

Cutter narrowed his eyes. "Someone is trying really hard to get a hold of you. There are a dozen messages. It looks like you missed the first rendezvous…in Paris."

"That must have been the trip the other Julian had gone on."

"Then apparently you were supposed to meet up around here at a place in Kensington."

Julian frowned. "So, the country is called New England. What's the deal with all of these British names?"

"It would take a while to go through the full history of this plane, but the short version is that after two failed attempts to gain freedom from the empire of Britain, the country finally negotiated a deal to become an independent country about one hundred years ago. There's still a very heavy British influence here."

"This place also has far more advanced technology than my plane."

"That actually played a large part in the country gaining independence."

"How so?"

"Most of the rapid advancement in technology in this plane came from New England. Before long, the British saw the writing on the wall. Even though they had successfully repelled the colonialists twice, a third try would result in a brutal and bloody, possibly devastating war. Instead, they negotiated a settlement, giving the colony its independence and securing favorable trade status that still exists today. You'll be interested in knowing that much of the southwest region of your United States including most of California is part of Mexico in this plane."

"No kidding. Well, I can't say that I'll be sad to leave. It hasn't exactly been friendly to me."

"It's not a bad place," Cutter said. "Trust me. There are far worst planes out there."

"So, what does this person want?"

Cutter looked up at the screen. "Actually, they still want to meet with you—in about an hour, not far from here."

Julian looked at the grandfather clock. "Do you want to come with me?"

Cutter nodded. "My afternoon is free."

"Before the day is over, Freena should have finished her speech and started a war."

"Cheery," Cutter said. "Sounds like a good time to get out of Dodge."

They entered Cutter's vehicle. Like Manny's, this was a quasi-land/air vehicle. Cutter drove to their destination, speeding through traffic. They arrived in thirty minutes with time to spare.

The day was breezy and chilly. Julian wished he had brought a jacket with him. He kept his hands in his pockets as they waited in a parking lot on the roof of a hospital building. He found it a strange place to meet. He wished they had chosen a coffee shop or a restaurant. He could use a warm beverage and a bite to eat.

"So, what do you think this is all about?" Julian asked.

"Not a clue, but I'm curious. I would like to find out more about your shade. He can't be married to Freena and just be Average Joe Citizen."

As they waited, Julian continued freezing his butt off. He spotted a flying vessel in the distance approaching them.

"Looks like we got company." Julian's heart was beating rapidly. One thing was certain—life had not been dull since he had left his home to do the Game Master's bidding.

Their car was the only one on the top floor of the parking lot. Julian glanced at his watch. There was thirty seconds left until the meeting time.

A sense of dread filled him as the vessel touched down on the asphalt. His eyes went wide a few seconds later when he realized what was causing that dread. There were four people in the vessel, and all of them were wearing the now familiar alien Power Ranger suits.

"Oh shit. We've got trouble," Julian said.

He glanced at Cutter, who pulled out a pistol. He had not even realized Cutter was carrying a weapon, but it shouldn't come as a surprise. Cutter seemed like the type of guy who prepared himself for all eventualities. He glanced at their vehicle, which stood twenty meters from them. They would never make it in time if they ran for it.

As if sensing those thoughts, Cutter said, "Let's find out what they want."

CHAPTER XV

Julian was too stunned to react when the alien in front of the pack removed his helmet. It was the same alien that had been in the vidmail, the one who was negotiating with the human in collusion to take over the planet. He had that peculiar crescent moon shaped scar below his left ear. It was the first thing he had noticed when he had seen this alien both in person and in the vidmail.

Cutter still held his gun, looking ready to fire.

He wasn't sure how this alien was able to move around without the suit, but he seemed to be breathing the air with no difficulty.

"Julian." The alien spoke with what sounded like a thick African accent and his voice was garbled. "Where have you been? I thought you were injured or dead."

Julian narrowed his eyes. This alien had some sort of relationship with his Julian counterpart. He had to learn more. The only problem was that he did not know if they were a threat to him and Cutter.

"What happened to you?" the alien continued. "We are living in desperate times. Despite our efforts over the past year, war appears imminent. I know that you want to stop this as much as I do, and that is why we must act."

Julian folded his arms. He didn't know if he could believe this Byraaky.

He glanced back at Cutter, who had narrowed eyes and a guarded expression. "I don't know what you're talking about. Your people are trying to take control of the planet."

The alien scrunched his face. His pale, green skin was furrowed in what Julian thought was a frown. "How could you speak such a thing? We have always been of the same mind. We both want peace and prosperity for our people. This is what we have been working toward."

"Then you have some explaining to do," Cutter said.

Julian nodded. "I have proof that that you and your people are going to invade Earth."

The alien's face grew dark. "This could not be further from the truth."

"Show them," Julian said.

Cutter put away his gun and brought out the vidmail player. The holographic image took shape. The aliens that had come from the vessel stepped back so that they could get a view of the scene playing before them. The first scene was the break-in, where they had stolen the Trulifiam 7. After that, the conspiratorial conversation played with the alien in front of him.

Julian studied the alien's reaction. The others in the group were unreadable since they still wore helmets. From the alien's facial features, Julian first read confusion, then recognition, and finally anger.

He spoke in furious bursts. "This is a deception, a forgery. I would have thought that the trust that we have gained would allow you to see through this lie."

"How is it a deception?" Julian asked.

"I spoke those words, true," the Byraaky replied. "But not to this individual and not in this context. You of all people should know."

"And why should I know?"

"I spoke those words to you. How can you not remember?"

"You'll have to excuse my friend," Cutter said. "He's taken a few blows to the head and his memory isn't so good these days. Well, there's one way to find out the authenticity of this all. I can analyze the data to see if it's been compromised."

Julian turned to him. "Why didn't you suggest that before?"

Cutter shrugged. "Had no reason to think it might be fake."

The alien grabbed Julian's hands, his large eyes pleading with him. "I beseech you. Time is running out. You must intercede on our behalf with your wife before many die. Please."

* * *

Julian felt like the dirt encrusted at the bottom of his shoe. He had thought he was going to leave this plane with a clear conscience, convinced he was doing the right thing. Now, he was filled with doubt. He was sitting on a chair in Cutter's house, which was a modest affair in comparison to the one he had been living in for the past couple of days. They had been there for the past couple of hours as Cutter busily worked on a computer system that looked way above Julian's level of comprehension.

Cutter took a deep breath and looked up at him. "The files on this chip have been compromised."

"Meaning what exactly?"

"Meaning that these are multiple files combined together. It will take time to recreate the original source file or tell where it has been corrupted, but it's definitely been manipulated. Very sophisticated level of manipulation here. This wouldn't be easily detected. Only by someone with serious expertise on these systems, which I have."

"But the folks at the World Council will be able to tell, right?"

Cutter shrugged. "They could find someone with the technical expertise to decipher, but I doubt they will. They have too many people there who want war to happen. And this visual should be enough to sway the fence sitters."

Julian shook his head. "That son of a bitch. The Game Master must have changed these files. He's played me like a fool again."

Cutter put his hand on Julian's shoulder. "Don't be so hard on yourself. It looked authentic. I certainly had no idea that it was a fake. Neither did Freena. Nor will anyone she presents it to."

Julian folded his arms, trying to think through the contents of the vidmail. "I get the part with the break-in. That could have easily been humans dressed in suits, but what about the conversation that the alien said took place with the other Julian Dawson?"

"Who knows," Cutter said. "Perhaps the Game Master had him abducted in Paris, stole his vidmail player, took that file, and then used it to create the one we saw. It's all guesswork, and it's not like your shade is here for us to ask him."

"I wonder where my shade is right now."

"I don't have the foggiest notion."

Julian buried his head in his hands and groaned.

Cutter rose from his chair. "It doesn't matter how the Game Master did it. It's too late."

"What do you mean?" Julian asked.

"The Earth forces have already attacked planet T478."

"Can't we do something about this? Maybe I can talk to Freena. Tell her about the fake video. Hell, tell her all of it, about the Game Master, too."

Cutter shook his head. "It's too late. People on both sides wanted this to happen. You can't put the toothpaste back in the tube. It's time to leave. For both of us."

Julian nodded. He wished there was something he could do, but Cutter was right. He handed Cutter the chip Manny had given him to contact the Game Master. "I need to go back to where I belong."

* * *

An hour later, Manny and Coyote picked him up in the same vehicle they had used when they first met. Once inside the vessel, Manny patted him on the shoulder. "Why so glum? You got the job done.

Surprised the hell out of me. Didn't think you had it in you."

Julian closed his eyes. "Leave me alone."

"No need to be so touchy. I'm paying you a compliment. I'm sure the boss man'll give you a nice reward."

"I don't want a reward. I just want to get home."

"Yeah, I heard that song already. So, tell me. How was that wife of yours? Did you get some on the side?"

Julian glared at him. He wanted so badly to slug Manny across the jaw. It would probably be the last thing he did because the big man could snap his neck like a twig.

Manny chuckled. "Who am I kidding? You couldn't get action at a brothel if you were carrying a fist full of hundreds."

"Do you try hard at being an asshole or does it come natural to you?"

Manny gave him an icy stare. He looked as if he was going to reach out and choke Julian until Coyote gave him a look that suggested he should back off. Julian had pressed his luck with that comment. He wasn't going to try it again, but it felt good.

There was little conversation the rest of the way, which suited him just fine. They landed in a parking lot in front of a shiny, tall building. There was nothing sinister or nefarious about it.

He and Manny took a high-speed glass elevator that seemed to shoot up into the sky on a rocket. The people on this plane had to be in a hurry because everything moved fast around here. When they exited on the twenty eighth floor, they entered a large open room with futuristic equipment that Julian couldn't even guess their application, but there was a whole lot of beeping and buzzing.

As they walked, Julian stared at a large, spherical, purple object that was shooting blue rays into an object the size of a marble. When he lagged behind, Manny pushed him forward.

Julian had to stop when he saw an orangutan sitting at a table, dressed in a suit, drinking from a cup, and eating with a fork and knife. He stood, open-mouthed, gaping at the bizarre scene, which

Manny paid no attention to, as if it was an ordinary, everyday occurrence.

The orangutan raised his glass to Julian. "Good day, sir."

Manny put a firm grip on Julian's shoulder. "What, you never seen a talkin' monkey before? Come on. Boss man's waiting for us. Nothin' to see here."

Julian gave him an incredulous look. "Nothing to see here? I've never seen anything like this before."

"That's right. You're not from around here. Well, maybe you can see some of our sights later. Right now, we got business to attend to."

Julian let Manny guide him through this high-tech play pen. Resistance would be futile.

The area was so vast that Julian could not see from one end to another. As they walked, he saw things that made his head spin. They reached a partitioned area, which Manny motioned for him to walk through.

He found the Game Master sitting on a plush sofa wearing a wide smile. He held a glass of champagne in one hand. On a narrow, round table stood another glass of champagne. He stood and handed Julian the second glass.

"Congratulations on another job well-done, Mr. Dawson. I had the utmost faith that you would be able to complete your task. Sit down. Share a beverage."

Julian folded his arms. "I don't think so."

"Why must you be so obstinate? I am congratulating you and expressing my thanks."

"That vidmail is a counterfeit. You manipulated it to make the Byraakys look guilty. The other Julian was working with them, trying to prevent this conflict from happening. Seeing as how I've seen no evidence suggesting that they are the aggressors, and knowing how treacherous you are, I'm guessing that their intentions are actually peaceful, and that I've condemned a countless number of people to die."

"This war is an absolute necessity." The Game Master raised one finger. "It is right and just. The Byraakys have been encroaching on this planet and aim to take it over. This will stave off their attempts. It is the people of Earth who must control their own planet."

"So, global domination isn't enough for you? You need interstellar domination."

The Game Master did not respond but maintained a smug look.

"Mostly I feel bad for Freena. She truly wanted to do the right thing, and thanks to my meddling, she wound up doing the wrong thing."

"You do not know that of which you speak. You can rest your conscience because she did the right thing, Mr. Dawson."

Julian shook his head. "Will you stop working me for once. Just get me home."

"Indeed." The Game Master motioned to the glass of champagne. "This is the beverage that you will need to take you through the door."

Julian frowned. "This looks nothing like the last brew you had me drink."

"You are quite right in that accord, but it will accomplish the same goal. Drink and you will see."

Julian closed his eyes, picturing his wife and daughter. He picked up the glass and drained it. This time he would be going home. When Manny and the Game Master led him to the door, he was ready to be back in his home plane for good.

CHAPTER XVI

Except it didn't happen that way. In his heart he knew the journey wasn't over. He was just trying to convince himself otherwise.

Julian felt like screaming when he found himself in a plane that clearly wasn't his. Instead, he inwardly groaned. He felt as if he were in the vortex of a tornado that was spiraling out of control with no way out.

This plane was the polar opposite of the previous plane, something made clearly evident when a horse drawn chariot passed him by. No, he was most certainly not home. He was standing on a grass field about a stone's throw away from a cobbled road. Nearby, a man herded goats into a circular building.

He looked around to find a man who looked like a Roman centurion walking in his direction. The man held a sword in hand and wore a mean scowl. Julian contemplated running, but where would he go? Julian looked down at the slacks, polo shirt, and sneakers he was wearing. He must look as strange to these people as the Byraakys looked to him.

He knew nothing of the geography of this land, nor did he know any of the people. If only Cutter were here, but he wasn't expecting his friend to bail him out today.

The centurion continued in his direction. He sized up the man. They were about the same height, but the centurion had forty pounds of muscle on him, not to mention the sword he was carrying.

He recalled his arrival on the last plane. The people dressed in Power Ranger suits who he had thought were aliens were probably just working for the Game Master. They may not have been Byraaky at all, and he doubted they were really trying to kill him. It was just another one of the Game Master's ploys.

With that in mind, Julian decided to stand his ground and take his chances with the centurion.

When the man was a few feet away from him, he said, "You are Julius Delessario?"

"Julian Dawson."

"You must exit here posthaste. Your mode of dress will land you in a prison cell. Follow me."

Julian hesitated. This man had to be working for the Game Master. Otherwise, he would not have known his name or where to find him. The question was whether or not to go with him. Undoubtedly, the Game Master was drawing him into another scheme.

Not far down the road, he spotted four men in a chain gang being led by a guard dressed similarly to the centurion. The guard lashed one of the men in the chain gang with a rawhide strap. The centurion was right. He wouldn't last very long here on his own.

The centurion did not wait for a response and began walking away. For better or worse, Julian ran after him. He would rather be with this guy than the fellow running the chain gang. Up ahead, a shepherd was herding sheep toward a market. Behind him was a beggar whose skin was pockmarked and ravaged with some type of disease, perhaps leprosy. The scent of raw sewage assaulted his nose. To the left of the path was a domed building with a statue of Neptune holding a trident.

Based on what little he knew of his circumstances, he shouldn't be in ancient Rome, but this place certainly invoked images of that time and place. The arches located throughout the area brought to mind pictures of ruins he had seen. He wondered if he would find a version of the Coliseum around here.

The centurion ushered him into a small house made of clay and mortar. The edges of the house were rough, and the roof looked flimsy. "Inside here, Julius,"

"My name is Julian."

The centurion frowned. "That's a queer name. Here you are Julius Delessario. You would be wise to remember that. And your mode of dress is beyond peculiar. We must remedy that immediately."

"I don't mean to be rude," Julian said. "Actually, I don't particularly care at this point, but who are you?"

The centurion gave him a severe look. "I am Marsanto Belez."

"I can't say that your name means a whole lot to me. Let me guess. You work for the Game Master."

Marsanto furrowed his brow. "The Game Master?"

"Yeah. He's a little fellow with a bald head. His nose is sharp and pointy. And he has this irritating way of clicking his teeth."

Marsanto's face lit up. "Ah, the Maestro."

"Yeah, well the son of a bitch has been sending me all over the damned place doing his bidding. I swear, if I ever get the chance, I'm going to tear his beak-like nose off his face."

"It would not be wise to speak ill of the Maestro."

"Yeah, I get it. Your Maestro pays you some serious coin to do his dirty work, so you feel compelled to defend his honor, even though he has no honor. The more things change, the more they stay the same."

"Your sharp tongue will get you in trouble."

"Look, Marsanto, you have to understand that this is my third go around with him. He has done nothing but lie and trick me, so you'll have to forgive me, but I'm getting tired of his act." Julian sat on the wooden stool.

"I understand your hardship, but if you wish to survive here, then you must do as I tell you. I have clothes that will fit you. Put them on and destroy the ones you have."

"If it's all the same, I would rather store these somewhere. I have the distinct feeling that when I leave this place, the clothes you give me will stick out like a sore thumb."

Marsanto frowned. "That is a curious expression."

"Yeah. I guess I should speak the way you do. As they say, when in Rome do as the Romans do. By the way, what's the name of this lovely city?"

"Delphi."

The name sounded close to Philadelphia, except this city looked nothing like any of the three versions of the city he had seen. He would have to ask Cutter about it the next time he saw him.

Marsanto handed him a blue wool tunic with short sleeves. Julian breathed a sigh of relief. He had seen men wearing togas earlier and was worried that he would have to wear one of those. He had worn one at a college party and had vowed never to make that mistake again.

Julian looked for a room in which to change in this small house. In one room sat a young man writing something on parchment with a feathered quill pen. In another room was a woman nursing a baby. He had no idea whose house this belonged to, but nobody paid him much attention. He shrugged, removed his clothes except for his boxers, and put on the tunic and a wide belt. Now he looked like a proper Roman citizen.

Marsanto folded his arms. "Julius, if anyone inquires, you just cut your hair and shaved your beard. And you recently fell ill."

Julian frowned. "I feel fine."

"How else will you explain your lack of complexion, Julius?"

"My name is not Julius."

Marsanto closed the distance between them. Their faces were within inches of each other. "From this point forward, you are Julius Delessario. Do we have an understanding?"

Julian tried to control his rising anger. "Right. I'm Julius Delessario. So, tell me more about this guy. And while you're at it, tell me what the Game Master, I mean the Maestro, wants me to do."

"You are an aid to Emperor Belesinto. In fact, it is said that you are the only one whom Belesinto listens to. You are thought to widely shape his policies. Your influence spreads far and wide in Delphi."

"Well, I'm glad that ole' Julius is doing well for himself." This seemed to fit the pattern of his other counterparts. "What else do you know about Julius?"

Marsanto took some cheese from the counter next to a brick oven, sat on a wooden stool by the table, and sliced it with a long knife. "You did not come from a wealthy family but have managed to attain significant wealth."

Julian furrowed his brow. "Is that sort of thing unusual around here?"

Marsanto nodded. "One's wealth is usually associated with their class and birth status. You started off as a merchant and through devious means, so I am told, managed to attain a fleet of ships. Your ability to attain rare and precious items made you a favorite with the nobility and aristocracy. Over a decade ago, you befriended Mauro Dechichio. By amassing a large fleet, you helped him repel the attack of the Nordic invaders. This was what led Mauro to becoming Emperor Belesinto after the line of the ruling family had died during the invasion."

"Well, thanks for the history lesson. What about his family? Where does Julius live?"

"You reside in a cottage on the estate of Emperor Belesinto. He likes to keep you close. My understanding is that you are often needed at strange times to help settle one crisis or another. You have three children, two of them of school age, one still a babe yet."

Julian peeked out the small window. Not far away, men were laying stone in the construction of a bridge. He noticed the arches typically associated with Roman architecture. "So, is Julius married?"

Marsanto frowned as if that should have been obvious. "Indeed, he is."

"Let me guess. Julius is married to a beautiful woman."

"Indeed, you are married to a fine woman. Almarella is renowned throughout the land for her beauty and grace."

Well, at least the other Julians were consistent. He would hate to go to one of these planes and find that he was married to a homely woman. "All right. So, we've established what Julius does, what his family life is like, now tell me why I am here. What does the Maestro intend for me to do?"

Marsanto smiled. "Your job is a rather simple one."

"There's nothing simple when the Game Master is involved. I have come to learn that the hard way. What does your Maestro want me to do?"

"Your duty is to kill Emperor Belesinto."

Julian's nostrils flared, his anger rising. He had already done things that he was not proud of for the Game Master, but this was taking it too far. "No way. Absolutely not. I am not going to kill anybody for that scumbag."

Marsanto stared at him with the dead eyes of a killer as he drew his sword. "You indeed will perform your duty. If you do not, I will kill you."

CHAPTER XVII

There was nothing to gain here by fighting Marsanto, other than his own death. The large man would run his sword right through him. Even had Julian been armed, he wouldn't like his chances against a seasoned warrior. He would bide his time and think of a way out of this mess by operating out of instinct and using his wits.

He gave Marsanto a cold stare, not ready to concede defeat. "Where is your Maestro? I want to talk to him."

"He will not be joining us."

"Fine," Julian said. "Where do I live?"

"I am glad that you are coming to your senses. I did not wish to administer your death on this morning. I will lead you to your house under the guise of your newly hired bodyguard."

Julian raised his brows. "My bodyguard? That's funny. You're just as likely to slit my throat as you are to protect me."

"Do your duty and you will find me the best ally you can have. As I mentioned, this land is quite dangerous, especially for a stranger. You will need protection, and I will provide that as long as you stay loyal to the Maestro."

Marsanto might be right about needing protection but having

him around would be troublesome. He wasn't going to kill anybody, but with this big meathead breathing down his throat, how would he be able to get away with not completing his task, especially with Marsanto already threatening to kill him if he didn't comply? There had to be a way out.

As they left the house, Marsanto said, "Act naturally. Your movements and countenance are stiff and unnatural, suggesting that you are not who you claim to be."

"Well, I'm not," Julian said.

"And publicizing that fact to the world will not serve you."

The skies had darkened since his arrival. Lightning struck in the distance, but that did little to stop the people from going about their business. After walking a mile, they reached a large, thriving marketplace where merchants were hawking a multitude of goods including leather products, livestock, and slaves. Seeing the slave trade did little to improve his distaste for this plane.

The place was loud and raucous. Those selling their wares and shoppers shouted back and forth. Several shop keepers tried to proposition him into purchasing their goods, but Marsanto quickly ushered him through the market.

More thunder rumbled. When rain started to fall, some of the vendors packed their wares and left. After Julian and Marsanto exited the market, the rain stopped. They entered what appeared to be a government center. The area was inhabited by domed, immaculate structures. Statues and sculptures lined the front of the buildings. They passed a magnificent fountain that was an architectural masterpiece. The roads and buildings here were statelier than anything he had seen in this land, the noise level had reduced considerably, and he did not encounter any disease-ridden beggars.

Marsanto said little to him as they walked. He began to wonder if Marsanto was a stranger in these parts as well. During the entire time they travelled, he had not greeted or spoken with anybody other than an occasional nod that did not indicate familiarity or friendship.

Maybe he was just an antisocial bastard.

They walked past the government district to a gated community filled with massive houses decorated with ornate statues. Equipped with soldiers at the perimeters carrying swords and spears, this was unlike any gated community Julian had ever seen. Many of the soldiers had hounds that looked capable of tearing out a person's throat.

"Act as if you belong here," Marasanto said. "After all, this is where you live."

Julian smiled and waved at the guards. They let him through without incident. "That was easy enough."

"These guards are not the only ones you will need to convince of your authenticity. Others may be more suspicious."

An older man with a ruddy complexion and a long beard ambled toward them. "Julius, where have you been? You were to preside at the Festival of Lights, and nobody knew of your whereabouts. Your wife thought the emperor had sent you on a diplomatic mission, but I told her that was not the case. And what happened to your hair?"

Julian reached for his hair, until he remembered Marsanto telling him that his Julian counterpart in this plane wore it long. He tried to regain his composure. "Ah, yes. My hair was starting to bother me so I decided to cut it. It's better this way. You should try it out some time."

The man frowned and gave him a curious look.

"As to your other question, I am afraid that one of my business interests pulled me away. There was an emergency situation that needed my immediate attention. I had to leave without informing anyone."

"Where did you go?" the old man asked.

That was a question that Julian had no way of answering, being wholly ignorant of the geography of this land.

"We just returned from Florenheim," Marsanto said. "The Ainglish were threatening his shipping lanes."

The older man gave Marsanto a hard stare. "Do you normally speak for your master?"

Marsanto bowed his head. "My apologies for speaking out of turn."

Julian glanced at Marsanto with what he hoped was a look of disdain. "It is hard to find good help these days. I will see to it that my guard is properly beaten. I had to make sure that if they were to consider such a thing, that I would smash the Ainglish into next week."

This time both Marsanto and the old man gave him quizzical looks. He had to watch his expressions around here. It would be one of the many things that could give him away as an imposter.

"At any rate, things are settled now," Julian said.

Julian's new home was one of the larger houses in the villa. It had a wide, arching gate. Inside the gates, the yard was filled with vines growing grapes in one section and tomatoes in another. He also spotted several lemon trees. In the middle was a large fountain of a statue of a naked woman with water coming from a spout in her mouth.

He turned to Marsanto. "Do we need a key to get in or something?"

Marsanto pulled out a skeleton key from his pouch. He used it to unlock the front door. Julian stepped onto the tiled floor. The furniture was made of plush velvet and dark leather. Numerous paintings hung in the interior room which led to an atrium with a large, brick oven. The scents of fresh bread wafted in the air. A fresh loaf was on the table. It looked tempting, so he helped himself to a piece, figuring this was his home.

The bread was amazing. It had a cinnamon-buttery taste and practically melted in his mouth. He offered some to Marsanto, who accepted a piece, and then helped himself to another.

While sitting at the table eating, he quizzed the centurion on things he needed to know. Who were the people Julian should be acquainted with? What did they look like? He asked about the buildings they had passed and which ones he should know about. He had Marsanto sketch him a crude map using a quill pen and parchment.

Unfortunately, Marsanto was not nearly as informative as he would have liked. By the time they finished eating and drinking from a jug of wine he had found in the kitchen, he still had more questions than answers. This conversation furthered his impression that Marsanto wasn't from this neighborhood. He knew a good many things, but not as much as a resident would.

The things he cared least about were Julian's relationship to the Emperor and how he would carry out his task, since he had no interest in fulfilling it.

"Where will you be staying?" Julian hoped the answer wasn't here in this house. That would make things more difficult.

"I have a place to stay not far from here."

Julian breathed a sigh of relief. "I'm going to need time to get oriented. What's the best way to contact you?"

"I will be here with you."

"Yeah, I appreciate that and all, but I don't think I'm going to need you all the time. I need time by myself. Look, I completed my last two tasks for the Maestro on my own."

Marsanto pursed his lips. "Remember that I am here to provide you protection and guidance on things you need to know, but also to ensure that you complete your task."

"Yeah. You already told me that if I don't go through with this that you'll kill me, and I don't doubt that you will, so that's all the incentive I need. Still, I don't need you hovering over my shoulder all the time."

"I will make myself available to you. You need not worry about finding me."

That still sounded ominous.

The ringing of chimes indicated the front door had opened. Walking toward them was a stunning woman of exquisite beauty with long black hair, big brown eyes, and an athletic figure. He could only presume this was Julius's wife.

"Julius, where have you been?" She had a melodic tone to her voice. "I have been terribly worried for you."

Julian removed his hat. "I apologize to you. There was an emergency with the Ainglish threatening our trade routes that I had to immediately attend to. I should have sent word to you."

Almarella put her hands on her hips. "The Ainglish again? I thought you made an alliance with them."

Julian waved his hand. "They're a stubborn lot, always trying to put one over on you."

Almarella frowned. "Put one over."

"Oh, it's just a saying the Ainglish use," Julian said. "It means to gain an advantage, often through unscrupulous means."

Almarella paused, as if to consider this. "Oh, I see. Put one over. I will have to use that."

"Feel free to use it whenever you choose."

Almarella's mood changed abruptly as she turned and saw Marsanto. "And who are you?"

"He is my bodyguard," Julian replied. "I hired him for extra protection with all of the tension with the Ainglish."

Almarella's eyes went wide. "Do we have something to worry over?"

"Not at all. I feel better having someone around who is capable of handling a rough situation in the slight chance that it would occur. It's better to be safe than sorry."

Almarella frowned.

He had to stop using phrases and expressions from his home plane. "I wanted to show Marsanto where we live. He will be retiring now to his quarters."

Marsanto gave him a hard stare but was hardly in position to refute this. Based on the cover story, he would be expected to take orders from Julian, not the other way around.

He rose from the table. "Yes, I will be leaving. I will return early tomorrow as you requested."

Julian walked him to the front door. When they reached it, Marsanto pulled him close. "Tread carefully. Remember your task. There is much you need to fear in this place."

Julian was glad to have the centurion gone. He needed to think of a way out and couldn't do that with that behemoth hanging around.

CHAPTER XVIII

He spent a pleasant evening with Almarella, dining on grilled sardines and potatoes cooked by a house servant, followed by a walk along the grounds of the estate. Although Julius and Almarella were prosperous and owned large parcels of land elsewhere, this estate was owned by the Emperor.

They took a walking path that wound across the estate. They passed through lush gardens and well-manicured lawns. One section contained an aviary with colorful birds that Julian had never seen before. The conversation was awkward, since most of the things that Almarella spoke about, the people and places she mentioned, were foreign to him. As a result, he mostly listened, trying to absorb as much as he could.

During their walk, they spoke of their three children. Their youngest child was two and their oldest ten. He was surprised that he had not seen them yet until Almarella informed him that they were staying at her mother's house and were due back tomorrow. They had the evening to themselves. Julian started getting nervous when she suggested what they should do with their free evening.

He had to quickly change the subject and the only thing he could think of to get her off-topic was his hair.

"I don't understand why you ruined it," Almarella said. "It was beautiful. Now…I don't like it so much."

"I can always grow it back." Julian wore his hair short and combed forward. Occasionally, he would put gel on it, but he had no hair care products here to use. "I felt as if I needed a change."

She tilted her head and looked up. "You will grow it back." She spoke it an insistent voice as if there was no debate on the subject.

They returned to their house just before dusk. As soon as they returned, Almarella began lighting candles and lanterns. It was going to be difficult getting used to being in a place without electricity. The bathroom situation was difficult enough to deal with.

When she was finished illuminating the house, Almarella poured two glasses of wine. "So where were we? Ah, yes, you were going to ravish me, I believe." She took a sip of wine and then slipped out of her dress with astonishing grace.

He stood open-mouthed, gaping at her. She wore nothing underneath other than silk undergarments. He grabbed the glass of wine, nearly spilling it. This was not good, not good at all.

Think of Nancy. Think of Nancy.

"I don't know if this is such a good idea. What if the children return?"

"The children won't return until tomorrow." She sipped her wine and slowly walked toward him. "What is wrong? Don't you find me attractive?" She tilted her neck and arched her shoulders.

That was the problem. She was stunning. The super-models of his plane had nothing on her. Damn Julius for having such a beautiful wife. "Of course I find you attractive. It's just that…"

He was at a loss for something to say. Fortunately, he was saved by somebody knocking at the door. He slowly stepped past her. "Um, I'll get that. You may want to get dressed."

As he walked to the door, his legs were rubbery. He felt light-headed and wasn't sure that he was going to make it to the front door.

He opened the door to find one of the few dark-skinned men he had seen since arriving here. This man was a giant, at least a foot taller than him. He was bald with a neatly trimmed beard. He looked lean but had hands the size of oven mitts. He vaguely remembered Marsanto describing a man like this. "Herelius?"

He stepped inside without invitation. The big man bowed slightly to him and gave Almarella a deeper bow. Julian turned to find that the she was now clothed. Thank God for small favors.

"What brings you out so late tonight?"

Other than saving my sorry ass.

"The Emperor requires your presence," Herelius replied.

Almarella put her hands on her hips. "Not again. The Emperor demands too much."

"He demands what he will," Herelius said. "And it is never too much."

Julian shrugged. "Well, he is the Emperor." He glanced back at Almarella. "Duty calls. I have to go."

Almarella had a pouty look as Julian left the house. He followed the large man and two guards who had accompanied him. In his short stay in this plane, he had seen many bodyguards and security guards. He imagined that this was a common occupation in this plane.

They passed a drunken group of young men and women walking up the street, singing songs and laughing. They seemed to be having a good time, which contrasted with Herelius's dour mood. He wasn't sure if that was his usual countenance or if there was serious business the Emperor required him for.

They remained on the grounds of the massive complex. This place was a town until itself, with shops, taverns, and restaurants. It even had an apple and a pear orchard.

When they finally made it to the Emperor's home, which was naturally the largest place in this compound, he spotted at least two dozen guards spaced throughout the grounds.

Herelius did a half wave, half hand-flip as they passed the guards. Julian tried to replicate the motion but wasn't nearly as graceful as Herelius. They entered through massive double-doors, which had to be at least twenty feet in height. There was no way someone would be able to get through the front door without being heard.

Herelius led him forward past a long room with a massive table that looked as if it could seat forty people. Along the walls were numerous portraits. The people in the portraits all looked alike, so he assumed that they were the Emperor's family. Centered in the room was a candelabrum. A winding staircase led to the upstairs. To the right came the scents of roasted meat and fresh bread.

They exited that room and entered a parlor. In one corner, on an elevated dais was a piano. A number of plush chairs lined the room. In the corner was a compact bar with numerous bottles and glasses.

After exiting this room, they made a right turn and followed a long hallway. At the end of a hallway, Herelius knocked on a door.

Someone from inside told them to enter. What Julian saw took him aback. A pale-skinned man wearing various shades of makeup sat on a chair. He held a glass in one hand and a bottle in the other. He had long, curly hair and wore a puffy toga and a fur vest. In the background, a fire crackled. Three beautiful women laid on the floor on a leopard skin rug. They wore either no clothes or almost no clothes. They paid him and Herelius little attention.

The man got out of his seat and walked forward. Even from a few feet away, Julian could smell alcohol on him. At first, Julian thought he had been drinking wine, but as he got closer, it smelled more like brandy. Julian could only assume this was the Emperor. "Where have you been? You should have been here hours ago."

"I had to take care of some shipping interests," Julian said, sticking with his cover story. "There has been trouble with the Ainglish."

"What problems are we having with the Ainglish?" The Emperor gesticulated wildly with his arms. "Why haven't I heard of this until now?"

Julian raised his hand in an attempt to pacify Belesinto. He felt like a chameleon switching in and out of roles. If he ever made it back home, he should sell his company, move to Hollywood, and become an actor. "There is no need to concern yourself. I have already taken care of the problem. I am just trying to make things easier for you by giving you less to worry about."

This seemed to appease the Emperor, but Julian had the distinct feeling that the man was like a ticking time bomb, ready to explode at any moment. He was going to have to tread lightly near him. The only good thing was that Julius was his most trusted advisor, something he hoped would give him leeway in their dealings.

"The Ainglish are not our problem now," Emperor Belesinto said. "We face greater threats from within. You must stay focused."

One of the almost naked women that had been lying on the floor got up and walked over to the Emperor. She had long, blonde hair and a slim figure. She looked to be no older than seventeen, while Belesinto appeared to be nearing fifty. "You're too tense, your Grace." She stroked his arm gently.

Without warning, the Emperor reared back and gave her a backhand slap that sent her reeling to the floor. Blood spurted from her nose. She stared at him, a hurt look on her face, tears in her eyes.

"Out," the Emperor screamed. "Out! All of you! Leave right now!"

Julian had never seen this level of rage in a person before. He was certain that if they did not comply, he would kill them, right here and now.

Julian put his hand on the Emperor's shoulder and drew him closer. "We need to focus on the business at hand. Don't be distracted by unimportant matters." He ushered the Emperor to another part of the room, away from the women.

"Of course." Emperor Belesinto waved his hand.

By that point the women had left, thankfully.

"Now, what troubles you so?" Julian did his best to not sound condescending, but he had no idea how to deal with an emperor.

"Urias and Febrino in the Senate." The Emperor's eyes had a far-off look to them. "I am sure that they are going to be making a move against me."

"Do we have sufficient proof to arrest them?" Plots against leaders were something Julian could work with. He had read enough about them in history classes.

"Not unless your sources have told you something new," Belesinto said. "What have you learned since we last spoke?"

Julian shook his head. "Unfortunately, I haven't learned anything that will be of use in this situation."

"What have you done to your hair?"

"It's a new style," Julian said. "I think it will catch on."

The Emperor tilted his head as if considering this. "Perhaps. You have always had a way with fashion that appeals to the masses. Regardless, I am certain that they are planning a move. I can sense it in the way they have acted lately. We need to do something before their plot comes to fruition."

"But if we do not have the requisite proof, then we cannot take action on them in a legal manner. You are the Emperor. You cannot be above the law. Think of how that would look to the commoners. If you do not obey the law, then why should they?"

He had no idea if what he said to Belesinto would set him off but he tried to put himself in the shoes of someone who had to advise this maniac and keep him in line.

"You and your legalities."

Julian was satisfied the fiery rage Belesinto had exhibited earlier was gone. Of course, the man seemed psychotic and could explode at a moment's notice.

"They must be stopped," the Emperor said. "I cannot tolerate any threats to my realm. I want them dead."

"Give me time to gather information. It is important that you give the situation a chance to be handled legally before we act."

They went on to speak about other issues. He had some familiarity with most of the topics from Marsanto's briefing, but once they got into the specifics of the situations, he was lost. He was doing his damnedest to keep up with what was going on, but for the most part he found himself nodding and agreeing with the Emperor. When he got back to his home, he would have to find a pen and paper, or whatever passed for that in this place, and take copious notes on all that they had discussed today.

By the time the Emperor was done with him, two hours had passed according to the watch he kept in his pocket away from prying eyes. He was thoroughly exhausted. It had been a long and trying day, as had each of them since he started travelling through planes. He needed rest. With any luck, Almarella would be asleep and not looking to continue what she had tried to start earlier.

He said his goodbyes and told the Emperor he would follow up on the two members of the senate who were trying to overthrow him.

On his way out, he ran into Herelius. Julian grabbed his arm. "Would you mind having some guards accompany me to my house? There have been threats made, and I would prefer the extra protection."

He mostly wanted the guards because he wasn't sure he could find his way home in the dark. He might wind up wandering around for hours otherwise.

If this seemed like a strange request, Herelius did not indicate it. He selected three guards for the assignment. Travelling in the dark, with torches to guide their way, he was convinced of his previous assertion. There was no way he would have been able to get home on his own.

Once inside his house, using the key he had obtained earlier, he quietly made his way to their bedroom where he found Almarella sleeping soundly. He quietly removed his outer layer of clothes and lay down beside her. As his head hit the pillow, he contemplated what he would have to do to get out of this mess.

CHAPTER XIX

Julian awoke to the scent of roasted bacon. His stomach growled. He shielded his eyes in the brightly lit house. He got out of bed and searched for clothes. He selected a tunic of simple design and began the laborious task of putting it on. The last thing he wanted was to ask Almarella for help.

He found something that resembled a comb and used it to for his hair. He could use a warm bath. He found a small foot bath, a jug of water, and soap, which he used to clean his feet, providing him a small relief.

He had used the outhouse the previous evening and would have to visit it again soon. The lack of electricity and plumbing was jarring to his modern sensibilities.

When he went downstairs, Almarella put her arms around his neck and kissed him. "Good morning, my husband. Unfortunately, I was quite tired last night and went to sleep before you returned."

That was the only good fortune he had since arriving.

"I'm sorry I was out so late last evening, but I had pressing business with the Emperor."

Almarella gave him a look of disdain. "The Emperor and his

business. None of it is ever any good."

He found it interesting that although her husband worked for Belesinto, and the Emperor was in all likelihood the source of their livelihood and income, his wife seemed to have a great deal of hostility toward the man. After last night's visit, he certainly shared a low opinion of the Emperor. The man struck Julian as a paranoid megalomaniac who was obsessed with power and had a distinct lack of touch with reality. Had he not intervened, the Emperor would have killed at least one of those young ladies.

Apparently, Almarella was not the cause of the delicious scents wafting upstairs. A short, stout woman with black hair was preparing food in the atrium of the house.

"Almarella, what do you think about the Emperor?"

She frowned. "Why would you ask me about him? You know full well what I think of Belesinto." She turned away from him.

"Why do you harbor such animosity toward him?" Julian asked.

She put her hands on her hips. "Of all people, you should know the answer to that question. I know that you have unwavering loyalty to Belesinto and have pledged your life to him, but do not pretend to ignore the evil he has done. The horrible things he has done to our people, to our family, to me."

Julian had hit a nerve. He wanted to learn more but was afraid to probe too deeply. For one thing, these were all things that his shade, Julius, would already know. Flat out asking what she was referring to would make her suspicious.

"You know that I owe much to the Emperor but I have a greater loyalty to you and our family."

This seemed to calm Almarella. Her shoulders sagged and her face softened. She motioned with her hand to their house. "I know this is all due to the Emperor. My life and the lives of our children are much easier as a result of your work for him, but it still does not make it easy to accept. I will never forget what happened. Roperto is a constant reminder of that."

"Roperto?"

"I love our son," Almarella said. "You know that I am devoted to him just as I am devoted to our daughters, but it is still hard to look upon him at times and not feel animosity. I know that life isn't fair and so many others have it worse. My plight is nothing compared to theirs, but it is still difficult to accept."

Julian put his hand on top of hers. He wasn't sure what to say as he tried to piece together all of this information.

He was about to ask more questions when a knock on the door interrupted him.

"I will answer," Almarella said. "Perhaps the children have returned."

He followed her to the front door. The house was spacious with high ceilings and marble floors. There were at least three fire places. The atrium, where the servants prepared food, was the size of a small apartment. There was a constant breeze that flowed through the house that seemed to hold off the outside heat.

She opened the door, and Julian nearly fell to his knees. He could have cried. It was Cutter.

Almarella looked at Cutter and then back at Julian.

"Almarella, this is my good friend…"

Cutter interrupted him. "Marco Grandine."

Almarella frowned. "You never mentioned a friend named Marco."

"That is because we have not seen each other in many years," Cutter said. "You probably thought me to be dead."

Julian nodded. "I did."

"But alas, I was able to escape the Nordic prison that I had been held in Stiebengard."

"How did you know to find me?" Julian asked a question that held more than one meaning.

"It was not hard," Cutter said. "The name Julius Delesandro is well known in this region."

Julian turned to his wife. "My friend and I have much we need to discuss. Would you mind?"

"Of course not. It is good to make your acquaintance, Marco." She excused herself.

Julian put his hand on Cutter's shoulder. "Thank God you're here. You don't know how glad I am to see you. I could kiss you."

Cutter raised his hand. "Please don't. I figured you might need some guidance right about now."

"You couldn't be more right about that. How did you find me?"

"It took a bit of time," Cutter said. "This was the seventh plane I tried."

"You had to capture my scent or whatever it is that you do?"

Cutter nodded. "Unfortunately, I ran into a false lead on the second plane. It was someone else who had recently traveled. I eventually landed here, and the signs of travel were prominent, so I suspected that I would find you. After that, it was a matter of figuring out who you were."

"Did you try checking my home plane first?"

Cutter shook his head. "Didn't bother. The chances of you returning were remote."

Julian sighed. "And how did you know I was Julius Delesandro?"

"It wasn't as hard as you might think. You look exactly like him minus the hair and your lack of skin tone. Delesandro is very prominent in Delphi."

Julian ushered him to a room filled with bound books and scrolls that he assumed was a library. "The cook is making breakfast. Let's grab some food. How familiar are you with this place?"

"I've spent time here," Cutter replied. "It's been a few years, but I am well enough acquainted with this plane."

"I've been wondering. This place looks like ancient Rome. Is this geographically the equivalent of the Philadelphia that I come from?"

Cutter nodded and looked around at the books in the room. "Let's see if there is a map here. You'll find this interesting." He found a scroll and unwound it. "Ah, this is it. The geography of this world is vastly different than the one you're used to. Look here."

Julian stared at the map. There was a vast body of water and one large mass of land. He saw places identified as Delphi, Ainglatera, Nubia, and Assyria. "I don't get it. Where are all of the continents?"

"There are no other continents," Cutter replied. "In this plane, there is one large block of land and numerous islands."

"That's amazing."

Cutter pointed at the map. "If you'll notice, this has the general shape of South America. This is where we're at, which looks more or less like North America. That's the Florida panhandle. If you keep travelling west, you get Europe and the equivalent of Africa."

"Is this a map of the entire plane?"

Cutter replied, "This map isn't entirely accurate. You can see how technologically deficient these people are. Their version of the Roman Empire seized power a couple thousand years ago and never relinquished it. Unlike the Ancient Romans of your plane, these folks were not keen on technology and innovation. Much like what happened in your Dark Ages, because of their customs and religious beliefs, technological progress has been minimal. To that end, their means of travel is also primitive. The entirety of this plane has yet to be fully explored. There are numerous islands that have not been charted, including a very large one nearly the size and shape of Australia. Other than that one large island, which can be considered a continent unto itself, there's one large continent. And I have no idea what's at either of the poles."

"And the folks around here don't know about it?"

Cutter shook his head.

"Then how do you know about it?"

"My family has charted this plane far more thoroughly than the people who reside here. You have to understand that there is a widespread belief that their world is flat and if one sailed too far, they would fall off the edge of the world. Members of my family knew better and did not harbor these same fears."

Julian chuckled. "So, in the last plane I was in, they had advanced space travel and contact with aliens, but on this one they don't even know the damned planet is round. I guess they inherited the slow genes. Just how many planes are there?"

"Eighty-six to my knowledge. Not all of them are habitable. Then there are some that you wouldn't want any part of."

"In that case, I'm glad it only took you seven tries to find me. So, what do you know about the Emperor, this Belesinto character?"

"Emperor Belesinto is a nasty piece of business. He's known for his callousness and cruelty. The people of the land have been prosperous enough, at least those who have sided with him, so there hasn't been a sufficient outcry to overthrow him, although I think that would be a reasonable action."

"I had the misfortune of meeting him last night," Julian said. "I can't say I like the man very much."

"If you would like a historical comparison, think of Emperor Nero from your home plane."

"Nero, the crazy bastard who let Rome burn?" Julian asked.

"To be more specific, the one who watched Rome burn while playing his lyre according to many historians, although that conclusion is in dispute these days based on a review of historical records," Cutter replied. "Belesinto's erratic and prone to violent outbreaks. And he's your lord and master."

Julian sighed. "Yeah, unfortunately I've already discovered that."

"So, now that our history lesson is over, what task has the Game Master given you to complete this go around?"

"Kill Emperor Belesinto."

Cutter's eyes went wide. "You can't be serious."

"I wouldn't kid you about that."

"I can't figure out why exactly does the Game Master have it in for Belesinto. I realize the bastard is always scheming, but these two seem to be cut from the same cloth. Power is his game. He doesn't care who he has to step over to get it. I think his aim would be to become the supreme ruler of the universe, if such a thing were possible.

Belesinto is the same way except that his ambitions only extend to one plane."

"I have no plans on following through with the task."

Cutter raised a brow. "No?"

"Come on, Cutter. I think by now you should know I'm not a killer."

"No, I don't suppose you are, but you do plan on getting out of here and seeing your family, which means that you have to convince the Game Master to send you home."

"Even if I accomplish this task, what are the chances that he actually sends me home? He'll probably just send me on another errand. I have to get home. This is driving me out of my mind. How do I get out of this?"

Cutter put his hand on Julian's shoulder. "I wish I could tell you, but I don't know the answer. If I could take you with me to your plane I would, but it doesn't work that way. And before you ask, I've tried. Believe me, I've tried."

A sadness entered Cutter's voice as he said that last part. Julian had the distinct impression that Cutter was leaving out something, and he didn't want to pry since he needed the man's help.

Cutter turned toward him. "I'll tell you this much. If you do kill Belesinto, you'll be doing these people a favor. I won't shed a tear."

"Would you be able to go through something like this, if you had to assassinate someone?"

Cutter regarded him. "What you're really asking is have I done this sort of thing before. Have I killed someone?"

"No, I didn't mean…"

Cutter raised his hand. "That's okay. And the answer is yes. More times than I care to remember. I haven't always lived the straight and narrow. I've done things I'm not proud of."

They dropped their talk of killing when Almarella joined them for breakfast. The bacon was heavenly. Just before breakfast ended, Julian had another visitor. This one he didn't welcome with open arms.

CHAPTER XX

When Julian opened the door, he wasn't thrilled to find Marsanto with his scarred face standing there. The centurion narrowed his eyes when he saw Cutter. "What is he doing here?"

Julian glanced at Cutter, who clenched his fists, looking ready for a fight.

"We have a score to settle," Marsanto said. "I do not forget. Step outside now, coward."

Julian stood between them. "Ease up. What's going on?"

Marsanto folded his arms across his chest. "How do you know this man?"

"He's a friend," Julian replied. "More than I can say about you. All you are is hired muscle for an evil bastard."

Marsanto pointed at Cutter's chest. "Marco Grandine is a thief and a liar."

Cutter shrugged. "I've been called worse. As far as I'm concerned, you were too dumb to know the score. That's your problem, not mine."

"What are you two talking about?" Julian asked.

"An old issue," Cutter said. "We were working on opposite sides of the fence. Ben-Hur here just couldn't figure it out."

Marsanto removed his sword.

Julian's eyes went wide. "Put that away. We're not going to have someone hurt or killed here."

Marsanto was not about to back down. "This argument does not concern you."

"Of course it does. Look, Marsanto, you have a job to do. The Maestro is paying you good coin to accomplish this task. He won't be pleased if you undermine it by settling an old grudge. I trust Cutter, I mean Marco, more than I trust you, and I'm going to need his help to kill Belesinto." Julian was adlibbing in an attempt to defuse the situation. He certainly did not mean what he had just said.

Marsanto tensed, ground his teeth, and put away his sword. "When this is over, it will be your head on my sword."

Cutter laughed. "You think I'm intimidated by the likes of you? I'll be waiting for you."

Julian glared at Cutter. He might be his only friend in these parts, but he wasn't making the situation better. Cutter stepped back, allowing Marsanto room to enter.

"Look, you two don't have to be bosom buddies, but I can't have you at each other's throats."

"Very well. What have you learned?" Marsanto asked.

Julian led them to the library. "Before we get into that, tell me why the Maestro wants the Emperor killed."

Marsanto pursed his lips and stared at Julian with cold eyes.

"I need to know this," Julian said. "If he wants me to accomplish this task, then I need to know the parameters."

After a few moments, Marsanto said, "The Maestro is trying to annex a large parcel of land to the south of Delphi as part of a larger attempt to expand his base of operations. Belesinto stands in his ways, and, therefore, the Emperor must be eliminated, something that has been increasingly difficult due to his security. The Maestro wishes to avoid a large armed conflict where many will die."

Julian rolled his eyes. What a crock of shit. He just orchestrated something that would result in the death of millions—something Julian unwittingly played a part in and now deeply regretted. "He's all heart. Sorry if I don't believe you. He's a malicious bastard who doesn't care who he rolls over."

"That is your misinformed opinion, but it does not reflect reality," Marsanto said. "Belesinto's oldest son, who is line for the throne, is more malleable and not quite bright. That is who the Maestro wishes to rule Delphi."

Julian raised his right index finger. "I have a solution. When I met with the Emperor last night, he indicated that Urias and Febrino were about to make a move to dethrone him. Belesinto wanted to take action against these two. Why don't we work with them to eliminate the Emperor?"

Marsanto shook his head. "That is unacceptable. They are not allies to the Maestro. It must be his son who takes over the line of succession, not one of them. It will be the least bloody outcome."

Julian was pretty certain that saving lives wasn't on the top of the Game Master's agenda, regardless of Marsanto's assertion.

"Look, this man's not a killer," Cutter said. "Let your boss hire an assassin to do the job."

"This is not your concern, scoundrel. Unless you have a suggestion on how to kill Belesinto, remain silent."

"It's little wonder your wife left you," Cutter said.

Marsanto's face flared with anger.

"Will you two stop it," Julian said. "Can't we act like adults here?"

"You have complete access to the Emperor," Marsanto said. "He trusts you implicitly. This should be an easy task."

"Except that Julian…"

"Julius," Marsanto interrupted him. "He is Julius Delesandro here. You would be wise to remember that."

"Fine, Julius isn't a killer. Your boss picked the wrong man for the job."

"That is not my concern," Marsanto said. "He will do as instructed or I will kill him."

"And I would like to see you get past me to try it," Cutter said.

"Look, this isn't the least bit productive. It's more than obvious the two of you can't be in the same room together." Julian grabbed Marsanto's arm and ushered him out the door. "You're going to have to give us some room to operate."

Marsanto pulled his arm away from Julian. "I do not like the way this is proceeding."

"And I don't particularly care. Cutter and I will come up with a plan. He's helped me before. We won't do anything until we run it by you first."

Marsanto wore a confused look.

"I'll let you know about our plan before I act upon it. I don't intend on dying in this dreadful plane, so I have no choice but to follow through on the mission."

Marsanto narrowed his eyes. "You are walking on a narrow ledge and you are very close to falling off. I strongly suggest that you walk a straight line."

Julian patted him on the back. "Excellent advice. I wouldn't want to fall off. See you later."

He ushered Marsanto out the door. "Asshole." He knew he had to be careful. Marsanto definitely struck him as someone he did not want to cross, even with Cutter here to watch his back.

Julian turned to Cutter. "What was that all about?"

Cutter waved his hand. "Long story. That bugger was working for the Game Master, transporting a highly illegal shipment of jungle mint, an extremely addictive narcotic. I seized it from him."

"You seized it?"

"Well, yes. We were originally working together on the job, but I felt it better if I had it instead of him. The quantity being transported was worth a small fortune. I used the shipment of jungle mint as a bargaining chip for the release of the princess of the Isle of

Mahii, this plane's version of Hawaii. I was well compensated for my efforts by her father, but just gazing upon the lovely face of the princess and accepting her personal reward was payment enough."

"How did you escape the Game Master's wrath for doing that?"

"By giving him something he wanted more. Our score was settled, but Marsanto was left bitter about the whole situation."

"Well, try to play nice. He's a bad ass who carries a big sword."

"He's not half as impressive as he thinks he is," Cutter said.

"All the same, I don't want to cross him."

"Are you really going to go through with this? Killing the Emperor?"

Julian sat on a bench in the library. "It seems like it won't be a big loss if Belesinto dies. I have yet to meet anyone who has a positive opinion on him. He's a maniacal tyrant, but that doesn't mean he should die. Or at the very least it doesn't mean that I should be the one delivering his death. Not to mention, I'm no assassin, or even a soldier or mercenary."

Cutter nodded but said nothing as he helped himself to wine from a jug on the table. Julian didn't mind this plane's wine but unlike Cutter, he wasn't a morning drinker.

"Even if I kill Belesinto, the Game Master's still not going to send me home, not as long as he has another scheme that he's going to involve me with."

Cutter drained half of his glass of wine before putting it down. "That's quite a dilemma you have there."

"I know. What can I do about?"

Cutter paused. "If it was me, I would just kill the bastard. I mean the Game Master, not Belesinto. Although I might just take the Emperor out for good measure and do this plane a favor."

"If I kill the Game Master, then I'm stuck here forever, and trust me, I do not want to live in this plane. I want to get out of here as quickly as possible.

"Catch-22 my friend."

"What I really need is a way to force his hand to make him take me back to my home plane. I wish I could get some sort of leverage, something I can use, but he's an amoral bastard. I can't imagine blackmail would work on him."

"Not likely," Cutter said. "The only thing that can stop him is a bullet to the head, and that has been tried before without success. He is well-protected and hard to get to."

They discussed strategy to kill the Emperor—only in theory of course. Cutter presented some options, none of which sounded appealing. If he were to kill Belesinto, he wanted to do it in a way that was not so obvious. The last thing he would want was for Julius's family to take the brunt of his actions.

After this brainstorming session, Julian needed a break. Not to mention that his children, or rather Julius's children, would be arriving soon. He still couldn't believe that there was a small part of him that was actually considering an assassination attempt.

Cutter must have sensed that he was getting wary of this discussion. He excused himself and told Julian that there were a few friends in Delphi he wanted to visit.

What Julian really needed was to write his ideas down and think it through. He was a visual thinker. His office had two big white boards, and his walls were always loaded with yellow stickies as he plotted his course of action.

He searched for something to write with. Even though the house had a library with a number of books and scrolls, he could not find anything in there. He continued to search the other rooms but didn't have any luck. If Julius was the Emperor's right hand man and a statesman, then he had to do some writing.

He found a house servant who was dusting. She had an olive-skinned complexion and appeared to be in her early twenties. Getting frustrated in his search, he called out. "Excuse me. I'm looking for some parchment and a quill. Can you please let me know where I can find some?"

She made some hand gestures to him, which he could not

understand. He repeated his request, this time more slowly. She continued to respond to him with more hand gestures.

He felt foolish. Julius would know that she couldn't communicate with him. He would know that the servant was either mute or did not speak his language. He retreated. "I'm sorry. I'll find it. Thanks for your help."

He sighed and went up the stairs. It was his good fortune that he found parchment, a quill, and an ink box. Before he had a chance to get some of his thoughts down on paper, it was time for him to meet the rest of his family.

CHAPTER XXI

Julian went to the entrance hall to meet his new family. He did not know for how long they would be his family, nor did he intend on getting attached to them. He had his own family to worry about, if he ever got to see them again.

Nine-year-old Analicia was a pretty young thing who looked like a younger version of Almarella. Her skin was a deep, olive color. She had long, black hair tied with a ribbon. Her face was free from blemishes, and she had a smile that lit up the room. So full of life, she ran around the house after greeting Julian. He had a difficult time getting an answer from her regarding how she enjoyed staying at her grandparents' house, since she would not stay still for more than a few seconds a t time.

Little Roperto was down by the edge of the fence picking rocks. All he could make out was the boy's mop of dark, curly hair. Roperto came running toward them.

Julian froze. He looked nothing like either he or Almarella. Yes, the boy had curly black hair, which he had seen from a distance, but far more distinctive was the crooked nose and the blue eyes with the slightly upturned slits. As Julian examined him closer, he came to the realization that the boy looked very much like Emperor Belesinto.

The conversation he'd had earlier with Almarella echoed in his head. She had mentioned that she loved their son, but every time she looked at him it was a constant reminder about the animosity she felt toward the Emperor. He was starting to piece things together. The Emperor was Roperto's biological father, not Julius. Julian was starting to have a bad feeling about this but was determined to learn more.

The boy ran up and leapt into his arms. Julian lifted him up high and kissed him on the forehead. Whatever the situation was, Roperto seemed to love his father. He put Roperto down, and Analicia ran up and hugged him as well.

Analicia put her hands on her hips. "What happened to your hair?"

"I gave it a little trim. Do you like it?"

Analicia walked around him, her eyes narrowed. "I do."

"You're the only one who seems to like it."

Julian had intruded upon their lives. He was an imposter in their midst, and depending upon what actions he took, he could ruin this family. He had been put in an impossible situation and did not know how to act. Whatever he did, he did not want to put these children in danger. He wouldn't be able to live with himself if he did.

When they all got inside, the children regaled them with stories about collecting berries off of vines in their grandparent's garden, as well as going fishing by a stream near the house. Analicia went on about a pretty, pink butterfly she had caught. Julian found the kids to be polite and charming and the baby, Impa, was as cute as could be.

When Almarella told them to put their belongings away, they immediately complied. He wanted to have some time alone with her. There was still more he needed to learn. With her parents around, he asked Almarella if she would walk with him.

She gave him a suspicious look. "You want to walk with me? For you, it is work all the time."

"Family is more important than work.

After Almarella put on a pair of sandals and a silk head cover, they left the house. On their way out, Julian saw the same pretty servant who could not communicate with him earlier.

Before he could think better of it and because his curiosity got the better of him, Julian said, "I was trying to ask her where to find parchment, and she did not answer me."

A stern look crossed Almarella's face. "Why would you do that? Are you trying to mock Firmina?"

"Um, no. I wouldn't do that."

"You know full well what Belesinto did to her."

Julian didn't know what to say. He gave her a blank stare.

"Why are you looking at me like that? You know what he did." When Julian did not say anything, she said, "How he cut out her tongue."

Julian's jaw dropped. "Cut out her tongue?"

Almarella ground her teeth. Her anger was palpable. "Yes. Cut out her tongue. After he raped her, and she wanted to come forward and tell her story, your precious Emperor had her tongue cut out. You were the one who put her in our employ since she had no other possibilities without a tongue."

Julian took a step back. He felt as if he had been smashed in the abdomen with a sledgehammer. He thought Belesinto capable of murder but had not thought the man capable of such savage brutality. The mere thought of cutting off another person's tongue made Julian's skin crawl. He was dealing with a whole different level of evil and barbarism than he had ever encountered before.

He had to learn more. His suspicion was overwhelming him. Plus, he had already agitated Almarella to no end. He might as well push it further. "When we spoke earlier, you had mentioned Roperto. The Emperor is his father."

Almarella gave him an incredulous look. Tears began to form in her eyes. "Of course, Belesinto is his father. What is your point? Are you going to blame me for the Emperor raping me and impregnating me with Roperto? Is that it?" Her last words were shouts. He had not been sure if this had been the case or if it had been an affair. He should have realized it would be the worst-case scenario. His naivete was getting him in trouble.

Julian held her shoulders and gazed into her eyes. "I am sorry. Please forgive me. I have not been myself today. I find myself forgetting things I should know. You resent my working for the Emperor."

Almarella looked away from him. "Yes. I know how much it means to you, but I hate that you have to work for him. You know I support your goals and ambitions, but I loathe the sight of the man."

"I understand. I have come to hate the man as well."

Almarella turned her head to look at him, her face shrouded with confusion. "I don't understand. You have always defended him."

Julian took her hand, and they continued walking. It was a warm, sunny afternoon. He did not know what season it was in this plane, but it felt like late spring. "Sometimes you need a fresh perspective on a situation. Sometimes you are so enwrapped in your plans and ambitions that you lose sight of what is really important. I think Julius Delesandro has done that very thing. I think Emperor Belesinto is an evil man. Would you not agree?"

She frowned. "Of course I agree."

They passed an orange grove. The oranges looked delicious, so Julian picked two, offered one to Almarella, and peeled his. "Then the question is what to do about it. Not what is convenient or what will be more profitable. What is the right thing to do?"

"I don't understand," Almarella said. "There is nothing to do. He is the Emperor. He has a divine right to rule."

"There is no such thing as a divine right to rule."

Almarella's frown deepened.

Perhaps he was speaking out of turn from the beliefs held in this plane, but he did not care. He felt a burning desire for justice. For too long a blind eye had been turned to this maniac. That type of inhuman behavior should not be tolerated. He also felt a growing resentment toward his counterpart.

The man was willing to work for somebody who had raped his wife.

What did that say about him? He knew it was easy to pass judgment when one did not walk in another's shoes, but in this case, he was walking in Julius's shoes.

"Do you agree that is time for the Emperor to die?"

Almarella stopped walking and gaped at him. "What are you saying?"

"I am simply asking you a question. Do you think Belesinto deserves to die?"

Almarella stared at Julian. "Yes. I do."

"I do as well."

* * *

Julian could hardly believe what he was considering. Furthermore, he could hardly believe his motivations. He would not kill somebody to satisfy the Game Master schemes. He would do it to deliver justice to Delphi and the woman married to his shade. He had never felt such a range of emotion as he had during his conversation with Almarella. It was a combination of anguish, rage, utter sorrow, and an unquenchable thirst for vengeance. He was determined to set things right.

Now the question was how he would enact this plan. Earlier, Cutter spoke the truth. He was no killer. In the end, he may not have the nerve to pull it off, but somebody had to put an end to this monster's reign of terror, and he was in the position to do so.

He wanted to discuss options with Cutter, but unfortunately they were only supposed to meet late that night at a pub near the market. Instead, Marsanto, sporting a mean scowl and a surly disposition, visited him.

They took a walk out of the gated community to an isolated area near a farm about a mile away. "What is your plan? Time is growing short, and the Maestro is impatient."

"You're in contact with the Maestro?" Julian asked.

"That is not your concern."

Marsanto was right about one thing. They didn't have much time. He had met with the Emperor and his inner circle shortly after his decision to kill the man. The Emperor would be traveling in three days for a period between three and five weeks, depending on how negotiations went. Julian was supposed to be accompanying him on that trip, something he had no intention of doing.

"What is your plan?" Marsanto asked. "I can provide you with assistance."

Julian was tired of this thug. "Relax. I'm still working on it. In case you're not aware, I'm new to this sort of thing."

"And I am not. That is why I can provide you with assistance."

"I don't need your assistance," Julian said. "I need to do this in a way that doesn't implicate Julius Delesandro or his wife."

"They're not of concern to the Maestro."

"Well, they sure as hell are my concern, and I won't do this if it means harm will come to them."

"You must have a plan for me by tomorrow at this time."

Julian rolled his eyes. "I will complete this task and I don't need your help. Marco will help me figure this thing out."

Marsanto's face grew a few shades darker. "He will not be escaping me this time. After he is no longer useful, he will meet his demise. I could have killed him once. I should have killed him. I will not make that mistake again."

Julian said nothing, but he would be damned if he was going to let that happen.

CHAPTER XXII

Cutter nodded slowly as he drank ale from his ceramic mug. He narrowed his eyes and looked up at Julian. "You sure about this? This is really what you want to do?"

"Yes," Julian replied. "It's not just to get home. This man is evil to the core, and I need to bring him down. Will you help me?"

"Of course."

"So how would you do it?"

Cutter tilted his head back. "Well, seeing as how close you can get to him, I would probably slip a dagger into his gut when we were alone and get the hell out of there as quickly as I could."

Julian looked somberly into his mug of ale.

"But I wouldn't recommend that course of action for you. If you hadn't done that sort of thing before, then trying it against the Emperor under these circumstances wouldn't be wise."

Julian nodded. "I would only do that as a last resort."

"Fortunately, there's more than one way to milk a goat. What you have working for you is that the Emperor trusts you, and you have access to him."

"Whatever happens, this can't lead back to Almarella and her family.

They did nothing to deserve this." Julian sat back in his chair. "What about Febrino and that other fellow in the senate? I can approach them and set up the Emperor for a fall."

Cutter shook his head. "Three things that are problematic with that scenario. One—you run the risk of incurring the Game Master's wrath. Two—they may not even want Belesinto killed. It may just be his paranoid ravings at work. Three—the more people you get involved, the better chance it has of unraveling."

As much as the thought horrified him, he would have to be the one to kill Belesinto. This wasn't a task he could contract out as he often did with things that were out of his expertise in his consulting business back home. "What about poison?"

Cutter slowly nodded. "That is certainly something that has been effective in many assassination attempts over the years. Of course, that means procuring the poison."

"Would you be able to get some?"

"I'm not sure I could. It's not every day that I buy poison. I know some rough folks in these parts, but poison wouldn't be their weapon of choice."

Julian rubbed his stubble. "I could get close enough to slip some into Belesinto's drink. He doesn't have anybody taste his food or beverage for him."

"True. If things go wrong, I could always get Almarella and the kids out of Delphi."

"Even if you do, what happens when the real Julius returns? He would be apart from his family and possibly on the hook for the murder of the Emperor."

"Which would land him an execution," Cutter said. "And if they ever find his family, they would probably be targeted for death as well."

They went through a number of different assassination scenarios. They all had their drawbacks. In the end, Julian decided that poison was his best option.

"One more thing you ought to know," Julian said. "That bastard Marsanto means to kill you before this is over. He told me in no uncertain terms."

Cutter took a long swallow of ale. "He won't be the first who's had that intention, and as you can see, I'm sitting here right beside you. He's welcome to try it."

"You need to protect yourself. I don't see you carrying a sword like he does."

"I don't need one." Cutter pulled back his tunic to reveal a pistol.

"Glad to see you come prepared."

Cutter grinned. "Mind you, I would never use a weapon in a place like this unless I absolutely had to, but what sense would it make to fight Marsanto with a sword. He's been carrying one around since he was six. I would be at a huge disadvantage therefore I'm not going to play his game."

"All right. Just be careful. Let's meet again tomorrow around noon. Same place?"

"I'll be here." Cutter finished his ale and put the glass down on the table.

* * *

"He's waiting for you inside his quarters," Herelius said. As if for emphasis, he pointed to a bronze door.

Reluctantly, Julian walked toward the door. He cleared his throat, then knocked on the door. A muffled scream came from the room. He knocked on the door again. "Is all well in there?"

He had the distinct feeling that things weren't okay. He opened the door to find Belesinto grab the arm of a woman, who was clearly trying to get away from him. He threw her down onto the bed.

The Emperor turned his head briefly to acknowledge Julian. "Ah, Julius, I was wondering when you would arrive. We have much to discuss."

Julian froze in place, looking from the Emperor to the woman on the bed to the door, completely at a loss as to what he should do.

"Perhaps now isn't a good time," Julian said.

"Of course it's a good time," Belesinto said. "We have much to discuss."

"Yes, but…"

"But what?" Belesinto slapped the woman and proceeded to tear her shirt off.

She protested but eventually gave in to the Emperor.

"Tell me more about this conflict with the Ainglish," Belesinto said. "Is this going to lead us to war? I fear that we have conflicts on too many fronts as it is."

Julian turned away in revulsion as the Emperor began to have intercourse with the servant. She was clearly in distress and not enjoying the experience. He was torn about what to do. He wanted to physically separate Belesinto from this woman, but that would likely be the last thing he ever did. Seeing how volatile he was, that would likely cause the Emperor to execute him on the spot. Instead, he made up some story about how he didn't think there was much to worry about, that he had been overly cautious. The blocked shipping lane issue seemed to be resolved. After a while, he excused himself, still feeling an utter sense of revulsion at the encounter and second-guessing his decision about not interfering.

He felt a terrible shame as he walked back to his house. He was more determined than ever to kill that insane megalomaniac. If such a thing were possible, Belesinto might be worse than the Game Master.

When he reached his house, he found Almarella picking tomatoes from their garden. She rose to greet him and kissed him. She quickly pulled away from him. "What is it? You have a haunted look about you."

"Walk with me." They left the gated community and took a long walk up a hill to a remote area that sported an amazing view of the ocean. The ocean had clear blue water, free of pollution. He counted a dozen boats in the bay and several more along the horizon.

The wind was gusting hard at this elevation although it had been calm before they started their journey. Neither of them spoke as they walked. He took a moment to savor the view before sitting on a stone bench. She sat next to him. He was surprised to hear himself recount what he had just seen. If this had been his Nancy sitting next to him, he would not have been able to tell her.

Almarella turned away from him and gazed at the ocean. "Something about you has changed. Ever since your return from the trip to meet the Ainglish, if that is what you actually did, you have been different. I can hear it in your voice, see it in your mannerisms, feel it in the questions you ask."

Julian didn't know what to say. He couldn't tell her that he was from another plane of existence and that he was impersonating her husband. She might be perceptive, but not that perceptive.

She reached for his hand and held it, a gesture that felt more intimate to him than when she had removed her clothes. "You mean to assassinate the Emperor. That is why you were asking those questions."

Julian opened his mouth but couldn't think of what to say.

"So, you do mean to kill Belesinto," Almarella said. "I was not sure, but your lack of response answers my question."

The last thing he wanted was to have her involved. "Look, I'm not sure why you think I would do something like that, but I can assure you…"

"Please don't deceive me. We have been married for fifteen years and have known each other our entire lives. I know you as well as a person can know another."

Julian could not help but grin. She didn't know him at all. "The less you know about my affairs, the better off you and the children will be. I would rather not discuss it with you."

"Husband, there is no one in this world who would like to see the Emperor dead more than me. Let me help you."

Julian sighed. She could be of use to him, and if she really wanted him dead as much as she professed, then it should be her choice to get involved. "Poison. I want to poison him."

Almarella paused for a minute before saying, "I can get aconite. My Uncle Respario, besides being a physician, is also an herbalist. Well, an herbalist of a different sort. He can provide me with it."

Julian had the distinct impression that she may have used her uncle's services before. "This aconite, how does it work? What does it look like?"

"It is better known as wolf's bane. In the north they use it to kill wolves. It comes from a flower, and its extracts are quite deadly. It takes very little of the extract to kill a person. The person who swallows the aconite will first experience a dry mouth, then will become numb in their extremities. They will die within minutes."

Julian glanced at her, still holding her hand. "You're serious?"

"I could not be more serious."

Julian released her hand and covered his eyes with his palms. For a while he said nothing. He didn't want to get her involved. On the other hand, she had more invested in killing Belesinto than anyone. If this is what she truly wanted, then who was he to deny her? He continued to internally debate the merits of using her in his plot and, in the end, decided he was in no position to turn down help.

"I would need this in the next two days. Can you get it for me by then?"

Almarella stared at him. After a few moments, she replied, "Yes. But I will have to leave now."

"Who will take care of the children while you are away?" With all his job-related responsibilities, he certainly couldn't do it.

Almarella frowned. "You are acting so strange. Firmina will take care of the children as she always does."

"Of course. I have had so much on my mind that I am becoming increasingly forgetful."

"No. It is beyond that. You are different."

He had to steer her away from this line of thought. "Tell me more about the aconite. What does it look like? How can I deliver it to him?"

"The extraction is in liquid form. You can place it in his beverage."

Julian would have ample opportunity to mix it into his wine. The bastard certainly drank enough of it.

"In that case, you should prepare to leave. I need the poison as soon as possible."

CHAPTER XXIII

When Herelius summoned Julius to an emergency meeting with the Emperor, he thought for sure that his plans were about to go up in flames. Almarella had yet to return with the poison she was going to obtain from her Uncle Respario. He was convinced that the Emperor was going to accelerate his plans to travel to the Kingdom of Xianapa. Belesinto ostensibly wanted to open trade with the underdeveloped kingdom, but in reality he wanted to exploit their resources. The land was rich in gold, diamonds, and iron, all things the Emperor coveted. Publicly, he claimed he was going to help the people of Xianapa, but his private conversations with Julian indicated his true intentions.

On the way, he thought of reasons to argue against the acceleration of this trip. He didn't think that claiming he had personal issues to resolve would sway the Emperor. He still was uncertain just how much personal influence Julius had with the man. Clearly, the Emperor sought his advice, but he did not know if he had enough stroke to postpone this trip. Instead, he contemplated official reasons of government business that dictated waiting another two days to embark.

In the end, his consternation was for nothing. This late-night meeting had nothing to do with the trip to Xianapa, at least not directly. Fortunately, when he arrived, there were no women present. Belesinto was alone except for an older man with a long beard playing the lute. Apparently, Belesinto did not have a problem with the lute player being present for their confidential conversation.

While the old man played his lute and sang about tales of battles and conquests, Belesinto poured him a drink. The Emperor always had a cup in hand, which played into Julian's plan. Julian accepted the cup out of courtesy, but only took the smallest of sips. The brandy was strong, and the last thing Julian wanted was to be inebriated during this critical time.

Belesinto paced around the room. He had a crazed, determined look on his face. He normally appeared dangerous, but now he looked downright frightening. "Something must be done, sooner than later."

Julian wasn't sure if he was supposed to know what the Emperor was talking about but he lacked context. He waited in vain for Belesinto to continue. "Something must be done about what?"

Belesinto abruptly turned toward him, a scowl marring his face. "Febrino and Urias of course. I am getting a worse and worse feeling about them. They mean to dispose of me and soon. We cannot let that happen. They must be eliminated."

"You mean assassinated?" Julian asked.

"I certainly do not mean that they should be brought here for tea."

"Of course not," Julian replied. "Why not have them arrested?"

"On what charges?" Belesinto asked.

"Treason."

"There is no proof. Just much supposition and my instincts, which, as we both know, are never wrong. They are guilty. Proving it, however, will be difficult."

Julian did not actually care either way and was only putting up an argument for appearances sakes. "Leave it to me." If Julian succeeded in killing the bastard, none of this would matter.

"This must be done quickly. I want them executed while we are in Xianapa. Therefore, it will appear less likely that I had anything to do with their assassinations. You need to make arrangements immediately."

"Consider it done. I have already been looking into the matter in case it was necessary to eliminate them. Urias and Febrino will no longer be a problem for you."

Because you will be dead.

The rest of the meeting centered on the goals and agenda for the upcoming trip, both the public ones and the ones that mattered to Belesinto. Julian volunteered to handle almost everything.

When they were done with official business, Belesinto told him that he had a surprise for him, a gift for all of his hard work. Julian had no idea what this gift might entail and didn't want anything from this monster. He didn't want to spend an extra minute than he had to in this thug's presence. Nonetheless, he followed Belesinto out of the chamber, which resembled a library with volumes of books and parchments on shelves, to a room with marble floors and a pool with clean, clear water.

Steam rose from the pool, so he assumed heated water was piped in, but he could not find the source. It made it difficult to see inside the room, and the air felt thick. He wasn't sure why the Emperor led him into this room unless his gift was supposed to be a hot and steamy bath. He bathed yesterday outside of their home in a public bath located inside of their gated community, and it felt wonderful to remove the dirt and grime that had been building up on him since his arrival.

He continued to follow the Emperor through the steam-filled area until he saw a girl chained to wall. Her breasts were bare, and she wore hardly any clothing. She looked to be no older than sixteen with dark skin and hair. She was thin and tall, and appeared to be utterly frightened.

He turned toward the Emperor, not even trying to hide his revulsion. "What is this?"

The Emperor smirked. "Why, this is your gift of course."

Julian tried to hide his disgust. She was a young girl, not some sexual object for a middle-aged man's depraved desires. "My gift?"

"Yes. She is just off the slaver ship from Xianapa. Isn't she perfect? I normally get the first pick from the slaver ships, but you have been working hard of late and deserve a reward. I wasn't sure if she was too old for you. I know how you like them young. If so, I will certainly add her to my collection."

Julian wanted so badly to slug this creep, but that would ruin his plans. He took a few moments to calm himself and remember who he was. He wasn't Julian Dawson. He was Julius Delesandro and, until he left this dreadful place, he would remain Julius. He smiled. His first instinct was to unequivocally say no to this offer, and he was about to do so until he stopped himself. Declining his offer wouldn't help this girl at all. She would just become Belesinto's sex toy. He couldn't let that happen. "You are most generous, your Grace. I have been under much stress of late, and I will gladly accept this most beautiful gift."

Julian was amazed that he could say that with a straight face. Seeing that girl chained to the wall enforced his overwhelming desire to murder the Emperor. He was not a violent man. He had never killed anybody, but he felt justified in his course of action.

"That is why I have you with me. You always have your priorities together, but you recognize having time to play is important."

The girl recoiled as Belesinto unchained her. Julian put his hand on the girl's wrist and drew her to his protective custody.

"I believe you will need time to prepare. You have very specific goals to accomplish on this upcoming trip. One thing you can do is write your goals on parchment and put them in order of priority. It will help you maintain focus."

Belesinto tilted his head. "Your idea has merit. Perhaps I will do that."

"If you don't have any other need of me, then I would like to enjoy this most wonderful gift of yours."

"I'm sure you do." Belesinto gave a lecherous smile that made Julian want to puke. He glanced at the frightened girl before he left with her and exited Belesinto's home. Looking at her made him think of Natalie. He tried to fight the rage that coursed through him, that threatened to consume him. That poor girl was someone's daughter, or sister, or grandchild.

He held the girl's hand and walked to the exit of the community. He said nothing to her until they were beyond the gates. He turned and faced her. That look of fear had not escaped her face.

"I'm terribly sorry that you had to experience this. I wish I had the time and resources to return you to your homeland." Julian reached into his pouch and took out a number of coins. The coins he pulled had significant value and he was confident they would be sufficient. He handed them to the girl. "Take these and return to your homeland. This should be enough to buy you passage. Be discreet and stay safe."

The girl had a stunned look on her face. She hugged him fiercely.

"Find a place to stay tonight. There are many sailing ships at the harbor. Hire one to return you home."

He watched as she ran off into the night. As he was walking back to his house, he recalled his conversation with the Emperor inside the room with the steamy pool. Belesinto had mentioned that Julius liked them young and thought this girl might even be too old for his tastes. He felt sick with revulsion. He already had doubts about his Delphi counterpart, but this had changed his outlook. He initially wanted to protect Julius, but no longer. Now, he only wanted to ensure that his family was out of this mess. As for his shade, when this was all over, if he was on the hook for the murder of the Emperor, then so be it. Let the bastard burn.

CHAPTER XXIV

"Where is she?" Marsanto asked.

"She'll be here soon," Julian replied.

Marsanto grunted. "I have dealings to attend to."

"Then go," Julian said. "I don't need you here. Almarella will arrive soon."

"She must." Marsanto handed him a dagger. "Or you will kill him with this."

Julian nodded and took the dagger from him before ushering the Game Master's henchman away. "Just remember, when this is over, you take me to the Maestro."

Julian anxiously awaited Almarella's arrival. Any delay could derail his plans, especially since he couldn't rely on Cutter to help him. If neither of them could procure the poison, then he would have no choice but to go with Marsanto's plan.

His anxiety festered like an open wound. Being stuck inside the house made him feel like a trapped rat, so he went outside to get air. He kept the dagger sheathed on his person. This plane was getting dangerous, and he felt reassured having this weapon. It couldn't be as difficult to wield as a sword. As he once heard on Game of Thrones, stick them with the pointy end.

During the course of his vigil, the children came out to spend time with him. He was too distracted to play with them, and eventually they abandoned him to their own pursuits.

It was nearing dusk when Almarella's wagon approached. He rose and walked to greet her. She was wearing a hooded robe that mostly concealed her face.

He helped her from the wagon and ushered her back into the house. In his home plane, if he had been involved in a conspiracy to assassinate a high-level political figure, he would be concerned about the conversation being bugged. There were no such listening devices here, and it was more likely that someone might overhear something while they were outside. Once inside, he made sure none of the servants were around.

"Do you have it?" Julian asked.

Almarella nodded and produced a small bottle. The top contained what looked to be an eye dropper. The bottle was dark, and he couldn't see inside. He didn't want to open it since the contents were lethal.

"What color is this liquid?" Julian asked.

"Clear, like water," Almarella replied.

"It is odorless, tasteless?"

"It has no noticeable smell," Almarella replied. "I am told it has a slightly bitter taste, but if you mix it with wine, then the Emperor won't be able to notice."

Julian put the bottle on the counter and began to pace. "Except that he might not be drinking wine."

"If it is not wine, then it will be some form of spirits. The substance should be similarly unnoticeable if mixed with spirits."

"You're sure of this?" Julian asked.

"Yes. Are you certain you can do this? You do not appear to have the same resolve you had when we first spoke about this course of action."

He'd had too much time to think about it since then. "I will do it. You can be certain of that."

"Good. This is something that needs to be done, but I never thought I would see the day that you would actually consider such action."

"Neither did I. Before this happens, you and the children must leave Delphi." Julian began to pace inside of their kitchen. "In case things go wrong, or they suspect that I poisoned the Emperor, I don't want you to be around."

"I can't leave you," Almarella said.

If Julius Delesandro was half the creep that Julian suspected him to be, then she and the children would be better off being far away from him anyway. On the other hand, they seemed devoted to him. Perhaps, he was a Jekyll and Hyde type and was an entirely different person around his family.

Julian shook his head. "It has to be this way. I can't risk you and the children."

"Can't you find someone else to do this?"

"No. I'm the only one who can do this."

The Game Master wouldn't have it any other way.

"I'm not supposed to meet again with the Emperor before we leave. I'll have to invent a reason to see him before hand."

Late last evening, he and Cutter met at his house. After Julian told him Almarella was going to procure the poison, they devised a plan for him to get it into the emperor's drink and leave as quickly as possible. After the deed was done, Julian would meet Marsanto at a predetermined location. It was a solid plan. Of course, there were many opportunities for things to go south.

"I don't want you in Delphi, so that rules out going to your parent's house. Where else can you go?"

"We can visit my Uncle Respario."

"Under what pretext?" Julian asked.

"He has fallen ill. I will take the children to say our final farewell."

"I know you just got here, but I need you to pack some belongings and leave." Julian took a deep breath. "I need to do this today. How quickly can you leave?"

Almarella looked particularly lovely on this occasion. He could drown himself in her soulful brown eyes. "Perhaps an hour or two."

"It must be quicker than that. Time is of the essence."

She sighed deeply. "Very well. Help me pack a travelling chest."

* * *

After seeing Almarella and the kids out to their horse-drawn wagon, Julian began the trek to the Emperor's palace, the small and unobtrusive bottle of aconite tucked in a pouch on his person. He couldn't remember the last time he had been this nervous. He couldn't stop his hands from trembling and had to keep them folded. At one point, his teeth even chattered.

Some assassin I am.

As shaky as his hands were, he wasn't sure that he would even be able to work the poison into a glass.

When he reached the estate, the guards let him pass. He had to act calm and natural. Julius Delesandro visiting the Emperor was no big thing. He did it all the time. There would only be suspicion if he acted strangely. He took a deep breath as he passed a guard and gave him the hand greeting that was commonly used in these parts.

Once he opened the massive front door, he met Herelius, the giant of a man who seemed to be omnipresent. "I have urgent need to see the Emperor. There have been developments in the Senate that he must be made aware of."

"What type of developments do you speak of?" Herelius asked.

"The Emperor's fears may be coming to fruition. I have learned that his enemies in the Senate may be planning to ambush his caravan on the trip to Xianapa. I need you to heighten security for the trip. Whatever you planned in terms of guards, double it. Arrange for some of the more seasoned warriors to accompany us."

"Are you certain of this?"

"You can never be certain of such things," Julian replied. "But the information I received came from a credible source."

"In that case, the Emperor should cancel the trip."

"I came to discuss that very thing. He won't cancel. He will see it as a sign of weakness, however I must attempt to dissuade him because of the danger involved. In the meantime, I need you to increase protection."

Herelius nodded. "It will be done. The Emperor is in the throne room."

Julian tried to remember how to find the throne room. He had been there once, but the place was so vast, he couldn't be sure if he could find it again. Asking wouldn't make sense since Julius would have a thorough knowledge of this palatial mansion. He thought of a different tactic. After Herelius left, he went to a different room, found a servant he recognized and said, "Take me to the Emperor now. I have urgent business."

"He is…"

Julian raised his hand, cutting off the servant. "No time. Just take me to him immediately."

The servant lowered his head and began walking. Julian followed. After they crossed through multiple rooms and made several turns, he was thankful he didn't try to make it to this room on his own.

His anxiety was eating away at him, culminating when they reached the throne room.

The servant left.

The Emperor was alone, peering over a map set underneath a glass case. When he looked up, a lecherous smile emerged on his face. "Ah, Julius, did you enjoy the girl? She was quite lovely."

"She was, but I have come here for urgent business. I received credible information that your foes in the Senate will make an attempt on your life during the trip to Xianapa."

Belesinto raised his index finger. "Those scoundrels. I knew they wanted me dead. We must eliminate them."

"It will be done. I am finalizing the details. I also instructed Herelius to double the guard detail for the caravan."

Belesinto nodded. "Good. Good. That is what I like about you. Attention to detail. Making sure all eventualities are covered."

"Thank you, your grace. But it is not all bad news that I have to share." Julian forced a wide smile. "Almarella is with child."

Belesinto came forward and embraced him. "That is truly good news. My blessings to your family. This requires a toast."

When Belesinto turned to retrieve a bottle and a glass for Julian, he made his move. He slipped the vial from his pouch concealed underneath his tunic, removed the eye dropper attached to the top of it, and drained its contents into the glass the Emperor had sitting on top of the table near the map.

Julian fumbled with the vial. It slipped out of his hand, and, for a moment, his heart almost stopped beating. He bent to one knee and caught it before it hit the floor. He looked up. Belesinto just finished pouring the glass and was turning when Julian shoved the vial into a pouch in his tunic. It wasn't fully closed, but there was nothing he could do about that now.

He stood upright as the Emperor approached. Belesinto handed him the glass. When the Emperor raised his glass, Julian raised his, and the Emperor toasted. "To a prosperous future, and another son."

Julian smiled and drained his wine.

Belesinto drank his and set his glass down. He staggered backward and clutched the table that held the map. "My throat."

He slowly approached as a look of terror grew on the ruler's face. "Your throat feels dry, yes? And you're having a hard time breathing?"

Belesinto frantically nodded.

"It's the poison I placed in your drink." The door was closed, and the Emperor was in no condition to yell for help. "You're an evil monster. Julius Delesandro never realized that, but I do."

A confused look covered the Emperor's face. "I…don't."

"Someone should have killed you a long time ago."

Belesinto reached out toward him.

Julian wanted the Emperor to know just what had happened and why despite the combination of terror and adrenaline coursing through his body.

"I want you to look at the face of your murderer." Julian grabbed his tunic and pulled him forward. "You're an evil bastard. You have raped and killed and brought ruin to people. Now, it's your turn to die."

Belesinto convulsed. Death was near.

He had to get the hell out of here now. He raced out the door and ran back the way he came from. He spotted several servants and began to yell. "The Emperor! He has fallen ill!"

He ran into the brick wall that was Herelius and grabbed the big man's arm. "The Emperor is severely ill. He needs medical attention immediately. There's no time to waste."

He thought for a second that the henchman might apprehend him, but Herelius immediately went to find help. He was banking on everyone trusting Julius Delesandro in order for his plan to work. All of the information he gathered suggested his counterpart's reputation was beyond reproach—except, of course, with his relationships with young girls.

As soon as Herelius left, Julian went the other way to his pre-planned exit. He continued to sound his alarm as he left the palace. He wanted complete chaos so nobody would pay him attention. He took a rear exit and ran a few hundred meters through a wooded area. Once the woods cleared, he encountered a stream, his meeting spot with Cutter. So far, everything was going as planned. He even started to breathe easier.

He found Cutter waiting for him. His friend held a sack with the same clothes Julian wore when he first arrived in Delphi. Wherever he was heading—hopefully home—he wouldn't need his tunic.

"How did it go?" Cutter asked.

"According to plan. Ding, dong, the witch is dead. You know, I can't say there is anybody, even the Game Master, that I despise more than the Emperor. He's a monster."

Cutter tossed the sack to him. "I never got to experience life in his inner circle, but I saw enough to know his wicked ways."

Julian began to remove his clothes and put on the old ones Cutter gave him. "It's weird. I mean, I've never killed anybody before this, but I don't feel bad about this. I feel that justice has been served."

As he finished putting on his clothes, Julian heard a rustling coming from the woods. With all of the commotion at the Emperor's palace he had not been expecting anyone, least of all Marsanto Belez, coming at them with sword in hand.

CHAPTER XXV

"What are you doing here?" Julian asked.

"Once you have completed your task, I told you I would settle unfinished affairs," Marsanto said. "Now step aside."

Julian stood his ground. "I don't think so."

Marsanto delivered a backhand that clipped the side of Julian's head. Julian hit the ground hard.

His head still fuzzy, Julian tried to shake it off and get to his knees. He looked up and saw Cutter draw his gun, but not quick enough as Marsanto knocked it out of his hand and landed a solid punch to the side of Cutter's head. Seconds later, Marsanto was on top of Cutter, raining down blows on him. He pulled out a dagger and attempted to stab Cutter, who held it back at arm's length.

"Son of a bitch." Julian found a large rock nearby, and did not give much thought to what he was about to do and its ramifications. All he knew was that he had to stop Marsanto.

Marsanto and Cutter were still engaging in a life and death struggle. He doubted either of them noticed him. He smashed the stone on top of Marsanto's head. He smashed him again. When the centurion flipped over onto the ground, Julian smashed his skull with the stone once more for good measure.

He looked down in a mixture of horror and revulsion as blood and brain matter leaked out of Marsanto's head. It was the most disgusting thing Julian had ever seen, and he had done it. He had been hesitant about killing the Emperor with a dagger, yet he just brained Marsanto with a large rock. He put the rock down and turned away, trying to keep himself from vomiting.

Cutter struggled to his feet and picked up his handgun. He moved Marsanto with his foot while clutching the side of his head. "This bastard's dead. Can't say as I'm going to miss him although he does have a nasty left hook. Should have seen that one coming." He slowly trudged toward Julian and put a hand on his shoulder. He spoke in a softer voice. "Thanks. The bugger took me by surprise. I shouldn't have let my guard down. Pretty stupid of me. It could have been a fatal mistake."

"I killed him," Julian said. "I can't believe it. I actually killed a man with my hands."

Cutter nodded. "Not to belabor the point, but you did just kill the Emperor."

Julian went his entire life without so much as a thought of taking another life, and in the span of a half-hour, he killed two people. What was becoming of him? Even if he made it home, what part of him would be left?

"But this…this is different. The Emperor was evil, and Marsanto…well, this death was brutal."

"It needed to be done. And if it makes you feel any better, I can assure you he was no choir boy. Trust me. You saved my neck. That's not something I'll ever forget."

Julian sighed. If it was a choice between Marsanto and Cutter living or dying, then it would be an easy choice. "How am I going to find the Game Master now? Marsanto was supposed to lead me to him."

"I have a pretty good idea where to find him. In every plane, he tends to have a handful of places he owns and spends time at. There's one such place outside of Delphi. Even on foot, we should be able to make it before nightfall."

"What about the body?" Julian asked. "Shouldn't we do something about it?"

Cutter shook his head. "Leave it. With all of the commotion going on with the Emperor's death, nobody is going to pay much attention to this piece of garbage. We need to leave now, before people start wondering what happened to the Emperor's right-hand-man. They will be looking for you before long. We have to take advantage of the chaos."

Julian followed Cutter. They veered away from Belesinto's palace and took a path around the perimeter of the gated community. Along the way, there were shouts, cries, and the sound of movement, both on foot and horseback. Commanders gave orders, and guards scurried about. He thought he was going to make it out of the complex unscathed until a senator, along with three men-at-arms, approached him.

"Julius, is it true about the Emperor?" the senator asked.

If he noticed Julian's odd clothing, he made no indication. He wore a cloak, which he hoped obscured the rest of his clothes.

Julian nodded somberly. He tried to look as sad as he could muster given the adrenaline rush he had been on for the past few hours. He hoped his acting chops were up to the task. "It is true. He is dead. I saw him at the palace. I fear someone has murdered him. That is why it is imperative that I protect his son to ensure the line of succession. No harm must come to him, or anarchy will reign in Delphi."

"Yes," the senator said. "That is a wise course of action. In this time of crisis, we must make sure Delphi doesn't fall into revolution."

"To that end, I require two of your horses. We must not waste time to find the Emperor's son."

"But…" the senator was about to protest.

"I insist that two of your men provide us with their horses. Time is of the essence."

The senator instructed two men-at-arms to comply with Julian's request. What Julian was quickly learning was that the key to impersonating somebody was being confident.

He and Cutter mounted the horses. Not that he was an expert, but Julian had experience horseback riding and could ride competently. After mounting his horse, without a further word, he and Cutter disembarked.

"Well done there, counselor," Cutter said. "You're getting pretty good at this game."

"This isn't a game. Everything about this is very real and dangerous. How long will it take to reach this place by horse?"

"Not more than an hour or two. We don't want to wear out these horses by running them too fast, but they should be able to keep a decent pace. You're comfortable with riding?"

"If I've made it this far without the horse throwing me off, I should be fine. How do I get home? What can I do to end this insanity?"

"I would suggest flaying the Game Master alive. That would get his attention." When Julian didn't reply, Cutter said, "That was a joke."

He was in no laughing mood.

"Truthfully, I don't know. But we'll be able to get a hold of the Game Master soon enough and see what we can figure out."

"I don't get it. Why me? Why did the Game Master have to include me in his evil machinations?"

"Because you're unique."

Julian frowned. "What do you mean?"

"What you have to understand is that most people are singular individuals. They don't have shades in other planes."

"Well, my wife, Nancy, had a shade on that first place."

"Yes, she did. But have you seen any of her shades in any other plane you've visited?"

Julian shook his head.

"It's not unusual to find someone with one counterpart on another plane. It is rare for a person to have shades on two separate planes. This is now your fourth plane with a shade. That's exceedingly rare. My guess is that there are more Julians out there. That they tend to have some level of importance would only further attract you to the Game Master."

Julian rode for a while in silence. He never thought of himself as unique. He had always been another face in the crowd, never standing out. He had never been great in sports, or overly intelligent, and had so far been moderately successful in business. He always considered himself a good-hearted, hard-working person with drive to make a better life for his family.

"You have to understand that it takes a convergence of many circumstances for a person to have multiple shades. In other words, the stars have to align. For them to align the way they have for you is pretty astonishing. When you find a person with multiple shades, that individual is typically someone of great importance who accomplishes great things."

"I haven't accomplished great things."

"I would beg to differ. You just rid Delphi of one nasty emperor and improved the lives of many in the process. Just consider the women he's harmed and would continue to harm in the future."

Julian shrugged. "My actions also brought two separate planes to war. So far, I've done far more harm than good, and I don't think I can ever make up for the destruction my actions may have caused."

"Yeah, well, you're not the first person the Game Master has duped. I can include myself in that group."

Julian waited for a further explanation, but one wasn't coming.

They left Delphi and took a dusty road. Along the way, they passed farms and houses, but nothing that resembled the large commercial enterprises within the city. They stopped when they reached a large temple with an onion shaped dome. It had a main building and a number of smaller buildings attached. They led their horses to a stable just outside the temple where a strong bull of a lad took them.

Cobbled stones led to the temple's entrance. The building was drab gray with nothing to distinguish it except for its dome. It seemed like just the place for the Game Master.

Julian kept his distance from the beggar with open sores wearing ragged clothes at the entrance of the building.

"What makes you think he'll be here?" Julian asked.

"I certainly hope he's here, because I'm not sure where else to look. I had some dealings with him on this plane, and this is where we met back then."

Julian followed him inside the temple. He wasn't familiar with the religious customs of this plane, but this did not look like a place of worship. Two people were at a table counting large sums of currency. A group of men negotiating a deal sat inside of another room. At the far end of the main room, a large man with a round belly displayed his wares to several shoppers. The wares in this case were prostitutes, based on their dress and how they carried themselves.

One of the prostitutes, who was a wearing a white dress that left little to the imagination and a slit on the side that ran up to her hip, approached them. "The Maestro requests your presence."

Julian stared at Cutter quizzically. "How could he possibly know we're here? We just arrived."

Cutter shrugged. "Probably has carefully concealed cameras."

She led them to the back of the temple. They went through a few rooms and corridors. Inside, the building was significantly larger than he expected.

When Julian saw the short bastard with the beady eyes and bald head, all of his anger and frustration overwhelmed him and he charged at the Game Master. He wasn't sure what he planned on doing, but it didn't matter. Before he reached the evil bastard, three oversized henchmen intercepted him. One tackled him to the floor. Another put his knee on Julian's spine. The third man stood like a wall in front of the Game Master.

"Hey, ease up on him." Cutter went after the man who had tackled Julian and physically restrained him. A scuffle ensued between them.

Julian tried to move, but the henchman had him pinned down. He looked up and shouted, "You son of a bitch. You said you were going to send me home. I've done everything you've asked of me. You said you would send me home, you lying bastard."

"Enough," the Game Master said in a shrill voice. "Lay your hands off each other."

Julian could not see behind him, but before long the sounds of Cutter and the other guy fighting subsided.

"Mr. Dawson, I told you I would send you home, and I remain true to my word. It is my solemn promise that I will return you to your family after the completion of the tasks I have set for you. I had additional work I needed you to perform, which delayed that promise, but I assure you that you will see your family. Now, will you behave if I tell my men to let you go?"

Through gritted teeth, Julian replied. "Yes."

"Release him," the Game Master said.

The man, who had his knee uncomfortably positioned on Julian's spine, eased off and lifted him to his feet. Julian glanced around. Based off the blood trickling down the nose of the man Cutter had been fighting, his friend got the better of their scrap.

"There is no reason we can't be civil. We are all gentleman here." The Game Master pulled out a gold bracelet lined with diamond studs and offered it to Julian. "Take this as a gesture of appreciation for a job well done. You can give it to your wife when you see her again."

"And when will that be? Where are you sending me off to this time?"

The Game Master grinned. "That remains a mystery, but as I'm sure your friend explained to you, your chances of getting home are increasing. There is a limit to the amount of shades one individual can have."

Julian glanced back at Cutter, who nodded.

"I can't vouch for the Game Master, since, as we both know, he is a serial deceiver, but it is true that there can't be many other Julians out there. I have a good idea of who your fifth shade might be. A sixth? I can't recall hearing of any person having that many shades, but I wouldn't rule it out."

"Take the gift," the Game Master said.

"I don't want the gift. I want to go home."

"Patience, Mr. Dawson. You will get to your destination."

"Send me home now, you demented asshole."

The Game Master shook his head. "Name calling will get you nowhere. Of course, I could just have one of my men snap your neck, then you will never get home."

Julian glared at the little man. He wanted to lunge at him and tear out his throat, but that would get him nowhere.

"Since you are so impatient, I suppose I should send you away. Follow me."

Reluctantly, Julian trailed the Game Master. Cutter and the goon squad followed. He led them to a room with a blue door that glowed ominously.

Julian raised his brows. "Why the doors?"

"They're portals. How they work is somewhere between science and mysticism, but that need not concern you." He handed Julian another foamy beverage that was bluish green.

"Why the beverage?" Julian asked.

"It's the only thing that is keeping you alive when you step through the portal. Doing so for one like you would be fatal without it."

Julian was sick and tired of these little games, but refusing would get him nowhere, and he already tried to take the Game Master by force to no avail. If he was going to see his family, he would have to continue playing this game.

Julian glanced at Cutter. "What do you think?"

"You're off on another one of his games. This door will get you to where he wants you to go, but it won't be home." Cutter had his fists clenched and his jaw was tight. His eyes narrowed as he looked at the henchman. He looked ready for a fight.

Julian sighed. "All right. Let's get this over with."

Cutter put his hand on Julian's shoulder. "Don't worry. Wherever you wind up, I'll find you."

The Game Master ground his teeth. "Do so at your own peril. I will not have you thwart my plans."

"You hurt him, and I won't do a damn thing for you," Julian said. "Try me."

The Game Master narrowed his eyes but did not say anything.

With some reluctance, Julian opened the glowing door. He stepped through to what lay beyond.

CHAPTER XXVI

With darkness surrounding him, Julian felt sudden panic. He was free-falling, or at least it sure as hell felt like that. He tried to look to the ground but could see nothing. He was surrounded in a fog so thick, he felt as if he could cut through it with a knife. The sense of falling stretched for an eternity. When the falling sensation finally ended, he landed on his posterior onto the dusty ground.

The fog almost instantly dissipated. He looked up and found that dawn was breaking in this arid land. Dust filled his mouth and throat, giving him a coughing fit.

"Take a deep breath, Julian. You'll be all right."

Julian turned, startled to hear his name. It was Cutter.

He looked up and grinned. Instead of being despondent about not being home, he was glad to see a familiar face. "Hey, what are you doing here? Where am I?"

Cutter extended his hand and lifted Julian to his feet. "Well, as you can see, you're not in your home plane."

Julian looked around. Nearby were a saloon, a bank, an inn, and a number of shops on the cobbled road. This seemed to be a populated area. Further along in the distance were numerous houses and other structures. A horse drawn carriage being led by a man wearing black trousers and a white buttoned shirt came in his direction. "Holy shit. I'm in the Old West."

"You're not far off the mark," Cutter said. "This place is what your country used to look like about one hundred fifty years in your past."

"But how did you know to find me here?"

Cutter motioned with his right hand and began to walk away. "Follow me. I can't stay long."

Julian followed Cutter into an alleyway at the side of a building. "What's going on?"

Cutter looked around as if to make sure nobody was in earshot. "Listen, I haven't been exactly forthright with you. You see, I'm not as benevolent as I might seem, something I feel guilty about since you saved my ass earlier. Ever since I figured out what the Game Master was doing, I was hoping you would wind up here. In fact, every time you crossed planes, I came here first, hoping I would find you. Fortunately, for me at least, you're finally here."

Julian looked around in confusion. He couldn't help but feel a sense of betrayal about Cutter's admission. He had come to think of him as a friend, a guide through these troubled times. "Why do you want me here?"

"I have a history in this plane, and not all of it's good. I'm a wanted man. If I'm found by the authorities, I will be arrested and hanged."

"Damn. What the hell did you do?"

"It's a long and complex story. We don't have time for the full-blown version, but I can give you a quick and dirty recap."

"Tell me."

"I settled back in this area when I was a younger man, which might seem strange based on options I have in other planes."

"Let me guess," Julian said. "It involved a woman."

"Of course it involved a woman. She was and still is the love of my life. Her name is Felicity. We have a child together." Cutter became choked up. Julian wasn't sure if he was going to continue, until he cleared his throat. "My daughter's name is Clarice. She'll be turning ten soon.

"Anyway, I needed work, and the Game Master had a job for me. It seemed straight forward, and I had worked for the Game Master before. Mind you, I never trusted the bastard, but I figured I could look out for myself. My assignment was to provide security and protection to the visiting ambassador and his family from Britannia, this plane's version of the United Kingdom. Around here, they remain the most powerful and influential country.

"The ambassador was here to help negotiate a peace treaty between the Confederation of Colonies, what you know as the United States, and the natives of this land after decades of bloodshed. The People, as they refer to themselves, have been warring with the Confederation for nearly a hundred years. They are far more organized and formidable than the native people from your plane were during a comparable period in the frontier days. The fighting between the two sides is much fiercer here, and the colonists don't have a measurable technological advantage as they did in the history of your plane."

Julian shook his head. "Is there any plane that doesn't have war and strife?"

"Just look at your own plane. You have terrorist attacks, fighting in the Middle East, a war in the Ukraine, that fella in North Korea who wants to blow up the world. There are always people who want what others have or use religion as a reason to go to war, or groups that have radically different philosophies and cultures. Then again, it almost always comes down to money. When you have been where I've been and seen the things I've seen, you come to accept that's the way of the world. I do my best to stay away when the animosity becomes too intense.

"Going back to what happened. It seemed like an easy job. It all went to hell when the train carrying the ambassador and his family exploded before arriving at its destination. I watched the explosion happen and could do little other than help carry out the dead bodies.

"It was a tragedy, and I felt horrible about it, especially with the ramifications, but little did I know that I would become the prime suspect in the bombing. All of the evidence conveniently pointed toward me. I had nothing to do with it, but once things get rolling, it's hard to stop the momentum, and they needed a scapegoat.

"I went underground, did some digging, and found that the real culprit was one of the men I hired for the security detail, a real piece of human filth named Edgar Smith. I had known Edgar for a while and thought I could trust him. If I run into Edgar again, he's a dead man. I strongly suspect that the Game Master paid him to blow up the train. Of course, I have no proof. Nothing I could take to the authorities.

"I faced the most difficult decision of my life. Ultimately, the only thing that made sense was to leave this plane. Leave Felicity and Clarice and never return. If I stayed, I would be arrested and executed for a crime I didn't commit. I would do my wife and daughter no good dead."

Julian put his hand on Cutter's shoulder. "I'm sorry to hear that. I feel for you, man. I guess I'm not the only one who has been forced away from their family."

Cutter tilted his head. "You have a better shot than I do. It's like I said before, I have no ability to take other people with me when I travel. If I could, I would have taken my wife and daughter to another plane. I didn't want them to lead a life on the run here."

Julian's early misgivings about having been betrayed by Cutter melted away after hearing his story. "What can I do for you, man?"

"I was hoping you would be agreeable." He handed Julian a brown, leather pouch. "This has gold. Quite a bit of it. If I can't be there for my family, the least I could do is help them financially." The next thing he handed Julian was a digital camera. "If you don't mind, I would like you to take some pictures of my wife and little girl that you can bring back to me. This plane has nowhere near this level of technology, but they already know about my travelling, so it shouldn't frighten them to see this type of device. It would mean a lot to me. I also have a gift for my little girl." He handed Julian a Rubik's Cube. "It's not much, but they don't have anything like this here, and I figured she would get a kick out of it."

"I'm sure she will."

"I would also like you to give them a message. Tell them that I love them very much, that I think about them every day, that I wish I could be here for them."

Tears began to form in Cutter's eyes.

"I'll do that. Where can I find them?"

Cutter handed him a piece of parchment. "This is a map. They're about two hours away from here by horseback. If you could deliver those to them, I would be grateful."

"Of course."

"Thank you. Unfortunately, I have no idea what the Game Master has cooked up for you this go around, and I won't be around to help, so you're on your own."

"I understand," Julian said. "I'll figure it out."

"The Game Master got that part about you right. You may be getting a raw deal, but you are certainly capable of performing these tasks."

Cutter offered his hand, and Julian shook it. "I don't know when we'll meet next. Good luck, my friend. I'll see you in another life."

Cutter turned and walked away. With his index finger, he pointed in the air and drew a pattern. Before Julian's eyes, Cutter stepped through the pattern and disappeared.

"What the hell?"

For a while, Julian stared dumbfounded at where Cutter had been. Eventually, Julian turned and walked back to the street in which he first arrived. He looked around and found a couple of men wearing wide-brimmed hats riding horses. Although this area seemed relatively quiet, further up the road there was a bustle of activity with people going in and out of buildings and merchants selling their wares. A woman carrying a baby entered a bank across the street. He stayed put. If history was any indication, someone representing the Game Master would soon be joining him to tell him about his next assignment. He tried to remain in the background since his modern clothes would stick out. Not so severely as in the last plane, but they would stand out nonetheless. A pretty lady passed him on the street, and gave him a double take, but didn't say anything.

After fifteen minutes, a man wearing a badge rode a horse in his direction. Julian cursed under his breath. The last thing he wanted was to attract the attention of local law enforcement. He hesitated, not sure what to do. Fleeing would make him look suspicious.

He held his ground and waited. The man wore a brown hat, and had a long black beard and mustache. He rode his horse in front of Julian. "James Dawson, you need to come with me."

"My name isn't James Dawson."

The sheriff stared hard at him. "You might think you're Julian, but while you're in my city, you're James Dawson. Now come with me so we can get you out of those ridiculous clothes."

Not that he had much choice. At least he found the Game Master's emissary. It was time to find out about the most recent scheme he was going to be involved with.

CHAPTER XXVII

Julian walked alongside the sheriff until they reached a stable where the sheriff had a horse waiting for Julian.

"I was told you know how to ride," the sheriff said. "Is that right?"

"I'm no expert but I can ride." Fortunately, this time Julian wouldn't be riding under duress with the threat of guards chasing after him to arrest him for the murder of the Emperor. Compared to that, this should be easy—except that it wasn't. Julian's horse kept kicking and snapping at him as he tried to mount it. It took several tries before he finally succeeded.

The sheriff gave a nice hearty laugh. "You all right there, partner? Maybe a donkey would be better suited for you."

Julian spoke through gritted teeth. "I'm fine." He noticed a distinct pattern develop. Everybody who worked for the Game Master was an asshole.

Once Julian was properly on the saddle, he followed the sheriff's horse out of the stable, off the main road, and through open fields. They rode at a brisk pace, and Julian had to fight to keep control of his horse. The land was arid, and wherever they went, a storm of dirt and dust followed in their wake. He figured the man would take him to the sheriff's office but realized that wouldn't be the case the further afield they went.

They had little conversation along the way. They passed through a corn field, a cattle ranch, a farm, and finally a river. By the time they reached their destination, Julian was tired and thirsty.

Whey they stopped, Julian asked, "Do you have some water?"

The sheriff tossed him a flask.

Julian took a long drink. The hot sun was beating on him. Unlike the sheriff, he wasn't wearing a hat or other appropriate clothing for riding in this type of climate.

After the sheriff dismounted, Julian followed suit.

"Where am I and why am I here?" Julian asked.

The sheriff motioned to the surrounding area. "This is Penn's Woods."

"Penn's Woods, as in William Penn?"

The sheriff narrowed his eyes. "I can't say I'm familiar with a William Penn. However, Joseph Penn was the founder of this great state."

Julian wondered if this person was of the same lineage as the William Penn of his plane. Ultimately, it didn't matter for his purposes. "That's wonderful. So, what exactly does the Game Master want me to do for him?"

"Game Master? I'm not familiar with anyone of that name. However, the Grand Magisterium provided me with instructions to give to you."

Julian rolled his eyes. "I don't give a damn what name he goes by. I would call him an asshole but you'll threaten to kill me if I don't mind my manners. You pricks who work for him are all the same no matter what plane you're in.

"I would watch that acid tongue of yours. It may get you in trouble around here."

Julian folded his arms. "Let's get this straight. I've been though all kinds of shit recently because of your Grand Magisterium. I don't care what you think about me, and more to the point, you don't scare me."

The sheriff revealed his revolver. "Maybe not, but this should."

Julian's temple throbbed. He balled his hands into fists. He was ready to attack this guy despite being unarmed. "Go ahead. Shoot me. I'm pretty certain your Grand Magisterium will be mighty angry if you do. My guess is that killing me will be your own death sentence. Now, cut the crap and tell me what I need to know."

The sheriff smiled. "Very well, Mr. Dawson. There's no need for us to be on unfriendly terms since we are on the same side." He extended his hand. "I am Edgar Smith, sheriff of the free city of Chester."

Despite the heat, a chill ran across Julian's body.

Edgar Smith. The man who had double-crossed Cutter.

He was about to say something then thought better of it. Better to hold that information close to his vest. Reluctantly, he shook the man's hands. For better or worse, they would have to work together, but he would remember what Smith did to his friend.

"Before we go into the task that is required of you, let me explain a few things. There has been a great deal of tension between us citizens of the Confederation of Colonies and those savage Injuns who pollute our land."

"Oh you mean those people who were here before you? The ones whose land you stole before you pushed them aside like they weren't even human? And now you're upset because they want to take back what you stole from them."

"I'm not so sure that the Grand Magisterium chose the right person for the job," Smith said. "But that isn't for me to decide. As I said, there have been many hostilities. The fighting has been going between us and the savages since my Grandpappy was a young man. He slew nearly fifty Injuns himself."

"You must be proud," Julian said.

"I sure am. Listen to me, Mr. Dawson. You're not from these parts; therefore you have no right to judge. You have no idea what it's like living here. I reckon that if you did, you would have a whole different outlook on life and this situation."

Julian had an immediate distaste for this man because he betrayed Cutter, but he had to concede that Smith had a point. His worldview was shaped by the plane in which he lived. Had Julian lived in this plane, undoubtedly his outlook on life would be different. Perhaps he shouldn't be so quick to judge, but he couldn't help himself.

"There are two major tribes of Injuns in the northeastern part of the Confederation of Colonies: the Wyotsoks and the Chynos. Historically, these two tribes haven't gotten along well and have fought each other over the silly things that Injuns fight over. God knows I stopped trying to figure them out long ago. It's impossible to understand these ignorant savages. At any rate, the Wyotsoks and the Chynos have a common enemy—the citizens of the Confederation. Together, well they can be a mighty formidable group to fight against.

"That's where you come in. You see, Mr. James P. Dawson is a prominent merchant, one of the wealthiest men in the country."

"Hmm, why doesn't that surprise me?"

"I am not sure why that should or should not surprise you,' Smith said. "However, he has done extensive trading with both the Wyotsoks and Chynos. My understanding is that he has a mutually beneficial relationship with them. My guess is that Dawson doesn't particularly enjoy the company of the Injuns, however they are necessary to further his business endeavors."

"All right," Julian said. "I get the picture. So, what does the Game Master or Grand Magisterium or whatever the hell you call him want from me?"

"I was getting to that. The Grand Magisterium needs you to convince one of the two tribes to join us and turn against the other. We are looking for complete and utter annihilation. My reading of the situation is that it would be easier to get the Chynos to side with us and turn against the Wyotsoks than the other way around. As James P. Dawson, you have resources at your disposal. You have significant wealth, influence, and holdings. These will be your tools to accomplish your goals."

Julian shook his head. "You have got to be kidding me. This son of a bitch wants me to start another war. I'm tired of his warmongering."

"You have it all wrong. You're not starting a war. We have been fighting for decades. Your job is to end the war. We wipe out the Wyotsoks, and then it won't be difficult to eliminate the Chynos as well. With those two tribes eliminated, the remaining tribes in the Confederation of Colonies will fall in line. That will end the cycle of death and violence and fighting that has been plaguing this great nation for as long as I can remember. We want nothing more than to move on as a peaceful nation, but that can't happen while we're fighting these savages. The only option is to eliminate them."

Julian raised his hand. "Enough with the savages. They're people."

"Well, I can see that you're a prickly sort. God forbid I offend you."

"This is bullshit."

"This is right and just. Do you have any children, Mr. Dawson?"

Julian nodded.

"As do I. A boy and two girls, all in their early teens. I don't want to have them fight and potentially get injured or killed in these wars. I want my grandchildren someday to live in a land without the constant threat of violence and death. Is that so wrong?

"Think of it what you may, but that is your task at hand, one that I am here to assist you with and also ensure that you complete."

Julian knew there was no point in arguing. Simply refusing would not accomplish anything, but he would be damned if he was going to be the Game Master's patsy again. Edgar Smith could spin it any way he wanted, but the bottom line was that the Game Master's scheme was going to result in a whole lot of people dying. The question was, how could he get out of it?

For the next two hours, Smith gave him detailed biographical sketches of the important people he would have to know among the People as well as politicians that Julian's counterpart had dealings with. Fortunately, Smith had pen and paper available. The pen consisted of a feathered quill with a small ink container, but Julian still managed to take extensive notes.

He asked Smith questions about James Dawson's mannerisms, how he interacted with people, if he had any quirks, how he spoke, but Smith could not provide much detail since he did not personally know the man and only knew him from his public appearances.

Julian had a severe headache by the time they were done. Smith offered to cook some pork belly on the wood stove, but Julian did not want to be in the presence of this man for any longer than he had to. He declined the offer but took the clothes Smith gave him. They consisted of britches, a wide-brimmed hat, and a white collared shirt. The outfit seemed as if it belonged somewhere in between Colonial times and the Wild West, but at least they fit well.

"Now, that looks much better than the clothes you came with," Smith said. "I imagine you must be ready to see your house and your pretty wife. You have a lot of work to do. I can't imagine this will be easy, but you seem to be a competent fellow, even if your values are misguided."

"My values are just fine," Julian said. "Please take me to my home."

CHAPTER XXVIII

Julian figured James Dawson was wealthy since his other counterparts had also been wealthy but he wasn't prepared for the massive ranch the man owned. It took fifteen minutes riding on horseback once they left the city limits before they reached it. He wasn't adept at gauging the size of land, but it had to be thousands of acres. It took a while just to get to the house from the edge of the property.

There were several houses on the property, but the main house dwarfed the others. The term mansion didn't do it justice. It was the biggest house he had ever laid eyes upon. The grounds close to the house was ornately decorated with columns and statues. He encountered several fountains and a cobbled rode that led to the front of the house. The most remarkable aspect of this property was the moat at the front entrance of the house. Seeing as how this plane didn't appear medieval, he guessed it to be decorative.

Smith circled in front of him with his horse. "It is quite grandiose."

"Just how rich is James Dawson?"

"I reckon he is the wealthiest man in the entire state. He owns about a third of the land in these parts."

Julian whistled. He was feeling wholly inadequate seeing how successful each of his shades were. He was clearly the underachiever of the group.

"Seeing as how you have dozens of horses on your ranch, you won't be needing this one."

Julian nodded. Besides the horses, he had seen hundreds of cattle and sheep. There were also numerous apple and pear trees. Outside of the grazing lands stood well-manicured lawns and a garden that would be fit for the cover of a magazine.

"I will leave you to get oriented to your new abode, Mr. Dawson. However, I will call upon you tomorrow so that we can set the plans in motion."

Julian waved Smith away. "Right. Right."

The less he saw of Smith the better. The man had a real creep factor to him with his talk of Injuns and Savages Julian wouldn't have liked him even if he wasn't pre-disposed to dislike the man because of what he did to Cutter. He would try to avoid the man as much as possible for as long as he was on this plane.

On his way to the front door, Julian encountered dozens of people he assumed worked here. Some took care of livestock, others tended the ground and garden, while others picked fruit. They all bowed and were deferential to him. Not knowing how James Dawson would react, he merely nodded as he passed them.

When he reached the front door, he was glad to find it open since Smith had not provided him with any keys. This way, he avoided the awkwardness of having to ask a servant to let him in.

The interior of the house was just as impressive as the exterior. The first thing he noticed was a massive chandelier filled with candles. To his left and right were winding staircases. The floor was made of marble. The walls were lined with paintings, and sculptures adorned many inside spaces. He walked around slowly. Even though it was his for the time being, he did not wish to break anything and felt a bit intimidated by the opulence of this house. He made sure not to put his hands on any expensive objects. He was trying to get a feel for James Dawson, but other than someone who collected pricey items, he could not detect much personality.

Footsteps sounded from above. He looked up and did a double take.

"James!" called out a startled voice.

The woman standing in the overhanging corridor was Nancy. Not a replica, but his Nancy. She even sounded like her. At least that's what his clouded mind interpreted. He tried to respond but could not utter a sound. He put his hand to his mouth and was about to move forward when he suddenly felt woozy. He stepped forward, but his legs gave out underneath him, and everything went dark.

* * *

Julian opened his eyes and found Nancy looking down at him, except that it couldn't possibly be Nancy since he was in this plane that resembled the post Civil War era of his time. Yet there she was hovering above him.

Without thinking about what he was doing, he reached up and touched her face. "Nancy."

She frowned and touched his forehead. "You aren't feverish, James, but you are certainly acting as if you are in a state of delirium."

Julian propped himself on his elbows and stared at the woman who could have been his wife. Except that she wasn't his wife. She was Elizabeth Dawson, the wife of James.

A dark-skinned woman approached him with a warm, wet cloth that she applied to his forehead. They had numerous housekeepers, and although Edgar Smith had given him many of their names, there had been too many for Julian to remember. "Are you feeling well, Master Dawson? You must have tripped and bumped your head."

He removed the towel. "I'm fine. Truly I am, but thank you for your concern."

Elizabeth tilted her head back and appraised him. "Are you sure that you are feeling well? Rowena, get James some water."

Rowena returned with water in a wooden cup. It wasn't cold the way he liked it, but he was dehydrated, which may have contributed to his fainting spell. He drank and handed the cup back to Rowena. "Thank you. I needed that."

"Yes, Master Dawson."

"Please, no Master Dawson. It's James."

She nodded curtly and walked away with an uncertain look.

Elizabeth helped him to his feet, displaying surprising strength. He had to remember that she wasn't Nancy, no matter how much they looked alike.

"Thank you." Julian couldn't help himself and hugged her.

"Are you certain that you are feeling well?" Elizabeth asked.

"I am. I think I was just dehydrated."

Elizabeth frowned. She even had Nancy's dimples on her cheeks. "Dehydrated?"

"I just need to drink some water."

Julian sank into a sofa that looked soft and inviting. He motioned to the spot next to him. "Please sit next to me."

Elizabeth hesitated before taking the spot next to him. "I was hardly expecting you so soon. I only expected you late this evening, if you returned at all."

"My plans changed. There is new business I have to deal with."

Julian closed his eyes. His head buzzed. When he opened his eyes, she was still there. "You have no idea how good it is to see you. I've had one rough day, but seeing you makes it all better. It's as if I had been held underwater and now I can breathe again."

Elizabeth's face flushed as she turned her head away from him. She folded her hands and settled them on her lap. She was wearing a full length pale blue dress and a necklace that sparkled with diamonds, no doubt an extravagant gift from her husband. She cleared her throat. "What business is it that brings you back so soon?"

Julian sighed. "It involves the People and the Confederation of Colonies, and it is one big mess. I'm not sure how to proceed, but I sure have my hands full."

"Your hands full? That is a queer expression."

He reminded himself that his colloquialisms would be different from how they spoke here. "Yes. Well, it will be difficult to accomplish this task. Tell me. What do you think of the People?"

Elizabeth sat upright. "It isn't right that the People have attacked us unprovoked."

The conviction in her words didn't ring true to Julian. "Don't tell me what you think James Dawson wants to hear. Tell me how you truly feel."

Elizabeth stared at him again. She seemed indecisive before speaking again. "The People were here long before we were. The land rightly belongs to them, and we continue to push them further away. We don't deal fairly with them. They have legitimate complaints that the Confederation routinely ignores. Is that what you wanted to hear?"

"Is that how you truly feel?" Julian asked.

Elizabeth nodded.

"Then that's what I want to hear. I value you what you have to say."

"You never seemed to value it in the past."

Julian imagined that if this plane was like the olden days of his plane, then the opinions of women didn't carry much weight. "What else can you tell me?"

"The People have a respect for us that we don't share for them. We have treated them poorly over the years since the first settlers came to the new world. What choice do they have but to fight against us? If things had been different from the start, if the attitude of the settlers had been to share and not to steal, then perhaps things would be different now. At this point, however, all we can do is fight them."

Julian smiled. He gently touched her face, which was unblemished and had no makeup. "Then I must have been a fool all of this time for not soliciting your opinion. That was logical, well-reasoned, and articulated perfectly. I beg your forgiveness for being so pig-headed."

Elizabeth stared at him with a look of bewilderment.

Julian lowered his head and ran his fingers through his thick hair. Thinking about his upcoming task depressed him. He didn't have a plan. Even when he came up with a plan, the negotiations with individuals he didn't know or understand would prove difficult. Edgar Smith had provided him an overview of the principals involved, but he would have to get a more in depth review of the players before he spoke with them. To further complicate matters, he had no interest in having one of the People tribes attack another.

Elizabeth put a hand on his shoulder. "Is there something wrong?"

"I just wonder if this task is bigger than me. I don't know how I can accomplish what I need to."

"You certainly have always been capable. You have proven yourself in political and business dealings repeatedly."

That was James Dawson, not him. This was out of his league. He would have to find a way to resolve this situation again. What choice did he have? He rose and offered his hand to Elizabeth. "Would you care to take a walk around our lovely grounds with me?"

She gave a smile that warmed him inside. "I would love to."

CHAPTER XXIX

With some reluctance, Julian allowed Smith to accompany him into the city of Kensington the following day. As Smith explained, although no longer the nation's capital, it was where most of the country's significant business took place. Julian did not want this loathsome man to accompany him, but he needed Smith. How else was he going to know who to meet with? In this backward place, he did not have photos or videos to identify these people.

They rode in via horseback. He'd had more practice riding in the past week, both here and the last plane, than he had over the last five years and was starting to get the hang of it.

Smith continued to school him on who he was meeting today. After a business luncheon with members of the state commerce committee, he would be meeting with several senators and congressmen about the situation involving the People. According to Smith, the men he was meeting with would be allies in the plot to get one on the tribes to turn against the other.

He had to find time to visit Cutter's family. Based on James Dawson's schedule, it seemed unlikely that he could make it out today.

The cover story they came up with for Smith's presence was that the Chynos recently made threats against James Dawson, and Smith was providing him extra protection given Dawson's status as a prominent businessman. However, he told Smith he didn't want him present while he was talking with these people since the conversations would be of a confidential nature, and it would not make sense to have a law enforcement official present under those circumstances especially if the things they were discussing were less than legal, which was his way of getting some separation from Smith.

The luncheon left Julian confused and frustrated from listening to a multitude of names and issues that had little meaning to him. He was able to pick up on the basics of these issues from the tutorial Smith gave him, but he was mostly in the dark. The principals asked his opinion on several matters, and he gave vague answers. At least the food was good. At the luncheon, they served baked chicken, cornbread, and fried potatoes.

After the luncheon, he and Smith mounted their horses to go to a meeting across town with Senator Hawthorn from the state of Baton Rouge and Congressman Anderson from the state of Duquesne. He wasn't sure where these states could be found geographically since he had yet to see a map of this place.

Senator Hawthorn had an intense look on his face. "The situation continues to grow more dire in Baton Rouge. Last week, the largest bank in the state was robbed by the Chynos."

"Are you sure they were responsible?" Julian asked.

Senator Hawthorn scowled. "Of course, I'm certain."

"So, if the robberies were performed by citizens of the Confederation of Colonies, then that would be acceptable?" Julian asked.

"To your point, bank robberies in Baton Rouge and elsewhere aren't uncommon, but this is the first time the Chynos have tried it. If word of this spreads, then other members of the People may also try, not just in Baton Rouge, but throughout the country."

"And we have seen an escalation of hostilities by the savages along the Andoran Mountains," Congressman Anderson said. "They're using the mountains as a base of operations since they can hide from us and attack when we are least expecting it. They drove us out of Fort St. Pierre. We need to stop them before they make further gains on our positions. They are like a disease that keeps spreading. If we don't stamp them out, then they will overrun us."

"To that point," Senator Hawthorn said, "Where do you stand in the proposal we made to you? I was given to understand that you would be amenable to having one of the tribes turn against the other, and that you would have the connections and ability to make that happen."

Julian eyed both men. This could only mean that James Dawson had not been part of these plans. One of the Game Master's emissaries must have reached these two politicians and told them James Dawson would go along with this scheme. Otherwise, the Game Master wouldn't need Julian. The only move he could make was to outwardly cooperate. He still hadn't figured out his strategy, but he vowed not to be a pawn once again in the Game Master's evil machinations.

Throughout the afternoon, he had to fight through boredom as he listened to lobbying from businessmen and politicians on topics he neither knew nor cared about. By the time he was done, it was too late to see Clarice and Felicity.

He was hoping to ditch Smith after his meetings were finished for the day, but he doubted he would be able to make it back to the estate on his own.

As they were riding back, Edgar asked, "So have you come to understand by now why these savages must be disposed of?"

"Can you do me a favor?" Julian asked.

"Of course."

"Please shut your mouth."

"A mighty bit sensitive there, aren't we Mr. Dawson?"

"I said shut your mouth. You and I have a working relationship for as long as I'm here. Nothing more. I'm tired of you referring to them as savages. They're just people, no better or worse than you or I."

Edgar Smith gave him a hard stare before turning his attention back to the road. "Very well, James. You remain willingly ignorant. I don't even believe you are trying to understand these matters. You don't even have a plan yet. When are you going to meet with the representatives of the tribes?"

"I'm working on that," Julian said. "I've been here for all of one day. Give me a break."

"There will be no breaks. I'm not sure you understand the gravity of the situation. This great nation is at war, even if it hasn't been officially declared. Action needs to be taken, and we can't wait. So yes, you have not been here long, but you do not have the luxury of sitting back and waiting."

"I'll get on it."

"And I am here to see to that," Smith said. "I am here to ensure that you do your job."

"If you really want me to do the job, then let me know what I need to know and get out of my way. Let me handle the planning and strategy."

"I don't think that's such a prudent idea. This is a whole different world for you. You're unfamiliar with the customs and the culture. You need a strong hand to guide you, someone to give you sage advice."

"Unfortunately, I'm no stranger to alien worlds, and I've proven to be quite resourceful in solving these problems. If not, then your Grand Magisterium wouldn't have sent me here. Everywhere he has sent me, I have successfully completed my task."

"I was warned that you may not be so receptive to this task and that I would have to watch over you closely."

"Yeah, I don't play nicely with others," Julian said. "Speaking of which, I need you to clear my schedule tomorrow morning."

"You have appointments tomorrow morning."

"Then you're going to have to reschedule them for me."

"I'm not your personal secretary," Smith said.

James Dawson had a secretary. He met her earlier. She was an austere woman in her fifties who did not give a hint of warmth and friendliness. "Well, then get Ms. Van Zant to change my schedule."

"I suggest you alter your demeanor," Smith said. "You are not in charge of the situation. Would you like to know what my orders are if you don't fulfill your end of the bargain?"

"What, you're going to shoot me?"

Edgar Smith did not respond. He merely smiled. Julian was tired of being threatened. He had other ideas in mind, and some of them involved vengeance for his friend.

Julian stopped riding and turned toward Smith. "I'm taking tomorrow morning off. Make it happen."

* * *

When he reached the estate that was his new home, he melted at the sight of Elizabeth. She radiated a certain warmth and fortitude that made her like a beacon shining in the darkest of night. She was standing near the main entrance. He couldn't be sure if she was waiting for him, but he was glad to see her.

He dismounted his horse and greeted her by kissing her hand. "After spending a day with vipers and sharks, you have no idea how nice it is to see you."

She put her arms around his shoulders and planted a kiss on his lips. He wanted to pull back but was powerless to do so. He was completely captivated by her and how remarkably she acted and even felt like Nancy. "It's nice to see you too. I've been looking forward to this all day long."

"Have you?" Julian asked.

"I have."

For a moment, he thought about stepping back but quickly discarded that idea. "You are a breath of sunshine to brighten my day."

After putting the horse in the stable, they walked hand-in-hand around the estate. Julian took an apple off a tree and bit it. It tasted delicious. He handed it to Nancy—or rather Elizabeth. As much as she looked like her, he had to remember this wasn't his wife. Despite that, he couldn't help but notice how soft and inviting her lips looked.

"Cassandra is preparing a special meal for us tonight. We will be dining on veal chops, asparagus, roasted potatoes, and her special sweet cakes that you always enjoy."

Julian smiled. "As long as I have you for company, I'm sure it will be delightful. I don't know how I deal with haggling with these politicians all day long. They're dishonest and devoid of integrity."

"You should be used to dealing with them by now," Elizabeth said.

"I'm not. How have you spent your day?"

"In our twelve years of marriage, you have never once asked me that question," Elizabeth said.

"Then shame on me. I should have asked you long ago. So, how have you spent your day?"

"Managing the ranch and estate as usual. There is always much to be done. Making sure the crops are being handled appropriately, the larder is kept full, and the horses tended to. Janice and Louise came over for lunch, and we continued the knitting we have been doing."

"Is that right? Well, I would like to see some of your work."

Elizabeth stopped and stared at him for a long moment. Perhaps he should hold back on his enthusiasm. Her husband probably didn't show her this much attention. "In that case, I would like to show it to you."

As they walked arm-in-arm back to the mansion, he came to a full realization that this chapter in his work for the Game Master would be anything but easy to resolve.

CHAPTER XXX

Julian fully expected to see Smith the next morning. If he did, the situation was likely to get ugly. Fortunately, Smith heeded his warning and did not make an appearance.

After a hearty breakfast of bacon, potatoes, fresh bread, and coffee, Julian got his map, provisions for the trip, the items Cutter asked him to bring, and a horse that was saddled and ready to go. He bade Elizabeth farewell and set off on his journey.

Last night with Elizabeth had been a harrowing affair. After dinner, they sat on the veranda and spoke at length. He enjoyed getting to know her better. It was remarkable that she not only looked like Nancy but acted like her in so many ways. As they were getting ready to retire for the evening, Elizabeth became amorous. His temptation level had been off the charts, but he managed to feign fatigue, kissed her goodnight, and went to bed. Being that close to her and not acting on his urges had been torture.

Following the map on horseback had not been as easy as he thought it would be. A guide would have been useful, but asking Edgar Smith was out of the question. He could have asked any number of people who worked at the ranch, and after a half-hour of travel, he regretted not doing so, but this seemed too personal a matter to include a stranger. In the end, he had to stop a few times to ask for directions.

He arrived in Dunksferry, a small town that boasted a general store, a saloon, a butcher's shop, and a handful of businesses. It wasn't hard to find Clarice's house, which was modest by most standards and downright puny compared to the estate of James Dawson.

A picket fence surrounded the yard to the rear of the house. He peered over the fence and found a girl in a green dress feeding pigs. Their eyes met. She was a pretty young thing with golden hair and sparkling blue eyes. Julian saw a lot of Cutter in the girl and knew this had to be Clarice.

He called out her name.

She frowned. "Do I know you, sir?"

Julian leaned over the fence. It was hard to have a conversation with the pigs making so much noise. "As it happens, we have never met. I am, however, well acquainted with your father."

"My f-f-father?"

Julian nodded. "I have come a long way and would like to speak with you and your mother.

Clarice nodded and ran into the house through a back door.

While waiting, Julian stared at the pigs as they ate. When he heard movement coming from the front of the house, he walked his horse toward it.

A tall, attractive woman with brown curly hair, high cheek bones, and a face that, although pretty, was hardened by years of labor, greeted him. She wore a deep frown as she stared at him. "Mr. Dawson?"

"May I come in?"

Felicity hesitated before regaining her composure. "Of course you may. It's an honor to have you in my house. You will have to pardon me since I don't understand the nature of your visit."

"He's a friend of Papa's," Clarice said.

"You're a…a friend of…my husband?"

Julian nodded. "I am. If you don't mind, I would prefer to explain the situation inside. It's a long story."

Julian followed Felicity into the house, while Clarice tended to his horse. Felicity motioned to her kitchen table, a modest piece of furniture made of wood that appeared to be hand-carved. "Please sit."

"I've been on a horse all morning. I prefer to stand."

Sitting at the table, Felicity folded her hands. "You'll have to excuse my surprise at your visit. I certainly never expected that my late husband knew you, Mr. Dawson."

"Yeah, about that. I'm going to take a leap of faith with you. I'm not exactly the Mr. Dawson that you think I am. I'm well aware that your husband is very much alive. We've only known each other for a few weeks now, but he has become a friend. He's a good man and I've come to depend on him. He asked me to help him, so I told him I would do whatever I could." Julian raised his hands. "I know. I'm making little sense. Let's step back."

Clarice returned through the front door.

"As I'm sure you are aware, your father and your husband travels through different planes of existence." If Felicity or her daughter were surprised to hear this, they did not show it. "I've been caught up in a scheme where I have to impersonate different versions of myself across planes. In yours, it's James Dawson, this wealthy and powerful merchant. Since he first met me, Cutter was hoping I would land here so I can visit you two. And I come bearing gifts.

"This is for the daughter he loves very much and wishes every day that he could see her." Julian pulled out the Rubik's Cube and handed it to Clarice. Her face lit up. "This is a special toy that provided me with hours of enjoyment as a child. You have to align all nine of one color on each side of the cube." He demonstrated. It had been many years since he used one, but he was able to get the hang of it quickly.

He handed the Rubik's Cube to Clarice, who was immediately

engrossed by it. Her bright, blue eyes radiated intelligence, and she had an intense gaze as she tried to solve the cube.

Tears formed in Felicity's eyes. "I wish he were here. It hurts so much that he isn't with us."

"I know," Julian said. "Much like him, I'm separated from my wife and daughter. I feel your pain just like I feel his pain. If there was a way to be with you, he would, but he fears that returning here would endanger his life as well as yours, a risk he's not willing to take. He loves you both dearly."

Felicity glanced at her daughter, who was still busy working at the Rubik's Cube. "It's been so difficult not having him around. Oh, I was used to him being away with his travels to worlds beyond this one, including the one you come from. When I first learned about it, it sounded so mystical and wonderful. As fantastical as it seemed, I believed what he told me, which makes it easy to believe what you are telling me, even though most would consider it an outlandish and fanciful tale."

Julian smiled. "I certainly would if I wasn't living it."

"It's hard not to resent my husband. He abandoned us." Felicity raised her hand to quell Julian's protest. "Oh, I know he had his reasons, but that doesn't make the hurt go away. Now that you're here, I can almost forget about that and remember how much I love him."

"I'm certainly not going to tell you how to feel. That's not for me to decide, however, I can tell you this. I have been ripped away from my family, and it tears me apart inside. I ache for them. This whole experience has been mentally and physically exhausting. I know what pain feels like, and when your husband was relaying his story, I could feel his pain."

"Thank you, Mr. Dawson. It is Mr. Dawson, isn't it?"

Julian grinned. "It is."

He pulled out the sack containing gold and put it on the table. "There is something else he gave me. I know it doesn't replace him not being here, but this sum of gold should make your lives easier."

Felicity glanced at the sack but did not open it. "It will. I run a store in town, but it is not always easy to make ends meet. I'm not sure what it is like where you come from, but being a woman and running a business is not easy around here."

"I can't imagine it would be. I have one more thing." Julian reached for the digital camera.

Clarice's eyes lit up. She put down the Rubik's Cube. "It's one of Papa's devices. What does this one do?"

"It takes photographs. Your father misses you terribly and wanted some photos to remember you by."

Clarice's smile faded. Her face was filled with a sadness that made Julian fight back tears. It wasn't like him to get weepy, but being in this plane was taking an emotional toll on him.

"I wish I could see him," Clarice said.

"May I take some photos of the two of you?"

Julian took dozens of pictures of Felicity and Clarice, playing amateur photographer. He enjoyed spending time with them and accepted Felicity's invitation to stay for lunch.

After eating a hearty meal of beef stew, he bade them farewell, got on his horse, and returned to Kensington where James Dawson's secretary, Mrs. Van Zant, was waiting for him with a severe frown, reminding him of all the appointments she had to reschedule. He apologized, saying that an emergency came up that required his immediate attention.

He had several meetings, including another conspiratorial one concerning the People. The man he met, a judge named Jeremiah Riggs—undoubtedly in league with the Game Master—gave him details of a clandestine meeting he was scheduled to have tomorrow with Joseph Lorca, one of the leaders of the Chyno tribe. Julian had a hard time concentrating and found his mind drifting.

He was mentally worn out by the time his appointments were finished for the day and returned to the estate of James Dawson. After putting the horse in the stable, he walked to the house, greeting several workers he now knew by name. Once inside, he found Cassandra busily preparing dinner. She put down her ladle and said, "Miss Elizabeth is waiting for you upstairs."

All throughout the ride back from the city, he couldn't get his mind off Elizabeth, who was another man's wife, something he was having a hard time reconciling.

He removed his boots before making his way up the stairs. "Elizabeth?" he called out but did not get a response. "Elizabeth?"

"In here."

The sultry voice came from the bedroom. He opened the door. It took him a few moments to catch his breath. Elizabeth was wearing a silk robe and not much else. He wanted to turn and leave before things got out of hand but found himself rooted to his spot.

"I know things have been difficult for you lately, so I thought I would do something nice to surprise you." Elizabeth partially opened her robe. "Do you like what you see?"

Julian closed his eyes. When he opened them, he felt his resistance waver before completely collapsing. He was tired of living someone else's life. He was tired of being a pawn in the Game Master's evil schemes. She looked so soft, so inviting. He moved toward her. "Yes, I do."

Elizabeth put her arms around his neck and pulled her close to him. "I was hoping you would say that?"

She kissed him deeply. He dropped all pretenses and surrendered himself to her.

CHAPTER XXXI

Julian stepped out onto the veranda and sat on a chair, staring at the countless acres of property owned by his shade. The property was beautiful, lush, and well-tended. As he sat, he was overwhelmed by guilt and his own personal misery. Although he enjoyed every moment of his time with Elizabeth as they were together in the throes of ecstasy, he now only felt regret and shame. No matter how much they looked alike, she was not his Nancy.

He felt Elizabeth's hands slide around his waist and her warm breath on his neck. So enwrapped in his thoughts, he did not notice her approach him from behind. "What's wrong? I thought you enjoyed that."

He buried his face in his hands. That was the problem. He enjoyed it too much. He started talking before he even realized what he was about to say. "I...I'm not your husband. I'm afraid I have been deceiving you."

A light kiss touched the back of his neck. "I know. If you were my husband, I would not have been so eager to make love to you."

He turned to stare at Elizabeth with stunned disbelief. She had an innocent smile that he found endearing. "I...I don't understand."

"I don't know who you are, my handsome stranger, but one thing I know with absolute certainty is that you're not my husband. You have shown me and those who work here nothing but kindness. The only thing my husband ever showed me was the back of his hand. You have solicited my opinion, whereas any time I volunteered my opinion, my husband met me with scorn and derision."

"When did you realize that I'm not your husband?" Julian asked, still hardly believing her words.

"Almost from the beginning. The first time I saw you was when you lost consciousness after first locking eyes on me—a distinct way to make a first impression, I must say. And I said to myself 'Why, that's a peculiar way for James to react.' What solidified my belief that you aren't James is that my husband has a scar right here." Elizabeth motioned to his side. "And you have no such scar."

Julian chuckled. "The first time I saw you I was mesmerized by your beauty. And by how much you look like me wife."

Elizabeth's brows rose. "Your wife?"

Julian nodded. His counterpart's wife on that first plane looked like Nancy but there were subtle differences. Elizabeth was identical to her, almost like a doppelganger.

"What's her name?"

"Nancy," Julian replied.

"Do you love her?"

Julian nodded. "Very much so."

"Then she's a lucky woman."

Julian regarded her. "I take it your marriage to James Dawson is not all you hoped it would be."

"Even in the best of times, my marriage has been loveless and bitter. In the worst of times, it has launched me into a deep depression. These days, I live for our children. That reminds me, you have never actually met my children."

"No, I haven't."

"Both of them are at boarding school in a different state. There is ten-year-old James Jr. and Joseph, age eight. They're adorable. Boarding school was my idea, although I tried to position it so that it seemed like it was my husband's. The truth is I want them as far as possible from their father so they won't adopt his bad habits."

"What is James like?"

Elizabeth turned and gave a weary sigh. "He is a loathsome man. Yes, he's intelligent, incredibly successful, persuasive, and also very manipulative. He is hungry for power and wealth and will crush anyone in his path to achieve his ends. He's mean and cold-hearted. Sometimes, I think he's incapable of kindness. At least, he hasn't shown me any. His words sting as much as his fists."

Julian touched her face gently. "That's awful. I don't understand. If James is as horrible as you describe him, then why did you marry him, and why would you stay with him?"

She eyed him curiously. "I had no say in my marriage. I come from a prominent family from Britannia. The marriage was arranged by my father, who was attracted to my husband's ambition and growing wealth. My family is old money. We have plenty of prestige, but our actual fortune was dwindling due to bad investments and bad luck. James Dawson has more money than you can imagine but he doesn't have the pedigree—a prestigious family that he was born into. As far as staying with him, I don't even know how to answer that. Where could I possibly go? My parents wouldn't have me back. To be on my own would mean that I would be homeless and penniless. Then there are my children. They need me. I couldn't possibly consider leaving them—especially leaving them in his care."

"I'm sorry you have to endure this. You're a good, kind person. You deserve better."

Elizabeth smiled. "I do have better—right now. In the last few days, you have brightened my existence and given me a different perspective on life. So, my mysterious stranger, who are you? Is your name even James?"

He chuckled. "No it isn't. My name is Julian—Julian Dawson."

"And how is it that you have entered my life, Julian?"

Julian looked out at the green fields and sighed. He wondered how much he could tell her, how much she would believe. It didn't take him long to come to the realization that he could trust her implicitly. Perhaps it was because she was so similar to Nancy.

"How do I even begin to explain all of this? Until the past few weeks, I led a normal existence. I was ripped out of my life by this rotten bastard known as the Game Master. From what I'm learning, there are many different worlds." He gestured to the area around them. "One of which is this one. Apparently, it is my luck or misfortune that there are different variations, known as shades, of me in some of these worlds. There are shades of you as well, including the one I'm married to.

"I have been given tasks to complete, impersonating my shades in these various worlds. I just want to get home and I keep being told that if I complete my next task it will happen, but so far it hasn't."

"So why have you been sent here to impersonate my husband?"

He told her about his latest assignment. "And the thing is, I have no interest in having the People war against each other. I'm not a pacifist, but I don't want men to fight and die for no good reason. And damn it, I'm not going to. I've been delaying this assignment but I just can't go through with it." Julian took a deep breath. "I won't do it."

"Then don't do it. You're a good man. Why should you bend your way in the service of an evil man? Why should you operate in a way that goes against your principals?"

Julian folded his arms. "I shouldn't. What's the point of going home if I lose who I am in the process?"

Elizabeth leaned in toward him. He could feel his desire for her stir within him once again.

"Why not do the opposite?" Julian said, almost too himself. "He wants me to pit the People against each other, to create more war. Why not try to unify instead? Create peace instead of war."

"Now that sounds like a truly inspired idea." Elizabeth laughed. "You are definitely not my husband. He would never say something like that."

"Then he's a foolish man," Julian said.

"If you were to do something like that, you would need to form a coalition of people from all the different sides: the People, business leaders, and government leaders. I think I could help you out with that."

"How so?"

"I pay attention. When my husband is meeting with and entertaining leaders of industry and prominent politicians, I listen closely to what they have to say. Of course, nobody pays attention to me since I'm a woman. Moreso, I listen to what they don't say, and how they say things. I know what motivates them. I have a pretty good idea who would be amenable to such a suggestion, and which of them would be receptive to such a message if it's coming from James. He does hold a great deal of sway and influence that you can use to your advantage."

By defying the Game Master, Julian put himself in serious physical danger, not to mention he severely reduced his chances of ever returning home, but there comes a time in life when a person has to take a stand for what they believe in, and Julian reckoned that time was now, despite the danger. Perhaps it was the presence of a good woman by his side, or maybe he was just sick of this whole game, but he was taking his stand right here and now.

"Let's do this," Julian said. "This is going to take extensive planning. Answer me this. I have told you a very outlandish tale, one that I can't imagine many people would believe. Hell, if I wasn't living through it, I wouldn't believe it. Yet you seem to have no problem accepting it. Why?"

Elizabeth grinned. "Then we are of very different minds, my fine sir. I don't find it difficult to believe your story. I meet a man who looks identical to my husband in every way yet clearly isn't James.

I know that he doesn't have a brother, let alone a twin. How can something like this be possible, unless there is something occurring far outside of the bounds of normal? Not to mention that you seem completely sincere and honest. So, if that is your story, then I believe you."

"You must be a trusting sort."

Elizabeth held his gaze. "Perhaps I just believe in you."

"I'm a long way from home, so it's good to have someone like you on my side. My one friend that I have been able to rely on as I've journeyed through these different places can't be here."

"Oh? Why is that?"

Julian explained Cutter's predicament while Elizabeth listened quietly.

"That's very sad. Then I must make it a point to visit his wife and child. That's quite a hardship to endure."

"You have your own hardship, being married to a heartless bastard like James."

"Look around. There are worse situations to be in." Elizabeth had a look of melancholy. "But enough of me. I'm not even sure what I should call you."

"I think you should stick to James. I don't want people to suspect anything in case you slip."

"Then you really ought to change your behavior. You're nothing like James, and that's a good thing. But if you want to convince others, then you need to act more authoritative, less kind. You need to look at people not as if they may be your friend, but only with an eye toward what they could do for you. The only relationships James has are transactional ones, and if there is nothing you can do to benefit him, then he doesn't have time for you."

"Sounds like a real asshole."

Elizabeth gave him a peculiar frown.

"Oh, it's just an expression where I come from. He seems like someone I would not want to share a shot of whiskey with. How's that?"

"Better."

"I think I can manage to act like that. It's easier to play a villain than a hero."

There was a twinkle in Elizabeth's eyes. "But it's more difficult to be a hero than a villain. What you are doing is heroic."

"I'm no hero, just a guy trying to get back home and hopefully do the right thing in the process and make up for the damage I've already done."

"The first thing we must do if you are going to be successful is to have you speak to the leaders among the People who would be amenable to your message of peace."

"And you know who they would be?" Julian asked.

"I do. They have been over to our house on several occasions. I know which ones have the appropriate influence and will be receptive."

"I'll approach them under the pretext of some sort of business dealings." Julian nodded. "If we can get them into the same negotiating room with members of the senate and congress and maybe a few business types, perhaps we can iron out a deal."

"Before we do that, we should resolve something first. Don't feel guilty about what you did, about we did." Elizabeth leaned into him. "We are two strangers in need of one another. Granted, our circumstances are different, and I realize this relationship between us isn't permanent. I assume at some point you will leave, and my husband will resume his normal life."

"I can only guess that will be the case."

"I am in need because of the lack of fulfillment in my life and marriage. Yours is borne of desperation and loneliness because of your predicament. We need each other. I don't regret what I did for one moment, and neither should you. I can't say whether or not your Nancy would understand, but if she is like me as you suggest, then she will. Nor do I think she should ever find out, but don't beat yourself up about this. You're a good man, Julian, and Nancy is lucky to have you."

Julian smiled. "Thank you for your kind words. I don't know that they are deserved, but I do appreciate the sentiment."

Despite what she said, he could not help but to ponder if he would tell Nancy about this if he ever returned, and what her reaction would be.

CHAPTER XXXII

Julian wasn't sure what to expect when he met Joseph Lorca, known among his tribe as Iron Eagle, the following day. He and Elizabeth had plotted out who he should approach among the People about this peace plan, and Lorca was not one of them. The fact that Congressman Anderson and Senator Hawthorn wanted him to meet Lorca told Julian where the man stood. However, he still could gain valuable information from this meeting.

That morning, Julian and Edgar Smith rode on horseback to the printing press factory that Lorca owned and operated. James Dawson was a minority owner in Lorca's company. As Elizabeth explained to him, James had a piece of so many different businesses and real estate ventures that it was exceedingly difficult to keep up with them, although her husband had a knack for such things.

It was a long ride, and Edgar spent the time chatting about some things that were relevant and others not so relevant. Every so often, he would stop, take out a spyglass, and scan the area. He would then make a comment about the terrain they were passing through.

Edgar elaborated about Lorca's life story. The man was of mixed birth. His father was white and a citizen of the Confederation of

Colonies. His mother was a member of the Chynos. He operated in both societies, having been raised among the People but educated at Radcliff, one of the most prominent universities in the country. He had success in the business world, dealing with both the citizens and the People. He and James Dawson apparently got along well, their common interest being to amass wealth.

He would speak to Lorca, pretending to go along with the Game Master's plan, while using it to gather intelligence. Meanwhile, he would arrange meetings with different members of the People that Elizabeth suggested—clandestine ones that Smith wasn't going to find out about. Since he didn't want to use Mrs. Van Zant, Elizabeth was doing most of the leg work to arrange these meetings.

At one point, Edgar Smith started laughing.

"What's so funny?" Julian asked.

"I can tell you have bedded Mr. James Dawson's sweet wife. There's no point denying it. It's written on your face whenever you speak of her."

Just hearing him mention Elizabeth flooded Julian with guilt. He wanted to stay faithful to Nancy but found it impossible when he was around Elizabeth. He said nothing, trying to maintain a poker face, something apparently, he wasn't good at. Of course, Smith could just be baiting him or phishing for information.

"Ah, so it's true," Edgar said. "You aren't even protesting. Well, I certainly don't blame you. I know that I would if I were in your position. You think she would protest much if I had a go with her."

Julian's rage simmered. He so badly wanted to thrash this asshole. "If you don't have anything productive to say, please keep quiet. You're about as irritating as taking a bath with porcupines."

Edgar chuckled. "I see I caught a nerve. Well, perhaps over a few bourbons your tongue will become looser."

"I'd rather share a drink with a viper than with you. You're a repulsive little man."

"And you just might regret saying those words, Mr. Dawson."

"When this is all over, we'll settle up. Until then, provide me with the information I need and nothing else. Do I make myself clear?"

"Oh, yes you do. Except I don't take orders from the likes of you."

Julian took his own advice and kept quiet. There was nothing to gain by bickering with Smith. He had to stay focused. There was a lot riding on what he was doing over the next few days. It was ridiculous to think that the fate of so many rested in his inadequate hands. He was hardly worthy of wielding this kind of power and certainly didn't want it. He had to make rational and logical decisions. He would listen to Elizabeth, who was both wise and intelligent.

Joseph Lorca looked more American businessman than a member of a tribe. He wore a pinstriped suit and expensive leather shoes. His English was educated and refined, and he carried himself with an air of superiority. He wore his long hair neatly tied in a ponytail. He greeted Julian and Edgar with a smile and a firm handshake, and welcomed them into his lavishly furnished office, filled with paintings and sculptures, that was attached to his printing press factory.

"I'm glad that you decided to meet with me on this most important and sensitive of issues," Iron Eagle said. "I was surprised when Mr. Smith told me the outline of your plan."

"You have to be ready to take advantage of opportunities when they present themselves," Edgar said. "I knew this was something you would want be involved with and would have the power and influence to make happen."

Iron Eagle poured brandy for each of them. "Don't mistake the intent of this meeting. I am not making any commitments. I am merely interested in hearing what you have to say, Mr. Dawson, out of respect for you and since we have worked well together in past business dealings."

Julian took the glass of brandy and drank. He thought his eyeballs were going to pop out of their sockets as he choked on the hellfire liquid.

Iron Eagle brought him a glass of water, and Julian decided it would be prudent not to try any more brandy. It took him longer than he would have liked to regain his composure, but his throat still burned.

"Before we start," Julian said, "I have to know why you want the Chynos and Wyotsoks to war against each other. It seems strange for someone who is part of the People to plot their demise."

"I may be of the People, as you say, but that is only a part of my heritage. I have been educated in the best schools and have learned the way of business and commerce. I can fit in equally among high society as I can with the People. To answer your question, I'm a forward-thinker. I see a vision for the future. We must move this nation forward, and that simply can't happen with the constant squabbling and feuding that occurs with the People and our citizens.

"Furthermore, I owe the Wyotsoks no loyalty. Before there was even a nation here, the Wyotsoks were raiding and killing my people. The notion that the People are peaceful is just ludicrous, and anyone in the Chynos or Wyotsoks or any number of tribes know this to be a lie. The tribes have been warring for centuries, long before any white man stepped foot on the continent. Any sentimentality I might have for the People as a whole would be utterly foolish, and if there is one thing that I cannot abide, that is foolishness. Therefore, I would like to hear your plan, a progressive one that will move this nation forward."

Julian stared hard at him. "Cut the bullshit. I know you better than to accept that kind of inane answer. What do you really want? What makes you tick?"

Iron Eagle looked flustered, the color draining from his cheeks. He took some time to compose himself, all the while staring at Julian. "Fine. Let us be open and honest. I want what you have. I want to be you."

Edgar gave Julian a sideways glance that indicated some level of unease with this line of questioning but Julian ignored him.

"Explain."

"I want to be able to associate with the upper crust of society. The decision makers. The power brokers. I want to wield the type of power that you possess. But due to my mixed heritage, I haven't been able to do so. You can help me with that. You can open those doors that have been to this point closed to me."

"Very well. I needed to know where you're coming from and now I know. I understand why you want this. I want all cards on the table so to speak." Julian folded his hands and leaned inward. "The idea is to proceed with two surviving entities, not three. The way I see it, there will never be peace with three major entities, and since The Confederation of Colonies is not going away, that only leaves room for either the Chynos or the Wyotsoks. If you can deliver the Chynos, then that would be the ideal scenario from my point of view."

Based on the narrowed eyes and sly grin on Lorca's face, this appeal seemed to have worked. It was all in the delivery.

"That is a sound idea," Iron Eagle said. "One filled with potential."

"The question at hand," Julian said, "is can you deliver the Chynos? That question is paramount, because if you cannot, then I may be forced to explore other options."

Lorca drank more brandy. Unlike Julian, he seemed to have no problem with the demon swill. "My influence among my people is quite vast. I can assure you that I can convince the tribe to turn against the Wyotsoks."

"Good," Julian said. "That is what I wanted to hear."

Julian felt sick with disgust. Lorca spoke of wholesale genocide as if it were no big thing.

"To make this happen," Julian said, "we're going to need a concerted attack between the army of the Confederation and the Chynos. Will they be willing to put aside past grudges and fight alongside the Confederation army?"

Iron Eagle leaned back in his chair. "They will if given the proper inducement."

"And how is that we will properly motivate your tribe?"

"The tribe will need its own sovereign land. The area west of the Andorran mountains through the Columbia River would be appropriate."

Julian whistled. "That's a steep price to pay." He was unfamiliar with the land's geography but thought that sounded like something James Dawson would say in a negotiation.

"The Chynos would also need the ability to trade with other nations as their own entity apart from the Confederation, as well as the unconditional right to bear arms."

"Oh, is that all?" Julian said. "Why don't you just ask for the moon while you're at it?"

The peculiar sideways glances that both Lorca and Edgar Smith gave him told Julian that he had probably gone too far with that comment.

"I am going to have to meet with leaders of the tribe, as I am sure you will have to speak to government leaders, but I believe we have the basis for strong ground with which to work. And, of course, all negotiations will have to be kept strictly confidential."

For the next hour, Julian drowned in the minutia of specific aspects of this plan. It was difficult for him to keep up with the multitude of names and places. Edgar frequently jumped in when Julian struggled, proving he wasn't completely useless. By the time they were done, Julian had a splitting headache and longed to see Elizabeth again.

When they left, Edgar Smith said from his saddle, "That went exceptionally well, I must say. You had your share of difficulties, but fortunately I was there to help you when you fell. You may not want to admit it, but you need me."

"I need you about as much as I need a plantar wart," Julian said.

"Insult me all you want, but you can't do this without me," Edgar said. "And your very life is dependent upon the success of these negotiations, so I would suggest you stay on my good side."

CHAPTER XXXIII

When Julian arrived at the sprawling mansion after a long day of business meetings, some of them involving the Game Master's conspiracy, he was weary and sick of it all. He needed a long, hot shower, which didn't exist in this plane.

He couldn't get his mind off Elizabeth, and was excited to see her, but she wasn't alone. She was in their parlor with two members of the People. She introduced Chief John, who held a seat on the high council of the Wyotsok nation and Fire Wolf, a similarly high-ranking member of the Chynos.

"I know you are greatly concerned with recent developments, so I thought it important to meet immediately with these two esteemed gentlemen," Elizabeth said.

He pulled her aside and whispered, "A little advanced notice would have been nice."

Elizabeth merely smiled and spoke softly. "You'll be fine."

He wasn't prepared to speak with them and was not sure what to say. He would have liked to come up with a game plan and go over it with Elizabeth first, but he was going to have to wing it.

Julian circled in front of the seated men. "Thank you for agreeing to this impromptu meeting. As my wife may have explained to you, recent developments concerning the People and the Confederation of Colonies have caused me grave concern. There is a grand conspiracy afoot that may bring doom to both of your tribes. I cannot stand by and watch this injustice happen and have made it my mission to make sure it doesn't come to pass." He was still getting used to how the folks around here spoke and tried to match his language and cadence to theirs.

The two men stared intently at him.

"While your reputation as a captain of industry proceeds you," Chief John said. "You will have to excuse my skepticism. You are not known for your benevolence."

"Perhaps not, but I assure you my motives are genuine." Julian said. "I fear that this nation may be torn apart by the actions of a few men who do not have the best of intentions, and what will my business endeavors amount to under such conditions? A healthy nation is a prosperous one, and that is what I intend to keep."

He had to remain consistent with the James Dawson character in order to pull this off. Why would James want to do this? He would only do it if it meant protecting his business interests.

Julian told his two guests everything he knew about the plot. He gave them the names of the principals involved, except of course, the Game Master. He trusted Elizabeth that these were two men who he could confide in and had the power to enable change.

Chief John circled around the parlor, a whiskey Elizabeth had served him in hand. "What you speak of is indeed a grave situation, one that we cannot let pass but you will have to pardon my skepticism."

Fire Wolf crossed his arms. "If what you say is true, then I do not see any alternative but the further escalation of war between the People and the Confederation of Colonies. We will fight for our existence. We will remove your people from the land we once held."

"You mistake my intentions," Julian said. "You speak of fighting for your existence, but there is a better way. This nation will only prosper when Chynos, Wyotsoks, and citizens of the Confederation all work together. I have seen a vision of the future, and that future is of one united nation."

He had to break through to these two and get them to trust him. "I do have financial motivation here but let me be frank. I have not always been a good man and have done many things that I am not proud of. I want my legacy to be more than just that of someone with great wealth. I would like my legacy to be one of a person who brought this nation together."

Chief John sighed. "Perhaps I am being too judgmental regarding your character."

Julian could see he had their attention. Now was the time to give them the hard sell. "What people need to realize is that our strength is our diversity. That is what makes this nation great. This is a place where people from other countries can come and worship in the manner they please, build a life and future for their family, where the only thing that will stop them is the limitations they put upon themselves. A place where everyone is entitled to life, liberty, and the pursuit of happiness. A place where people are free to create their own destiny and not the one that was provided by their birthright where their only limitations are the ones they place upon themselves based on their ambition and work ethic. But this can't happen if we fight among each other. I know what this country can be. But in order to achieve this vision we must stand united. Will you join me? It starts with us and will spread like wildfire."

"If what you say is true, and I don't doubt you, then we must oppose those who stand against this ideal," Fire Wolf said. "I will do anything that is necessary for the survival of my people. We have been facing our potential demise ever since the white men landed on these shores. My people don't want war, but we will fight for our future. However, I would like nothing more than to have peace between the People and the Confederation."

"It's more than peace," Julian said. "We must integrate our society if we are to thrive. We must live together as one and celebrate our differences instead of letting them divide us."

Chief John refilled his whiskey. "What you speak of sounds ideal, but I don't see how it can be possible. There are too many among your kind who distrust the People and would never dare to even break bread with us, let alone live together."

"Those walls can be broken," Julian said. "It will take time and the effort of many, but it can happen."

"I never knew you held these beliefs," Fire Wolf said. "In the past, your interest has always been in business and commerce, and how to further your success in those endeavors. You were always ruthless in your dealings, although, to be fair, you were always honest and fair with us, so I do not complain, unlike most of your counterparts, who only look to cheat the People."

"Times change," Julian said. "People change. The situation changes. We must adapt to these changes. I want to be a better man. I know that I have evolved a great deal in recent days." He spoke those words sincerely. He was a different man since his travels through alternate worlds started. He had done things he would have scarcely thought possible just a few months ago.

"People's opinions and attitudes can change as well." He harkened back to his own world where there had been large upheaval in various social issues in recent years. "I believe that we and other like-minded people of influence can start own revolution."

Julian was proud to be an American, and always felt that the thing that made his nation great, above all other things, was that it was a place where people from all over the world travelled and immigrated to in order to fulfill an ideal, a dream, and once the people of this world came to that realization, they would prosper as well. They just needed a catalyst.

Chief John rose and extended his hand to Julian. "Then we will be the catalyst. The three of us will be the spark that ignites the fire. But there is much work to be done in order for that to happen."

"Well, actually there will be four of us." Julian motioned for Elizabeth to join them. "None of this would be possible without my wife."

A bright shade of red colored Elizabeth's face. No doubt, she had never been included in such high-level discussions and negotiations. If Julian was going to change the way the Confederation of Colonies acted toward the natives of this land, then he might as well change the way they felt about women as well.

Fire Wolf rose to his feet. "Then let us get to work."

* * *

They went well into the evening plotting out the course of events over the upcoming days and weeks. Julian was glad to see that neither Chief John nor Fire Wolf excluded or talked down to Elizabeth. Julian looked at her not as his equal but more than his equal since she knew a hell of a lot more about this world and its customs than he would ever know. Not only that, but she had also known which two men to invite to kick off their plan, for it became evident that Fire Wolf and Chief John were excellent choices. He was going to have to continue to lean on her going forward. He couldn't do this without her.

When they finally finished, Ezekiel, one of their butlers, led their guests to a guest cottage. Elizabeth had the foresight to have the rooms prepared for them, even furnished with sleepwear for their esteemed guests.

He and Elizabeth stood hand-in-hand watching them depart. He felt strange holding a woman's hand, one who wasn't his wife, but nobody else reacted to it since they all thought he was married to Elizabeth.

"That was exhausting," Julian said.

Elizabeth turned to appraise him. "I thought you performed

admirably, considering you have little experience dealing with political leaders. This is far different than what you did in your old life. What was that again?"

"I was a marketing consultant."

"I have no idea what that means," Elizabeth said. "But it sounds so charming when you say it. Regardless, you did well tonight."

"I did well? You were amazing. You have a knack for cutting to the heart of the matter and persuading people to come around to your way of way of thinking. And I'm quite certain you have never been included in these types of discussions either."

Elizabeth smiled. "I learn by staying in the shadows."

"Well, you need to come out of the shadows." Julian looked up at the wall clock. "I missed a few evening appointments. I'll have to feign illness."

"There's no need. I sent a messenger to tell Ms. Van Zant telling her that you were indisposed and would not be able to make any of your previously scheduled evening appointments in town, and to send your regrets to those you were to meet with."

Julian raised her chin with his hand. "You are indeed amazing. Is there anything you haven't thought of?"

"I'm sure there are many things. The one that comes to mind right now is what will become of us. I know how I feel about you, and I have a pretty good idea how you feel about me. The question is where do we go from here now that we know who we are? Well, I suppose you knew all along who I was, but I was at a bit of a disadvantage in that regard."

Julian took a deep breath. "We have to deal with the elephant in the room."

Elizabeth folded her arms. "Elephant in the room?"

"It's an expression. It means the uncomfortable thing that nobody wants to talk about."

"On the contrary, I do want to talk about it. Understand this. I have strong feelings for you. You're everything that my husband is not, but the last thing I want to do is force you into something. I fully understand your commitment to your wife and I would never want you to do something you're uncomfortable with. Having said that, my desire for you hasn't waned in the slightest."

Elizabeth gazed up at him. He found her sparkling green eyes mesmerizing. He could lose himself in those eyes. She was in so many ways like Nancy, almost like a clone, yet more mysterious and exotic in some ways.

"My desire for you is as strong as it has ever been. The problem is my guilt eats away at me. It's a battle I fight on a daily basis since I've been here."

"I won't convince you to join me in the pleasures of the flesh. However, I will extend an invitation." Elizabeth pulled away from him slowly.

Their hands lingered until they were no longer touching. Julian felt a terrible loss. Perhaps what he was doing was completely wrong. Perhaps it showed a weakness of character. Perhaps he was not the person he wished to be—faithful, loyal, trustworthy. Also, there was the possibility that defying the Game Master so blatantly would either lead to his death or being stuck in this plane. But none of those things mattered right now. What mattered was that he craved Elizabeth in a way that was downright frightening. He tried not to think about anything as he followed her into the house and up to her bedroom.

CHAPTER XXXIV

The next few days were a whirlwind of activity. Julian met with Chief John and Fire Wolf on a daily basis. They coordinated their activities through Elizabeth, who proved to be invaluable. She was hyper-organized and had a remarkable recall of names, faces, events, and, more importantly, an ability to intuit people's positions on matters.

Besides meeting with men locally, he sent invitations to prominent politicians and industry leaders who they thought they could lure to their side. The goal was to create a powerful coalition both within the Confederation of Colonies and The People. A big enough coalition could enable the change they were seeking. Julian did his best to avoid Edgar Smith, who was expressing strong irritation that he was available so infrequently. He still met with Edgar's people—those who wanted war between the two groups—but Smith expressed frustration at their lack of progress.

The man was a growing problem that Julian had to deal with. He just wasn't sure how. The avoidance and subterfuge couldn't last forever. He loathed the man, but Edgar was his link to the Game Master. How would he be able to go home without that creepy weasel?

Not to mention, how would the Game Master react when he realized what Julian was plotting? Edgar had already hinted that he would kill Julian if he did not complete the assignment.

It was one large conundrum.

One afternoon, he and Elizabeth congregated in the study. They had a strange dynamic between them. They were lovers and business partners. Julian found it difficult to separate these two things, although Elizabeth seemed better equipped to compartmentalize.

"This truly seems to be working," Elizabeth said. "We have found those who have never spoken out before about ending the war but are amenable to the idea."

"True," Julian said, "but there are strong factions who vehemently oppose our plans. You haven't been speaking with them as I have."

"Oh, but I have. Perhaps not those who hold power, but in my day-to-day discourse I encounter people who have hatred toward the People. They hate those who are different from them, who they don't understand. It's an irrational hatred, but one that exists in the hearts and minds of many. They will have to be won over."

"First things first. We have to convince the decision makers and influencers. In time, people will come to accept it. I have seen this in my world. My society, albeit with all of its flaws and problems, is an integrated one. In my country you can find people of different races, religions, and countries of origin. It's not always peace and harmony, but generally, people live and work with others who are different from them without much strife."

Elizabeth leaned in toward him and rested her head against his shoulder. "It sounds like a wonderful place. You should take me there some day."

"I'm incapable of taking you there with me. Even if I were, that would create a multitude of problems, such as the wife and child I have in my home plane."

"Do you think I would like Nancy?"

Julian kissed the top of her head. "Most definitely. Besides the fact that you two look identical, with exceptions being your hair style and mode of dress, you're very much alike. She would be like your twin sister."

"Then I think I would like her."

$$* * *$$

Julian was amazed at how quickly the plan was progressing. The President of the Confederation of Colonies was arriving later this week under the pretense of opening ground on a new university—there weren't many of these in the country, so this was a big deal—but in reality it was to meet Julian, who had requested an audience with the man. He now had support from powerful allies and was going to use that to create a united front when dealing with the President. He was convinced that if he could get the President's support, then his bold plan would come to fruition.

With the primitive communication equipment in this plane, he had expected this process to take months, but the plan was coming along far quicker. He could feel momentum building in this movement like a blooming flower about to burst.

It was early in the morning, and he drank coffee that Rowena prepared for him, along with toast and marmalade. Rowena was a strong-willed woman. She had escaped slavery in this plane's equivalent of Haiti and sailed into the Florida panhandle by boat with other slaves. Here, she found employment and a husband, but had been too old to start a family.

Although there were too many servants in this place to get to know them all personally, he'd had a few quality conversations with Rowena. She was smart and perceptive. He was convinced that she suspected he was not the actual James Dawson but hadn't said anything about it yet. Whereas the other servants kept their distance and maintained polite formality, she had opened up to him as if he were just another person, not the rich and powerful James Dawson, and he was convinced she would not have done so if she thought she was talking to his shade. Of course, he would not tell her his true identity. Just letting Elizabeth in on that secret was taking a huge risk.

As he was getting ready to go into the city, his butler, Ezekiel, came rushing inside. "Master Dawson, you have an unannounced visitor."

As he was tying his shoes, Julian looked up at him. "Who?"

"Sheriff Edgar Smith," Ezekiel replied.

Julian cursed under his breath. He managed to avoid Edgar all day yesterday but would not be so fortunate today. He had to ditch him in order to meet with a federal court e who he hoped to secure as part of his alliance.

Julian walked outside to meet Edgar. The mean scowl on Smith's face told him this would be no social call.

Edgar charged at Julian. With two hands, he shoved Julian to the ground.

Before Julian could rise, Edgar delivered a kick that landed squarely on his ribs. "Did you think I wouldn't find out what you have been scheming, you rotten scoundrel?"

Julian grunted in pain, then looked up to find spittle flying from Smith's mouth and a look of sheer hatred in his eyes. "What are you talking about?"

"I know all about your secret meetings. I know all about this plan of yours. You think you can hide something like that from me? I know everything that happens around here."

"Really?" Julian decided to drop the charade. "Because it took you a while to figure it out, you dumb shit."

Smith snarled and went to kick him again. Julian was ready this time and lunged at Smith, delivering a shoulder tackle to his mid-section. Julian got to his feet and cracked Smith in the jaw with a straight right. He didn't have any formal fighting training but had been in more street fights growing up than he could remember. He never sought trouble, but trouble always seemed to find him.

Julian pivoted, landed two punches to Smith's ribs and then an uppercut that sent a tooth flying out of his mouth. Smith's head rocked backward, and he hit the ground. Julian pursued him and was about to smash the son of a bitch into next week, when Smith, still on the ground, knocked him senseless with a boot to the face from an upkick.

He struggled to regain his composure but found himself on the receiving end of numerous punches and kicks. All he could do was cover up and hope to somehow get back into this fight. He held his arms up but was only successful in blocking about half the blows that came his way.

Smith pulled away from him. Julian looked up at him through blurred eyes to find blood coming from Smith's mouth. He may have inflicted damage on his adversary, but there was no doubt that Julian had gotten the worst of this scrap. His entire body throbbed with pain to the point where he could hardly move.

Julian had to mount a comeback, or Smith would kill him.

Smith circled around him. "I told you what I would do if you didn't complete the task the Grand Magisterium gave you. I told you! But what did you do? You're actually helping these vermin, the People. They need to be eradicated from this world like the pestilence that they are. Instead of sticking with the plan, you had to sneak off like a thief in the night making these secret meetings behind my back. You really thought you would get away with it?"

Julian winced. "Well, you are pretty damn stupid."

That comment earned him a boot to the face. He went back to the ground in a heap. His head was cloudy once more.

"Do you have anything else humorous to say? If so, I suggest you do so now since these will be the very last words you speak. It will be the last will and testament of Julian Dawson, the man without a plane of existence."

Julian staggered to his feet only to be kicked by Smith once more.

Smith pulled out his revolver.

"Prepare to die, Mr. Dawson."

Julian was getting ready for a desperate lunge at Smith with whatever reserve of strength he had left, but before he could do so, a shot rang out. A big, bright splash of red covered Edgar's chest. He collapsed as blood spilled from his mouth.

Julian turned to find Elizabeth standing behind him holding a smoking rifle.

She had a look of fierce determination. When their eyes met, her face softened. She dropped the rifle and ran toward him. She fell to her knees and hugged him. "Oh, Julian. I though he was going to kill you. Are you hurt? You, you don't look so well."

He put a hand to his battered face. "I've felt better." His face felt as if he had been smashed a thousand times by a baseball bat. His vision was blurry, and his breathing labored. He probably had broken a rib or two during the fight.

"I, I killed him, didn't I?" Elizabeth asked.

"I sure as hell hope so." Julian gingerly moved toward Edgar Smith to make sure he was dead. Yes, the man had definitely bought his ticket. He didn't need to take a pulse. Smith's vacant eyes were a testimony to his demise. Good riddance. The world certainly wasn't going to miss this bastard.

"I can't believe I actually killed a man," Elizabeth said.

Wincing, Julian slowly rose to his feet. "If it makes you feel any better, I hadn't killed anybody until just before I got here. It wasn't easy. I can't imagine it ever is." Julian put his hands on his knees and took a deep breath. "We have bigger problems to deal with now. A sheriff is dead on your property."

The stunned look left Elizabeth's face. "We can fix that problem."

"How so?"

"Get Ezekiel," Elizabeth said. "He has been working for our family since he was a young child, and his family before him has been working for mine for generations. His loyalty is beyond doubt. We will take the body and bury it deep within the property in a place nobody ever goes to. You are James Dawson, a wealthy and prominent captain of industry and commerce. You will not be a suspect in the disappearance of a sheriff."

"But he's been seen hanging around me since I've arrived here."

"You are a very busy man and you have no idea of his whereabouts. Furthermore, you don't have time for such questions. You will have to feign illness so that you don't have to go out in public until your facial injuries heal. If you don't show signs of guilt, nobody will further question you. Remember who you are pretending to be."

Julian nodded, trusting Elizabeth's judgment. He walked with a heavy limp, still unsure just how severely he had been injured. Fortunately, he didn't have to go far to find Ezekiel, as his butler came running forward.

"I heard a gunshot." Ezekiel stared wide-eyed at the dead body lying in the dirt.

"He attacked me," Julian said. "I had to shoot him. There was nothing to be done. However, if such a thing were made known, it would not bode well for me or my family. Discretion is of the utmost importance. Can I trust you?"

Ezekiel appeared insulted by the question. "Of course, Master Dawson. I would never betray your trust for any reason. Ever."

"Thank you," Julian said. "Now please help me remove the body."

In Julian's current condition, Ezekiel would have to do most of the work.

Elizabeth told Ezekiel precisely where she intended to bury him. Julian could only hope that Elizabeth was correct, and that if only the three of them knew about this, they could contain the fact that she had killed Edgar Smith.

CHAPTER XXXV

Rowena was still in the kitchen cooking what was sure to be one of her amazing signature meals for Julian's special guests, Chief John and Fire Wolf. The mood was decidedly celebratory, and the three of them along with Elizabeth were having drinks. Julian found a whiskey that he found passable and shared it with his guests. Interestingly, it was a less expensive brand that most of the common folk drank.

It had been a crazy month since Elizabeth had shot Edgar Smith dead. Since then, that surreal scene had replayed in his mind a thousand times. Elizabeth was still feeling the effects of her actions. Every so often, a deep sadness would overcome her, and Julian had to give her a pep talk, telling her he would have died if she hadn't shot the sheriff.

The past month had been of a whirlwind of activity. One day blended into the next. Julian had taken part in so many clandestine meetings that he had a hard time keeping track of who were the good guys and who were the bad guys. There had been many ups and downs during that time. It sometimes felt as if he were part of a script of some Hollywood movie.

What got him through the endless plotting and speaking to high-ranking government officials and leaders of industry was the knowledge that when the day was over, he would be in Elizabeth's arms and in her bed. It was a type of bliss he had never experienced. And damn if he didn't feel guilty as sin for it. He reconciled that some things couldn't be helped, and that he and Elizabeth were destined to be together, just as he and Nancy were destined to be together.

Fire Wolf raised his glass. "I must say, James, I misjudged you. I had preconceived notions of who you were based on our previous interactions, but you have shown yourself to be a strong-willed man whose interest lies in promoting peace and justice. Quite frankly, I always thought you were greedy, but you have proved me wrong."

Chief John put his large hand on Fire Wolf's shoulder. "You were being too hard on our young friend. You need to see the good in people."

Fire Wolf frowned. "You expressed those same doubts to me when we first started this venture."

Chief John laughed. "Then I suppose we were both wrong."

"You three have worked very hard to accomplish this. I still can hardly believe that we are on the eve of signing this historical peace treaty, one that will change our nation's history." Elizabeth was practically radiant as she spoke.

"Now, young lady," Chief John said. "It would be improper of you to not take credit for the peace treaty. You have worked just as hard as anybody here to make this come to fruition and you deserve an equal share of credit. Modesty is unbecoming of you."

"Thank you," Elizabeth said.

Julian knew that this was the collaborative effort of many people, not the least of which was the President of the Confederation of Colonies. It took some convincing and quite a bit of concessions, but in the end, he became a powerful advocate to make this plan happen. Julian knew that once he won the man over, others would fall in line. He was very much looking forward to seeing this treaty get signed.

Still, he was filled with doubt and uncertainty. After Edgar Smith's death, he had not heard from either The Game Master directly or anybody representing him. The people such as Iron Eagle that he had been meeting in order to fulfill the Game Master's edict had faded into the background once it became clear which way the political winds had shifted. He feared that retribution would be in his future, not the least of which would be an inability to get back to his home plane.

Elizabeth seemed to sense his consternation and did her best to assure him that things would turn out fine, but he had his doubts. He tried to tune out these doubts and enjoy the moment. It wasn't every day that he changed the future of an entire world.

* * *

On the morning of the signing of the peace treaty, Julian was putting on one of James Dawson's finest suits. The man had quite an extensive wardrobe and many to choose from. Elizabeth, meanwhile, was between two dresses. She asked his opinion, but he thought they both looked great on her.

As he was getting dressed, someone knocked on the bedroom door. It was Ezekiel. "Sir, we have an urgent situation."

Julian glanced over to make sure that Elizabeth was decent before opening the door. He did not, however, get the chance to do so. There was a loud bang that startled Julian, and the double doors flung open.

Three men wearing bowler hats and sporting pistols stood at the entrance. One man had a handlebar mustache, another sported an eye patch, and the third one towered over his two cohorts like the Berlin Wall.

"I tried to stop them," Ezekiel said. "But as you can see, they are well-armed."

"You're coming with us, Dawson," Handlebar Mustache said. "Dead or alive. It doesn't much matter to me."

"I don't think the President would appreciate it too much if you killed me before his peace treaty signing."

"There ain't going to be a signing for you," Handlebar Mustache said.

Julian rolled his eyes. "It was a joke, you dumb shit. I didn't think you came here armed like that to escort me to a ball. Let me guess, the Grand Magisterium isn't happy with me these days. Doesn't like the fact that I haven't been playing ball with him and his grandiose schemes of world domination."

"You have gotten yourself in serious trouble," Handlebar Mustache said.

"Well, my fourth-grade teacher always told me I would amount to no good. I guess she was right after all."

"You disobeyed the wrong man." Mr. Eyepatch yanked him by the wrist and twisted it.

Julian tried not to wince or show any signs of pain, no easy feat given the man's grip strength.

Ezekiel grabbed the man's arm. "Lay your hands off of Master Dawson."

That was all the incentive the giant needed to grab Ezekiel by the throat, lift him off his feet, and fling him against the wall. Ezekiel's eyes rolled to the back of his head as he slumped against the wall. A picture frame that had been hanging above his head fell and crashed on top of his head.

Julian pulled away from the man holding his wrist. "Hey, that's enough. I'm coming with you assholes. There's no need to hurt Ezekiel or anyone else around here."

"There's reason if you give us one," Handlebar mustache said.

"I will go willingly to the Grand Magisterium," Julian said. "Just give me a minute to say goodbye to…" He was about to say his wife before thinking better of it. More softly, he said, "Give me a minute to say goodbye to Elizabeth. Please. Then I'll go with you. I won't resist."

"You can say goodbye to your wife," Handlebar Mustache said. "But just to be sure that you have no more ambitious plans, we will take your loyal servant, Ezekiel, with us while you bid her farewell. If you try to escape, which would be a foolish proposition, we will kill him. Then we'll hunt you down and kill you as well. Then we will kill that pretty wife of yours."

"Have you ever heard of the expression you can catch more bees with honey than with vinegar? Judging by your lack of expression, I'm going to say you haven't. Anyway, you play nice, and I'll play nice."

Handlebar Mustache glared at him for a few moments before he and his goons left the room with Ezekiel as hostage.

Elizabeth was in tears. "I can't believe this is happening. Those men mean to do you harm. You have to escape."

Julian shook his head. "That's not an option. They would hurt you as well. Look, I'll be fine. I don't think the Game Master is going to injure or kill me."

He wasn't so sure about that last point, but didn't want to overly worry her. The Game Master very well might kill him for his defiance.

Tears formed in Elizabeth's eyes. "This is awful. We should never have gone down this path. It has only brought ruin."

Once more Julian shook his head. "Not at all. I knew from the beginning I was playing with fire, but I have no regrets. We've done some incredible good here. I consider myself blessed to be able to accomplish this. And furthermore, I don't regret the opportunity to be with you. I love you, Elizabeth. Being able to be with you is one of the greatest things that has ever happened to me."

"Then this is it?" Elizabeth asked. "This is farewell."

Julian nodded. "I don't think I'll ever see you again. Look, you need to see this thing through. We've done too much good work now to have it fall apart. Promise me that you'll work closely with Chief John and Fire Wolf to make sure this treaty and everything we worked for doesn't get derailed. Finish what we started."

Elizabeth nodded. "I will. But that is not my greatest concern right now. After all these years of a loveless marriage, I finally found the man I love, one who fulfills my soul in a way that nobody ever has. I can't bear to lose you."

Julian sighed. He held her closely. "I don't know what the future will bring, but I know that I'll never forget you. You touched my heart and soul."

"Be safe, Julian. I love you."

He kissed her softly. "I'll do my best. I have the feeling that if the Game Master truly wanted me dead, then I would already be dead. The fact that I'm still alive probably means he's not done with me just yet."

Handlebar Mustache called out, "Enough, Dawson. You're leaving now."

Julian kissed Elizabeth again before they dragged him away. As they were escorting him out of the house, he felt a terrible longing for Elizabeth even though they just separated. He was going to miss her terribly. And if he ever got home, he would have to reconcile the time he spent with her.

As they were about to saddle up, a half-dozen armed men—all James Dawson's servants—approached with their guns drawn. No doubt they had seen three armed men who appeared to be looking for trouble and came to his defense. He had told them to be on guard after the incident with Edgar Smith. They were at an impasse when the Game Master's men drew their weapons as well.

Julian raised her hands, trying to defuse the situation. The last thing he wanted was a shootout on his behalf. He waved his hands frantically but stopped sort of actually jumping in the middle of these two groups. "There is no need for any shooting today. I am going with these men of my own free will. Please lower your weapons—all of you."

It took a few minutes of hard stares between Dawson's servants and the Game Master's goons before they actually lowered their weapons. Even then, he wasn't sure that violence wouldn't erupt at a moment's notice. The henchmen had to tread carefully since they were woefully outnumbered, not just here, but throughout the ranch, which held dozens of armed men who would surely kill anyone who meant to do James Dawson harm. It would be easy for Julian to tell them to take out the Game Master's men, but that wouldn't solve anything. The Game Master would just send more reinforcements to get him—probably even kidnap him when he wasn't suspecting it. It was futile. The man would never stop coming after him. Julian had to eventually see the loathsome toad, unless his intention was to stay here permanently—a thought that had crossed his mind a time or two, but he still desperately wanted to be with his wife and daughter again.

The journey out of the ranch on horseback was treacherous. They encountered more men with rifles, and Julian had to talk them down. For all of James Dawson's faults, his hired hands certainly seemed loyal to him. He wasn't sure who was in charge among the Game Master's goon squad, but coming here with only three armed men was idiotic. Perhaps Edgar Smith was the true brains of the operation, and these guys were the B team.

"Where are we going?"

"To meet your judgment," Eyepatch said.

"I was hoping for an actual location," Julian said.

"You don't need to know that," Eyepatch said.

"Can you at least tell me if it's going to take a while?" Julian asked.

"We will be there when we arrive," Eyepatch said.

"You guys are amazing conversationalists."

They travelled for over five hours mostly in silence with a couple of stops along the way. Feeling sore, Julian used the breaks to stretch as best he could lest his legs get cramped. They finally arrived at their destination—a white house that stood on a plot of land of immense size, so massive that there were no other properties as far as the eye could see.

They dismounted, and Eyepatch turned to him. "The Grand Magisterium awaits. If I were you, I would pray for leniency."

CHAPTER XXXVI

It felt as if these men were leading Julian to his execution. Each man held one of his arms while Handlebar Mustache led him inside. Perhaps he had misjudged the Game Master's intentions. In that case, it was too late to attempt an escape. They were located in the middle of nowhere, and he couldn't outmuscle his three captors. His only option was to figure out what that evil bastard wanted and how to get out of this mess.

They walked through a sparsely decorated parlor with little more than a clock hanging on the wall, and into a small kitchen that had several empty pots and pans on the counter along with a jug of water. They led him further inside until he entered a room with a familiar electronic whirring sound—an odd sound for this plane.

Sitting at a circular table was the Game Master, typing on a laptop computer, something that looked as out of place here as a stone tablet and chisel would on his own plane. When the Game Master looked up, they locked eyes. He closed his laptop and stood—all five feet of him—barely visible above the table he stood next to. He gave Julian a hateful glare, a look that lacked intimidation given the man's slight stature.

The Game Master stomped his way toward Julian. His face was bright red. When he spoke, spit flew from his mouth. "Julian Dawson, you are a liar and a cheat. You have betrayed me."

That was all Julian could take. Any rational thought escaped him. He broke free from the men holding him, lunged at the Game Master, and knocked him to the ground. Before he could get his hands around the man's thin throat, the giant of the trio lifted him by the back of his head and slammed him hard to the wooden floor.

Julian tried to fight losing consciousness. He wasn't sure if his eyes were closed, or the world went dark. All he knew was that his mind was jumbled. He tried to open his eyes but found this task to be beyond him. He felt pressure against his chin and jaw. When he finally opened his eyes, he looked up to find the giant, who looked impossibly tall from Julian's position, stepping on his jaw.

Julian cried out and tried to grab the giant's leg, but it was as futile as grabbing the trunk of an oak tree.

The Game Master loomed over him. "Off of him."

Mercifully, the henchman removed his massive foot. Julian clutched his jaw, which screamed in pain.

"Get him to his knees," the Game Master said.

The giant lifted him as if he were a small child. Julian's balance was shot to hell, so they had to hold him upright.

The Game Master slapped Julian's face. "How dare you defy my orders! I have been planning this action for years. All of that work has been for naught. You are nothing but a scoundrel."

Instead of speaking, Julian chuckled at the comical sight of the Game Master standing next to his oversized henchman, who had to have at least two feet in height over his employer.

Julian tested out his mouth first. When he finally spoke, his voice was hoarse, and he couldn't speak as loudly as he wanted. "I'm a liar. I'm a cheat? Are you kidding me? You have been nothing but dishonest with me from the start. Every time you had a new task for me to perform, it was with the promise of going home. But every time

I find myself in a new plane with a new task. And you wonder why I didn't follow through with your last scheme. Why should I? You'll never send me home. If you want me to do your dirty work, then you have to make it worth my while, and the only thing I want is to go home and stop working for you."

"Why shouldn't I kill you now?" the Game Master asked.

"The answer's obvious," Julian replied. "The same reason I didn't go through with the last assignment, bringing mass extinction to a race of people just to serve your purposes. You need me for something else. Some other task. Well, I'm done working for you. I'm not one of your hired goons."

The Game Master got in his face. "Oh, you are far from done with me, Julian Dawson. Nobody refuses me. I own you."

"Bullshit. I'm not your servant, and I am done working for you."

"Is that what you think?" the Game Master asked. "Let me explain something to you. I have one final task for you before you get what you want, and this is truly your final task since you have no other shades in any additional planes."

"I'm not doing it," Julian said with as much defiance as possible.

"You have no choice, Mr. Dawson. I know everything about you. I know your strengths and weaknesses. And do you know what your greatest weakness is?"

"Not being able to get past your goons so I can grab you by your neck and choke the life out of you."

The Game Master glared at him. "No, you fool. Your biggest weakness is how much you care for your family. And that is how I can control you." He returned to his laptop and typed on the keyboard, then turned to Julian. "Observe."

The giant pushed him toward the laptop. Julian felt cold dread. A video was playing on the screen. He wanted to look away but found he couldn't. He gave a gut-wrenching cry when he saw his daughter in the backyard of their home. She was on the swing set they had given her a couple of years ago. She seemed to be singing a song, although he couldn't make out the words. The camera panned over to his wife, who was speaking on her cell phone. For a few moments, he felt as if he were plunged into some vortex of the weird. It was like he was watching Elizabeth, wearing his wife's clothing and talking into an instrument she would never have seen before. He had to remind himself that this was Nancy, not Elizabeth.

Nancy's face was etched with worry. Although he could not hear what she was saying, the conversation was animated. She seemed to be yelling into the phone. She was normally composed and calm. It was a rarity to see her in such a frantic state.

He turned to the Game Master. "Just how long have I been away from home?"

The Game Master's face formed a grin that would fit well on a weasel's face. "Not as long as it would seem to you, but long enough to concern."

"I hate you more than I have hated anyone or anything in my life."

The Game Master shook his head as if disappointed with a wayward child. "Hate is such a wasteful, negative emotion. You should replace it with an emotion more befitting your current situation—terror. You see, if you don't do this thing for me, I'm going to kill your wife. But it won't be by my own hands. You see, I employ certain individuals whose methods, shall we say, are a bit crude. Normally, I don't associate with these types, but I have found them to be effective at performing certain jobs. I'm afraid that a couple of them really enjoy their work. I personally find how they violate their victims to be repugnant, but everybody has their own way of working. You have to understand, I do not like to micromanage. One particular individual in my employ—now these are only rumors mind you—but I understand that he especially enjoys hurting and killing young children.

"No doubt, it will be a horrific way to die. To spice things up, I can instruct them to have Nancy watch as they kill your daughter before they finish her as well. As for Elizabeth, perhaps my three men who escorted you here today can have their way with her before they slit her throat."

Eyepatch gave a lascivious grin. "Yeah. I'd like that."

"Of course you would," the Game Master said.

Julian fought a battle of emotions roiling inside him. One was the complete and utter rage that was threatening to explode. The other, perhaps more powerful emotion was naked fear. The Game Master had henchmen in every plane he had travelled to thus far. There was no doubt that he could follow through on his threats.

Julian cursed under his breath. What choice did he have? He couldn't risk Nancy and Natalie's well-being. Now he couldn't risk Elizabeth's as well. He doubted he would ever see her again, but she would forever be in his heart, mind, and soul. "What's this one final task you have for me?"

"Ah, so you are agreeable then?" The Game Master asked.

"I haven't agreed to shit, yet," Julian said. "I'm willing to listen to what you have to say. So far, every one of your schemes has been twisted and lethal to the people who live in that plane, with the end result being the death of many."

"Well, this will not involve death. It will, however, involve some level of danger."

"So, what war do you want me to start?" Julian asked.

The Game Master smirked. "There's no need to start a war. Where you will be travelling, war is very much in progress. This is, in fact, a war of epic proportions. Think of World War Two from your own history, except at an even grander scale."

"Cheery. You seem to thoroughly enjoy that fact."

The Game Master grinned.

"So what diabolical scheme do you have planned for me?" Julian asked.

The Game Master intertwined his fingers. "I have a horse in this race, so to speak. I have brought the leader of one of the factions to power, and he seems to have forgotten that. He is drunk with his own power and overestimates his position, forgetting how he got there, and, truth be told, perhaps mentally unstable."

Julian frowned. "Mentally unstable? Like Emperor Belesinto."

"Worse."

"Oh, that's just wonderful. That's exactly what the world needs—some crazy, demented ruler under your control."

"In fairness, he has been an effective leader who has the collective will of his people behind him. Sometimes he uses fear and coercion, but the people are attracted to his strength. In a world at war, his ability to defeat his adversaries is something that has consolidated the backing of his people. His fatal flaw, however, is that he thinks he no longer needs me. He, of course, is dead wrong."

"So what? You want me to kill him?" Julian asked. "I killed for you once. I won't do it again."

"Not at all. I want him to be kept alive and well. He just needs to be brought back into the fold."

"And what exactly am I supposed to do? Espouse upon him your greatness and tell him how wonderful you are."

"No," the Game Master replied. "What I need for you is to bring him to me. I will deal with him in my own way and bring him back on board."

"That's it? You want me to bring him to you?"

"Yes," the Game Master replied.

"Pardon my skepticism, but that hardly seems like something you would need me for. What's the catch?"

"There is no catch."

"Then why did you need me for this task?" Julian asked. "Why don't you just send your goons in and snatch him?"

"That would not work. He would know who my men were and would recognize them before they got to him. Not to mention he keeps himself very well protected, so brute force would not be an option here. "

"You mind if I stand?" Julian asked.

The Game Master motioned to Handlebar Mustache to help Julian to his feet.

"Let me guess. You see, I've seen this movie before. A few times actually. Your goons can't get to this leader, but my counterpart in that plane can because he has access to this guy. He's an advisor of his. Someone that man knows and trusts."

"In a way you are correct, but not in the manner that you think. Your shade on this particular plane happens to be an ambassador of a country that is on the opposite site of Von Ryan. If they know each other, it would be a very casual relationship. However, based on your shade's position, he would be able to arrange a meeting with Von Ryan, especially since his nation's allegiance in this war is potentially wavering. That is what I will have you do."

Julian chuckled. "So, when I meet with him, I'm supposed to hit him over the head with a frying pan and drag him away? Or wait, maybe you want me to give him a tranquilizer."

"None of those things," the Game Master said. "You will merely use your influence to arrange a meeting. Further instructions will be provided to you when you arrive on the plane. I will have someone there when you arrive to give you the details you will require in order to complete this assignment."

Julian took a deep breath. The last thing he wanted was to do more of this monster's bidding. He was sick of the schemes, sick of the wars, sick of people getting killed as he played a role in it. On the other hand, there was nothing stopping the Game Master from killing him and those he loved if he didn't comply. However, he couldn't give in so easily.

"How do I know that once I finish this assignment, you won't kill me?" Julian asked. "If, as you say, this is my final shade, then what incentive would you have in keeping me around?"

"Mr. Dawson, you are a bright man. You have just gone thought all these planes and seen your different shades with their wide-ranging levels of power, influence, and success. Do you not think I could make use of such individuals? There will always be opportunities in the future, therefore you still have significant value to me. The last thing I wish to do is to kill you, unless, of course, you betray me again."

Julian gritted his teeth. "All right. I'll do this, but so help me God I'll kill you no matter how many of your goons I have to get through if you screw me again."

The Game Master laughed. "I can rest assured knowing this will never happen. Do not fool yourself. You could never touch me. "

"I can sure as hell try."

"It would be a futile attempt. I assure you."

"All right, enough of your jibber-jabber," Julian said. "Let's do this, already."

The Game Master nodded to Handlebar mustache, who left the room. A sudden idea flashed across Julian's mind. With one of the Game Master's henchmen out of the room, if he could overtake the other two and get to the door that would transport him…but it made no difference. He wouldn't be returning to his home plane. He would be going to the one the Game Master was sending him to for his next mission. The best laid plans…all of them futile.

Handlebar Mustache returned with a glass with a purple beverage.

The Game Master laughed. "Drink up. I tried to make this one especially tasty."

Julian rolled his eyes. "You're so thoughtful." He gulped the beverage. "Take me to the door."

"It's right here in the room," the Game Master said.

Julian's vision turned blurry. The entire room spun. He likely would have collapsed to the floor, except Handlebar Mustache prevented him from falling. When the room stopped spinning, and Julian's vision cleared, he found a bright red door, completely unsupported by any frame or hinges standing on its own in the far corner of the room.

He released himself from Handlebar Mustache and walked toward the door. Just before he turned the handle, he turned and glared at the Game Master. He then opened the door and stepped through.

241

CHAPTER XXXVII

Julian heard a loud shriek that threatened to burst his eardrums. He remained perfectly still. It was as if his mind was already in this place, but his body had yet to catch up to it. He smelled smoke and felt burning heat from a fire several blocks away.

When he opened his eyes, he witnessed complete chaos. A shrieking man was lying on the ground. Half of his left leg was severed, and he clutched his stump. The man's face was the color of charcoal, and his hair was covered in soot.

He jumped as an explosion erupted in the background some distance away.

He looked around and found others in similar predicaments. The people on this cobbled street had severed limbs and wounds that would surely kill them if they did not get treated soon.

A siren wailed in the background. He went to help the man with the missing leg but wasn't sure what to do. A large, wooden crate covered the man's chest. He tried to heave the box off the man, but it wouldn't budge He lowered his shoulder and tipped the box, but feared he might move it in the wrong direction, and this would cause him to suffocate.

Julian turned when he heard someone call his name. The voice had a refined accent. When the person called out his name again and began to walk in his direction, he was sure this was the guy the Game Master sent to meet him.

The man had a thick beard and short curly hair. He wore a tweed jacket and bifocals. His suit was filthy from the dust and soot from the explosion. Julian glanced back at the wounded man.

"I need you to come with me."

Julian shook his head. "I can't. This man needs help or he's going to die.

"It appears that he is going to die regardless of whether or not you help him."

"All the same," Julian said. "We can't leave him here like this. Let's at least move this box off of him."

"Very well." The whole time he worked with Julian, the man had a look of utter distaste. After a great struggle, they managed to rid him of the box.

"Now, let's go. I have to brief you on your mission."

"No. We have to take him to a hospital," Julian said.

"Are you being purposely obstinate?"

Julian shook his head. "Just ask your boss. I'm always this way."

"Well, it will be of no use. The hospitals in this area are over-crowded and are not accepting new patients, especially ones so close to death. This isn't the first bombing we've had in recent days, but I suppose you wouldn't know about that."

An airplane flew overhead. This plane wasn't as primitive as the last one he had been to. "Do you have a car?"

The man frowned. "A car?"

"Yes. An automobile that you use to get around with." Julian pantomimed driving.

"Ah, yes. My wagon is nearby. I wasn't precisely sure where to find you."

"Let's put this man in your wagon and take him to the hospital."

The man folded his arms. "I will not allow that fellow in my wagon. I'll never be able to remove the blood stains."

"Look, if you want to tell me about about this mission the Game Master is having me undertake, then first we have to help this man." Julian looked around. There were others that needed help, but he appeared worse off than the rest.

"You're a fool, you know. And you're going to get yourself killed with that do-gooder attitude. It won't work around here."

"Well, let me be the one to figure that out. In the meantime, help me carry him. Besides being a do-gooder, I'm also very stubborn and can't be talked out of doing something once I've made up my mind."

Muttering curses, the man helped carry the wounded fellow to his wagon. They set him in the back seat, and the Game Master's emissary crank-started the wagon. This plane may not be as primitive as the last one, but it sure as hell wasn't modern.

"What's your name?" Julian asked.

"Charles." The man kept his eye on the road, which was a good thing since he had to swerve past numerous wreckages in the process. To say that the city they were driving though was war-torn was like calling the Amazon a stream. All around him were destroyed buildings and roads shattered by bombs. The sounds and smells of death and decay permeated the air.

They approached a small white building.

"We have reached our destination," Charles said. "We are dropping him off, and that is all we are doing. Do you understand me?"

Julian raised his brows. "This is a hospital?"

"I'm sorry it doesn't meet your standards, but yes this is a hospital. We will leave him here. Whatever happens beyond that is neither of our concern."

"Right. Right." This sure as hell didn't look like any hospital he had ever been to. They managed to find a nurse who took in the man with the missing leg. Charles was right about that point. Whatever was going to happen with his guy now was beyond their control. Perhaps the actions they took on this day would save this man's life or maybe it wouldn't. This was all he could do.

Charles looked nothing like his previous handlers. Usually, they were massive fellows who looked like they could bench press a Buick. Charles was of average height and build and looked more like an attorney than someone who cracked skulls for a living.

"You're not the muscle, are you?"

As they entered the wagon, Charles gave him a quizzical look. "I beg your pardon."

"You don't go around hurting and killing people for the Game Master, do you?"

Charles chuckled. "Good heavens, no. What in the world gave you that idea? No, I work for parliament."

"Then why do you work for that slime?"

"That slime, as you call him, makes the world go round. He controls more things than you can possibly imagine."

"Oh, I have no problem imagining all of the things he controls. I've seen it firsthand in more places than here. I'm well aware of his reach and influence."

"Very well. Then you should understand why I have allied myself with the Master of Keys. It is how I get things done around here. If not for my ties to him, I shudder at how ineffective my efforts in parliament would be."

"Master of Keys?" Julian asked. "That's a stupid name. What, he ran out of creative names?"

Charles rolled his eyes. "Get in the wagon before we get hit by a stray bullet. This is not a safe area. It is a war zone, after all."

"Really? I thought we were at some tropical beach resort."

Charles crank-started his wagon again. "You are a difficult person to deal with."

"I'm a little bitter, too. I've had to go on a number of missions with the promise of returning to my wife and daughter, and that promise never seems to come to fruition. My patience has run thin."

"My understanding is that your performance of late has left a bit to be desired. We won't have any failure this go around. Do I make myself clear?"

"Or what? You're going to kill me?" Julian stared at Charles. He had little doubt that he could pound this pencil pusher into oblivion.

"Nothing so crude or vulgar. I believe a sufficient threat has been made on the wife and daughter you previously mentioned that you love so dearly."

Julian gritted his teeth. "How can you work for the Game Master, or the Master of Keys as you call him? He's an evil son of a bitch. If you're working with him, then you are perpetuating evil as well."

"Good and evil is relative. As I mentioned earlier, his influence can make things happen. And the sad fact is that my nation is on the losing side of this war effort. The time to switch allegiance is upon us. Our very lives and the future of our children and generations to come depend on it. I am trying save my nation and the lives of millions. Does that sound evil to you?"

Julian had seen enough of the Game Master's machinations to know that he was evil with a capital E. His schemes typically ended with a whole lot of people dying as he played his games and pulled strings. It made him wonder just how deep he had sunk his tendrils into the politicians, governments, and businesses of his home plane. It would certainly explain a lot.

They drove out of the city into a less ravaged area that didn't look as if it had been blasted to hell by bombs. There was still wreckage here and there, but not nearly as widespread or as severe.

"Your counterpart, Jarvis Dawson, does not live in this country, but is visiting and staying at this hotel. You will be safe, since this is far from the danger zone. But you never can tell when a stray bomb might fall."

"Well, that's reassuring."

The street they were walking on was well paved and had not been destroyed by bombs. Tall buildings stood on either side of the street.

Wagons large and small were parked alongside the sidewalks.

A kid, who looked to be in his late teens, ran up the street toward them. He was looking over his shoulder as if being chased. The kid, who had long hair tucked behind a cap, kept advancing in their direction. He wasn't paying attention and—Julian tried to sidestep him, but he and the kid collided, and they both crashed onto the cement.

Charles, who went unscathed, glowered at the kid and raised his fist. "Watch where you're going, you ruffian."

Charles was about to extend Julian a helping hand, when Julian noticed a folded white piece of paper in the kid's hand. He glanced at the kid, who winked at him.

Julian quickly rose to an upright position. "I'm fine. Don't worry about me. Let's just get on our way and settle into my hotel so you can give me the rundown on what's going on."

"Very well." Charles turned and resumed their walk.

Julian fell into step behind him. When Charles wasn't looking, he opened the note. He tried not to reveal his stunned surprise at what he read. It had one line, written in black ink, "Meet me at the Arenson building tomorrow at 1000 hours." It was signed by Cutter.

Julian grinned. It would be good to see his old friend again.

CHAPTER XXXVIII

"**N**ow, let me give you a history lesson," Charles said as he poured tea. "Or rather, let me update you on current events, which would be more appropriate given the circumstances. The Unified States…"

Julian cut him off. "This country is called The Unified States? Not the Unified States of America or the United States?"

Charles frowned at him. "No, the Unified States. Anyway, this nation is part of a three-fold war that is being fought quite literally around the globe. I can't think of any area that is not in some way affected by the war or has not seen its share of fighting and violence. Anyway, there are three different factions or alliances, if you will, and every nation is tied to one of these three factions."

"You mean there are no Switzerlands?"

Charles put down his saucer and cup. "Switzerland joined the Brigan pact along with Unified States. Anyway, we are fighting a war that we will inevitably lose. The other sides are too powerful and too ruthless. We simply lack the stomach to persevere with our current allies."

"So, you want to betray your allies and jump aboard the winning side? That's exactly the sort of thing I would expect from someone aligned with the Game Master."

Charles gave him a cold stare. "He has not taken sides per se, but has influences on all three factions."

"Even better," Julian said. "That way he can't lose. He's gamed the system."

"I am not sure what that means, but I can tell you that the nations that are part of the Brigan Pact are facing inevitable doom and destruction. In the long run, Von Ryan will prevail. He has military might, cunning, and ruthlessness that the other sides lack to ultimately win the war."

"But Von Ryan isn't playing ball with our Master of Keys, is he? That's not acceptable. He has to fall in line with our mutual friend."

"Yes, that is correct. When he first took power, Von Ryan was more or less an apprentice under the Master of Keys. His ego has grown substantially, and he believes he can rule the world without having anyone to answer to."

For the next two hours, Charles filled Julian's head with all sorts of details and minutia about this plane, most of which didn't seem relevant to his current situation. However, Charles, being a politician, had to be long-winded about every topic.

Fortunately, he ordered dinner to be delivered to Julian's suite. By that point, Julian had built himself quite an appetite. As Charles droned on about one uninteresting topic after another, Julian devoured lamb chops with considerable zeal. He had not eaten anything in over twenty-four hours. After eating, he got quite drowsy, something Charles picked up on.

"I will leave you to retire for the evening then. I will see you in the morning where we can discuss further plans, including making contact with Von Ryan."

That woke Julian out of his stupor. "What time in the morning?"

Charles looked at his time piece, a fancy pocket watch with a gold chain. "Let us meet at nine thirty."

That wouldn't do if he were to meet Cutter at ten. "Earlier would be better. I'm a bit of an early riser and I don't need much sleep. Can we move up this meeting to seven AM?"

"That won't work. I have a meeting with my nation's ambassador."

"Look, I'm much more of a morning person. How about eight?"

Charles checked his pocket journal. "Very well. We will have to make it brief, however, since I have another meeting at ten in the morning."

"Brief works better for me anyway. As you can tell, I was starting to drift during your history lesson."

Charles looked down at him with disdain. "I noticed." He straightened his long tie and smoothed out a lock of his curly hair.

Julian ushered his handler out of the building. He could hardly believe his good fortune that Cutter was here.

He went to the balcony of his suite. Out in the distance, a fire was raging. He wondered if it would spread this far but found it unlikely. Overhead, vintage looking fighter planes flew. On the drive here, he had seen several military vehicles. He had never been in a war zone before, and after what he had witnessed, he hoped to never be in one again.

He tilted his head back and closed his eyes. He had never felt so desolate and alone. He missed his wife and daughter horribly but missed Elizabeth as well. If truth be told, his heart ached for her more than it did for Nancy. He couldn't imagine making it through the last couple of months without her.

He heard the distant rumblings of what he thought might be an explosion. He looked in the direction of the sound and saw a bright light followed by more smoke. Just what the hell had he gotten himself into?

* * *

He found Charles to be supremely irritating the next morning as they had tea and pastries in Julian's suite. Charles had an air of superiority about him and treated Julian like an imbecile for not knowing basic things about the war and the plane they were in. Of course, he didn't know anything about the place. He had just arrived yesterday. To make matters worse, his morning meeting had been canceled, so they started at seven, and this extra time allowed Charles to be even more verbose than usual. Julian wanted to speed him along but couldn't tell him he had a meeting with Cutter that morning.

Charles had brought a blackboard, which seemed more than a little pretentious. He detailed it with names of places and countries that had no meaning to Julian, except when they happened to correspond to a similar place in his plane. Charles seemed to be in his element, pontificating and theorizing about the reasons for the war, and the strategies that some of the nations employed. If it wasn't for the three cups of tea, Julian would have fallen asleep.

As best he could discern, between the three factions involved in this conflict, a staggering one hundred and twelve countries were actively at war. He couldn't recall off the top of his head how many countries were involved in World War Two, but this seemed like an extreme amount. The aggressors in this war and the ones who started it were the country of Rotgard and their leader Von Ryan, who Julian would be meeting in the near future.

Charles was a member of parliament of the Silver Isles, this plane's version of the United Kingdom. He was in the Unified States as an emissary from his country, but his real reason for being here was to help Julian set up a meeting with Von Ryan.

Knowing what he knew about Von Ryan, and the fact that the Silver Isles and the Unified States were both on the same side and on opposing factions to Rotgard, Julian was still having a hard time figuring out why Charles was helping him. That was until Charles explained that he was part of a secret coalition with members from several nations including the Silver Isles to switch sides and join Von Ryan and the nation of Rotgard.

"Isn't that treason?" Julian asked.

"No. It is complete and total pragmatism. My nation is on the verge of annihilation and in danger of being wiped off the globe. I am doing what I can to make sure that does not happen. If it can't be done militarily, then it can be done diplomatically. If the current leaders do not see that, then we need new leaders."

"Wait. Let me guess. The Game Master, or the Master of Keys as you call him, is going to help remove your current leaders and put his own in place."

Charles raised his brows but did not say anything. Julian guessed he was on the mark with that last statement.

"All that I do, I do for the good of my people," Charles said. "I am wholly ignorant of this place you come from, but I can tell you that I have seen unending suffering. My brother just died. Two uncles, and my young nephew and niece have all died in this horrid war. I would like to see it come to a conclusion, and I would like to see my nation survive."

During his lesson, Charles meandered off into subjects that weren't pertinent, so Julian had to reel him back in and keep him focused on the topic. He kept glancing at the clock on the wall. He couldn't miss this meeting with Cutter. On the previous evening, he had spoken with a woman who worked at the front desk of the hotel. She informed him that the Arenson Building was a fifteen-minute drive and told him that they could provide a taxi rental to take him there.

Trying his best not to appear either rude or suspicious of doing something untoward, he managed to usher Charles out of there and not give him the bum's rush. With time ticking down, he grabbed a billfold that Charles had provided him which contained identification papers as well as currency he would need to secure a taxi. He rushed down the stairs to the lobby and found the front desk woman he had spoken with previously, who introduced him to a gentleman who would secure the taxi for him.

When he exited the hotel, Julian stared in bewilderment. He expected one of those primitive automobiles, such as the one Charles had driven him in yesterday, but instead, a horse drawn carriage met him out front.

Julian turned toward the hotel employee, who he assumed was the equivalent of a valet. "This is the taxi you arranged for my transport?"

"But of course it is, Mr. Dawson."

"But it's got a horse."

The valet frowned. "Certainly, sir. All taxis for hire in the city have a horse."

Julian cursed under his breath. "This is going to take a while."

"It shouldn't take more than fifteen minutes to reach the Arenson Building, sir, road conditions permitting."

Julian sighed, took the travelling bag he brought from his suite, and threw it in the back of the carriage. The valet provided the driver with instructions, and they were off. He hoped Cutter would understand the difficulties he might face in travelling in this foreign plane and stick around beyond their meeting time, in case Julian arrived late.

As they progressed through their slow journey, he spotted numerous troops marching. Some were on foot. Others were in motor-powered vehicles. He even saw a handful of armored vehicles that looked like tanks—something that took him aback given the level of technology he had seen thus far in this plane. Perhaps they were not as primitive as he thought, despite his horse-drawn carriage.

A fire burned in the direction in which they were traveling. As they drew closer, the heat from the conflagration became more prominent.

"Have to take a detour," the driver called out.

Julian sighed. He saw the necessity of the detour, but now he would definitely be late. The detour turned out to be a roundabout route. They had to double back and take a large loop around a park, where soldiers were conducting military drills, before resuming the path to the Arenson Building.

By the time they finally reached their destination, Julian was over a half-hour late. He paid the driver the fair, although he was not happy with the ride. It wasn't the driver's fault. It was this world at war and their primitive transportation. He walked up the marble steps of the Arenson Building. Large concrete pillars lined the entrance of the building. The exterior of the building was mostly gray, and there was a large fountain at the bottom of the steps.

He looked around, unsure where to go. Although there were only a few people walking along the paved area and the stairs leading to the building, inside it was bustling with activity. Several men sat reading newspapers. To the right was a bank of desks, mostly attended by women, who sat in front of typewriters, keying away. Two men were involved in a heated argument, while a third appeared to be mediating the situation.

He cautiously moved inward, looking for Cutter. Then it occurred to him that he might not find Cutter. Perhaps he would send another messenger to deliver further instructions. Or worse, maybe this was all a ploy by the Game Master to trap him.

He had to step around scaffolding. On top of the structure was a man in drab, off-white workers' clothes with buckets of paint, brushing the wall. Julian scanned the area as he walked around the scaffolding. He jumped, startled by a loud, crashing sound.

"What the hell?"

A bucket of paint dropped from the scaffolding. Fortunately, the lid was on, and the paint had not spilled. Given his proximity, had there not been a lid, it would have gotten all over him.

He began to move forward until he froze when the worker said, "Pardon me, Julian. Didn't mean to nearly hit you with the bucket."

Julian stared upward and did a double take at the man in the workman's outfit. By God, it was Cutter. He hadn't noticed at first since he now had dark hair instead of his customary blond hair—obviously a wig.

Julian smiled. "Glad to see you're trying to earn an honest living."

"That will be a first." Cutter climbed down the ladder from the top of the scaffolding. "It appears that I am in need of more paint. I could use a hand."

"I would be glad to oblige," Julian said.

"Good. Follow me. We have much to discuss.

CHAPTER XXXIX

"**I** have much to tell you about the world you're in," Cutter said. "But first I need to know about what you just went through? Did you see my wife and daughter? How are they? Did you give them what I asked you to give them?"

Julian nodded. He told Cutter all about his experiences in the previous plane. Rehashing the events of the past few months felt cathartic. After he finished telling Cutter about the death of Smith and the peace accord he helped ratify, he told him the details about his relationship with Elizabeth.

He stared at Cutter for a long moment. "Did you know about Elizabeth, my counterpart's wife?"

Cutter nodded.

"You knew she was a shade of my wife Nancy?"

Cutter nodded.

"Then why didn't you say anything?"

Cutter shrugged. "I don't see how it would have helped. Whatever was going to happen, whatever you were going to do, it would be up to you to decide how to proceed."

"But if I had known…"

Cutter cut him off. "Would you have done anything differently? Look, I'm not going to judge you and your relationship with Elizabeth. I've had more than my share of indiscretions and things that I've done that I later regretted. I'm the last person to pass judgement on another."

"I need to get back home, but at the same time, I crave seeing Elizabeth again. She's…I feel as if she's my soulmate."

"There's something you need to understand. Certain people are drawn to each other. There are three separate planes where your shade was married to your wife's shade: you and Nancy, of course, then there was the woman in the first plane you visited that looked just like your wife, and Elizabeth in that last plane. That's not a coincidence. It's something I've seen repeatedly in my travels."

Julian pondered that for a while in silence.

"There's something else I need to tell you. While you were away in the last plane, I travelled to your home plane. I found out where you live and visited your house to see your wife and daughter."

"You saw Nancy and Natalie?" Julian took a deep breath as his heart raced.

"I just wanted to let them know that you're okay. That you're still alive."

Julian stammered. "How long has it been since I've been away?"

"It's been about three weeks since you've been gone from home."

Julian stared incredulously. "Three weeks? That's impossible. I spent more than three months on the last plane alone. There's no way in hell it's only been three weeks."

In a wistful voice, Cutter said, "Time works differently in the various planes. There isn't a linear relationship. I have tables and charts that my family has tabulated over the centuries which detail the time relationship between planes. It's quite complex, and I couldn't rattle it off from memory. I have to reference these tables frequently when I travel. Bottom line is your family thinks you've been away for three weeks."

Julian took a deep breath. "What did you tell them?"

"As you can imagine, it wouldn't be wise to tell them the truth. If I went into details about what you've been doing lately, they undoubtedly wouldn't believe me."

"Undoubtedly,' Julian agreed.

"I told them you were safe and well. Otherwise, I tried to be as vague as possible. I told them there was something you had to do, and there was no way for you to contact them until you completed your task. I told them that you would be home as soon as humanly possible and that there was nothing that you wanted more than to be back with them. I also insinuated that you were working for the United States government."

"All true, except for that last bit about the government." Julian said. "How did that go over?"

"Not well. Your wife was a bit hysterical. Your daughter seemed to take it better."

Julian closed his eyes. "Natalie. I miss her more than you could possibly imagine."

"Oh, I could imagine quite well."

Julian nodded, remembering Cutter's family. "Of course. I enjoyed the time I spent with your wife and daughter. They're good people. And they had no problem believing my story. Elizabeth has already befriended your wife, and I'm sure she will look out for them. She has a heart of gold. With Smith out of the way, can you return."

Cutter shook his head. "If that was all it took, I would have killed that bastard long ago. I won't shed a tear that he's gone, but unfortunately it doesn't change my situation."

A wave of sadness hit Julian as he thought about his current situation and the people he left behind, so he changed the subject. "How did you know to find me here?"

"Because I know your shade in this plane, so I, or rather my network has been tracking his movements and reporting back to me. I'm almost certain this is your final shade and that the Game Master would eventually send you here."

"That's what the Game Master told me. So, he wasn't lying?"

"About this?" Cutter shook his head. "I don't think so. I'm sure he has been lying to you about everything else. You can't trust the little bastard. Anyway, I figured you would eventually wind up here. This is the most vital of all the missions the Game Master would send you on. The stakes are quite high on this plane."

"I can see that. So, I'm a bit confused about this network."

Cutter folded his arms and began to pace. The room they were in had a long, wooden table with matching chairs surrounding it. There was little in terms of decorations on the wall except for a simple clock. The walls were painted sterile white.

"You remember when we first met, I told you I try to stay away from politics in the various planes I visit. Well, I wasn't entirely being truthful."

"It seems as if there was a lot you weren't being truthful about."

Cutter nodded. "I won't deny it. I felt bad about you and your predicament, but being the selfish bastard that I am, I saw it as an opportunity to accomplish things as well. But you've saved my ass and have proven that you're a true friend. I'm sorry for not being forthcoming."

Julian waved his hand. "You didn't owe me anything and I couldn't have made this through without you."

"I promise to be truthful in all our dealings going forward. As I was saying, I do try to keep my distance from political wheeling and dealings. It's more trouble than it's worth, and there's little a person like me can do to affect any kind of change. This plane is an entirely different story. There's some seriously bad shit going on here. It's a world on the verge of complete and utter destruction, and I have too many friends and even some extended family here to see it go by the wayside.

"Most of it has to do with the dictator that has his sights set on taking over the world. This guy is a real piece of work, let me tell you. You remember the funny looking bloke with the mustache who started World War Two back in your home plane?"

"You mean Adolf Hitler?"

"Yeah that guy. Well, Hitler is a lamb compared to this monster. Let me show you something."

Cutter placed a leather carrying bag on the table in front of them. He pulled out a portable video player with a flip top screen.

Julian frowned. "This doesn't exactly look like technology from this plane."

"Of course not, but I figured it wouldn't stand out as much as a holo projector. At any rate, I took some reel footage I obtained here and digitized it."

"Why?"

"So I could show you. Take a seat."

After Cutter pressed play, the next twenty minutes were filled with the most horrific images Julian had ever seen. He saw scenes of people being burned alive by the gray coats, Von Ryan's secret police. There was shocking footage of poor, huddled people with haunted eyes—old men, women, young boys, girls, it seemed to make no difference—being taken to open fields where soldiers torched them with flame throwers. On the screen, enemy combatants were flayed alive. What they did to prisoners of war was so brutal that it almost defied description.

Julian had to turn away at footage of a Silver Isles soldier being questioned by an interrogator, who took a nail and twisted it into the soldier's eyes. Unfortunately, it did not end there. In a city that Cutter told him was the equivalent of Paris, Von Ryan's secret police went from house to house abducting children that Cutter informed him were used in the sex trade. If anyone in the household tried to stop this from happening, they were brutally beaten.

After a while, Julian closed his eyes. "This is awful. I can't watch anymore."

Cutter obliged him and turned off the portable video player. "I've been to many planes and have seen many terrible things, but nothing at this level. He is a maniac in a class all of his own. I can't tolerate the tyrant's existence so much that I violated a policy I hold sacred—don't get involved in politics and world events. So, I became part of a network made of travelers like me but also groups from this world from all three factions including Von Ryan's own alliance dedicated to trying to stop him."

Julian opened his eyes. "And I'm supposed to meet this this psychotic son of a bitch. The Game Master thinks he can reel him in."

"That's folly. The Game Master is far too confident in his own ability to manipulate people. It won't work with Von Ryan. Tell me exactly what the Game Master is planning for you."

Julian relayed all the information he had.

When he finished, Cutter stroked his goatee. "Hmm. I think I can make this work to our advantage."

"What do you mean by our advantage?" Julian asked.

"Me and the network I work for."

Julian leaned back against the chair. "I noticed you didn't include me in that equation. I've been given an ultimatum by the Game Master. If I don't come through and deliver Von Ryan, then he will kill not only Nancy and Natalie, but Elizabeth as well. And their deaths won't be pleasant. I have no choice in the matter."

Cutter narrowed his eyes as he stared at Julian. "Screw the Game Master. Are you going to be his slave for the rest of your life?"

"I stood up to him last time, and it didn't work out so well for me. I put myself in a far worse position. What choice do I have?"

"How can you say it didn't work? Cutter asked. "From what you told me, you affected great change that will impact that nation for generations. That's something amazing and tangible. Don't forget I lived in that plane and favored it so much that I got married to a woman and had a child there. To do what you did is very impressive. Now is your opportunity to once more affect great change, and I would say this situation is quite a bit more dire."

"That's all well and good, and perhaps noble, but there's one little problem, or rather a really big problem with me going against the Game Master and defying him a second time. There's no way I'm risking my family or Elizabeth. I'm willing to take a chance with my own life, but I won't allow harm to come to them."

"Listen to yourself Julian. You're willing to allow millions of people die just for the safety of a few. That's not the person who gave the Game Master the middle finger and helped the world you were just in. That's not the person you are."

Julian went silent for a while. He couldn't ignore what he just saw and not do something about it. If there was a way to save all of these people, then he had to do something to try to save them. He eventually broke the silence. "What if there is a way to do this—to defy the madness the Game Master is trying to perpetrate here and still get back to my family?"

"I already told you that I can't take you with me when I travel."

"I know that. I have an idea—well, it's not a great idea yet, but if what the Game Master is saying is true and this is my final task before I return home—something that you think is likely—then I don't need him. I need his portal. So, what if…what if I go through with this and make it seem like I'm delivering Von Ryan to the Game Master, but instead your people actually take him."

Cutter nodded slowly. "Okay."

"I'm sure the Game Master is going to be well protected."

Cutter nodded once more. "No doubt."

"But if he thinks that everything is going as planned, he won't be suspecting anything. And you have this network of people, right?"

"I do."

"So, do you have enough people that would be able to overtake him and his guards if he's not suspecting it."

Cutter thought about this for a few moments. "Yes. For sure."

"We're playing for keeps this time. I have one shot to take him out. I think we can flesh out a plan where we can take down both Von Ryan and the Game Master, but I'm putting my life in your hands."

"Julian, I promise you that I will do everything possible to get you home safely if you're willing to do this."

"Okay. Let's do this. Let's stop Von Ryan and kill the Game Master once and for all."

CHAPTER XL

It was late in the afternoon by the time Julian finished his lengthy and in depth conversation with Cutter. They had gone though many eventualities, and by the end, Julian was satisfied that they at least had a reasonable plan. He wasn't entirely confident it would work. Many things had to fall in place, they made some massive assumptions, and Julian would have to rely on people he had never met with the only assurance that Cutter knew and trusted them. Cutter had become a friend to him, but he also hadn't always been honest in their dealings, but in these lands of strangers, Cutter was the one person he felt he could rely on.

Cutter had arranged for someone to drive Julian back in a wagon to the hotel, which was a far better mode of transportation than the horse drawn carriage he had taken to get here, even if it did move slower than cars from back home and the driving was treacherous on these damaged roads.

He let out a long yawn when he arrived at the hotel. A man at the front desk informed him that Charles had been there twice looking for him. They weren't scheduled to meet, but knowing how high the stakes were, it came as little surprise that Charles was stalking him.

He might have the appearance and mannerisms of a lawyer, but he was very much the Game Master's man. That meant he was not to be taken lightly, even if his appearance suggested he was a lightweight.

After getting back to his suite, Julian fixed himself a drink from the bar. It was a nice set up with various liquors and liqueurs. He had not heard of any of the brands, so he picked up a bottle that called itself brandy and poured a couple fingers into a glass. He settled into a comfortable chair and sipped his drink, pondering the course he had chosen. It was an all or nothing proposition, involving extreme risk. If it worked, he would be home free. If it didn't, then he was a dead man.

If he was being completely honest with himself, the chances of it working were slim. There were so many pieces that would have to fall into place like a properly set structure of dominoes.

On the other hand, he was pretty damned desperate. Even if he completed this latest mission, he would still be under the control of the Game Master. The Game Master would only let him live if he remained useful. That meant he would never be free. He would forever have to go on these Godforsaken missions on behalf of that sociopath whenever a situation presented itself. It was an untenable situation.

A knock sounded on the door. He wasn't expecting anybody. Julian inwardly groaned when he found Charles at the door.

Julian opened the door, and Charles immediately stepped inside without being invited. He folded his arms in a gesture that reminded Julian of a cross college professor. "Where have you been? We are short of time, and you have been gone all day long."

Julian tried to play it cool. He sat back on the chair and tilted his head back. "Relax, man. You never told me you wanted to meet again today. You want something from me, then I suggest you make your intentions clear. As for where I was…" Julian shrugged. "This is a whole new world for me. I wanted to check it out. Get a lay of the land. I can't imagine I'll ever return to this plane of yours."

Charles's face puckered so much that Julian thought it would implode. "Are you insane, man? We are in the middle of a God damned war. You could get yourself killed out there. And then this whole mission would be for naught."

"If I get myself killed, then the mission is the least of my concerns. And I am fully aware that this is a war zone."

Charles paced back and forth. "From now on, you do not leave here without my consent. Do you understand me?"

"Yes, Master."

"Your sarcasm is not appreciated."

"And the fact that you're an asshole isn't appreciated."

Charles stared at him incredulously. "A what?"

"Never mind. So what exactly do you want now that you have me here?"

Charles took a deep breath and tilted his head, almost transforming back into the career politician. He spoke in a more measured tone. "I have been working on plans for your meeting with Von Ryan."

"Ah, yes. The psychotic dictator that I have heard so many lovely things about."

"Yes, well for obvious reasons you can't meet with Von Ryan in the Unified States. They would have him shot on sight if he ever stepped foot in this country. However, I have been working on arranging a meeting in the country of El Santo Del Sol." Charles paused and stared at Julian. "And based on that blank look on your face, I assume you don't have a clue as to where that might be."

"Yeah. Never heard of it."

"You have, actually. I have mentioned it a few times."

Julian shrugged. "Whatever. What's the pretext of the meeting?"

"The pretext?"

"Yes. I'm assuming Herr Psycho Von Ryan is a busy man conquering nations. Why would he take time out of his busy schedule to meet with little old me?"

"Ah, a good question. That is because you—or your counterpart—is plotting a coup attempt on the Unified States."

"Very ambitious of Jarvis Dawson. Does he know about any of this?"

Charles shook his head. "Not at all, and there is no coup attempt." He wheeled the portable blackboard that he had used earlier and began to sketch a map outlining the Unified States. This country was about half the size of the United States of America and didn't include almost any of the southwestern states and half of California. He went on to draw a host of other countries and their capitals before he finally got to El Santo del Sol. By his best estimation it was around the equivalent of southern Mexico in his plane.

"Don't take offense," Julian said. "But your plane seems a bit primitive by my standards."

Despite his plea to not take offense, Charles gave him a wicked glare.

"Anyway, how exactly would I travel to this country?"

"It will take too long by wagon and the journey will too treacherous, therefore you will have to travel by aeroship."

Julian swallowed hard. He didn't like the sound of this. "Aeroship? That isn't some steam powered airplane?

Charles wrinkled his nose. "Steam powered? Heavens no. Aeroships use a special form of petrol to power their engines. Where did you ever get such a notion?"

Julian ignored the question. "All the same, I'm not too keen on the idea of flying given the primitive level of technology involved with your transportation."

"Perhaps you don't understand, Mr. Dawson. You will be going on that aeroship to meet Von Ryan. You are not in a position to dictate terms."

Julian grumbled. "Fine, if I die, then the mission is over."

"You will be fine. I have flown in aeroships many times, and as you can see, I'm still among us. When we arrive in El Santo Del Sol, I will have transport waiting for us that will take us to meet Von Ryan. The truth of the matter as far as safety is concerned, the aeroship is not my primary concern. Rather, it will be travel through El Santo Del Sol. There is constant guerrilla warfare taking place in that nation."

"Lovely," Julian said. "So, what you're trying to tell me is that it will be even more dangerous there than it is here."

Charles hesitated. "Yes."

"That's awesome."

"I will arrange an armed guard as part of the transport. There will still be danger, but I am confident we will manage to reach our destination in one piece."

"How reassuring. When do we leave?"

"Tomorrow. Here is our itinerary." Charles laid out several sheets of paper on the table.

Julian scanned them briefly. He inwardly thanked Charles for these papers. This way he would be able to show them to Cutter.

"Do you have any questions?" Charles asked.

"Yeah. You keep saying we. Does that mean that you're going with me?"

"But of course. How else can I ensure that you complete your mission?"

"Let's say this actually works, and I can deliver Von Ryan to the Game Master, then what? How do I get out of this hellhole? No offense."

"I have little doubt that you intended offense. Regardless, if you successfully complete the mission, then I will then transport you to the Master of Keys. He assured me that he will return you to your home."

That was exactly what he wanted to hear. He needed that to happen to ensure his plans would be successful.

"Is there something wrong?" Charles asked.

Julian shook his head. "No. I was just thinking about everything I've been through."

"Well, it appears that your journey is almost over. I'm not going to say that this trip won't be without danger, but it isn't anything that I am not willing to undergo myself, and I can assure you I have no intention of dying. I have a few things to attend to, but we will discuss the plans in greater detail tomorrow before we depart. Are you ready for this?"

"I'm ready for all of this to be over."

Charles smiled. "Good. This will soon be over, for you and for me."

CHAPTER XLI

Julian was jittery the following morning. He had met with Cutter the previous evening after Charles left. Cutter had sent a courier to Julian's hotel with a message to meet him in a shady part of the city about a mile from the hotel.

He relayed everything he knew to Cutter. Precision was vital for his plan to succeed. Unfortunately he couldn't give him an exact location but gave him the city in El Santo Del Sol where they would be landing.

"More than you would imagine," Cutter had told him. "This isn't like the plane you come from. There doesn't exist anything resembling an airport as you would know it, but there aren't many landing strips in El Santo Del Sol, so we'll figure it out—hopefully."

"Okay. I'll proceed with the Von Ryan meeting," Julian said. Will your people be nearby when we meet?"

Cutter nodded. "I'll have people on the ground shadowing you."

"Will you be there as well?"

"You're damn right I will be," Cutter replied.

Julian had to operate in faith that his friend would be doing his part. Hopefully it wasn't blind faith. In a worst-case scenario, he would give the Game Master exactly what he wanted. That still could at least land him a ticket home unless it was all a ruse and the Game Master planned on killing him after this last task.

Still, there was so much that could go wrong. His stomach churned as he and Charles drove to the airstrip. Hearing and seeing several bombs explode in the distance did nothing to settle his nerves. What if they took enemy fire on the flight? Did this aeroship even have defensive capabilities, or would they be defenseless in the sky?

Charles seemed to be rather cheery, talking about how bright the future would be when his goals came to fruition.

The airstrip consisted of about a dozen runways. The surrounding field was lined with numerous primitive looking aeroships, the type with double wings and propellers. The one they approached near the runway was orange and black. It had a cockpit and room for six passengers. He didn't think there was going to be any room service aboard.

"You sure this is capable of flying?" Julian asked.

"Of course it's capable of flying," Charles replied. "Why would I select an aeroship that wasn't capable of flying?"

Julian grunted. "It looks…primitive."

"Well, I assure you that it will take us to our destination."

A short man who looked like he should be a jockey approached them.

Charles walked toward him and shook the man's hand. "Edmunds, is the aeroship prepared for flight?"

"Indeed it is," the little man replied.

Julian put his hand on Charles's shoulder and spoke in a low tone. "Don't tell me this guy's our pilot."

"He is our pilot," Charles replied. "You have a better one?"

"You can't be serious. He's like five feet tall."

Charles raised his brow. "Five feet?"

"What? You don't use that unit of measure in this plane?"

Charles shook his head.

"Well, this guy is really, really short. How's he going to see over the controls?"

"He has flown dozens of flights and has not had any incidents."

Julian's unease grew as Edmunds continued to dicker around with the aeroship.

"How does this contraption even fly?" Julian asked Charles.

"Well, I'm no aviator, but it uses petrol for fuel and the propellers spin and in goes in the air. We shall be fine. Just prepare for the flight. There is little room for cargo."

"That's okay. I packed light." Julian motioned to his carrying bag that held some papers, a change of clothes, and a few other small items he picked up along the way.

Less than an hour later, Julian was on board and strapped into his chair, wearing the helmet the aviator gave him. He couldn't believe that this was an open vessel. Like it wasn't terrifying enough being on this death trap. The fact that he wore a helmet to wear did not calm his nerves. Julian took his seat on the aeroship, mouthing a silent prayer. He tried to control his breathing but he was on the verge of hyperventilating. He was going to die in this primitive flying vessel. He was sure of it.

The little jockey of a pilot actually had to go outside and spin the propeller blade to get the aeroship started.

Doesn't he have an ignition key?

When the aeroship began to move, it sputtered and nearly stopped. Julian almost wished it would stop and he wouldn't have to go through with this ordeal. Much to his chagrin, it picked up speed as it went down the runway.

The aeroship leapt off the runway, and, for a half second, Julian thought it was going to crash right back down. It tilted and dipped before Edmunds managed to right it. Julian's heart dropped to his stomach as the aeroship ascended rapidly into the sky. He leaned over and vomited out of the side of the plane. His face felt as if it had been ripped off his skull. He closed his eyes and prayed that he would survive.

The first half hour of the flight was sheer torture. Julian's stomach did backflips, and he nearly vomited three more times but managed to hold it in. Then, at some point, he settled into the flight. It was still harrowing, but his fear and revulsion diminished to tolerable levels. Perhaps he would survive this experience after all.

The flight was a long ordeal, and he even fell asleep during part of it. There was a certain rhythm to flying in this deathtrap, and he had not slept well since his arrival. It had been difficult with the constant barrage of explosions. By contrast, he had slept great with Elizabeth by his side. He felt an aching in his heart just thinking about her.

It was nearing nightfall when they began their descent. He was so anxious to be back on the ground that toward the end he felt as if he was crawling out of his skin. His stomach had been thrown into a million loops. He kept glancing at Charles, who seemed calm and relaxed.

It was a blessed relief when they finally touched down on the airstrip, although that experience was harrowing enough as the aeroship tilted back and forth before finally righting itself just before hitting the ground.

Once on the ground, Charles turned toward him. "You don't look so well."

Julian glared at him, too numb to answer. When he exited the plane, he kissed the ground. He vowed to never fly on an aeroship again.

"I suppose my first flight was rather challenging as well, but one gets used to it."

"I doubt it," Julian said.

The second leg of the journey would be done using a military vehicle, but that wouldn't be until the morning. They were staying overnight in a hotel for diplomats and their families. He was in dire need of a good meal, a shower, and a solid night's sleep. Showers weren't all that readily available on this plane, but fortunately, both the place he had been staying at and the one they would be staying at tonight, had them.

Unfortunately, his dinner companion for the evening was Charles. The man never stopped talking. On the one hand, Julian did not feel like speaking and didn't have to say much. On the other hand, the man was a pompous windbag who was confounding to listen to. Julian found himself nodding off on a couple of occasions and had to bail out early, much to his companion's chagrin. Apparently, he wanted an audience to listen to him pontificate.

There was no word from Cutter that evening. He was not sure how Cutter would communicate with him. They had never established that. Cutter only assured him that he and his people would be on the ground. Still, in a foreign land in a strange plane, it would be comforting to talk to the one person he trusted.

He was still asleep the following morning when Charles knocked on his door. Apparently, the man was always chipper. He was dressed in a suit and had a cup of tea in hand. He seated himself at the table in the parlor sipping his tea. "I must warn you that we will be undergoing the most treacherous part of our journey."

Julian stared at him incredulously while eating a pastry prepared by the hotel's kitchen staff. "You've got to be kidding me. You mean that aeroship wasn't the most treacherous part of the journey?"

"Not at all. We will be traversing through some very hostile territory."

Julian sighed. "Then why didn't you select a safer place to meet with Von Ryan?"

Charles replied in his most condescending voice, and he was the master of condescending voices. "I am not quite sure if you are aware of this, but we have an entire world at war. There are no safe places. El Santo Del Sol is right in the thick of the conflict, and it happens to be the place that Von Ryan is willing to meet with you."

"So what? We're going to be shot at down here?"

"There is always that possibility. However, we will be travelling with a military convoy. They will do their best to keep us safe."

"That's reassuring."

Julian wished that Charles hadn't told him that. It only made him feel more trepidation. His plan would all be for naught if they got killed before he even got to Von Ryan.

After breakfast, they were on their way. They travelled with a convoy of military wagons, which looked like antique trucks to Julian. They were slow and temperamental but seemed to manage the rough terrain well enough. Inside the trucks, Julian could hardly describe the accommodations as luxurious. In the back where he sat with Charles, there were long benches that lined each of the walls. There was no cushioning on the wall, so they had to rest upon metal. The benches were long slabs of steel with legs welded into the bottom of the truck. A wire mesh grid separated them from the driver and passenger seats. There was a rack of guns hanging on the mire mesh, so if they were under attack, at least he could grab one of the guns to defend himself.

The ride was bumpy, and it did not take long for Julian's back to ache. The only source of entertainment was Charles and his constant monologue on the politics and history of this plane. By this point, Julian figured he knew everything that had happened in this world for the past two hundred years. The only useful aspect of the monologue was his information that he provided about Jarvis Dawson,

"Tell me more about him," Julian said. "Do you know him?"

"We've met a time or two. He's a good fellow. He's genuine in his beliefs and has dedicated his life to improving the lives of others. He hails from a prominent family, but instead of the pursuit of wealth, Jarvis has instead chosen a path of philanthropy. Before the war, he was involved in a half-dozen philanthropic organizations, and was very vital in the emancipation of slaves from some of the lower countries. He was vital in the decimation of slave trade, which still exists, but is not nearly as prevalent as it had been."

By this point, he felt as if he knew Jarvis fairly well and actually liked the guy, a distinct improvement from his feeling toward some of Julian's other shades.

Four men with dark complexions and mean scowls sat on the bench opposite them. They had little to say, either to Julian and Charles or each other. One of them wore an eyepatch and kept staring at Julian as if all the bad shit that was happening to him with this war was somehow Julian's fault.

They had been driving for almost an hour when the driver hit the brakes, turned toward them, and began yelling a series of expletives in Spanish. Apparently, this was the command for the men to act, since they grabbed guns from the rack.

Julian turned to Charles. "What's going on?"

"Nothing good I'm afraid."

Someone began opening fire on their truck.

The men on the other bench opened the rear door, poured out, and began firing their weapons.

"Now what?" Julian asked.

For the first time, Charles lost all composure and hid underneath the bench. "Take cover."

After hearing rounds ping off the truck, that was the last place Julian wanted to be. If he stayed, he would be a sitting duck. He grabbed a rifle from the rack. He had done quite a bit of hunting in his youth, but it had been nearly a decade since he had gone hunting with his father and uncle. Not to mention, he had no idea if these guns would be the same as the ones he had used back then. There was no use worrying about it now. He exited the truck and into the fire.

CHAPTER XLII

The first thing Julian did was survey the situation. There were four military wagons in his caravan. He anticipated similar vehicles from whoever was shooting at them, but there were none on the road. Instead, a host of armed guerrillas fired at them from the bush at the side of the road.

Shots flew from every direction. It was hard to tell where the enemy combatants were situated. He took cover behind a wheel of the military wagon. He couldn't tell who had the more soldiers on their side—his group or the guerrillas.

One of the men from his military wagon, who stood not more than ten feet from him, took a bullet to the neck. Blood spouted from it like a fountain. The man jerked back and fell to the ground.

Julian's heart drummed faster. Although he had seen his share of death since his adventures in plane travel with the Game Master, this was way too real and too close for his liking.

An enemy combatant, presumably the one who just killed the man near him, emerged from behind the truck. Just as the guerrilla was leveling his gun—a long gun like the one Julian had—he pulled the trigger of his own rifle. From point blank range, there was no way he could miss, and the shot took the guerrilla in the middle of the chest.

Julian crawled toward the guerrilla and was about to put another bullet into him, but his dead eyes indicated that was unnecessary.

The surrounding area was a shooting gallery. Julian was having a hard time telling who was winning this skirmish. He shuddered at the sound of more vehicles coming in his direction. "Shit." The opposition had reinforcements coming. Julian was about to start firing at the newcomers when he saw Cutter driving one of the vehicles—a military wagon even larger than the one he was travelling in.

A swarm of soldiers emptied out of the military wagon and opened fire on the guerrillas. It did not take long for the guerrillas to go into full retreat mode as they toppled like dominoes. The fighting did not last long after that, and the enemy escaped into the bush. Cutter and his people did not linger, leaving just after the fighting died down.

This created a great deal of confusion. Julian understood a bit of what the soldiers were saying in Spanish. From what he gathered, they had no idea who had assisted them, and Julian wasn't about to clue them in. They seemed to conclude that it must have been their own people patrolling the area.

About twenty minutes after the fighting had ceased and the enemy combatants had fled, Julian was back in the military wagon as they prepared to depart. The attitudes of those sharing the opposite bench, even the soldier with the eye-patch, changed dramatically. Instead of looking at him with suspicion and derision, he was one of them now. They slapped him on the back and patted him on the head. He wasn't sure what they were saying, but it seemed as if they were reliving the combat they had just been though, and every once in a while, they would point at him and nod their heads.

Julian leaned over toward Charles. "What are they saying?"

"Apparently, you acquitted yourself quite well out there. They are saying that you are much fiercer than you look. What happened?"

Julian gave him a brief accounting of the events, excluding any mention of Cutter.

"They weren't sure who came out to help them, but whoever it was, their assistance was much needed and appreciated," Charles said. "I, for one, am glad the fighting is over. That was quite a scary scene."

Julian rolled his eyes. How would this clown know? It's not like he was out there when the battle was raging. He had only come out of the rear of the wagon well after the shooting had stopped, and the opposition had retreated.

He was glad that the men on the opposite bench had a more favorable opinion of him. There was no telling if that might come in handy. Despite the fact that a few of them had been killed, their general attitude was jocular and upbeat. He had never served in a military unit, so he could not relate.

With the excessive break in the action, he had no idea how much they had deviated from their timeline. He wasn't overly concerned because he knew for certain Cutter and his people were here and would be there to fulfill his end of the bargain. Now, all he had to do was survive the rest of this trip in order to get to his meeting with Von Ryan.

"So, what do I do when we get there?" Julian asked. "We haven't really gone over that part."

"There's not much to go over. When you meet with Von Ryan, you will exchange pleasantries, and he will take you to the location of the meeting. At that point, I will contact the Master of Key's people, and they will intercept Von Ryan and bring him to meet with the Master."

That part was still unclear. Von Ryan did not want to have this clandestine affair at the place in El Santo del Sol that Charles had selected. Instead, they would travel elsewhere. When Charles had pressed Von Ryan's aid on the location, he had told Charles it was a secure location nearby.

"Well, what do I say to him while we are travelling to this undisclosed location?"

"There is an even chance that you won't even be travelling in the same wagon, assuming that is the mode of transport that he would select to reach the destination," Charles said.

"Fine, but if I do travel with him in whatever mode of transport he chooses, what do I do then? I'm not exactly well-versed in dealing with megalomaniac rulers." That wasn't entirely true. He'd had a bit of experience with that very thing in recent times.

Charles waved his hand. "Just make small talk."

"Small talk? Seriously? That's the best you can come up with?"

"He wouldn't expect any serious negotiations to occur until you arrive at the designated location, so until then engage him in small talk. And you will never get to the point of any actual negotiation. The intercept will happen before then."

Julian frowned. "What if he starts talking about things I'm not familiar with?"

"Von Ryan most likely has never met Jarvis Dawson. At the very least, he would be nothing more than a passing acquaintance. It's not like he is a good friend of Jarvis and would have intimate knowledge of him. At any rate, there is no way he would know any more about Jarvis than you do with all of the information I have given you."

"Yeah, but I've only been living in this plane for less than a week. I could be either exposed as a fraud or, at the very least, an idiot who doesn't have a clue as to what's going on."

"I'm confident that you'll manage."

Julian gave a low growl but did not reply.

"I don't understand why you are so concerned. You just blew up these Bushmen to bits from what I understand. Surely, that's a more terrifying experience than talking about the state of affairs of this place with Von Ryan. By now, you should be well-versed with what's going on here. We've certainly had our share of conversations on the matter. I haven't been spouting off about the current state of the world just because I like to hear myself speak. I have been doing it so that it would be fully engrained in your thick cranium when you needed it."

Julian rolled his eyes. "And here I thought you were just thoroughly trying to annoy me."

The bumpy ride became smoother. Without being able to see the outside, Julian discerned that they were getting out of the less developed area and approaching something more modern and urban.

"We should be arriving at our destination in just a few minutes," Charles said. "Are you ready?"

Julian nodded, despite the fact that his stomach was roiling and his head and back ached. Although he was anxious about what was to come, he wanted to get this over with.

Although the drive did not last much longer, it still felt like forever to Julian. Various scenarios ran though his head. Most of them involved Von Ryan discovering he was an imposter and killing him on the spot, even though it was highly improbable that Von Ryan would even know how to realize that Julian wasn't who he purported to be, let alone uncover the truth.

When they got out of the military vehicle, Charles brushed dirt off Julian's suit. "You're all disheveled. You look as if you have been playing in the mud." When he tried to fix his hair, Julian drew the line at that and told him he would be fine.

"We're in the middle of a war. I'm sure Von Ryan will understand."

"I suppose you're right," Charles said. "He does favor the use of a military commander's uniform. And it's not like he doesn't have blood on his hands. He's very active in putting down those that oppose him."

"That's reassuring."

Their military escort took them to what could only be described as a skyscraper by the standards of this plane. There were other tall buildings, but the rest looked insignificant in comparison to this one.

"This was built about ten years before the war started," Charles said. "It was supposed to be the new Community of Countries Center, a place where representatives of various nations could congregate, discuss, and resolve the most pertinent issues of the day.

The level of distrust that started this war ultimately brought down the Community of Countries before it ever got off the ground. The building still stands, but it is now used by various business enterprises to execute commerce."

As they walked through the building's lobby, they encountered mostly well-dressed men in tailored suits. Some of the men were Caucasian, but most looked Latino. This building was a striking contrast to the jungle he had just traveled though. One would hardly think that world was less than an hour's drive from here.

He and Charles entered a primitive looking elevator. It was small and narrow and had an attendant who sat at the front. There wasn't enough room for their entire military escort, so only one armed guard entered with them. The others walked up the stairs that stood to the right of the elevator.

There was little room to move inside of the elevator. It was slow and cranky, working its way against gravity as if it held a grudge. There was an opening to the rear of the elevator that allowed Julian to see it creeping upward. He had been in glass elevators before, but this was more disconcerting than any elevator he had ever ridden.

A fraction of an eternity passed by the time they reached their destination. He followed Charles out of the elevator. Their armed guards stood waiting for them. Apparently, walking was the quicker mode of travel.

Julian's pulse quickened. It was hard for him to not be intimidated by the man he was about to meet. He had heard so much about him, and none of it was good. He was a tyrant, a ruthless conqueror, and a cold-blooded killer. He had seen videos of what the man's people had done—horrid acts of violence and depravity that had frightened him to his core. And now he was going to see the man for himself.

CHAPTER XLIII

On the trip to El Santo Del Sol, Julian had contemplated at length the best way to approach an authoritarian dictator who was hell-bent on conquering the world. He decided the best approach was to use flattery. Treating him as an equal wouldn't suffice. He probably thought of himself as a god. What self-respecting megalomaniac wouldn't enjoy hearing about his awesomeness?

Von Ryan was shorter than he expected. Julian was no giant, but he still had about five inches on the dictator of Rotgard. Von Ryan had flaming red hair and a handlebar mustache. His hair was longer than Julian would have expected for a world leader, and it rested just above his shoulders.

Julian smiled as he approached. "Chairman Von Ryan, it is a pleasure to meet with you on this most auspicious of occasions. I have been looking forward to it."

Von Ryan shook his hand then unexpectedly pulled Julian into a bear hug. Julian found this odd since the dictator was not a friend of Jarvis Dawson, and Charles wasn't even sure they had met. Perhaps this was the way Von Ryan greeted all his allies. "It is good to meet you. I hope your trip was well."

Von Ryan's English was rough to understand. Charles had told him earlier that he would be using a translator. Julian assumed that was the thick-necked man standing next to him.

"The trip was not without its difficulties. We came under a bit of fire, but as you can see, we are here in one piece."

Von Ryan slapped him on the shoulder. "Yes. Yes. One piece. I see." Von Ryan spoke in German to the translator. Julian knew just enough German that he could pick up some of what he was saying, but not enough to carry on a full conversation without the presence of the translator.

The translator said, "Chairman Von Ryan would like to thank you for your diligence in making your journey. He is well aware of the dangers of travelling in El Santo Del Sol's countryside."

Julian nodded. "I am a great admirer of Chairman Von Ryan. I respect his idea of a new world order and have been working diligently behind the scenes to convince those in my government that it would be in our best interest to work with the Chairman instead of fighting him. Unfortunately, those currently in power seem unwilling to listen to reason and logic."

This time it was Charles who translated. Julian didn't realize that Charles knew German. Perhaps this was the etiquette on this plane. Each party was supposed to provide their own translator.

After Von Ryan spoke, the thick-necked translator said, "The world has changed, and those that cannot accept change will cease to exist. Chairman Von Ryan has a gift for you. He understands that you share an interest in the prominent Rotgardian philosopher Helmut Schmidt. This is a copy of his latest work."

The translator handed him a soft pouch. Inside was a hardback copy of a book. The title of the book was "On Wings of Angels". The title suggested a book of fiction, but he took the dictator's word that it was a work of philosophy.

He opened the book and saw the signature of the author.

Holy Shit!

Here was the most powerful and dangerous person on this plane giving him a gift, and he did not have anything to reciprocate.

Just when he was about to hyperventilate and lose it, Charles produced a pouch of his own. He handed it to Julian.

"That was very kind of you. He is my favorite philosopher, and I have not read his latest work. And this gift is for you." At least he hoped it was a gift. Although he was grateful that Charles was prepared for this eventuality, Julian wished he had informed him that he had a gift ready to give the Chairman.

Von Ryan opened the soft cloth wrapping and inside found a dagger made of ivory. It was ornately carved with letters that looked as if it could have been written in an ancient language. The dagger also had finely carved symbols. He saw what looked like the sun, a snake, and an eye inside of a triangle.

The smile on Von Ryan's face indicated his approval. He spoke to his translator, who said, "This is a most generous and thoughtful gift. I will display it in my headquarters in Rotgard."

Julian remembered Charles talking about Von Ryan's fondness for weapons of war. He had a large collection of pistols, rifles, and swords.

Von Ryan spoke once more, and the translator said, "I would like to express my sincere condolences about the death of your wife and your young daughter."

Julian froze. The horror of the situation hit him like a two-ton sledgehammer. He knew he was breaking character but couldn't help but turn and glare at Charles. Why hadn't the son of a bitch said anything about that? This was hardly the time to find out about Jarvis's misfortune. He had a newfound empathy toward his shade. That must have been devastating for him. He could only imagine what it would be like losing Natalie and Nancy.

Through the translator, Von Ryan said, "This war has taken a toll on all of us. Yours was an especially heavy price to pay. By working together, I hope to avoid more of these tragedies."

"Thank you," Julian said. "It has been a trying time. These last few months, in particular, have been some of the most difficult of my life."

Von Ryan put his hand on Julian's shoulder. "We go to do serious talk now. We travel together."

Julian, Charles, Von Ryan, and the thick-necked translator got in the most luxurious vehicle he had seen during his time in this plane. It had leather seats, wood panels, a roomy interior, and a ride that could justifiably be described as plush and comfortable.

He sat in the back seat of the vehicle. The translator sat between he and Von Ryan. Charles sat in the front seat, across from the driver. During the ride, Von Ryan spoke of childhood vacations spent in the same Silver Isles that Charles hailed from. He also spoke about a new pet Rottweiler he had been training.

The truth was that Von Ryan came off as friendly and affable in a one-on-one situation. This was hardly what he had been expecting. He thought he would be meeting Satan incarnate. He did his best not to temper his earlier feelings about the dictator. The videos Cutter had shown him were appalling. What he had read about Von Ryan clearly showed him to be a tyrannical dictator, if not a madman. Not to mention, this was his chance to finally get home and out of the clutches of the Game Master. There was no turning back now.

The drive was longer than Julian had anticipated. Von Ryan seemed relaxed during the trip. With his arms spread out and his head tilted back, he had the appearance of someone going to a ball game rather than someone having a discussion with ramifications to the fate of his planet. If he suspected betrayal, he certainly didn't show it. Perhaps he was confident in his own security—they did have two vehicles following them, or he had confidence that Jarvis Dawson was genuine in his effort to negotiate with him.

The vehicle came to a stop nearly a half hour after the trip began. Von Ryan had been talking nearly the entire time, and Julian only had to add the occasional comment, so it had not been an overly taxing experience. The driver parked on the dirt alongside a narrow road. To their right was a white building that could best be described as nondescript.

As they exited the car, Julian's heart raced. He had no idea what to expect. He did not know if Cutter would make his move here or if it would be while they were inside the building, or perhaps afterward.

The translator explained that this was a safe house used by high-ranking members of the Rotgardian government. He heard several vehicles coming in their direction. Julian wasn't sure whether or not he should run for cover. Moments later, he did when the bullets started flying.

CHAPTER XLIV

About twenty to thirty men and women poured out of cargo vans and unleashed hellfire on Von Ryan's security detail. It was like the shootout at the OK Corral.

Charles grabbed his arm. "Inside the building. Quick!"

Julian hesitated, scanning the crowd to find Cutter. It was hard to see much of anybody since those that had emerged from the vans were taking cover behind them. Von Ryan's guards had already suffered heavy casualties in this brief skirmish, and it was easy to tell which way this battle was going.

Charles tugged at him. "I know you got yourself in the middle of the fight last time and fancy yourself as some sort of hero, but now is not the time!"

Von Ryan turned to them and shouted in German.

"What did he say?" Julian asked.

"He said go inside the house," Charles replied. "They have reinforcements nearby."

This time he did go inside with Charles, but not before he took a rifle from a dead Rotgardian. As the fighting continued, the four of them entered the drab white house.

Once inside, Von Ryan locked the deadbolt behind them. "Safe in here. There is secure room downstairs."

The shooting had died down outside, which meant Cutter's forces must have overtaken the Rotgardian guards.

Charles's voice was on the verge of panic. "They're going to storm this place and take us before long."

Von Ryan raised his hand. "Troops twenty minutes away. I call downstairs on radio. We safe there. It is bunker."

Julian shook his head, raised his rifle, and pointed it at the dictator's head. "You'll do no such thing. In fact, we're all going outside."

Charles's eyes went wide. "What do you think you're doing?"

The thick-necked translator was about to make a move on Julian until he gave him a sharp look, keeping his finger pressed against the trigger and the gun against Von Ryan's temple. "Don't even think about it. I have no problem killing this nasty son of a bitch right here and now."

He and Cutter had discussed this possibility, and Cutter had suggested Julian take out Von Ryan. Julian did not want to be the trigger man, although if he didn't see an alternative, he agreed to kill the dictator. After killing before, the task no longer seemed so daunting, and there was no doubt in his mind that Von Ryan deserved to die.

"I don't understand," Charles said. "Why are you doing this?"

"I have no interest in delivering this evil piece of shit to your Master of Keys," Julian said. "I'm not going to contribute to the destruction of your world, and I'm not going to let the Game Master have his way. I'm not going to be a pawn in his schemes anymore. Sorry, Charles, but I made a better deal."

Von Ryan snarled at him, a look of pure hatred in his eyes, but with the barrel of the gun pressed against his head, he had no choice but to comply or wind up six feet under staring up at the daisies.

"You traitor scum," Von Ryan said.

Julian pushed the dictator forward. "Shut the hell up. I'm not even Jarvis Dawson, you fool. And I can't imagine he would ever be a party to helping you in your quest for world domination. Now, let's all move forward, nice, quietly, and orderly. There are some folks out there, one of whom happens to be a friend of mine, that are interested in chatting with you. Do the right thing and I won't kill you."

Von Ryan muttered what Julian thought were German curses through gritted teeth, yet still walked forward.

"Open the door, Charles. And you…" Julian glanced at the translator. "You go out first. Charles, you follow him. Von Ryan and I will exit last."

Julian thought his voice held some assurance. He was getting better at these intense, high-risk situations. He had no idea how this thing was going to break, but at least he was under control. If Von Ryan or the translator made a move…well, he hoped it wouldn't come to that.

"Who the hell do you even know in this plane? You have been here for less than a week?" Charles asked.

Julian did not answer.

"And how could you possibly have been able to arrange this?"

Julian almost felt bad for Charles. He seemed completely and utterly flabbergasted. Here was a guy who thought he was always the smartest guy in the room and had all the answers. He was starting to find out the hard way that wasn't true.

"I have a friend who is a traveler," Julian replied.

Charles's face scrunched up. "A traveler? What in the devil is that?"

"Not sure if you're familiar with the term, but it means he can travel from plane to plane. A special talent of his." Julian smiled. He couldn't help it, but he was enjoying rubbing this smug bastard's nose in the situation just a little too much. "With all of your preparation, deliberation, and pontification, you didn't cover that angle? I guess not. That's very disappointing, Charles."

Charles asked, "Do you have any idea just how powerful the Master of Keys is? You are like a pesky fly to him, and he is a giant in comparison to you."

Julian raised his brows. "Really? He's shorter than that little jockey of a pilot you had flying our aeroship."

"I'm speaking figuratively," Charles said.

"Yes. He crush you," Von Ryan said.

"I may be a pesky fly, but I'm one that just might bite him in the ass."

They walked outside in the order Julian had told them to. When they did, a swarm of soldiers were pointing guns at them. Cutter stepped forward. "At ease. The situation is under control."

A half-dozen soldiers stepped forward and seized Von Ryan. Their treatment of the dictator was anything but gentle.

Cutter walked up to Julian and put his hand on his shoulder. "Well done, my friend."

"I don't want to count my chickens before they're hatched. This is only the first phase of the plan. I have a feeling the next one is going to be even harder to pull off."

Cutter shrugged. "Perhaps. But the plan is sound, and with some luck, it will work."

Julian closed his eyes. He didn't want to get his hopes up. Chances were, it would all go up in flames.

"How about we talk to your good buddy, Charles?"

Julian nodded.

Two women wearing masks covering most of their face held Charles at gun point. Most of the people with Cutter were Latino or of Caribbean decent. The group seemed to have doubled in size compared to the initial wave that had been shooting it out with Von Ryan's guards.

Charles wore a mean scowl as they approached. "Who the devil is this? Is this your friend, the traveler?"

"I'm Cutter, and I am indeed a traveler, which means I can visit places like your God-forsaken world, but I don't have to stay."

"Do you understand who you're crossing?" Charles asked. "Do you understand just how powerful the Master of Keys is?"

"Sure do," Cutter replied. "I've been dealing with him for a long, long time. I know all about him. The little bastard screwed me over. Now it's time for me and Julian to do the screwing."

"Hmph. All you two will be doing is digging an early grave. So, what are you going to do with me now? Kill me?"

"Of course we're not going to kill you," Julian said. "We need your help. In fact, you're vital to our plans."

Charles crossed his arms. "I have no interest in helping you."

"You haven't even heard what we want you to do," Julian said.

"What do you want me to do?" Charles asked.

"Take me to the Game Master like you would have done had I actually fulfilled my end of the bargain and delivered Von Ryan to his people."

"He'll kill me if I try to deceive him," Charles said.

"I don't think you're going to have to worry about him for much longer," Julian said.

"Well, I won't do it," Charles said. "He's essential for my career and what I am trying to accomplish here."

Cutter put his arm around the politician from the Silver Isles. "Charles, you don't have much of a choice. If you don't go along with the plan, we'll kill Von Ryan."

"You mean, you weren't going to kill him?" Charles asked.

"No," Cutter replied. "The plan is to use him as a bargaining chip. He's worth more to us alive than dead. We don't want him to be a martyr for his obscene cause. Instead, we're going to use him to broker a peace agreement and hopefully, an end to this war."

That was a lie, but Cutter stated it convincingly. Von Ryan wouldn't live to see tomorrow. Good riddance, as far as he was concerned. The look on Charles's face showed his own skepticism.

Nobody said anything for a time. Charles folded his arms. His brow was furrowed, giving him the look of a professor focusing on a task with intense concentration. "I would like to see my nation align with Rotgard and Von Ryan, but my life is at stake as well, for surely the Master of Keys will kill me if I cross him."

"Like I said, you won't have to deal with the Master of Keys for much longer," Julian said. "We're going to kill him."

"I don't believe you," Charles said.

Cutter leaned in closer to Charles. "In that case, let me sweeten the pot for you. If you don't do as we say, you'll give me no choice but to kill you. You strike me as someone who's number one priority is saving his own skin."

"In that case, you don't understand me at all. And you are nothing but thugs," Charles said.

Julian's lips flared. "Who are you calling thugs? You're trying to get in bed with Von Ryan, and you're a tool for the Game Master. Those two are the biggest thugs I've ever met. Charles, you seriously need to reassess your outlook on life."

Charles did not reply. Perhaps he understood the absurdity of his statement. At least Julian hoped so.

"So, what's it going to be?" Cutter asked.

"I don't appear to have a choice, as you so rudely pointed out to me. I will help you with your folly, even though I am certain it will not work."

"Maybe, we'll surprise you," Cutter said. "You never know."

"Good choice, Charles. I don't want to see you get hurt. I think you're a decent guy, just seriously misguided."

Charles stammered. "What do you know about the state of affairs here? You have been here for less than a week. Just because this ruffian gave you his perspective on the way things are around here; it doesn't make it so. I have been trying to teach you about the harsh reality that we are facing, and it is more than apparent that you haven't listened."

"I have listened and have come to my own conclusions," Julian said. "And I considered the history of my plane. We also had a maniacal leader who tried to take over the world. His name was Adolf Hitler. Fortunately, there were some brave people back then who had the courage and tenacity to stop him. I'm doing my part to stop Von Ryan before he does irreparable damage to this plane."

Cutter nodded. "Well said, Julian. We don't have time to waste. Me, you, and your good friend, Charles, are going to pay the Game Master a visit."

CHAPTER XLV

Charles delivered the message to the Game Master to let him know they had delivered Von Ryan to his people and were in route to see him. Julian and Cutter were with him when he made the call on the old-fashioned telephone. He delivered the message clearly, coherently, and without any attempts at deception.

There was no way of telling if the Game Master would be able to track them. Julian didn't see any reason for him to suspect foul play, so it was unlikely that he would check the veracity of their story. Charles found that scenario to be unlikely as well.

A convoy of vehicles followed them at a distance. The vehicles were filled with Cutter's soldiers, who were well armed with guns, rifles, and explosives.

Perhaps resigned to his fate, Charles seemed cheerier. "You do realize this little plot of yours is doomed to fail. You think you can outsmart the Master of Keys, but I assure you that you can't. You won't be the first who attempted to thwart him."

They were all in the back seat of a roomy wagon. It wasn't quite as plush as the one they had ridden in with Von Ryan, but it was still a comfortable ride.

"We're smart and highly motivated fellows," Cutter said. "We just might be able to thwart him."

"So, how did you know where we were going to be?" Julian asked. "I never had a chance to pass a message on to you."

Cutter pulled out a small, black device. "I inserted a transponder onto the vehicle in order to track it."

Charles peered at the transponder with a look of intense concentration. "What is that and how does it work?"

Julian's brow furrowed. "But don't you need satellites and GPS technology for that?"

"This isn't GPS at all, and it's not from your home plane. The device emits radio waves, and the receiver detects the radio waves."

"I should have realized you would have something up your sleeve."

"We were following you since you got in the wagon. And, as you could see, we were prepared for an assault."

"You are nothing but bandits and gangsters," Charles said.

"That's rich considering who you work with." Cutter shook his head. "I know you're well-intentioned, but you're on the wrong side, my man. Von Ryan is a vicious sadist. You think you'll be safe because your country is on the winning side of this war. How long will that last? Von Ryan wants it all. He might give the Silver Isles and the Unified States a brief reprieve, but it won't last. He's like a wolf stalking the hen houses. Eventually, he'll take your countries as well. Removing Von Ryan from power and killing the Master of Keys is your best opportunity for a safe future for you and your people. If you're being honest with yourself, you know I'm right."

For once, Charles didn't say anything.

Julian said, "We need to have a plan for when we see the Game Master."

They spent the next fifteen minutes devising a plan of action for their arrival at what Charles described as an abandoned factory that the Game Master and his people had commandeered. Surprisingly, Charles was actively involved in the discussion and even made helpful suggestions. Perhaps he was starting to realize the errors of his ways. It was just as likely that he would betray them, but Julian was willing to give him the benefit of the doubt.

When they were five minutes from the destination, Cutter instructed the diver to pull over. He would be going in one of the other vehicles trailing them. Julian and Charles would go alone.

Before exiting, Cutter put his hand on Charles's shoulder. "Don't even think about freelancing and not playing your part in this. I can't predict what's going to happen, but I can assure you this much, if you don't play along you won't make it out alive."

They continued driving to the factory. Julian looked back several times for the other vehicles that were part of their caravan. Eventually, they faded from view. The transponder made it unnecessary to be in such close proximity. His throat turned dry and his heart thumped. The adrenaline rush from the shootout had worn out, and all he felt now was emptiness. One way or the other, this would all be over soon. He longed to see his wife and daughter again and prayed that he would.

"When we get inside, act natural," Julian said. "He won't have any reason to suspect that Von Ryan hasn't been delivered to his people unless we betray this fact."

"I am a seasoned politician," Charles said. "You need not worry about me. Acting is part of the course. I will be fine. Worry about yourself."

Julian had been doing nothing but acting since taking on the various roles of his shades. He had no formal training, nor did he lie for a living like Charles, but he thought he was capable of doing the job.

They parked in a lot that had seen better days. Massive chunks of asphalt had been torn from the ground. The perimeter was surrounded by barbed wire fence. There were about a dozen military vehicles inside the lot, scattered throughout the patches of unscathed asphalt. Their driver, a woman who spoke no English, dropped them off near the entrance of the building.

"Are you ready for this?" Julian asked.

"Indeed I am," Charles replied. "And I give you my word that I will not try to undermine you. I am quite interested in learning if you are as resourceful as you think. If I were a wagering man, I would place my bet on the Master of Keys prevailing."

"Well, I look forward to proving you wrong," Julian said.

They approached the armed guard.

Charles pulled out papers and handed them to the guard, a large, scary looking Latino with an eyepatch. "Charles Whitfield here to see MK. I have the package."

Julian could only assume he was the package.

The guard looked over the papers and handed it back to Charles. He grunted and nodded for them to go through.

"Can that guard even read or understand English?"

Charles shrugged. "Whether he can or cannot is not my concern. Most of it is the presentation. If you sound confident and appear as if you belong, most people won't question you."

The interior of the building was nothing like the exterior, which could accurately be described as a rotting carcass. He found screens and monitors that did not belong to this time and place. Cables and wires ran along the walls and ceiling. Some sort of robotic device whose base was a series of wheels wrapped in rubber that reminded him of the bottom of an armored tank wheeled past him and through an open door.

Charles stared, wide-eyed at the tech. "Fascinating."

"Stop gaping. Didn't you say how important it is to look as if you belong?"

Charles straightened his tie. "True."

"So where exactly is the Master of Keys?"

"He provided me instructions to proceed to the fifth floor of this facility. We are to take the lift at the left of the lobby and down the hall."

Charles walked in that direction, and Julian followed. Julian was wearing a tracking device that Cutter had provided him with. He and Charles were to approach the Game Master as if the job had been completed and he was ready to go home. Cutter and his people would then invade and breach the facility. Julian would have liked to plot this part of the plan in greater detail, but they ran out of time. He took some solace in the knowledge that Cutter's soldiers had performed admirably thus far.

There was another armed guard at the entrance to the elevator. This one was smaller and thinner, but he carried what looked like a machine gun, so Julian wasn't going to make any sudden or threatening actions. Charles introduced himself and handed a paper to the guard. He scrutinized it closely, then told them to follow him to a room, where he picked up an antiquated looking telephone and made a call. Given some of the advanced technology that existed in this factory, Julian was surprised that this guard wasn't equipped with something more technologically advanced, like a two-way radio.

The guard put the phone receiver back in its holder. "You are expected upstairs. I will escort you."

Julian and Charles followed the guard. He tried to keep his breathing and heart rate under control. Adrenaline could serve well in life and death situations, but now he needed to be composed and in control.

They got into the lift, which was far sleeker and more modern that the last one he had been on. Once inside, Julian's legs began to shake. He had to get under control. He could not meet the Game Master like this.

"Experiencing jitters?" Charles smirked.

"I'm fine." The lie even sounded hollow to him. He was not fine. It was distinctly possible that he was going to his death.

When they exited the lift, a striking woman holding a machine gun greeted them. She had Eurasian features and long, dark hair.

Charles's face went white. He looked as if he was going to soil his pants.

Julian stepped past Charles. "We're here to see the Master of Keys."

"And you are?" the woman asked him.

"I'm Julian Dawson."

The woman did not seem impressed. "Give me your weapon."

"I'd rather keep it."

The woman snarled. "And I don't give a damn what you want. Give me your weapon or I'll shoot you."

Julian gritted his teeth. He didn't want to give up his firearm but didn't see an alternative. He pulled out the pistol and handed it to her. She tucked it away.

"You might want to put that down," Julian said. "I just delivered Von Ryan to your boss's people less than an hour ago. He owes me a ticket home, and I fully intend on cashing in."

Keeping her machine gun raised, she motioned for them to follow her.

Charles whispered, "Her name is Chloe. She's an assassin of serious repute. Rumor has it that she has over a hundred kills in her resume."

"Good to know," Julian said.

"I don't know about you, but I've had enough guns for one day," Charles said.

"And I wish I had one right now," Julian said.

They walked down a long hallway with white walls. Someone grabbed Julian's leg. He gasped and jumped away from the gripping hand. "What the hell?"

The hand belonged to an older man. He was bleeding from a nasty head wound. Julian nearly vomited when he saw that the man's left arm was partially severed.

Without hesitation, Chloe shot him in the head.

Charles fell back and nearly fainted. Julian had to catch him before he crashed onto the tiled floor.

"Was that absolutely necessary, for Christ's sake?" Julian asked.

Chloe glared at him and kept walking.

More than ever, Julian wanted to be done with this madness. The fear he had felt on the elevator was gone. He was ready for this. He was going to kill the Game Master.

Julian felt a surge of pure hatred flood through him when he saw the Game Master surrounded by a trio of men in combat fatigues walking in his direction.

The Game Master wore a wide smile. "Ah, Julian, so good to see you again. By your presence, I take it that you have completed your mission."

CHAPTER XLVI

This was the proverbial moment of truth to see if Charles would be true to his word or if he would turn on Julian. There was nothing stopping Charles from revealing the truth, but despite that, he had the distinct impression that Charles had changed his mind in the past few hours about the war and those he served. His demeanor, body language, and level of enthusiasm had changed when they were in the wagon driving to this location. Julian had gotten to know the man quite well in the past week. He was intelligent and calculating, and must have been playing out the scenarios and percentages in his head. He also believed Charles was genuine in his desire to do what was best for his people. And now, helping Julian, was what was best for his people. It was a gut instinct, but he had faith in the man.

Charles cleared his throat. "Yes. Everything today went as planned. Chairman Von Ryan has been safely delivered and is waiting to speak to you."

The Game Master clapped his hands and held them together. "Now, that is the outcome I was looking for. There is no better story, Julian, than one of redemption. You failed me before, but with the right incentive, I knew you would complete this task. I salute you on a job well done. Now, follow me. I will call to verify that our friend Von Ryan is in safe hands, and then we will see about getting you home."

Julian tried not to betray any emotion but he silently cursed under his breath. He felt intense pressure in his chest. The jig was up. When he called, he would find out that nothing had happened according to the original plan. He almost expected Charles to blurt out that this was all a ruse, but he did not say a word. Instead, he trudged along the hallway just as Julian did.

When the Game Master opened a door, Julian half-expected to see people being tortured, but instead, they entered a room that was large enough to be a small sized factory floor and seemed ordinary other than a computer and tablet that were ridiculously out of place here sitting on a table.

"So, how was my friend, the Chairman?" the Game Master asked.

"He was actually quite charming," Julian replied. "He wasn't the evil monster I anticipated. I mean, he is an evil monster, but he didn't present himself that way in person. I found him to be personable and engaging."

The Game Master gave him a sharp stare. "So quick to judge. Things are not always as they seem in your narrow understanding of the world. You don't have all the answers."

"Perhaps I don't, but I can still decipher right from wrong, good from evil. Those are universal truths, and as usual, you are on the side of evil."

"You really are an irritating individual. Mr. Dawson, I believe that I will be glad to no longer have to deal with you…for now anyway." The Game Master grinned. "Although, I imagine I will need your services again at some point in the future. I think we both require a bit of distance and a cooling off period. All the same, you have been quite useful. Now, I will have a chat with Chairman Von Ryan. He has been rather disobedient of late."

Julian had to stall for time for Cutter to enact the plan. Once the

Game Master made the call, it would all be over.

"This is going to be the last time that I do an assignment for you. Ever." Julian approached the Game Master, but Chloe stepped in his path and pointed her gun at him. Julian did his best to act as if she didn't intimidate him, although inside he was quivering.

"And what gave you this silly notion that you can dictate terms to me?" the Game Master asked. "Perhaps you don't understand the precarious position you're in."

"Then why don't you spell it out for me," Julian said.

"Very well. This is the reality of your situation. You can only get what you desire—to get home to your family—with my assistance. When you are at home, I may, from time to time, require your services again. You are in no position to deny these requests, because I can and will hurt those you hold dear. I have people who do my bidding, who I pay handsomely, who have no qualms doing very bad things to a pretty wife and an adorable daughter."

Charles, who had been quiet in the background, stepped forward. "Look, we are all reasonable people here. I don't think these threats and hard stances are productive. Perhaps, we can come to an agreement that if Julian cannot refuse the assignment, at least you will give him sufficient time to put his affairs in order prior to him having to leave. Furthermore, as this type of assignment may put undue hardship upon him and his family, that he will be given sufficient compensation for his time and efforts."

"Naturally, I would have no problem with providing compensation," the Game Master said. "I certainly have more than my share of men and women on my payroll, and none of them complain about not being properly compensated. As for the timing, I can possibly work with him depending on the time sensitivity of a given project."

"It's not just that," Julian said. "Your schemes are inherently evil, and I don't want to be involved in them. They invariably wind up with people dying, and oftentimes the ones who die are innocent."

"Then perhaps we can come to an agreement that if Julian finds the assignment truly detestable—let's say if it involves assassination or people perishing at a large scale—then he would have the right to refuse a given assignment."

The Game Master started to object until Charles put up a finger. "You do have to admit that a willing participant will far more likely yield the results you desire. Previously, you mentioned that he had sabotaged an assignment. You want results. Well, the best chance to get those results isn't through threats and coercion, but buy in."

The Game Master turned toward Charles. "He has no choice in the matter. I have all the leverage in this relationship."

"Indeed you do," Charles said. "But often a hammer is not the most appropriate tool to use when constructing something. A relationship of mutual trust is often most beneficial. Now in our dealings, I know that your motives are genuine, and thus we have worked together on mutually beneficial projects."

They went on for some time. Charles was at his pontificating best, making an argument as if he were in parliament. It was truly a sight to behold. Julian had never appreciated until this moment just how superb he was at his job as a politician. Meanwhile, the Game Master made point and counterpoint. They seemed to be enjoying themselves with this negotiation. For once, Julian was grateful that Charles was so long-winded.

When the conversation had run its course, Julian asked, "So, do you have a beverage prepared for me so that I can walk through a door and go home?"

The Game Master pulled out from his vest what looked to be a pack of cigarettes, which was odd since he had never seen the little man smoke before. As he took one of the items out of the pack, Julian saw that what he removed was not a cigarette but gum.

"I have actually been experimenting with a new delivery mechanism. I know the beverage is a bit distasteful, so I have put the formula into this gum."

Julian was about to snatch a stick before the Game Master pulled it back from him. "Not so fast, Mr. Dawson. Trust but verify. Is that not what your President Reagan once said when dealing with his foreign rivals?"

"Right, right," Julian said. "So, that's it. Just chew on some gum, go through a door, and I'm home. Is it in this room or do I have to go elsewhere to find it?"

"Mr. Dawson, you will find out in good time." The Game Master put his fingers together. "Now if you don't mind, I will have a brief chat with our mutual friend Chairman Von Ryan."

Julian cursed under his breath. What the hell was taking them so long? He had stalled the Game Master for as long as he could. He tried to think of what else he could do but nothing came to mind that did not smack of desperation. He followed the Game Master to a small office inside of this larger working area that was filled with workbenches, filing cabinets, and a handful of modern electronics sprinkled about. Chloe remained close to him, keeping a wary eye on him as if she fully expected Julian to make a move against her boss. She was right to be wary since he was thinking that very thing.

The Game Master used a phone that looked like it came from the desk of Alexander Graham Bell. He picked up the bell-shaped mouthpiece and put the other end up to his ear. With any luck, this relic of technology wouldn't work.

But luck was not on Julian's side as the Game Master spoke with somebody, presumably an operator who would connect him to the party he was trying to reach.

Just when Julian was about to go into full panic mode, a massive explosion ripped through the building. He could not tell where it had come from, but there was a large flash of light followed by a deep rumbling sound. The entire building shook. For a second, he contemplated running for cover, but could not find anything that resembled shelter.

More explosions rocked the building. Gunshots soon followed coming in all directions. They walked out of the office to see what was going on. Chloe held her automatic weapon at the ready, stand-ing in front of the Game Master. Before long, six additional guards joined her, forming a protective ring around the evil bastard. Julian wished he had his pistol, but there was no opening to take a shot at the Game Master anyway. He would have to wait this out and take his opportunity when it presented itself.

CHAPTER XLVII

Seconds later, Julian's ears were filled with the screaming of bullets being fired. He couldn't tell how close they were, but nobody was shooting in the room he was in—yet. It wouldn't last. The prudent thing would be to take cover somewhere, but he was beyond doing the prudent thing. He kept his eye on the Game Master. If the opportunity presented itself, he would seize it.

Chloe was conferring with the evil genius. With all of the noise in the background, he couldn't tell what they were saying, so he inched his way toward them.

"It's too dangerous," Chloe said. "We have to get you out of here now."

The Game Master seemed unconcerned. "We don't know the nature of the threat yet, and I have business to conduct."

"Whoever is attacking can storm in at any time," Chloe said.

A large man with a bald head who was bleeding from the scalp came through the door. "They're nearly upon us. We're outnumbered and they're heavily armed."

Chloe turned to the Game Master, her eyes wide and pleading. "We have to go now."

The Game Master shook his head. "No need to worry. If it gets bad, I will walk through the door and leave this place. The rest of you can sort out this mess when I'm gone."

The door.

That had to be the portal to get back to his home plane. The Game Master was going to use Julian's way home as an escape hatch.

Not if I have any say about it.

The door burst open, and soldiers streamed in. Julian took cover behind a metal desk when both sides began to shoot at each other. He kept his eye on the Game Master. Despite his earlier bravado, there was no way he was going to stick around for this shootout. Chloe and the other guards were shielding the Game Master while returning fire on their attackers. More people poured in, from both sides as far as Julian could tell.

The pinging of bullets and the overall cacophony of gunfire was deafening. More of Cutter's people came forward though the entrance, but many of them were getting picked off by the Game Master's guards in the process.

Apparently, the Game Master decided to heed Chloe's advice as they retreated down the hallway. He saw the room at the far end of the hallway to the left that they were about to enter. This was the time for Julian to make his move. He knew there was a decent chance he would get hit by one of the many flying bullets, but he could not let the Game Master escape. After all, he was playing for keeps.

He took a deep breath and sprinted toward the Game Master. With all of the noise inside the room, he couldn't imagine they heard him running, and the Game Master and his guards didn't turn in his direction. Julian shoulder-tackled one of the guards, the man with the bald head who was bleeding from his scalp, out of the way. He dove and tackled the Game Master from behind. They skidded down the linoleum floor.

A mountain of rage coursed through Julian as he rained down punches to the back of the Game Master's head. He couldn't be sure how many he landed but didn't think it was more than four or five before somebody grabbed his hair and yanked him away from the Game Master.

A mean snarl filled Chloe's face. Intense rage and hatred radiated from her. Protecting her benefactor had to be more than just a job for this type of visceral reaction. She had an attachment to this repugnant man.

"How dare you!" She slapped his left ear. All he could hear was a loud, ringing noise. She raised her rifle. "You dare lay your hands on the Master of Keys. You will die for this."

Julian weighed his options—which weren't many—dropped to the ground and grabbed the Game Master. Fortunately, the man didn't weigh much. Julian lifted him off the floor and put the man in front of him, doing his best to create a human shield. As expected, Chloe or the other guards weren't going to shoot at him with the Game Master blocking their line of sight—not yet.

For the moment, they were at a standstill. The Game Master looked groggy and was babbling something incoherent.

"I'll kill you," Chloe said.

Julian slowly put his left arm around The Game Master's neck. "And I'll kill him."

"What do you want?" she asked.

For the time being they were out of the general range of shooting, but Julian did not think that would last. As Cutter's soldiers continued to press forward, it would be only a matter of time before they made it through the Game Master's defenses.

"I want to go home," Julian replied.

"You were going to go home."

Julian shook his head. "No. He's tricked me time and time again. I don't trust him."

"Well, now you will die." Chloe and the other bodyguards all pointed their weapons at him.

Despite using The Game Master as a human shield, he knew there would be openings for them to shoot him. His situation felt desperate as his mind scrambled for another way out of this mess.

Out of the corner of his eye, Julian spotted Cutter bursting forth with a rifle in hand. He aimed it at the bodyguard who was pointing a gun at Julian and put a massive hole into his bald head. Another shot took one of the Game Master's guards in the chest and a third bullet took out another guard. That left Chloe, who spun to the ground and aimed her pistol at Cutter. Julian lunged for her and knocked the gun out of her hand.

She scrambled for the gun, but Julian grabbed her by her waist to prevent her from reaching it. She wriggled free and kicked him in the face, causing Julian's head to rock back. She continued forward. This time Julian grabbed her foot. She shook him loose and once more kicked his head. For good measure, she also kicked him in the nose. Blood trickled down his eyes, obscuring his vision. Still, he held onto her, this time grabbing her left ankle. She continued to kick at him until Cutter lifted her and thrust her off him.

"Enough of that." Cutter pointed his gun at her. "I strongly suggest you refrain from moving if you want to remain alive."

As Julian struggled to his feet, Chloe glared at Cutter. Julian staggered and fell again. The room was filled with smoke, and breathing was becoming increasingly difficult. Blood and tears filled his eyes. For a moment, he thought he was going to suffocate, but the smoke was from the guns, not from an actual fire.

"You okay?" Cutter asked.

"I've felt better." Julian replied.

The shooting was dying down from its fever pitch. All the same, there were still more bullets flying uncomfortably close for his liking.

Out of nowhere, Chloe lunged at Cutter like a cornered animal. As calm as could be, he pivoted and shot her in the head.

Julian stared at her vacant eyes as she slumped to the floor.

During the commotion, Julian had lost sight of Charles, who now crept toward them. "Is she…um dead?"

"As dead as dead can be," Cutter replied.

"Probably for the best," Charles said. "She scared the dickens out of me."

The Game Master began to crawl away, but Julian caught up to him and stepped on the small of his back, causing the mastermind to groan. Julian grabbed him by his shirt collar and yanked him to his feet. He looked very much the worse for wear. His head was covered in blood.

"Looks like you lost this game," Julian said. "Pun fully intended."

"You think you can butt heads with me. I will destroy you. I will kill your family and make you watch as they are brutally murdered."

Julian cut him off before he continued his diatribe. "You'll do none of those things when you're dead." He reached into the Game Master's shirt pocket and took out the chewing gum that had the formula he would need for transport.

The Game Master muttered a series of curses.

How undignified.

"You know," Julian began, "I can't really say that I enjoyed playing your games, although I think I managed to do some good in a couple of places, but I'll be glad to be finally done with them."

The Game Master struggled to break free, but he wasn't exactly a physical force, and Julian had little difficulty restraining him.

"Charles, do something," the Game Master pleaded. "Help me!"

Charles shook his head. "Sorry. I'm with them. I was on board with the plan to have the Silver Isles join Rotgard since I thought it was the best scenario of some very bleak options. With Von Ryan out of the picture I believe this war can end without my country having to grovel to Rotgard. There are those in their nation who opposed Von Ryan but were afraid to speak against him. With him dead, I believe I can help facilitate their attaining a position of power in Rotgard. So, I am done with you."

The Game Master gave his former lackey a malevolent glare.

Cutter patted him on the back with his free hand. "I have to say,

Charles, I didn't trust you." He nodded toward Julian. "But he believed in you, and I think you've justified that belief."

"Thank you," Charles said.

"Would you like me to put an end to his misery?"

Julian shook his head. "I owe it to the people I've harmed in these journeys to kill this bastard myself. This is my penance."

Cutter handed his pistol to Julian.

He knew he should just shoot him and be done with it, but he couldn't help but to add a cheesy line that he might hear in an over the top Hollywood blow 'em up movie. Still clutching the Game Master, he said, "Game over." Then he pulled the trigger.

CHAPTER XLVIII

Cutter looked down at the Game Master's dead body. "Good riddance, I say. You just made a whole slew of planes better places. You okay?"

Julian nodded. "I'm just relieved that this whole nightmare is over. I'm glad to be done with this monster."

"You seem a bit melancholy."

Julian turned away. By now the fighting had ended. The last bullet fired was the one he used to finish The Game Master's reign of terror. His guards had been overrun. Those who weren't dead had surrendered.

"I suppose I am. I mean I am truly glad to be finished with the Game Master, but..."

"It's Elizabeth, isn't it?" Cutter asked.

Julian nodded. "It is. I can't help it. I love her. It may make me a bad husband, but I can't help it. I've been disloyal to my wife, even though she is Nancy's shade and is close to her as a person could ever be to another human being, but damn if I don't love her. And I'll never see her again. I...I guess I don't know what to think. But I suppose you can understand."

"I know full well what it's like to love someone and not be able to be with them. I feel that ache in my heart every day. But at least you have two people to come home to. Two people who miss you very much. So now what?"

Julian removed the gum from his breast pocket. "I chew this and walk through the door."

"Which door?" Cutter asked.

"I'm pretty sure I know the one. The Game Master was prepared to escape if things when south for him. He didn't react quickly enough."

Charles had taken charge of the scene, directing the soldiers on where to detain the prisoners even though he wasn't part of their military apparatus. He broke away and put his hand on Julian's shoulder.

"Well, that was some work there. I am not going to revise history and tell you that I thought this would be the outcome all along, but you excelled under pressure, and I am pleased that you rose above my expectations."

"Thanks for going along with it," Julian said. "You could have easily given me away, but you chose not to."

"I gave you my word, and as a gentleman, I take my word very seriously."

"You take many things very seriously," Julian said.

Charles chuckled. "Perhaps I do. I also believe that you presented me with a different path, a better path. With Von Ryan out of the picture, I believe there is a way to bring less warlike factions to power in Rotgard, and I may have the ability to influence that ascension to power. There may yet be an end to this war and an achievement of peace, even if it is not long lasting since there are many issues yet to be resolved. So, I thank you. And I wish you the best in getting to your destination."

"Good luck. You have a big task on your hands."

They shook hands.

"You ready for this?" Cutter asked.

"I am. I'm feeling a bit of trepidation. I mean, how do I explain all of this?"

Cutter shrugged. "You could just piggyback off the story I told your wife about you working for the government on a secret project."

Julian rubbed his beard. He had been growing it out since he had not been able to get used to shaving with a straight razor. "I'm thinking the truth might be a better alternative. Either story is going to be hard to believe, but at least one is real."

"Tell you what," Cutter said. "I'll pay you a visit in a couple of weeks and bring with me some incontrovertible proof that you have been to some of the places you claim to have been to. Perhaps technology that does not exist in your world."

Julian paused to consider this. "That could work, but hopefully my wife trusts me enough to know that I would never conjure up such an outlandish story. What about you? With Edgar Smith and the Game Master dead, maybe it would be safe for you to visit your wife and daughter in the last plane I visited."

Cutter took a deep breath. "Maybe. Even with Edgar Smith dead, I am likely still wanted. But at least for the first time since that fateful day, it's a possibility."

Cutter pulled out an envelope from the flap jacket he was wearing and handed it to Julian.

"What's that?"

"You've been away for about a month and I'm sure your family has suffered financially as a result. It's some US currency from your plane. I figured you could use it to get back on your feet. Plus, I owe you a debt of gratitude for what you did here and for helping me out with my family in the last plane."

"You don't owe me anything," Julian said.

"Regardless, you're taking the money. Don't try to outstubborn me because it won't work. I can be as hardheaded as they come."

Julian chuckled. "Okay. Thank you. I appreciate it and I'm sure it will come in handy."

They walked to the room the Game Master was preparing to escape from.

"You're a mess," Cutter said. "That assassin sure did a number on your face. You may want to find a restroom to clean up before you go see your family."

Julian waved his hand. "I'll be fine. I just need to go home and see them. It's been a long time."

"That it has." Cutter put his hand on his shoulder. "Be well, my friend."

"Where do you think I'll be landing?" Julian asked.

"Who can say, but you'll be home, so I think you'll be able to find your way back."

They shook hands, and Julian opened the door.

* * *

After walking through the door, Julian found himself in the familiar and comfortable environs of his backyard. He looked around, hardly believing his eyes. He was finally home. There had been so many times during his journey when he thought this day would never come.

He turned toward the front of the house.

"Daddy! Daddy! Daddy!"

Natalie jumped off the swing set in a fit of near hysteria and ran toward him. She leaped at him, her momentum so great that it nearly knocked him over despite her small stature. She hugged him as if the world would end if she let go. However, that did not last all that long as she pulled away from him. "Daddy, you're bleeding."

He put his hand to his face, and, predictably, his hand became covered in his own blood.

At the other end of the yard, standing by the fence, Nancy turned in their direction. She dropped the cellphone she had been holding. Her face held a look of stunned bewilderment. She stood there, as if frozen in time.

He lifted Natalie off the ground and slowly walked in Nancy's direction. She ran toward him, tears filling her eyes. By the time she reached him, she was sobbing. He put down Natalie and embraced his wife. She had lost a good bit of weight since he last saw her and she didn't have much to lose. When he held her, she felt frail and withered. He could only imagine how his time away must have been for her.

"Julian, where have you been? What happened to you?"

She began to cry, and he did not know what to do or say to comfort her.

"I thought you were dead. I thought we would never see you again. And then that guy showed up and said that you were working for the government." Nancy sobbed once more.

He held her close to him. "It's okay. I'm back."

"What happened? And why do you have blood all over your face? And how did you just appear out of nowhere?"

Julian wiped away more blood that was getting in his eyes. He should have heeded Cutter's advice and cleaned up before leaving.

"It's a long, long story. And I've been far, far away. Let's go inside. I have a story to tell you, but know this, I'm never leaving the two of you again."

ABOUT THE AUTHOR

Carl is the author of nine published novels which span the horror, fantasy, and science fiction genres in no particular order. He lives in Central Pennsylvania with his wife and the two most awesome boys you have ever met. When not feverishly conjuring stories about monsters, aliens, and things that go bump in the night, he works as a quality engineering manager for a medical device company.

Find out more about him by visiting his website at www.carlalves.com

BEYOND RAGNAROK
BY CARL ALVES

After a doomsday virus wipes out most of the human population, all of the world governments fall, and John Madison, considered to be a madman by some and a savior by others, has seized control of the world after manufacturing a vaccine for this deadly virus.

His rule is tyrannical and brutal. Rebel groups around the planet form in order to oppose him and his new vision of leadership.

The Battle of Ragnarok was meant to be the end of days—the destruction of the old world, and the creation of the new world. At the final battle, Odin and Thor would lead the Aesir against the giants and the forces of the underworld, commanded by Loki. Except Loki never shows up for the final battle.

In Beyond Ragnarok, an epic, post-apocalyptic fantasy novel that is steeped in Norse Mythology, Thor's sons, Magni and Modi, are among the few to survive the final battle. They must travel to our world to stop Loki and his diabolical plot for conquest. Separated from each other, they must rally the remaining people to rise up against Loki and the frost and fire giants under his command in order to take back control of the planet.

THE INVOCATION
BY CARL ALVES

The Invocation is a thrilling combination of Stranger Things and The Exorcist.

When Kenna Trigg plays with an Ouija board, little does she know that she is about to unleash a malevolent spirit upon the world, leaving her and her older brother, Jake, to stop the spirit as it leaves a trail of dead bodies in its wake.

In The Invocation, a supernatural thriller, Kenna Trigg and three of her friends from the fourth grade manage to befriend a spirit named Mia, who died in her late teens in a drowning accident, using of an Ouija board. Cotter, a malevolent spirit who had been a con-man and criminal in life, tricks Kenna and her friends into releasing him into our world by posing as Mia. Cotter has the ability to take control and possess people he comes across. With this new power, he begins a vicious crime spree. Kenna turns to her older brother, Jake, a professional mixed-martial artist who has recently been released from prison. Now, Kenna and Jake must stop Cotter from unleashing havoc in our world.

BATTLE OF THE SOUL
BY CARL ALVES

Andy Lorenzo has no family, few friends, poor social skills, and drinks and gambles far too much. But in a time when demons are becoming increasingly more brazen and powerful, he has one skill that makes demons cower in fear from him—he is the greatest exorcist the world has ever known.

In *Battle of the Soul*, a supernatural thriller that is a combination of Constantin and The Exorcist, since graduating high school Andy has left a long trail of demons in his wake while priests are dying while performing traditional rites of exorcism. Andy is the Church and society's ultimate weapon in combating this growing epidemic. He needs no bibles, prayers, or rituals. Andy is capable of going inside the person's soul where he engages in hand-to-hand combat using his superhuman abilities that only reside when he is in a person's soul. When eight-year-old Kate becomes possessed, Andy finds an elaborate trap waiting for him. He will do whatever it takes to win the most important fight of his life—the battle for Kate's soul.

"Ready for a lighthearted Battle of the Soul? *Andy Lorenzo's got the requisite exorcism skills, but he's no single-minded zealot nor cynical bleak arts practitioner. He gets the biz done with a deft touch and a wink and a nod to family values. It's not John Constantine here but try Cary Grant in Monkey Business.* Battle of the Soul *is a fine, fun supernatural read!"* — Mort Castle, Bram Stoker Award Winning Author of *The Strangers*

AVAILABLE NOW

BEYOND RAGNAROK

READ A SAMPLE HERE

CHAPTER 1

John Madison, the CEO of BioInception, scanned the auditorium at his company's headquarters. He addressed the crowd from a podium. "Welcome, my friends. Many of you have travelled a great distance to join me in the eve of our triumph. I want to thank each and every one of you because you believed. You have kept true to the teachings of your forefathers and their forefathers before them. As the world entered the modern era of high technology, it would have been easy for you to give up the old ways, but you have stayed true despite society's temptations. Look around the room. You will be the leaders of our brave new world."

For a moment, the audience took their eyes away from him. Some clapped. Others greeted their fellow followers. People from over thirty countries and six continents had gathered here. They were the chosen, the ones who would carry out his mission. He would share control of the planet with them, but he would leave no doubt who was in charge.

After all, they were mere mortals.

John moved around the room, making eye contact with his followers. "The planet has fallen to imperialists, terrorists, and those who loathe the principles we hold dear. It is time we take it back. I will reshape this world in my image, and you will be my vessels to bring about this change. There will be no need for war since the survivors will follow me alone. There will be no starvation since we will rid the planet of its gross overpopulation in one sweeping effort."

The audience chanted his name. Not his given name of John Madison, but his ancient one that he had been known by for centuries. Their rapture was intoxicating. He could tell them to commit suicide now, and they would obey.

At the moment of his greatest triumph, he had to remain the forceful leader of his fervent and devoted followers. He struggled to control the boyish exuberance he felt, wanting to gloat in vindication before those who had tried to thwart him. For they would soon be dead, and he would rule what was left of this world.

The auditorium was filled with the eager faces of his followers, who had come from every corner of the globe to enact his plan of mass destruction. They looked like junkies needing a fix, and their drug was power. Pure, unabated, and eternal. He would give it to them. His foes had so woefully underestimated him. While they were about to wage a battle for the ages, he would bring this world to its knees.

John opened a briefcase and removed a vial containing clear liquid. He held it up for all to see. "What I hold in my hands is the lifesaving vaccine. While others around you perish in a most gruesome fashion, while society crumbles, you will be immune. Tonight, we will administer it to each of you. In two days, you will count your blessings that you received it."

John pulled back his long blond hair, which had been tied into a ponytail. He wore an Armani suit for this festive occasion. He sat back and watched as they assembled into four lines at the corners of the auditorium that led to four stations where his people administered the vaccine. His followers rolled up their sleeves and spoke in low, eager tones.

After receiving the vaccine, they would get a briefcase containing additional vaccine to bring back with them. They would provide it within the next twenty-four hours to a list of people who had already been informed of their privileged status. Each briefcase included a doomsday device, an engineered mix of the Ebola virus and the avian flu.

John's team of scientists had been working on the deadly compound for the past decade. They had tested and perfected it to the point that it was ready to be unleashed on the planet's population. Its effects on test subjects exceeded his wildest expectations. Everyone who contracted the virus would die violently and painfully, just the way he wanted it. This was his coming out party, and he wanted to make it unforgettable. An airborne virus would have been more effective than Ebola, but the beauty of Ebola was that the deaths it caused would be so horrific that it would create widespread fear and panic. The masterstroke of his team of scientists was to engineer it with the avian flu, combining the deadly properties of both viruses.

Within seventy-two hours, after the necessary people had been vaccinated, the third phase of his plan would commence. For the last two years he had been scouting locations around the globe to unleash his doomsday device. He had chosen spots that would maximize the most damage: airports, stadiums, places of commerce, and popular tourist venues. Within two weeks the virus would reduce the Earth's population to a fraction of what it was now. Within a month, people would become sparse. Within a year, the population would drop to levels it had not seen in a few thousand years. And most importantly, it would be his to rule with an iron hand.

For the last few centuries, the world had eroded to its current abysmal state. It needed to be cleansed. It needed a leader that would restore it and bring about fundamental change that would endure.

The prophecies foretold that the world would be destroyed after the great battle. He was determined to change fate. The survivors would be his chosen ones and those resistant to the virus, which his scientists estimated to be less than one percent of the population.

John stared at the faces of his followers. Oh how the gods had underestimated him.

⟨HAPTER II

Magni gritted his teeth as he backed up against the wall of the courtyard. Each time his brother thrust his sword at him, he went into a defensive posture to parry it. On the few occasions when he mounted his own attack, Modi easily deflected the blows. This was about technique, not strength. If it was about strength, then nobody could beat him.

Magni focused on his form, and turned the tide of the duel, making Modi back up.

The brothers had been dueling since dawn. Besides the ongoing threat from the frost and fire giants, Magni had heard disturbing rumors lately that chilled his immortal blood.

The clang of swords echoed loudly. They continued to battle as the momentum shifted between them. Magni practiced different stances and techniques, knowing a real battle would be far more chaotic. Still, the better his skill, the greater chance he would prevail in a life and death struggle.

He took his eyes off Modi when a vision of blonde loveliness blinded him. She was like the sun, holding the world together. Her eyes were a shade of violet blue that mesmerized him. She smiled at him. He never had to question the sincerity of that smile since truth was deeply rooted into her being. It was Freya, his beloved. No matter how often he saw her, she still had the same spellbinding effect on him.

His distraction allowed Modi to knock him down, who stood over Magni and glared. "She'll be your undoing. You can't take your eyes off your opponent in combat."

Magni dusted himself off. He rubbed the bruise on his chin from Modi's latest blow. "If this were a real fight, I assure you I wouldn't."

"It's time to get serious, brother. The end of days is coming. I can feel it in my bones."

Magni sighed. This was all anyone spoke of lately. How could they be so sure after all this time?

He forgot about his conversation with Modi when Freya sauntered toward him. No being in any of the nine worlds could touch her beauty.

Freya put her arms around his neck and kissed him. "If that had been a real fight, you would have been killed."

Modi threw off his gloves. "My point exactly."

"We've been dueling all morning. It was fatigue."

"You can't afford to have fatigue against a fire giant," Freya said. "They won't allow you to recover from a mistake. What good would you do me if you were dead?"

"Very little, I suppose."

"Perhaps you could teach my brother some sorcery," Modi suggested.

"The way I perform magic, I'm just as likely to hurt a friend as a foe," Magni said.

"You perform that little illusion spell where you project another person's image fairly well," Modi said.

"Which is great as a practical joke," Magni said. "Little good it would do me in battle."

Modi stretched his powerful muscles. "To what do we owe this visit?

I assume you have a good reason to interrupt."

Magni rolled his eyes. Besides being a great warrior, his brother was also a brilliant poet, writing poems that enchanted the Aesir, yet he lacked tact and could be blunt to the point of being rude.

Freya remained unaffected by his gruff manner. "I come with a message from the Allfather."

Magni's brows rose. Why would Odin send Freya to deliver a message when a valkyrie would have been sufficient for the task?

"And what does Odin want?" Modi asked.

Freya shrugged. "You'll find out when I do. It's important. I could see it in his eyes. He wants the Aesir to meet tonight in Valhalla. No exceptions."

"We will be there," Magni said.

"Good. I'll see you then."

Magni knelt on the ground, staring at Freya as she left, admiring her curves. When she was gone, he turned to Modi. His entire body was tense, just like a feline ready to strike.

"It could only be one thing," Modi said.

"And what's that?"

Modi scowled. "Don't play the fool. The battle."

"Why are you so fixated on Ragnarok?"

Modi frowned. "What a foolish question. Ask Heimdall, or Odin, or father. They've been preparing for this for centuries."

"Odin has been trying to stop this for centuries."

"You know how much I respect Odin, but his best efforts won't stop it from happening." Modi stared into the distance. "The Battle of Ragnarok will define us. And we will be a monumental part of it. That's why we must be ready. We can't lose. If we do, then Loki and the giants will rule not only Asgard, but all of the worlds. We can't let that happen. That's why I've been tough with you."

Magni put his hand on his brother's shoulder. "When the final battle comes, I will fight with the spirit of a thousand warriors. And we will prevail."

◇ ◇ ◇

As Magni and Modi approached Valhalla, they encountered Tyr, who wore his usual surly expression. "This had better be good. I was about to embark on a great hunt."

"I'm sure you won't be disappointed," Modi said.

Tyr was the bravest of the Asgardians, sacrificing his hand when they had bound Fenris, the giant wolf that terrorized the Aesir. He could do no wrong in Magni's viewpoint even if he wasn't the friendliest person Magni knew.

Once inside Valhalla, Magni sought out Freya, who stood next to her brother, Frey. Her eyes appeared troubled as she avoided his gaze. Perhaps she knew more of what Odin intended to say than she had let on.

Magni wore a broad smile when his father appeared. He walked across the room and hugged Thor. Thor patted him in the back, nearly knocked Magni over. They often had tests of strength. Although Thor was reputed to be the strongest of the Asgardians, Magni often bested him in these contests.

"It's good to see you, father." It had been many months since he had last seen Thor, which was not unusual since he was often away on one quest or another.

Thor nodded. "How have you been?"

"Good."

"And your brother?"

"Fretting as usual."

"Understandable given the circumstances. And Freya?"

Magni smiled. "Doing well."

Thor ruffled Magni's hair. "Take care of her."

"I will. So, why have you been away for so long? You never even told me you were leaving."

Thor took a deep breath. "I'll explain later. First, we must listen to Odin."

"So much mystery." Magni meant that to be humorous, but Thor did not smile. Usually, his father was a jovial sort, always being in on the joke.

Other Aesir entered the room. The gatherings at Valhalla were gallant feasts with gourmet food and lavish entertainment. Today, the mood was grim as evidenced by the dour expressions on the faces of his brethren.

After the Aesir entered the great hall, Odin closed the doors. All eyes fell upon the Allfather. He took his usual seat at the head of the table next to his wife, Frigga. Magni was struck by how old they looked.

The others sat at their normal places around the table. Some valkyries were also in attendance. When the time came, they would be called on to fight, and Freya would lead them. They would be a valuable asset against their enemies.

All conversations came to a halt when Odin called for silence. "Thank you for joining me in Valhalla tonight. As you know, or have heard, or speculated, dark times are upon us. For many years I have fought against this. I have done everything I could to prevent it from happening."

Magni's heart ached. Odin had tried so hard to avoid this conflict, but it was impossible to fight fate. What was destined to happen was going to happen, and not even Odin could prevent it.

The Allfather shook his head. "I have tried to make peace. I have made concessions, even though it would have been politic not to, all in an effort to defy the prophecies. Thor and I have been monitoring this for some time, and the signs are undeniable."

Magni glanced at his father, who had a stony face. Unlike Odin, his father welcomed the battle ahead. He was Asgard's greatest warrior, and this would be the ultimate test of his prowess in battle.

Odin looked around the room and made eye-contact with his brethren. "The Battle of Ragnarok is upon us, and I can no longer stop it. This is a battle we can't lose. We can't let Loki gain control of Midgard and the other eight worlds. I shudder to think what kind of darkness Loki and his ilk will create if we fail.

"I ask that each of you remain near Valhalla in the upcoming days and weeks. Prepare yourself for battle. Join in devising strategy to destroy the enemy."

Odin took a deep breath. "I love all of you. My children, my friends, my comrades. Few seated among us will survive this battle. I have lived a long and fruitful life. I cherish the time I've spent with you."

There were nods and somber expressions throughout the room. Even the unflappable Thor wiped tears from his eyes.

"The Battle of Ragnarok will test the strongest and heartiest to their limits. When I look around this room and see your fortitude, I know we will prevail."

The Aesir raised their fists and shouted. Even Magni, who was not prone to such outbursts, joined in. Before long, echoes filled Valhalla with chanting and singing.

Odin waited until the great hall quieted. "It will be time to fight soon enough. Now we will feast."

Magni searched out Freya. If their time was limited, then he wanted to spend as much time as possible with her.

⟨HAPTER III

The feast at Valhalla lasted until the morning. Magni held back during the debauchery. Unlike most of the others, he was not in a celebratory mood. He toasted and broke bread with his brethren, but Odin's words remained in his head. This was the last time he would feast with many of his friends and family.

When it was over, he started to return to the hall he shared with Modi, but his father stood before him wearing a melancholy expression. Behind him stood Odin, tall and imposing with his one eye. He had gained eternal wisdom after sacrificing his eye in order to drink from the spring of Mimer. His eye patch was an example of how much Odin had sacrificed for the Aesir. Magni, in turn, would sacrifice anything for Odin.

"We must talk, son. Get your brother. This is important."

"I'll find him." If this was so important, then why hadn't they spoken about it earlier?

He walked through the hall. It did not take him long to find Modi. He often knew where his brother was even when they were miles apart. When Modi wounded himself in battle, Magni felt it. When his brother experienced great joy, Magni's spirits also lifted.

Modi's favorite valkyrie was sitting on his lap. She whispered something in his ear, and he laughed.

When they made eye contact, Magni motioned with his head. He did not need words to communicate with his brother.

"I hope you have good reason to ruin my revelry."

"Father and Odin want to speak to us now."

"Very well." Modi kissed the Valkyrie and strode toward him. "I shall return."

The brothers walked in silence. In the main hall, Odin and Thor waited for them. They then went into Odin's private quarters within Valhalla.

Odin instructed the brothers to sit. He folded his hands. "As you both know, we have been preoccupied with the battle that lies ahead of us. For many of us it will be the final battle. I'm certain that I will not make it out of Ragnarok alive."

Thor nodded. "Nor will I."

Magni felt a twinge in his heart. What they said was true if the prophecies were to be believed, but he had a hard time accepting it.

Odin continued, "I fear we may have been short sighted, an inexcusable mistake. We have only seen Ragnarok, but what lies beyond is of greater importance than the battle itself."

Thor leaned into the table. "Over the last several months, I've been trying to learn what Loki and the giants are scheming. They will stop at nothing to ensure that there are no survivors on our side. They do not merely want to defeat us. They want complete annihilation."

Modi's eyes narrowed. "Then they intend to take Asgard?" One of the nine worlds united by the tree, Ygdrassil, Asgard was the home of the Aesir.

"No," Thor said. "They intend on seizing control of Midgard."

Magni gasped. The Aesir were the guardians of Midgard, a sacred pact made many centuries ago. Throughout the ages, they had intervened to defend Midgard from outside threats, but he had never thought Loki would be one of those threats. Magni could only imagine the havoc Loki could wreak in the world of mortals.

Odin closed his eye. He appeared to be in slumber. When he opened his eye, his face held tight concentration. "As you well know, you two are to survive Ragnarok."

Magni had always wondered if that was a blessing or a curse. He and Modi would survive the battle, but their loved ones would die. Was that worth it?

"But fate isn't a constant thing," Odin said. "It is like the shore of an ocean. The tide rises and falls. Erosion changes the landscape. What you see one day may be different the next. We need more information. That's why we will journey to Yggdrasil."

Yggdrasil was the tree of life. The guardians of Yggdrasil were the Norns, three maidens who were as old as creation. The Norns could see into the future and had decreed many prophecies. Although prophecies were destined to happen, they could be influenced by external factors. Still, whatever the Norns said almost always came to pass. Magni and his brother had only been to Yggdrasil once. It was on that occasion they learned of their special role at Ragnarok.

Thor stood. "We have to go at once. I have already arranged for provisions for the journey."

"What if Loki and the giants attack while we are gone?" Modi asked. "Without us, the Aesir will have no chance. You decreed that we remain in Asgard."

Odin shook his head. "This is too important. We must see the Norns. Tyr will lead in my absence. As for your concern, Heimdall has assured me that our enemies are not ready to attack. They will be soon, however."

Magni glanced at his brother. "Then let's not waste time."

They left Valhalla, leaving Magni to wonder if the great hall would still stand after Ragnarok. If it did, would there be anyone left to fill it?

They entered a massive chariot pulled by stallions. In the lead was

Odin's powerful, eight-legged steed Sleipnir. The stallion was one of Loki's offspring and had made the journey numerous times in the past.

During their travels, Thor told them about his activities for the past several months. Magni was stunned to learn he had journeyed to Niflheim, the underworld, the dominion of Loki's daughter, Hel. To journey there and back must have been a harrowing experience, especially in this time of high tension.

"How did you make it out of there?" Modi asked.

"With great stealth." Thor clutched his mighty hammer, Mjolnir. "And I had to smash a few heads."

Magni stared at his father's deep brown eyes. They looked as if they held all of the world's secrets. "Is it true then? Is Loki in Niflheim?"

Thor shook his head. "However, Hel is preparing the monsters of the underworld. They were in full battle mode."

Modi folded his arms. "Then where's Loki?"

"It bothers me to no end," Odin said. "He's supposed to lead the forces of the underworld against us. I can't imagine he would let others determine the outcome of the battle. He may be my blood-brother, but I know he wants our doom."

For a time, no one spoke. Odin's relationship with Loki had long been a sore spot among the Aesir. They had tolerated him because long ago he had aided Odin, and they had become blood-brothers, a bond even stronger than kin. Loki had always been mischievous, looking to create mayhem, but he had usually been harmless. That all changed when his actions led to the death of Odin's beloved son, Balder. Since then, his behavior had become increasingly treacherous and sinister. He was no longer welcome in Asgard, although his reach was far and wide, and he still managed to create havoc. Magni would give anything to know what Loki was planning.

Sleipnir never tired during the journey. Unfortunately, the rest of the stallions waned, and they had to stop for the evening. While the others pitched a tent and prepared a fire, Modi rode off on Sleipnir.

By the time they had pitched the tent and grew a large fire, Modi and the stallion returned with a large boar.

They roasted and ate the bore. Afterward, they drank fine wine, and Modi entertained them with poetry. Magni had always envied his brother's ability with words. Even their father, who was not one for poetry, seemed to be moved tonight. Perhaps he was sentimental because the end was near.

They left early the following morning. The stallions were rested and traveled with blazing speed. By mid-day, they neared Yggdrasil, the separating point from which the first humans had spawned thousands of years ago to populate Midgard.

Dusk was beginning to settle when they reached the giant tree. Magni looked in awe. He could hardly see the top of it, which was thin and wispy. The trunk was thick and course, about fifteen meters wide. Woven into its bark were depictions of great warriors and battle scenes. Magni smiled at the sight of his father striking down a frost giant with Mjolnir. Another had Odin leading the Great Hunt. He glanced at Modi, who appeared to be staring in equal fascination. Under different circumstances, Magni could have spent hours studying the tree's carvings.

As if to remind them of what they came here for, the three Norn sisters, Fate, Being, and Necessity, emerged. Although they were not beautiful by normal standards, each had her own attractiveness. Their faces were serene and eternal. They were older than Odin, as old as time. Regardless of what transpired in the days to come, they would still be there, retaining the memory of what had once been and harboring knowledge of things to come.

Odin and Thor bowed and placed their fists above their hearts. Magni and his brother replicated the gesture. The Norns, in return, curtsied.

Necessity, taller and thinner than the other sisters, was the first to speak. "Allfather Odin, thank you for coming in this time of great distress."

Fate, short and plump, stepped forward. "And, Thor, thank you for bringing your sons. They must know their part in what is to come."

Magni shifted uncomfortably. This attention was new to him. He was one of the least important among the Aesir. Things were taking a dramatic turn, and he and his brother would be front and center on this new stage.

Being grabbed Odin's hand. "Please rest."

Odin shook his head. "We appreciate your kind gesture, but we must do what we came here for and be on our way."

Necessity bowed. "Of course, what you say is true. The Battle of Ragnarok will start in ten days."

Magni took a deep breath. Ten days. That was too soon. He stared at Thor and Odin, and realized they had been preparing for this their whole lives.

CHAPTER IV

With his feet up on his mahogany desk, John Madison let out a loud laugh. He pressed the intercom button. "Klaus, you have to see this." He chuckled as Klaus walked into his office.

"Yes," Klaus said.

John motioned with his fingers. "Come here. Look at the television screen."

The big German folded his arms. His eyes remained expressionless and his face impassive. It was hard to faze Klaus. He had been a clandestine operative in the German intelligence organization, taking high risk operations around the globe. All along, he had been one of the faithful, one of the silent people who had followed John before his rebirth into this world. He would do anything John asked of him, having already killed dozens of enemies upon his order.

A middle-aged woman appeared on the television screen coughing out blood and bleeding through her orifices. The cameraman kept his distance from her. As her fits became more violent, the cameraman backed further away from her. Four others were dead, lying in a pool of their own blood, on the steps of the state building in Albany, New York. They had been staging a protest to demand an audience with the governor. While waiting, a few of their members had died from the hideous disease that plagued humanity, the one John had unleashed.

"This is beautiful." He glanced at Klaus, who remained expressionless. "Don't you find anything humorous? She was demanding that the governor do something about this disease, and while waiting for him, she bled out and died. Don't you see the delicious irony?"

Klaus shrugged. "The governor of New York is already dead."

He patted Klaus on the back. "Exactly. The whole thing is futile. I still haven't figured out why the governments are pretending some of their more prominent politicians are alive. They can't hide it forever. Can't these people just die with dignity?"

"They're weak and stupid. I would put a bullet in my head before letting the disease take me."

"I know you would." John pointed at the woman on the television screen. "Look at her. She looks like a slaughtered pig." John kept laughing, but Klaus's expression didn't change. He waved the German away. He was a valuable asset, but the man had no sense of humor.

John flipped the channels on his remote control. Many stations had gone off the air. He put on the BBC, which was still broadcasting.

Things were not faring better in Europe. The death, destruction, and chaos was exhilarating to watch. They estimated the death count to be four million in Great Britain alone, surely a conservative estimate. There was mass death in Germany, Spain, and Russia. Martial law had been declared in most countries, something that was hard to enforce since law enforcement officers in those countries were dying as well. Lawlessness plagued major cities. Hamburg was burning to the ground. He had seen footage of the nasty conflagrations. Human nature was a beautiful thing. As if it was not bad enough that he had unleashed this doomsday virus on the populace, they were destroying themselves. All the better. He wanted the Earth's population to be reduced to a manageable number. There would no longer be vast overcrowding.

The BBC showed the spreading of the disease in Asia, Africa, the Americas, and Australia. There was footage of Antarctica. He made a note in his tablet to send a team to investigate the frozen continent. Although there were no permanent residents in Antarctica, scientists and researchers stayed there. Because of the continent's isolation, they probably had not been infected. They would be a welcome addition to his new society—if they met his demands and accepted him as their leader. He would give them the option of falling in line with him and receiving the vaccine or be exposed to the virus.

He flipped through the channels and frowned after discovering Fox News was no longer broadcasting. What a shame. Although he enjoyed the footage from all of these valiant reporters, Fox News had provided the goriest and most revolting coverage. They had been instrumental in spreading terror and fear. He poured Scotch in his glass and offered a toast to the departed network. May they rest in peace.

Before long, all of the television stations would be off the air with nobody left to operate them. The survivors were desperately hanging on to survival in this disease ravaged world. After a few days with no communication from any television broadcasters, his people would commandeer the current broadcasting networks, and he would address the survivors, a monumental address that would live in the annals of history.

He turned off the television. As tempting as it was to watch this footage, he had work to do.

He took out his laptop. A few days after the pandemonium had ensued, he introduced himself to various world leaders and begun negotiations. He reviewed the detailed notes he made of conversations with them.

His phone rang. There were constant interruptions, making it hard to get any work done. It was his personal assistant, Inga. Besides being efficient at her job, she was a beautiful blonde who was more than eager to please him in whatever way he desired.

He answered the phone. "Yes, Inga."

"It's the president of the United States. He said it's urgent that he speak to you."

John rolled his eyes. "Of course, it's urgent. His country, or what's left of it, is falling apart. His once mighty power base is slipping from his hands. These are dark days for the president. Have some sympathy."

Inga giggled as she transferred the call to him.

"William, to what do I owe the pleasure?" John refused to acknowledge the man's title. As far as he was concerned, there was no longer a United States of America, just as there was no Great Britain, Saudi Arabia, Japan, or any of the old countries. The old world was dead. The new world belonged to him.

"You have to stop this, Madison. You're a madman."

"I'm a madman who holds all the cards."

"People are dying by the thousands."

John sighed. What a silly little man. How had he become the leader of the most powerful nation in Midgard? "Of course people are dying. That was my intent."

"How can you let this happen, you heartless bastard?"

John smiled. "With ease. Actually, I've enjoyed watching the coverage. Haven't you?"

"This is insane."

"Let's get to the heart of the matter. I've given you time to consider my proposal. When will you hand over control of your military weaponry?"

The former president breathed heavily on the other end. John smiled, picturing the man squirming. He had no option, really. The US military had virtually disbanded. There were still skeleton crews of troops in a handful of military bases, but they were struggling just to survive and maintain the peace. They were certainly in no position to strike against him.

"What you're asking for is impossible," the president said.

"Is that so? The way I see it, you have little choice. If you had met my demands earlier, your wife and oldest son would still be alive. I could have given them the life-saving vaccine before they died so horrifically. You still have a chance to save your own hide as well as that of your daughter and youngest son. Can you live with yourself—for however long that lasts—if you let them die in such a gruesome manner? I don't think so. Now give up control of your weapons. It's not like you have any power left. Your military forces have been virtually disbanded."

There was a long pause on the other end of the line. "I need time to think about this."

John laughed. "Time is a luxury you don't have. You're tucked away in a bunker, yet your people are still getting infected. How long will it be before the virus spreads to the remainder of your family? Tick Tock. Time is running out. If you want to live, then you must agree to my demands. Willie, face it. Your country no longer exists. You're the president of nothing. You're the commander in chief but have no one to command. Save yourself while you can. You may think it was noble that the captain of the *Titanic* sunk with his ship, but I think the man was an idiot. If you get infected and die, I'll still get what I want. Your vice-president is dead. The Speaker of the House has gone into hiding. Most of your cabinet is dead."

"How do you know that?"

"I know all. I'm a god. Now, Willie, make the right decision. This is my final offer."

John rolled his eyes. He was already bored with the conversation. He began typing. He had too much to do to get bogged down with this silly little man.

The president said something, but John was no longer paying attention.

"What did you say?"

The president sighed. "I'll do it. I'll give you what you want."

"A wise decision. I'll transfer you to my assistant, Klaus. He'll work out the details of the exchange."

Without a further word, John transferred the president to Klaus. He couldn't bother himself with this negotiation. That's why he surrounded himself with good people. They handled the details. John was a big picture thinker. He had an entire world to run, after all. Fortunately, his intelligence and capabilities far exceeded that of ordinary mortals.

This president was beyond a fool if he thought he would survive. John wanted to remove any symbols of the old power structure. The last thing he wanted was for somebody to rally the survivors.

He walked over to a large map of the old world and put a pin on the United States. One more country down. They would join France, China, Saudi Arabia, and more than a dozen other nations who had surrendered their military infrastructure to him. He rubbed his palms together and smiled. The world was crumbling faster than he thought it would.

His plans were in place. He had people ready to take over the legacy governments after their leaders surrendered power. His team was armed and organized. The survivors would look for guidance in the weeks and months ahead, and he would provide it.

Soon, all broadcasting outlets would be off the air. Then he would address the world and proclaim himself as their savior, the new messiah. He would lead them through this tragedy. His rules would be strict and his penalties harsh, but after all the people had been through, they would more than welcome his firm hand.

John's vision was coming to fruition, and there was nothing that could stop him.